Sons of Jabir

RAJA MIAH

Hyena Press

© Raja Miah 2002
Sons of Jabir

Visit our website:
www.sonsofjabir.com

ISBN 0-9540473-1-1

Published by Hyena Press
221 Kensington Street
Rochdale
Lancashire
OL11 1QS

Raja Miah asserts the moral right to be identified as the author of this work in accordance with the Copyright, Designs And Patents Act 1988.

All rights reserved. No part of this publication may be reproduced in any form or by any means – graphic, electronic or mechanical, including photocopying, recording, taping or information storage and retrieval systems – without the prior permission in writing of the publisher.

Design & production co-ordinated by:
The Better Book Company Ltd
Havant
Hampshire
PO9 2XH

Printed in England

Cover design by MusicPrint

Sons of Jabir

Sons of Jabir is about three brothers trying to struggle free from their traditions, but at the same time trying to understand their religion and obey it.

Suna and Bassha are twins, but Suna is more of a materialistic young adult, whilst Bassha likes to enjoy every moment of his life.

Rajah has suffered a broken heart in love and has recovered. But he wants to fall in love to experience those indescribable feelings again. At the same time he is scared. Can he handle more scars upon his heart?

Author's Acknowledgement

I dedicate this book to my father who suffers from schizophrenia and to my mother who cares for him in spite of her own poor health. Gratitude and love also go to my sister Saliah Begum for her belief in my writing and her constant encouragement. Not to forget my two younger brothers Bassha Miah and Suna Miah for their recognition and appreciation of my book.

Importantly, many thanks to my editor Jill Field for guiding and advising me through the production of this book. Thank you.

Raja Miah
June 2002

Prologue

"Raj what's wrong with you?" asked Bassha. Rajah was giving Bassha a haircut, what nowadays is called a David Beckham cut. Rajah worked for Daniel now and then as he had just finished his Barbering course at Hopwood Hall College, Rochdale.

"What do you mean, nothing's wrong with me," replied Raj as he put the clipper down and picked up the Wahl trimmer to complete the haircut with the finishing touches.

"Well you married Jazmine, I told you not to get married so young. Then you divorced her and on Mum's emotional blackmail you married Rowsonara, not to mention Kajol…"

"Look I don't want to talk about it, please," said Rajah and taking off the cutting square and collar from Bassha added," That'll be five pounds Bash."

Bassha gave a ten-pound note. Rajah returned a five-pound note in change. As Bassha walked out he concluded, "Hey Raj I didn't mean to upset you, right, see you next week."

Bassha being the last customer, Rajah didn't even bother to say 'bye. He locked up and sat on the empty battered settee as he transcended to his past.

Rajah asked himself, why does he have to be attracted to two women at the same time. When one has broken his heart and the other cannot think of anything but him.

Kajol fulfilled his teenage life with colours. The magic they had together was indescribable. She made promises, but really she was playing with his emotions. Things would have been different with Kajol, they could have had so much fun together, and the chemistry would have never faded away. They could have lived happily forever, that Rajah was sure of.

Now, he wished he had never met Kajol. Beautiful she was, but she wasn't faithful. Rajah has experienced when you get a broken heart, the pain is unbearable. You experience a pain that no doctor in the world can mend. A pain that cannot be overcome by conventional painkillers. He has understood it is the consequences of experiencing love that he is going through now. A pain only time can heal. In spite of all this suffering, because of falling in love with Kajol, Rajah has the courage of falling in love again. In the hope that this time things would be better, because he is not getting any younger.

Chapter One

"Hey, give me more chai (tea)," a shout came from one corner of the café-bar. "I wan' my bill," another screamed. "Get me pan, waiter," requested another. Waiters running around, to fulfil every desperate customer's need. Waiters were wearing lungi, instead of trousers (petticoat without strings, wrapped on the waist.)

A medium built gentleman dressed in khaki shirt and trousers, sitting alone near the café's kitchen, looked very impatient. He celebrated his thirty-first birthday a fortnight ago with his only friend. Dark brown oval face, light brown eyes, five-feet eight inches high, black hair. A scar right across his left cheek, the result of a past investigative story.

"Like, to order." The gentleman looked up at the exhausted waiter, replied, "Please, give me five minutes more." He picked up the menu and looked through it again, the fourth time. He pulled his left shirtsleeve, stared at his Seiko, the fifth time, "Where's Jabir?" He tried to relax, as he gazed his eyes around the café. He saw broken spider webs at each corner of the ceiling. There was a crack on the opposite wall from where he was sitting. Daddy Long Legs were flying about. Sweet odours from Indian deserts were coming from the kitchen. Tears formed from sweat dripping from waiters' foreheads. Customers talking over each other's voices.

The gentleman got his pocket comb out, removed his camera from his left shoulder. Placed it at the side of the timbered table. "You can't comb here," said a waiter as he hurried to the kitchen. The gentleman swallowed a laugh, replaced his comb back. "Huh talk about hygienic, look at the place." A waiter overheard him, ignoring the comment.

The waiter approached half sneering, "Ready to order, Sir." He glanced at his Seiko and replied, "Five past four, emmh, I'd like cup of tea."

Anything to eat, pastries, samosa, onion bhaji?" asked the waiter. "Not yet, make my tea Indian, put cinnamon and bay leaves also elaichi," the gentleman replied giving a smile.

"Ek-chai, Indian," shouted the waiter as he entered the kitchen.

As his eyes changed direction they looked at the entrance door. There Jabir Khan standing six feet one, dark brown eyes, semi-oval face with a sharp long nose, in his late twenties. His hair misplaced, a numb look on the depressed face. Jabir walked through the door ignoring the greeting of the cashier.

"Jabir-what took you so long, you know well this appointment is more important to you, than me." Jabir sat down and breathed slowly.

"I am sorry as usual, Chander my friend..."

"No I demand an explanation for neglecting punctuality-Jabir," Chander looked angry. Jabir paused for a few seconds as no words escaped his mouth, but puzzled in someone's thought. Chander added;

"Is something the matter, yes, yes-your temper you lost it again?" Chander handed a handkerchief. Jabir wiped sweat from his face with the hanky as he replied; "She's done it, she has done it again – I couldn't resist slapping her," Jabir's voice rose at the last two words.

"Now calm down a bit, tell me what happened," Chander requested.

"There's nothing much to say or tell, Ayrina insisted to go shopping, she wouldn't care about my concerns, always manipulative, do this do that. She even called me crazy today, I have had it up to here." Jabir dramatized his right hand to his neck.

A waiter approached their table; spoke in an arrogant manner; "Ready to order or not?" holding a pen impatient to scribble away on his pad. Jabir browsed the menu, as Chander ordered; "First of all please cancel my tea. Now we shall have one chicken bhuna, one sag-methi-ghosht, two boiled rice, six chapattis and a bindi bhaji side dish with a plain raitha." Jabir added;

"Also two glasses of sweet lassi, dhon-ya-baad." They gave the menu to the waiter and smiled at each other.

"I presume you are hungry, Jabir."

"Starving, no doubt about it." Changing the subject Jabir spoke again;

"Never mind, ah did you get hold of Mr… now what's his name? – forgot!"

Chander naturally broke out laughing;

"He,he,he-You know Jabir, your moods are no different from our country's weather."

"All right cut the cheekiness and answer my question, please Chander."

"I did, Mr Uddin told me to meet at six pm. He did say it's not difficult to get a visa, despite it may cost a little but I'm sure he'll be reasonable."

"Where are we meeting Mr Uddin," asked Jabir in relief.

"In front of Akbor's shoe store," Chander paused, he added, changing the subject,

"I assume your marriage is falling apart, is it not?"

"It seems to be, but Allah is witness, I don't think or want it that way. Now where's the food," groaned Jabir. Other customers were waiting too, all the waiters are under pressure as usual.

"Be patient Jabir, you always told me, the idea of love and marriage is romantic, and you're never in favour of arranged ones. But, never gave a slight indication of your married life, the problems, call yourself my best friend," said Chander with accused eyes.

"It's not how you think! It began a few weeks after the wedding night. I told her about my mother's illness, first I expected she'd care; show empathy, I was wrong. Nevertheless, thought she'd change with time. I was wrong again. I would have told you, I didn't want to make you worried. You already show too much concern for my mother, than my brother Rokiv and me. You've got your own problems to tackle, like when are you getting married?" replied Jabir obligingly.

"Now I understand, but you are not the only one that bear sorrow alone, it's not good. One should share the burden of his wounded heart. Anyhow you told me you've got an uncle in Chansirkapon and there's a communication gap in between, but keeping things inside your heart, I didn't expect."

"Chander don't push me, I already regret what I've done a couple of hours ago," Jabir paused, his tone changed as his volume increased, "The hell with her, I shouldn't have raised my hand, couldn't help it, she wouldn't stop nagging me."

The waiter came to serve their order, nothing like the service in Hilton. Instead he banged everything on the table in a flash. Before they could thank him, the waiter left.

Jabir starving, mixed the Bhuna with boiled rice, simultaneously Chander began to scrape rice on the tin dinner plate. Chander's eyes couldn't resist staring at Jabir, because he could see an expressionless face as Jabir gobbled a piece of cubed chicken. Probably Jabir cursing himself marrying Ayrina in the first place, one couldn't blame Jabir. Jabir couldn't break his late father's word and shame the Khan family. His mother wouldn't allow him. Resenting the fact he admired his cousin Shamina's attributes. Probably once loved!

"What are you wondering, Chander," said Jabir as he gulped his sweet lassi.

"I was just in deep thought, nothing more."

"And don't tell me you're thinking about my stubborn, heartless wife, she's not worth a thought." Jabir shouted for another glass of lassi, this time a sour one.

It felt to Chander after years of friendship, he never knew too much to judge his friend, when Jabir remarked 'stubborn wife', Ayrina must have got on Jabir's nerves. Chander interrupted Jabir as his friend was busy eating, and almost ate four chapattis.

Sons of Jabir

"Jabir, now tell me did you really slap Ayrina, I just can't imagine it."

"Yes I did and I don't want to talk about it any more," replied Jabir, showing no remorse. Chander managed to nibble half a chapatti with bindi bhaji, he wondered why does Jabir's mood change, like it does!

"Jabir now, don't get angry, what if Ayrina does something foolish?" said Chander.

"I don't care nor bother, and you stop showing any sympathy for Ayrina, you talk to me like I treat her, like a servant, but it's the other way round," Jabir scraping his tin plate and the dishes with a fifth chapatti. Jabir did have a big appetite but he wasn't himself today. Chander's friend was not like this, most of the time he was a modest, charming person with a distinctive personality and an emotional heart, not that he had a heart condition.

Chander first met Jabir, two years back at a conference in Dhaka, when Iyub Khan visited the Ram Mental Hospital and donated large sums of money for more doctors and nurses. Chander wrote an article that the hospital was dominated by females than males and had more of Bengalis, than Pakistanis.

Chander glared at Jabir. Jabir wouldn't look into his eyes, maybe because Chander's intrusion into his personal life upset Jabir. It feels to Chander his friend Jabir has never been so naïve than at this particular moment.

"Sorry Chander, I didn't mean to be rude, I just like to relax." "Neither did I mean to make your feelings worse." Chander paused and added, "I'd like to know and be wise of your intentions of going abroad," Chander trying to change the subject.

Jabir finished eating and soaked his right hand into a bowl of liquid water; he twitched because the water was cold. Then he shouted for a towel. The same waiter who took their order brought a towel. "Here," throwing it to Jabir. Chander had just finished; he shouted to the waiter "Bring me a bowl of

Sons of Jabir

water please, hot if you can." "Got it," replied the waiter as he walked into the kitchen with the dirty bowl of water, in case he slips. In those days even in the rush hour one single mistake and you would be sacked. Being Bengali it was not easy to get another job and is impossible if one is an undergraduate, only because Pakistanis have their own way of approaching everything.

The waiter returned with warm water and before he could vanish Chander said, "I know you're in a hurry but we would like our bill, now tell me as a matter of curiosity despite the fact that you run like a mouse, do you usually address customers with no manners, or is it just us." The waiter sneered and replied, "Neither am I prejudice nor a Pakistani, to me it felt like talking to my own race, like I do, is being friendly. You want manners in the future?" He gave a hint of a smile and walked away.

"So much for my cheek" muttered Chander.

Jabir left a tip whilst Chander paid the bill. As both were to step out Jabir asked the cashier;

"Hey, can you tell me what time it is," casually as Jabir combed his hair. The reply was arrogant; "I'm, not here to tell time," Chander swallowed a laugh, but Jabir got angry and said; "What kind of attitude do you call that?" Both then stepped outside and Chander requested; "Never mind calm down, we have business to handle." The cashier was arrogant almost every time, only because Jabir wasn't himself today. Chander wondered would Jabir be able to cope in England.

Chander glanced at his Seiko; "We haven't got much time, pull a rickshaw over now." On the street every rickshaw was almost occupied and litter was floating about on the muddy pavement. Finally Jabir waved at an empty rickshaw and shouted; "Oy oy oy," the time now five thirty six. The driver parked at the kerb of the muddy pavement, he spat red saliva onto the edge of the kerb. It was not blood; chewing paan and beetlenut together causes it. "Where to?" the driver asked as he untied his lungi from his waist and tied a tighter knot.

"Akbor shoe shop, opposite Qasim Tailor," Jabir requested. "Oh there, charr-taka," said the driver as he knew where to go and demanding his rate, Jabir disagreed and replied, "No, I'll give three taka," the driver nodded and they jumped into the rickshaw.

Both of them could have walked there with little or no sweat, if they were not short of time and despite the fact that the weather was too warm.

"Jabir, you believe you can establish a career or find a reasonable job in England?" asked Chander, still wanting to talk about Ayrina. The driver's bare feet sweated as he peddled into the crowds of rickshaws. "I hope so," replied Jabir becoming impatient and scratching his back as it itched.

Jabir is Chander's only hope to go to England, when Jabir is there, settled. Jabir has a brother named Rokiv Khan; soon Rokiv sends sponsorship for accommodation and a letter offering a suitable job. Then getting a visa shouldn't be too difficult.

"Akbor shof-Akbor shof," shouted the driver as the rickshaw halted beside the footpath. Jabir paid three taka. Chander's watch then struck five to six as both of them stood at one corner of Akbor's shop in Zindabazar Road, facing the variety of shops opposite. Zindabazar Road is pretty stretchy; one end passes the chain of shops leading to Iyub Khan's great mosque, named after Pakistan's present President. The mosque had a semi-circle gold painted tomb on top, white pillars constructed from the roof coming down onto a marble patio. Steps in the middle lead to a steel double door entrance inside the great mosque.

"Why isn't Mr Uddin here yet?" said Jabir anxiously. "He should be here any minute, he is a man of time," replied Chander.

The opposite end of the road came to a T-junction leading onto Chattak Road. There was a Dhaaba (like a Balti House) on the left side of Chattak Road and onto right side Dr Khashi's Surgery next door to Ibrahim's Pharmacy.

Sons of Jabir

Transport of all types travelled through Zindabazar Road, from bicycle to auto-rickshaw and cars to coaches. There were no traffic lights or pedestrian crossings. The location of Akbor's shop was in the centre.

"Assala-mu-alaykum," a voice greeted them from behind. They turned around and Mr Uddin stood in front of them.

"Alee kum salam," they both replied. "Mr Uddin, this is Jabir Khan as I have told you previously," Chander introduced.

"Yes, yes of course let's go into Akbor's shop where we can talk," said Uddin. The three of them stepped into the shoe shop and were greeted by Akbor himself;

"Salaam, who need what, sandals, shoes or boots?" neither Jabir nor Chander uttered.

"Assala-mu-alaykum, my name is Akram Uddin, if it is possible we would like to use your backroom," requested Mr Uddin. Akbor hesitated at first then he recognised;

"Ah Mr Uddin and Mr Chander, sorry I see so many faces every day, of course you can," Akbor gave them a single key and pointed to his backroom door saying; "Over there."

Akbor Ali was a respected entrepreneur in Sylhet. He was the only Bengali who specialised in all types of footwear amongst several Pakistani shoe shops and survived in perfect competition. One time or another every Bengali had purchased a pair of shoes or sandals from his shop. He had no fear of the Pakistani Government or of its republicans. He was a very helpful person, when needed. Why should he fear from their constituency? He ran a profitable legitimate business and paid all the necessary taxes.

Chander turned the key unlocking the backroom door and the three of them stepped in. The room not so large had a small rectangle window on the wall opposite its door. The three of them sat on white plastic chairs forming a triangle. Mr Uddin placed his brown leather briefcase on his lap and fiddling with the combination he spoke;

"I regret to inform you but I am short of time, now let's deal with Mr Jabir shall we," he glanced at his Casio watch and stared at Jabir for a while. Maybe because his eyes never met a handsome client before. To break the silence Chander said;

"Mr Uddin my friend Jabir wants a Visa for England, he believes his future is unstable in East Pakistan." Mr Uddin clicked open his briefcase as the numbers matched and said;

"Firstly any certificates of education, secondly any disabilities or medical record showing a minor or major illness and most importantly I require your mother's and father's names. My service of administration will be roughly twenty thousand taka." Jabir took a deep breath, exhaled and replied;

"Oh Allah-twenty."

"It's not much, normally it is more, Chander knows me well and that is why I do it less for you," Uddin said to the relief of Jabir.

Seeing Jabir's anxiousness, Chander asked; "Should money be a problem, I'll be glad to help." For a few seconds Jabir did not speak, as he was deep in thought.

"It's just money is a bit tight at the moment, I guess I will have to wait for the harvest which is two months away, then it should be all right."

"I will also need details such as a sponsorship from somebody residing in England, if you have a relative it's convincing. Along with a letter offering you a job from say a factory or restaurant," explained Mr Uddin.

"Yes I have an elder brother named Rokiv, he shall be providing necessary documents and my late father's name Ghulam Mustafa Khan and my mother's name Nessa Khan. I have also recently been to see my doctor and I feel he is being hesitant in making a diagnosis on me," said Jabir.

Mr Uddin, scribbling notes of what Jabir had just stated, his eyebrows stretched as he widened his grey eyes, spoke;

"Are you trying to tell me that you have an illness, which has not reached its peak? Or are you just being overcautious and protective?"

Chander interrupted;

"I think what he means, is his temper and change of moods. At some stage we all have a temper, don't we Mr Uddin?" All three of them started to sweat as the room temperature rose by their breaths. The room had no ventilation, and the small open window wasn't helping. Jabir questioned;

"My temper is sometimes uncontrollable, and afterwards I feel guilty."

"As long as there isn't medical evidence to prove an illness. Certainly it should not be a matter of worry until a future date" said Mr Uddin, as he put his biro and note pad back into his briefcase.

Knock-knock.

The door opened with a squeak, a little boy entered the room.

"Chai-chai," the boy said, holding a wooden tray with milk, tea and sugar. They all replied;

"No – say thank you to Akbor."

"So Mr Jabir and Chander, we will meet here after two months at the end of the Harvest. That is a nice camera you've got, Mr Chander." Mr Uddin complimented Chander on his camera. All of them walked out of Akbor's shoe shop, Chander returning the back-room key. Mr Uddin hailed a rickshaw and went to see his next client. Most of the shops were closed, so Akbor rolled his shutters down. Chander advised Jabir to go home, but Jabir requested to stay and spend some time. Maybe because he wants his wife Ayrina to go to bed when he gets home, which Chander doesn't know.

The night became silent, as time passed it grew darker. A lone auto-rickshaw drove past Jabir's home as its headlights sparked onto Ayrina Akthar. She had almost dozed off, if it had not been for the glimpse of the sparkling lights. She sat upright in a pine chair, near the front door, in the corridor, looking out. All she could see was the tomb of the great mosque, through the corridor's window.

Her unwilling dark brown eyes searched for the man she never really loved. Thinking of where he has gone? What's taking him so long? Is he dead? Pity for her, that's what she said hours ago, if she meant it or not! As if she bothered for another minute! She thought, "why should she?" he has been stubborn for a while.

Her belief now is undoubtedly that Jabir Khan doesn't care nor bothers about her feelings or her interests. He only cares that the food is on the table, the house is clean, tidy and shining. One shouldn't ask for anything, unless given by him. You cannot question him, or argue. What he says is right.

Ayrina's mind clicked to the day of their engagement. It was the first time she saw Jabir. What a handsome, religiously cultured figure he was, and still is. But she hates to admit it now. Charming in the way he talked, and his manners made her think a man of modesty, full of attributes, but not anymore, to Ayrina. Were his mannerisms and personality a mask, or was Ayrina flattered on the day of their engagement? Now, she is confused at their happy-go-lucky marriage.

Ayrina, herself having a background of respected high class family the Chaudharies. Her father an ex-colonel, served in World War Two. Her mother teaches Asian History and Advanced Bengali at a high school in Srimangal. Her late grandfather was an Airline Traffic Controller at the Pakistan International Airlines.

She never thought that her marriage had another miserable face to it. Primarily she was delighted by Jabir's good looks. When, she later found out that Jabir was not a graduate, she felt embarrassed to her friends because all their husbands have BA, B.SC, M.B.B.S, and the rest, after their names. So she reluctantly, on occasion, had to lie. Ayrina herself had got a degree in Sociology from Dhaka University before she married Jabir.

It was only because Ayrina's father promised Jabir's father, minutes after the time of her birth, to change friendship and become family. Ghulam Mustafa Khan and Ayrina's father were best friends, known in their regiment of the eastern frontier.

Sons of Jabir

Ayrina vaguely remembers at the time of Hitler's evilness and genocide, that her father was madly grieving because his friend, Jabir's father, was a victim of the atomic bomb, which allied forces dropped on Hiroshima.

From her engagement day until now, her every dream has been downtrodden, crushed. She just can't tolerate another day with Jabir, "even if I'm six weeks pregnant." She felt pity that she hadn't told Jabir. She sometimes thinks Why Jabir? Only because her father gave a word of promise.

The night became colder. The gust of wind rattled the litter outside. A cat walked past Ayrina's eyes, in a stare. She gave a shrewd smile. The paan leaves on the windowsill shivered as she shut the window and sat back. She rubbed her sobbed eyes dry. Her make-up washed away with countless teardrops. She was hungry, but didn't feel like eating.

Down memory lane, there were moments she wanted to go on holidays. She wanted a family. All the good things in life that her friends took for granted. All those glittering sarees she desired, Jabir once promised, that never came! But now, all she wanted was out of Jabir's solitary life.

From noon up until now, there hadn't been a split-second her mind hadn't thought of Jabir in hatred, hatred and hatred. Jabir's slap was a total shock. In her entire life no one pointed a finger at her. Not even her parents. Jabir did it, and it is final, a settlement needed to be reached.

Eventually Ayrina walked to her bedroom. She felt tired and drowsy climbing the stairs. She sat facing her dressing-table mirror;

"Ah, wooh, ah, wufhh," she agonized, touching her right cheek, which formed a pinkish bruise. Ayrina pulled her drawers, searched for a pen and pad, wrote a brief letter to her parents, that she wants a divorce and that's final. Then, changed and crawled into bed. As she snored away she mumbled:

"I hate you, hate you, hate you…"

The door handle clicked, it screeched as Jabir walked in slowly. He switched the light on and gazed into the kitchen, staircase and the living room. He sighed in relief; the corridor's wall clock struck twenty past eleven. He assumed Ayrina was sound asleep. He tiptoed into the kitchen, silently. Frying pans and pots were empty as he expected, so he prepared all the ingredients, ready to cook. Within half an hour he cooked himself Aloo-gobi and a few chapattis. If he had been in a chef contest he probably would have won a prize for the fastest cook. Previous times he cooked were when his mother became mentally ill, and after she was institutionalised. The thought of his mother makes him emotional, and he shivers every time. He wondered, could he become a chef in England, an Indian one.

When he finished eating he said a short prayer;

"Oh Allah, it is up to you, bless me always, make my mother well – Allahu-amin."

He trotted upstairs, the bedroom door was open. He tiptoed in, not disturbing Ayrina, grabbed a couple of pillows and a blanket from their bed, and returned to the living room. He made the couch as comfortable as possible. He took his shirt, shoes and socks off, yawned several times, and slept deep into the glittering night.

The disadvantage or annoyance of living near Sylhet was that the traffic was horrendous in the mornings. The sun glowed, casting the living room furniture. Jabir woke up, rubbed his brown eyes, ran to the bathroom to drain his bladder, brushed his teeth, rinsed, washed his face and combed his hair flipping it back. Out of the bathroom he put on his shirt, dusted his trousers and put his socks and shoes on. He picked the pillows up, grabbed the blanket and went up the stairs to the bedroom. He was surprised, Ayrina still sleeping, unusual of her.

"Are we still snoring" Jabir said irresistibly giggling, throwing the pillows and blanket on her. Ayrina promptly opened her eyes, leaned on the headboard and replied;

"What's it to you, as if you care! – Get lost."

Sons of Jabir

Jabir already regretted waking her up. He wanted to turn around, to get out of there. Natural or not, his mood intruded his thoughts;

"It seems to me you are asking for another one, on your left cheek." Jabir wondered, would he strike again, pretending to ignore her right cheek. Ayrina became self-protective;

"Oh yes-yes-yes, you sure can, slapped me yesterday. This is becoming a ritual, is it? I am not your mistress, understand," Ayrina said, raising her eyebrows. Jabir raised his voice with a simultaneous change of tone;

"You dare talk to me like that again, play with my patience. I had reason to slap you, despite my temper." To Ayrina it seemed some sort of a challenge. She increased her volume;

"You what – you had a reason to slap me, your damn temper my foot. Was I intolerable? I only asked you to take me shopping." Jabir felt guilt, sensed mixed emotions. His voice reduced;

"Ayrina, but I had to see some-one, important meeting, shopping and shopping, you are all the same, women, never give up, live in a material world, like money grows on trees." They were both arguing as if a Python and a Cobra wrestling.

Ayrina snapped her teeth;

"Yes – I know, had to see, good-for-nothing friend. That dumb, Ali." Ayrina crawled towards Jabir.

"My friend is not good-for-nothing. If you cannot respect someone, don't humiliate. He's an investigative reporter, independent." Jabir turned possessive about friendship. His brown eyes stretched wide. Ayrina wouldn't stop for nothing. They both began to sweat. The colour of her cheeks turned red. Jabir's face became elated. Ayrina turned furious, ignoring the consequences;

"You call him a friend, a rat, snake, lousy bachelor." For a moment Jabir's mind clicked to yesterday's conversation. "Is this what one is rewarded, poor Chander."

"Shame, ridiculous Chander showed sympathy for you – uncaring animal. And you – rat, lousy, what else, calling him." Ayrina's voice rose to its peak;

"I don't give a damn or care, if the two of you burn in hell. Miserable psycho – the only reason I married you was because of my father's promise, an honour. No wonder your mother is in a mental hospital."

A thunderstorm was nothing compared to what Jabir felt, struck by his wife. He instantly slapped Ayrina with a great anger. A sudden silence fell upon. "Listen bitch – don't dare refer to my mother like that again, ever."

He hit her so hard his hand stung. He immediately ran out of the bedroom and out of the house, slamming the doors behind. He ran straight to his wheat fields and knelt down, covering his remorseful face with both hands. Emotion took over, he began to weep. He felt awful about the whole incident

"Shouldn't have said it, she shouldn't have said that."

In the bedroom Ayrina remained silent. Bewildered, shattered and shocked, not surprised. She could feel pain. Her cheek felt like a wasp's sting. Sitting upright on the bed in a form of a statue. Finally she snapped her mind from the trance, shaking her head. Her long, straight black hair, rocked side to side like a raging bull. Ayrina screamed and screamed, turning into a wild horse. She kicked the dressing table. In seconds everything in the room was a mess. Then, gradually she came to a halt, her temper reduced;

"Bastard – bastard!" she shouted, panting. Her patience controlled her anger. She calmed down, collapsed on her dressing stool and looked at herself in the pink triple mirror, as it gave symmetrical reflections, images like zombies.

"That's it, that is it," Ayrina spoke out. She made her final decision. She ripped up last night's letter, dressed herself quickly and pulled a large PVC suitcase from underneath their bed. She unzipped the suitcase and dusted it with a pillowcase. She opened all her drawers and the metal wardrobe and grabbed her sarees, blouses, petticoats and her cosmetics. She threw them in, pressed the top cover down hard and zipped up the suitcase.

She wrote a letter and left it for Jabir on the dressing table. For the final time she looked at the triple mirror;

"Damn, bastard, go-to-hell, hell." She walked downstairs carrying her overloaded suitcase. She put on her raincoat, walked out of the house and locked the door. She posted the key through the letterbox. As it dropped to the wooden floor Ayrina began to walk, carrying the suitcase, towards the coach stand towards the town. She glanced at the wheat fields; her eyes saw Jabir on his knees. She sped up and covered her face with a black veil, fortunate to find a coach standing by, and the conductor shouting

"Dhaka, Dhaka, Dhaka…"

The conductor helped Ayrina with the luggage. The driver gave her a ticket, charging eighteen-taka. She sat in the middle next to an old woman, sighed with relief, she was gone forever.

An old man walking down the aisles under the shadow of his umbrella, across the fields, protecting himself from sunrays. As he came nearer to Jabir, he thought, "Must be a devoted Muslim."

"You, it's not time for prayer is it?" Jabir looked up, embarrassed, he blushed;

"No, no I was just – nothing." The old man passed by puzzled, not curious. Jabir wiped his wet eyes and face with his cotton hanky.

"Oh Allah, help me!" shouted Jabir, rising to his feet. He wondered what's Chander up to. He thought about Ayrina. "Must be cursing me." His mind didn't jump to any conclusions. He might have to cook for a while. Make sure, to control his anger and rage in the future. He hoped, prayed, and doesn't want anything serious to happen.

As Jabir couldn't afford to waste time, thinking of the near future, going abroad, he needed 20,000 taka within eight weeks. He looked around, farmers already started to plough

Sons of Jabir

their wheat fields. "Just two months to go, just two months." Hopefully all his financial worries would be over, he anticipated.

Working in the fields was not his idea, but his circumstances gave him no real alternative. He considered himself lucky in one way. He inherited the house and the fields from his father a long time ago. What amazed him was his elder brother Rokiv didn't claim any share. "Probably he adores me very much."

Actually it's part of an ancestry inheritance. His grandfather left his father two acres of farmland. From that his father, through sole labour, built the house, just before he went to war. Over a few years up to now, Jabir had managed to purchase another acre through the good harvests in the past. He wanted to work as a clerk or a bank teller. It was his misfortune; his mother became paranoid, resulting in him failing his diploma in commerce.

Sweating all over, Jabir reached his timbered shed, about eleven metres from his home. He rolled his trousers to his ankles and took his satin shirt off, which was damp with sweat, and hung it on a nail inside the shed. He picked a large bag of seeds and a digging fork, determined to plough a full acre.

As he emerged in the sunshine from his cool shed, both hands occupied, beads of sweat started to drip from his backside. Jabir liked to work in the open when the sun shines. The wheat fields are on the opposite side of the Surma River divided (in-between) by the main road leading to Jabir's house, approximately sixty yards from his acres diagonally. A couple of hours passed by in devoted labour. Jabir never felt like taking a break, continuously ploughing. He aimed to seed at least half an acre today, to achieve a full harvest, and a good one. He didn't even feel hungry.

Opposite Jabir Khan's detached house, faced several other detached houses taking a right direction abreast with the main road. The main road went across the Surma Bridge entering Sylhet. Behind the detached houses, there is the Surma riverbank.

Sons of Jabir

In winter the river reaches its high peak, sometimes resulting in holding up transport services. It overflows its embankment endangering agriculture, destroying vast amounts of wheat. The main road from Sylhet leads to numerous villages passing Lalabazar and Bishwanath, finishing beyond Joganathfur Road.

Jabir's forearm ached. He would have done more if the night glittered. For the past several hours water hasn't touched his dried lips. He only stopped to wipe his sweat beads from his forehead.

"I wonder what Ayrina's doing. I wonder how my mother is coping," mumbled Jabir. The next thing he did was to lock his shed, putting the farm equipment in place as his stomach grumbled. He buttoned his shirt leaving smudges of dirt from his fingers. He jogged home, so hungry now he realized. When he entered neither his left nor his right foot stepped on the key that lay on the wooden floor. He walked straight to the kitchen, turned on the gas and placed yesterday's Aloo-Gobi to heat. He quickly washed his hands, and then rolled five chapattis. The frying pan sizzled as it condensed the front of the cupboard besides the cooker. He switched the gas off, in stress he didn't know what he was doing, partly desperate. Jumping up and down he ran to the bathroom to drain his bladder. 'Has Ayrina eaten' crossed his mind. 'Probably.' He returned, feeling drowsy. He usually eats rice because he finds chapattis easy to make. He is not very fussy about eating, though not aware he may be getting indifferent day by day. "Oh Allah bless me always and those I adore," a short after dinner prayer. His body began to ache, he felt hot and euphoric. He thought of nothing, assumed Ayrina was asleep. He forgot to check his front door. He stumbled straight to the lounge and collapsed on the couch. He only managed to take his shoes off, too drunk in his tiredness, and within minutes had dozed off.

"Wake-up you lazy," said Chander. Poking Jabir's tummy for the last half an hour. Jabir opened his eyelids slowly, yawned and groaned, sat up.

"What are you doing here?" asked Jabir. He rubbed his eyes, still sleepy.

"Never mind, surprised how I got in," Chander said, wondering about the key he found on the wooden floor. 'Possibly Jabir dropped it.'

"Hey wait a second, how did you manage to get in?" Jabir suddenly aware.

"That's what I'm on about. The door was wide open. I noticed it coming out of next door for a news article. Got burgled last night."

"How could I be so careless? Lucky they didn't rob me."

"Sure, missed a good opportunity," replied Chander. He handed the key to Jabir. Jabir took the key and dropped it in his right pocket. Jabir puzzled, questioned;

"Where did you find the key?"

"On the floor, near the door, assumed you dropped it," replied Chander. Struggling to get the film out from his camera because the auto-wind has jammed.

"I even dropped the key. I could not be more careless. You know what Chander, I feel so, can't express. Yesterday, terrible, awful, never mind." Eventually Jabir stood up from the couch.

"Phew, you smell disgusting. Look at yourself, crinkled shirt, and dirty pants – no offence. Go and get dressed, we will go for a walk." Chander couldn't believe the ridiculous way Jabir slept last night. Chander added;

"I'll make us tea, get ready." Chander walked to the kitchen. Jabir walked to the bathroom, as he hummed;

"If only had millions, or win the lottery, only if, – if, at least got a friend."

Jabir's reflection in the mirror made him decide to have a shave. Good or a bad habit, Jabir liked to talk with his reflection, especially in an elated mood.

"Always admire Chander, when he comes to the rescue at time of disasters. Sometimes think Chander is all I have. Ayrina likes playing with my anger from the day of our wedding, despite yesterday's tragedy, pity she's still asleep. All that foul language, neglecting my mother. Brother Rokiv wouldn't have liked it. Every so often reminds me of her father's promise. If she had a different husband he probably would have done worse things to her."

Jabir finished shaving and had a quick bath. He towelled himself and leaped out of the bathtub and bathroom. Hs wet feet left footprints as he walked up the stairs. When he reached the landing the bedroom door was open.

As he entered the bedroom his brown eyes stretched wide open, and his mouth became agape. "Jabir, one day I'll be gone. You'll regret it for the rest of your life."

In the kitchen Chander was busy making tea and toast. The water took a while to boil. Chander was familiar with the Khan's kitchen. He opened the cupboard beside the gas cooker, selected a couple of tea bags from the bottom, as the top ones were pretty dusty. Something touched his right wrist as he withdrew his hand. The item fell on the floor;

"Ttunghhh,"

Chander looked down and saw another key. He threw the tea bags in the boiling water and turned off the grill. He bent down and picked up the metal key. "Maybe an extra key they keep for emergencies," thought Chander. Chander put the key back in the cupboard.

Finally he came out of the kitchen with four slices of toast and two mugs of steaming tea, leaving the aroma of bay leaves and cinnamon behind. Both his hands occupied he walked slowly past the bathroom. He noticed Jabir's clothes in the bathtub. He arrived in the lounge and freed his hands putting the breakfast on the glass oval table beside the couch. He sat on the couch removing his camera, putting it next to him. He really adored the camera because Jabir gave it him on his thirty-first birthday. He sipped his Indian tea, 'perfect.' He took a large bite from a slice of toast, 'not crispy enough.'

He leaned back, relaxed. He stared out of the window and began to wonder about Jabir. He glanced at his watch, "He'll take his time, oiling his body, combing his hair until every single strand is in place, pressing his shirt sleeves to get a permanent crease, same with the trousers, confident Jabir." Chander waited for his friend patiently, despite the toast and tea going cold. "Surely hope they're not arguing."

Earning a living as an investigative reporter, income varies. Independent, it is challenging, exciting and sometimes dangerous. Waking up early in the morning. Weekends lucky to get hold of an exclusive. Pity my sources are loyal. Only the motivational ones reach the top of the media ladder. I've still to climb high to compete against Suleman Qureshi, the well-known reporter of West Pakistan.

'Now what is taking Jabir so long, let's inquire', Chander walked to the stairs and shouted:

"Jabir, breakfast has gone cold." There was no reply. Chander thought maybe Jabir and Ayrina want to give him a surprise. Taking long strides up the stairs Chander reached the landing. The door was wide open, Chander stepped in, 'God', Chander was astonished. He froze, didn't know what to do! Startled. His eyebrows rose as his eyes stretched. Chander bit his tongue, couldn't utter a word, speechless. Is this a delusion, nightmare. Is Chander hallucinating? Certainly not, it is real! Jabir lying in bed unconscious, a towel wrapped round his waist. The fear of complete silence made Chander breathless. Jabir's one hand clenched to a fist, the other lay open flat. His face looked white, his body pale and bleak, and his brown eyes stationary.

Chander tried to snap out of his sudden physical trance, but couldn't. What Chander encountered before his eyes made him helpless. Drawers were open, half empty. The wardrobe was wide open with hangers tangling. Jabir's clothes were all over the bedroom floor.

His eyes returned to the unconscious body. Chander slapped himself. 'God help me', his trance broke, and he crawled besides the bed and instantly checked Jabir's pulse. 'Thank God', he felt Jabir's heartbeat. He immediately ran

Sons of Jabir

down straight to the kitchen and returned with a glass of water, spilling some on the stairs. He sprinkled some water on Jabir's critical face and held Jabir's head with his right palm. As the wet rim of the glass touched his dried lips Jabir breathed slowly. Chander sighed with relief as Jabir drank a little water. He gathered all the pillows and piled them. He put the glass on the table. He stretched Jabir, lying on his backside on the pillows, near the headboard, putting him upright. It is the most critical moment of Chander's life, his friend Jabir having a near death experience.

Despite the circumstances, questions crossed Chander's mind. Where is Ayrina? Why is this room messy? Never mind. What mattered to him is saving Jabir's life. Chander raced out of the house and stopped the first auto-rickshaw available. "Dr Khashi's surgery, hurry up." Chander was sweating from head to toe. He had never experienced such a devastating situation before.

In a matter of minutes, hailing through the rickshaws and idiot road crossers, the auto-rickshaw halted in front of Dr Khashi's surgery. Chander ran straight to the reception. He desperately asked;

"Tell Dr Khashi, matter of life and death." As Chander was panting Dr Khashi overheard and responded promptly. In no time, both of them were with Jabir in the bedroom. Jabir still seemed unconscious.

Chander felt relieved, as Dr Khashi knew what to do. Patient nor impatient, in worry, Chander began to pace up and down. Dr Khashi got out a syringe from his medical bag. He plunged the sharp needle, an inch long, into a bottle of liquid. He pumped until it reached the ten-millilitre mark of the eight-centimetre cylinder syringe. He then injected Jabir just below his right shoulder. After a few seconds Jabir closed his eyes.

"I have tranquillised him, hopefully he should recover when he wakes up," said Dr Khashi.

Chander asked;

"Can you tell me what has caused this? What is it a result of?"

"Probably an emotional threat, led to a sudden nervous breakdown." Dr Khashi wrote a prescription and handed it to Chander. As Chander paid the doctor's fee,

"I warn you, keep him away from bad news," requested Dr Khashi.

"I will try, thanks, bye."

The doctor left as Chander sat beside Jabir. He breathed a sigh of relief, still panting. Reluctantly relaxed he felt thirsty. As he reached out for the glass, Chander's eyes discovered a torn envelope on the dressing table. He picked it up, nothing inside, neither had the dressing table anything on it.

He turned, looked at Jabir and felt his heartbeat. It sounded a bit slow. His face began to regain colour. Chander took a tissue from the box lying on the floor. He wiped Jabir's face and the dried lips. Chander covered Jabir with a cotton blanket up to his shoulders bringing his arms out as Jabir lay in a tranquillised sleep. A piece of crumpled paper the size of a golf ball fell on the bedroom floor from his right hand. Making sure Jabir was comfortable, Chander picked up the paper. He opened it, stretched the crinkles and began to read...

"Jabir,

I hated you from the moment you slapped me for the first time. I never loved you and never will. I said it many times, saying it again; I only married you because of my father's word. I lost trust in you the day you told me your mother is in a mental institution. I am not the kind of woman you men treat like typical housewives. If I were aware of your mother's illness then I would have even broken my father's promise. This to you I don't know, but to me it's an accident that I am carrying your offspring. One thing is definite; you and me are finished forever, for good. Don't come and hassle me in Srimangal. Your mother is a psycho-whatever. No wonder you are turning into one. If your child becomes like you then I'll

kill that child. I could not care less if you burn in hell. Bye – I mean – forever.
   Ayrina"

Chander's eyes dropped tears as he looked at Jabir. He could not estimate how hurtful Jabir must have felt when he read this letter. Chander could never imagine Ayrina being so stonehearted, absurd, and shrewd. Not anticipating the consequences, self-respected selfish person. How could she be so cruel? Jabir's ambition and hope of going to Britain may have come to an end. Along with Chander's dreams of becoming a reporter for a national newspaper in Britain. For better or worse Chander determined to encourage Jabir to go abroad.

How could she be so inconsiderate? Jabir sacrificed his love to keep his family pride. Yet she constantly reminded him of her father's promise. Is it his fault that his mother is ill; it's bad enough for him. Chander remembered the occasion a day or two ago, when Jabir said;

"When I come on vacation from England, I'll buy her all the sarees she wanted that I promised her." It astonished Chander; Ayrina never knew the inner most feelings of Jabir's heart.

An hour passed by, Chander finished tidying the messy bedroom. Chander left Jabir in a deep sleep and walked to Ibrahims' Pharmacy. He returned with Vitamin C and Antidepressants, prescribed by Dr Khashi. After several thoughts Chander decided to write a brief letter to Jabir's uncle in Chansirkapon. It took Chander less than a couple of minutes. Chander waited in case Jabir woke up, another hour gone and Jabir was still in a deep sleep. Finally Chander walked to the Post Office and asked at the counter for a first class recorded delivery postage.

Chapter Two

Chansirkapon, a village surrounded by hundreds of tropical trees. January is the season of tangerines, bananas and coconuts, from a bird's-eye view the village looks like a green island, spring time, approximately half a kilometre from Bishwanath. The village has several extended families, except the Khan family.

All the homes are like bungalows. The first house in the village belongs to Anwar Khan. The walls are constructed of tin with wooden pillars structured in the centre. All the rooms are equal, first room, the kitchen. Gas lines have not reached the village. Cooking apparatus is made of clay, moulded from the ground shapes as small volcanoes. Holes are dug in the ground underneath the clay made cooker. Timber is used for the fire to cook. The second and third rooms are double bedrooms. The fourth, guest room, is used as the living room. There's a concrete patio in front, above the extended roof overlooks the landing, the size of a tennis court.

Several yards from the landing, there's a footpath going in both directions. One end leads to an inadequate non-concrete road full of bumps. The other end passes through the remaining families to a different village. From the left end of the footpath, approximately twenty metres, where the road crosses, is a local store, opposite a mosque. A few metres from the end of Khan's landing, crossing the footpath a staircase made of pebbles goes down to a large shallow swimming pool, similar to a small reservoir.

Villagers find it adequate and sufficient to swim, bathe, and no alternative but to wash their clothes in the same water, from the swimming pool. Amongst the eight homes there are four swimming pools in Chansirkapon. There is the bond of unity within all. Anwar is popular, well known for his attributes towards his fellow villagers. He takes honour of being a farmer, very vulnerable occasionally. Forty-four and looks after his health. He used to work for the East-Pakistan radio years ago. He has a wife and an only daughter.

A thin, short man in khaki uniform, peddling on a bicycle arrived in front of Anwar's guest room, parked on his landing;

Tring-tring-tring.

A young woman in her youth in a sky-blue saree came out. Her pale brown eyes refreshed in the morning breeze. Her long straight black hair covered her pink cheeks as the wind blew towards her five-feet-four, slim body.

"Letter, recorded for Anwar Khan," said the postman, breathing heavily.

"You can give it to me," replied the pretty female smiling.

"I need a signature."

"Oh will mother do. Father has gone for his morning walk."

"That will be all right." The postman got a biro and receipt pad out of his breast pocket.

"Ma-, maa, maah," she shouted aloud. Her mother came running, holding her breath and stood beside her daughter. They both look alike, the mother an inch shorter with grey-silver hair. The mother's cheeks puffed as she drew breath and exhaled;

"What what's the matter Shamina?"

"Registered letter for Pa."

The postman interrupted;

"Adaab," handed the pad and pen. Shamina's mother scribbled a very short signature. The postman handed the brown rectangle envelope.

"Dhanyo-baad," said Shamina as she slit the envelope with her index finger. She read the four short sentences quickly.

"Who is Chander, Ma?"

"I have no clue, where is the letter from."

"Sylhet."

Neither of them noticed as Anwar entered the landing.

"Ma, who's Jabir, famil…" Shamina got interrupted.

"Shamina-Asia, can't you read the letter inside, give it to me. I bet it's from my in-laws," said Anwar as he sneered at his wife.

"It's from Jabir, Shamina he's your cousin's brother," replied Asia.

Anwar read the letter, then;

"Jabir is ill, I have to go to see him."

"Shamina what did the letter say," asked her mother.

"It said, no time for introduction, Jabir is in critical condition. I'm his friend, my duty to inform you. Please come Sylhet, Jabir's house as soon as possible, from Chander. That's all Ma."

Asia looked at Anwar's worried face and spoke;

"You go and visit him, poor Jabir, take Shamina with you."

Anwar thought his wife may object because of the years of miscommunication.

"Ma, how can I not remember cousin Jabir," asked Shamina.

"You saw him a few times – you were small then. Jabir was nine to eleven months old when Uncle Mosthafa died in the war. Then Jabir and his mother moved to Sylhet to live. Shamina interrupted;

"Ma, I remember Nessa Auntie, and Grandpa gave the village house and fields to my Pa cause Pa likes the village atmosphere. Nessa Auntie came ill, hasn't Jabir got a big brother? Isn't Jabir married – Ma?"

"Shamina, enough of your questions, go and get ready, let's set off before noon," insisted Anwar. 'What critical state could Jabir be in, the last time Jabir sent a letter, explained he had admitted his mother in Ram mental hospital', Anwar stopped thinking.

"Ayrina had better be taking good care of him," mumbled Anwar.

"Pa, I am ready, who's Ayrina?" questioned Shamina, now wearing a pink saree.

"I shall tell you on the journey, let's go."

Sons of Jabir

Asia packed a carrier with fruits for Jabir. She stuffed a tiffen-carrier with rice, fish and curry and gave an umbrella for the journey.

Father and daughter reached the local store, less than five minutes by foot.

"Baishab Anwar – where are you going?" asked the shop owner curiously as he returned the cigarettes and change.

"Sylhet with my daughter, you know Ramu – long story."

A rickshaw peddling along, parked besides Shamina. A passenger jumped off. Shamina tried to negotiate a fare to Bishwanath.

"Stubborn driver demands char-taka, pa."

"I shall give him three, only three, not a paisa more on this bright day."

"Acha-acha." Shamina was pleased with her father as the driver agreed on three taka.

The bare sweated feet peddled quickly. After fifteen minutes or so Shamina and Anwar arrived at Bishwanath. The bazaar was not very busy; it was diverted with traffic usually. The rush begins just after twelve. Anwar paid the rickshaw driver. Anwar grabbed the umbrella and the tiffen-carrier. Shamina carried the cotton carrier bag of fruits. As they both were about to step inside the coach signposted SYLHET ALL STOPS, a boy not more than two feet, in rags with dirty hands and smudged face, pulled the edge of Shamina's saree from her back. Simultaneously they turned around.

"Have'n' eaten in days," the boy said glaring at Shamina.

"Give the child some money pa."

"Beggars I thought I'd escaped this time, here." Anwar gave the boy a taka reluctantly, and then purchased two adult returns. They both sat at the front behind the coach driver.

For the last time the conductor shouted; "Sylhet-Sylhet-Sylhet." The driver started the ignition and drove on his way to Sylhet. It was Shamina's second time going to a great town with her father. The first time was on Sheikh Mujib's conference at Zinda-bazaar last month.

****

Cutting through the dry clouds, the sun shone upon the uneven town. Chander suddenly woke up as Jabir still snored. Chander didn't anticipate he would carelessly doze off besides Jabir, despite that he was awake most hours last night. Pity Jabir ate a little before dawn. Chander glanced at his watch 'ten-thirty-five.' Chander checked Jabir's pulse and gladly opened the bedroom window. Chander yawned, stretched his anxious body as he walked downstairs. He washed his face and went in to the kitchen.

As Jabir turned his body facing the window, the sunshine brightened his face. Jabir squeezed his eyes then opened his eyelids gently. He smeared his dry lips, rubbed his eyes and gazed around. He saw Chander's camera on the dressing table. He confidently drank some water and waited for Chander.

A while passed, Chander returned with breakfast on a tray.

"Chander, how can I ever thank you?" said Jabir.

"Jabir, thank me by recovering and forgetting the tragic past."

"I'll try my best," replied Jabir, as he folded his legs on the bed and leaned his back on the headboard. They both ate toast and drank tea.

"Don't have to tell me anything. Think it's kismet. I insist you have a shave and bath. You'll feel better," suggested Chander.

Jabir went to get freshened up. The bathroom seemed clean. Jabir began to shave, without talking to his image in the mirror. There was a knock on the door.

"Cha-ander, some one is at the door," shouted Jabir.

"Aaah, sure I'll get that," replied Chander from the kitchen.

"Are you expecting anybody?"

"Take your time bathing yourself." After a second knock Chander opened the door. Chander noticed Shamina as he studied Anwar. 'Five-seven, dark brown eyes, definitely over forty.'

Sons of Jabir

"Asla-maly-kum, you must be Jabir's uncle!" said Chander.

"Correct, I am Anwar Khan, and this is my daughter Shamina. You must be Chander, I suppose."

After the bath Jabir felt fragile, so he slipped back in bed.

"I am pleased that both of you have come, it's an honour, please step in." Shamina and Anwar handed the tiffen carriers to Chander, as Shamina questioned;

"Where is my cousin Jabir and my sister-in-law?"

"Is he better?" said Anwar, as the three of them walked to the bedroom.

"Much better today. You are wondering why the urgency? Please bear with me," said Chander.

"Yes, by the way I don't see Ayrina!" inquired Anwar.

"Ayrina is the cause of all this mayhem. I shall explain things in due time. I request under the dire situation, not to mention Ayrina. I am hoping to cheer up Jabir by a surprise." They all entered the bedroom. Jabir was gazing out of the window.

For a moment Jabir stared at Shamina. His eyes blinked a few times as he spoke;

"Assala-malaykum uncle." Despite being surprised, Jabir was stunned suddenly of Shamina's beauty and body. To his eyes she looked like Marylyn Monroe. The last time he saw Shamina, she was recovering from measles.

"My dear nephew, you've got a very concerned friend here," said Anwar.

"How's auntie. Why didn't she come along? asked Jabir. Though they've not met in some time, it seems like they saw each other frequently.

"Ma, she's all right, left behind to look after the house, you know – besides she doesn't like journeys," replied Shamina. She felt charmed by Jabir's appearance under his critical condition.

Jabir questioned;

"How is your study, Shamina?"

"Struggling with English and Bengali grammar, everything else is all right."

All of them chatted for hours. They had a lot to talk about, mostly Shamina. Chander was pleased to see a miraculous recovery of Jabir's health. The reunion made Anwar realise the lost affection between him and his nephew. Jabir, for some reason, felt pity on himself. Every time Jabir glanced at Shamina one by one Ayrina's memories began to fade from his broken heart.

"I was wondering if you would like to come with us, visit Chansirkapon, and see your auntie Asia," suggested Anwar.

"That should be wonderful, yes, why don't you cousin Jabir," insisted Shamina.

"First thing I will do is get out of bed. I'd love to see auntie Asia, let me think Shamina."

Chander realised a break from ploughing was perfect for Jabir. There again Jabir wasn't very easy to persuade, despite harvest coming up.

"Almost forgot about Rokiv. How is he coping abroad," asked Anwar.

"Acha Rokiv bit busy as always. As a matter of fact he's preparing for me to go to London." Chander left them and sneaked to the kitchen.

"I received a letter from Rokiv a month back. To find out the value of the pound to the taka," said Anwar. Anwar wondered if it was still a secret or if Rokiv had broken it. Pity and good to know Rokiv looked out for Jabir's needs. Anwar promised Jabir's mother, he will not reveal to Jabir, that Rokiv was adopted.

In the kitchen Chander had prepared a small feast. Concluding what Asia stuffed in the tiffen carrier. Jabir reluctantly warmed up, and then slowly dressed. Chander returned and escorted Anwar and Shamina to the kitchen table. Chander explained to Anwar and Shamina about the cause of Jabir's nervous breakdown. "I never imagined Ayrina would turn so

Sons of Jabir

heartless," Chander finished saying. Anwar and Shamina were naturally shocked.

"I feel I can plough like a tractor," mumbled Jabir as he entered the kitchen.

"One surprise after another. Where did you learn to decorate a table like this – friend Chander?"

"I learnt from women's magazines, cooking columns."

"You should not have gone through this difficulty," said Anwar.

"Pa is right," supported Shamina.

"Please eat a little, I insist – it's no hassle at all," replied Chander.

"He's right, come on Shamina and uncle, you too. After all, little hospitality does no one any harm," suggested Jabir. Shamina smiled. They all sat down around the table and began to nibble.

"Nephew, I insist you should come with us. Village atmosphere will restore your complexion in no time," suggested Anwar.

"Think not yet, possibly in a day or two," replied Jabir.

"Are you hard to persuade cousin Jabir," said Shamina.

"It dee…" Chander interrupted;

"I know what's on your mind, the ploughing and harvest. I can look after that – time being. Now if you really want to thank me, I too insist you should go to Chansirkapon and relax, some days there."

"Do I have a choice?"

"No, and it's for your own good," said Chander.

Jabir glanced at Shamina and said;

"Well Shamina, am I hard to persuade? – yes. But I cannot disappoint my only friend."

All were pleased, including Jabir. Chander realised informing Jabir's uncle made things a lot better.

"Nephew, everything Allah does is for the best," quoted Anwar. Shamina nodded.

Chickens, hens put back in their cages by Asia. Grasshoppers twittering as the sun went down. Pigeons nibbling breadcrumbs on Anwar's landing. Jabir with uncle and Shamina walked through the landing, frightening the pigeons into the house.

"Assala-malay-kum," Jabir greeted his Aunt Asia.

Asia was pleased to see Jabir after a long time. Later, when Shamina told her mother about Jabir's unfortunate dramatic story, Asia could not stop her tears from falling.

"First father died, then his mother became ill, and now Ayrina did this. Only Allah knows who may have cursed Jabir," Asia finished saying.

"Why would anyone curse cousin Jabir Ma?"

"I mean it is his fate."

After dinner, lanterns were lit. Outside became dark; Jabir familiarized his uncle's house. As childhood memories flashed in his mind, it reminded him of his mother. At night he could not go to sleep. He found the change of bed uncomfortable. Finally after a tug of war with the pillows, Jabir managed to close his eyes.

"Cockle-doodle-do," the cockerel went. "Quack-quack, quack-quack," the ducks went. Jabir especially could not sleep any more. Just past dawn, Jabir lay resting in bed. Shamina entered the guest room with a cup of steaming tea.

"Assala-malaykum cousin Jabir, I hope you slept well. What would you prefer, toast or forota, for breakfast," said Shamina, as Jabir took the tea from her by its saucer.

"Anything, thanks for the tea. Not fussy what I eat for breakfast."

For the first day or two, Ayrina's torments and thoughts haunted Jabir. Whilst Shamina made him feel alive again, with her superstitious humour, talking about things in general, such as, would East be better off if run by Sheikh Mujib.

Uncle Anwar was busy milking the cows and working in the fields. Aunt Asia, cleaning, cooking and washing. Occasionally Shamina helped her mother. Three days struggled along, each day the clouds threatening to rain. Unfortunately Jabir couldn't forget what Ayrina had done. Though he had forgiven her, he felt his fields needed him.

On his uncle's introduction, Jabir managed to socialise with others in the village. Often in Bishwanath bazaar, they played caromen (similar to playing pool, instead the hand is used instead of a snooker cue.) Already Jabir began to benefit from the village's atmosphere.

On Saturday morning lightning struck, rain came pouring down. It rained continuously through the day, making the villagers daily routine a misery. Sunday morning the rain lightened.

Shamina was joyfully dancing on their landing. When Jabir saw her he foolishly joined her. They danced a while and got wet through. A few hours later unfortunately the foolishness caused them both a cold.

"What a stupid thing to do, Shamina," said her mother. Shamina laughed softly and replied;

"I felt excited, as I was in heaven, you know Ma."

"No I don't know," Asia finished saying and left. Jabir deeply embarrassed, swallowed a laugh.

"Cousin Jabir, why did you join me in the rain?"

"Why? I don't know. Maybe I felt as you felt."

At night after dinner a wolf howled outside in the darkness, which made Jabir concerned about something.

"Shamina, do you believe in ghosts?"

"Why do you ask?"

"Just."

"Partly yes, not like physics or voodoo. If one is to protect from Satan, then designated prayer-beads will help, believing in Allah."

"I am impressed of your religious knowledge," replied Jabir. Shamina smiled as usual and left the guest room.

The rain poured down heavily as days passed. Jabir began to worry about his wheat fields. He insisted on going home to Sylhet. Cousin Shamina reminded him, Chander would take care of them. Jabir's flu was still lingering. The shower of rain came thundering down. It made the road, which ended in Bishwanath, muddy.

On a rainy period, villagers especially suffer the most. They groan and moan because rickshaw drivers triple their rates. They have ploughing difficulties. This kind of climate was very unexpected in Spring. Jabir anticipates if the weather in Sylhet is worse then things could go wrong.

****

In Sylhet the wind, over seventy with heavy rain hailing across the town. Several continuous days of rain overfilled the Surma River. Inevitably the embankment overflowed as it flooded the wheat fields.

Chander had a reasonable day, getting hold of new stories. He became disappointed when he found out the calamity of Jabir's wheat. Now harvest was impossible. It was a pity Jabir won't confront the mayhem himself.

Destructive weather held up all types of transport. After considerable thought, Chander decided to wait for Jabir at his home. Having alternatives, it is not the end of the world for Chander or Jabir. For some solely dependent on agriculture, because of the flood it was.

January passed, the rain didn't stop. Beginning of February the rain lightened, after a horrific thunderstorm. On the third week it stopped completely.

Shamina told Jabir about the act of God;

"Allah doesn't want us to suffer in rain, when we Muslims will be fasting."

"You are saying, due Ramadan Allah stopped the rain. It could be co-incidental you know," replied Jabir.

"Maybe."

The moment the rain stopped, impatient and anxious Jabir wanted to leave. One, he missed Chander. Two, he had a bad feeling about his fields. His flu vanished a few days ago. Jabir in his misery of thoughts. The last words he said before setting off to Sylhet;

"Promise to visit before I fly, hospitality more than enough."

Jabir felt more of a guest, rather than a nephew. Over the past rainy days Jabir had come to adore Shamina. Though he pretended not to reveal the admiration.

Taking the first coach into the town from Bishwanath, in a hurry Jabir didn't glance at his fields. As he saw Chander from his lounge, before he could knock, Chander promptly opened the door.

"How did you know I was coming today?" said Jabir. He walked in and put his belongings on the couch.

"I knew – no rain, so I was expecting you. Did you notice anything? Never mind – I have good and bad news. Now I'll brew the tea – you rest."

As Chander brewed the tea, Jabir wondered what possibly could be the bad news. Chander returned with two mugs of steaming tea.

"Relax and hear me out. The process of life has not come to an end. The road to success is always under construction," said Chander as he sat down and handed a mug to Jabir. As both sipped, Jabir spoke;

"Tell me the good news first."

"Good news, I am investigating a top story, abduction of females. I think Jabir, it could be my biggest break."

"Very good, what is the bad news," Jabir thinking of the philosophical lecture by Chander minutes ago. 'The process of life...

Chander slipped his right hand into his right trouser pocket, leaning forward; he pulled out a bundle of crisp notes.

"Do not jump to conclusions. This money, my savings over the past months. I want you to accept it."

Jabir puzzled, un-sensed said;

"I will accept it, but what is it for?" Jabir paused. Instinctively he gazed out of the window. As Chander monitored Jabir's facial expression he added;

"Chander – oh Allah, why me?"

"Jabir, relax. Too much rain, incidents happen."

"Unfair, how many times is Allah going to test me."

For a moment Jabir stared at his wheat fields. Chander patted Jabir's back, in assurance and said;

"Stop feeling unworthy, cheer up. This money is enough to take care of things to go to Britain." Chander paused and got out an envelope. "Your documents arrived this morning."

Jabir accepted and agreed;

"All right – before I fly, we have to visit mother. Also Chansirkapon."

Chander nodded, then replied;

"Perfect."

Days passed as usual, only better than before. For Chander every day was sparkly dangerous and challenging, discovering leads towards the abduction story. Busy in thoughts, Jabir. 'Ayrina to Shamina, Mother to Rokiv – Allah bless them all.'

Eventually Jabir and Chander met Mr Uddin as promised in Akbors' shoe shop. The administration sorted out, a week later Jabir's visa and passport arrived in the mail. Jabir shopped for bits with Chander. Finally they booked a single flight on seventeenth April with the P.I.A.

Jabir was pleased, so they both caught the first coach to Dhaka from Sylhet, after dawn. Surprisingly not a single seat was empty. The coach driver was puffing smoke every half an hour. More than half the coach was smoking. The coach windows seemed as if they hadn't been wiped in months. Despite Jabir and Chander's detest, they were unfortunately passively smoking. If they had chosen rail it wouldn't have made any difference.

"This is intolerable, coaches have no regulation of how many passengers should board," said Jabir.

Sons of Jabir

"It is because the drivers and conductors want to make some on the side," Chander paused, changing the subject added;

"You know Jabir, some stupids say they think better when they smoke."

"Was that meant to be a joke," replied Jabir laughing.

"Not at all, my colleagues, they smoke pretty obsessively, when they get stuck on ideas."

"Sree-mangal, Sree-mangal," the conductor shouted as the coach stopped for service.

"Let's visit Ayrina, only teasing," said Chander laughing.

"So much for her, I'd still pray for her happiness. May Allah bless her desires."

They both admired the bright morning. The sun shining full upon the large Srimangal tea gardens. Green glitter all around, sparkling in the reflection of sunshine from the gardens, as they gazed through the greasy coach window.

The remaining journey travelled smoothly, except for a few minor bumps and crossing a river by ferry. After more than six hours the coach had arrived at its destination, Dhaka. The extensive journey made them both stiff. They couldn't nap because the conductor screamed stops at every station. One by one, passengers jumped off with their belongings. Jabir and Chander were last to get off the coach.

"It is off Co-me-sial Road, the hospital," asked Jabir, reassuring himself. Chander nodded. The conductor opened the bonnet to check the engine.

"What time do you return to Sylhet?" inquired Jabir as Chander glanced at his watch.

"Six, after sundown," the conductor replied.

Both of them walked to the auto-rickshaw stand.

"How many cigs do you think the driver smoked in the last six hours," said Jabir. He glanced at the contents at his side and carrier bag.

"Forty or more," replied Chander.

"Where to?" intrusively said the auto-driver.

"Ram Hospital, off Co-me-sial Road." Jabir paused, checked his wallet. He added;

"How much?" was not in the mood for bargaining.

"Sixteen taka – busy now, soon rush come."

They both jumped in the back, placing their belongings on their laps.

The auto-rickshaw hailed through the busy traffic, halted in front of a five-storey building. It had rectangular windows, a small car park and a main steel entrance. Jabir paid the driver generously and they leapt out. Both stepped in, pushing the steel door in the hospital. They walked up four sets of stairs arriving at the second floor. They walked to Reception.

Jabir cleared his throat as the woman looked up and spoke; "Yes."

"My name is Jabir, we've come to visit my mother. She is a patient here."

"Your surname please."

"Khan," replied Chander intrusively.

"Ahh, Nessa Khan, she's under Dr Naidi Hassan."

"Where can we find Dr Hassan," asked Jabir.

"Along the corridor, turn right after the old conference room."

As directed they found Dr Hassan by his nametag, just coming out of the Psychiatry Ward. Dr Hassan was a thin man with half moon spectacles hanging over the bridge of his nose and wearing a grey suit. His English was fluent, except, he pronounces 'a' as 'e' most of the time.

Chander broke into introduction;

"I am Chander, my friend Jabir, we have come to visit Nessa Khan." Jabir was already feeling depressed. He wondered what state his mother would be in. 'High – low.'

"Pleese come this wey, Nesse Khen is my petient." They both followed the doctor into the ward.

Jabir noticed his mother, he didn't like what he saw, tied down on the bed talking to no one. "She is talking to herself again, why is she tied down?'

Sons of Jabir

"We hed to strep her for her own sefty" said Dr Hassan. Chander questioned;

"Will she ever recover?"

"Recovery, not much hope," replied Dr Hassan. Jabir took a step towards his mother, stared at her, after a moment of hesitation; Jabir said a word; "Ma," no response. Jabir left the carriers on top of his mother's bedside cabinet, as tears streaked down his cheeks. What his mother was saying sounded pretty clear to him;

"HE WILL COME, YOU LIAR, HE WILL COME, IT'S NOT TRUE," but made no sense as always. Jabir controlled his emotions and wiped his cheeks.

"Let's walk to my office, gentlemen, follow me," requested Dr Hassan.

The three of them entered, one at a time in the office, neat and tidy, at the end of the corridor. Dr Hassan sat on his worn leather chair.

"Do sit." Jabir and Chander sat opposite the doctor, as Chander spoke;

"Are patients like Nessa Khan a threat to other patients?"

"Thret, no, ebnormel – yes. Telking historically the illness, I'll term it – Melencholy, or it wes referred as."

"Is the illness caused by some sort of past trauma?" questioned Jabir.

"Pertly yes, but could be spiritual…"

Chander interrupted;

"Evil-ism is that what you mean Dr Hassan."

"Not exectly, in the pest people believed were unewere of melencholic moods. Therefore they understood Seten end devil cen overteke the humen mind. Today, not so, from Greek times end scepticel people es Socretis, they understood the mind cen operate enti-socially, depressive sometimes, euphoric other times."

Curiously Chander asked;

"So how did they treat depressive patients in Greek times?"

"With voodoo, psychics, leter probebly hypnotherapy" replied Dr Hassan.

"Why does Mother talk like she does?" Jabir questioned quizzically.

"I believe end essume she is, bit eutistic – lives in her own little world."

Dr Hassan opened his right hand top drawer of his worn pine desk. He flicked through a dozen or so files, stopping his search when his eyes hunted in capital letters NESSA KHAN. Dr Hassan began again;

"When she wes diegnosed, ceuse her pest devestetingly treumatic. Looking at her file now, Mr Jebir, you've steted that your father died in the wer." With the window being open, the office had a cool breeze atmosphere. Chander listened attentively as Jabir replied;

"That was a long time ago, but she is still suffering."

Dr Hassan continued his summary explanation;

"Yes, but over the pest yeers efter your fether's deth, she reised you. In fect she wes depressed ell thet time. Then six yeers ego your Mother's perents pessed ewey. Then your brother went ebroed in his teen-ege," Dr Hassan finished as he choked in puffs. The two friends felt pitiful and full of sorrow.

"Is there no cure?" said Chander, fidgeting with his camera.

"It is herd to sey cos in a long term illness, one out of ten get cured. Like tea or coffee?" Chander glanced at his digital and indicated to Jabir with his stretched eyes.

"We have to go. If anything drastic happens please notify me," requested Jabir. The two friends stood up to leave.

"Heve I got your home address?" asked Dr Hassan concerned. Chander and Jabir shook hands with the doctor as Jabir replied;

"You have in my mother's pre-file," sarcastically. As both of them stepped out of the five storey building Chander started to giggle…

Sons of Jabir

"You heve, ah Jebir, some humour eh."

The two friends booked an adequate twin bedroom in a six-storey Two Star hotel, where one is lucky to get cold water from the shower, though the hotel was named after the Royal Bengal Tiger. They ate, drank and rested for an hour or two. Chander persuaded Jabir to visit Dhaka Airport, as Jabir would be flying soon, hopefully.

Both of them were disappointed as the airport offered little or no tourist attractions, except a few duty free shops. Chander purchased the Pakistani Times on their way to the exit from a newspaper boy. They returned to the Royal Bengal, exhausted and slept a while.

"You-two, I thought you'd catch the next one," said the coach conductor, smiling as he revealed his even stained teeth formed by nicotine. Jabir and Chander jumped on the coach, half drowsy, with their belongings. They sat at the back of the coach to avoid passive smoking. Within half an hour the coach began to roll as it fell behind its schedule. Chander opened the back window to wear off sleep. Hours passed, the coach driver crossed the river MEGNA, by ferry, along with other motor vehicles. Chander, too occupied reading the Pakistani Times, as of a sudden interest Chander spoke;

"Look, you know the story I'm working on,"

Jabir interrupted; "The female abduction, any news?"

"It says here two young females did not come home after an evening dance class. Three days missing." Chander showed the article to Jabir.

Jabir's eyes searched the news page as his eyes stopped at a black and white photo.

"Isn't that Bongo-Bondu Sheikh Mujib?" questioned Jabir.

"That's right it is," in reply Chander viewed the passport sized photo and added;

"Let's see what he has to say."

By this time the coach just passed Srimangal. As Chander cleared his throat and began reading the first sentence of what Sheikh Mujib has to say.

Sons of Jabir

"I Sheikh Mujib stand before my fellow Bengalis and the generation to come against the Pakistani government. Not with prejudice but the interest of our views, which are not getting better, but worse on those circumstances that our young female daughters and sisters are being kidnapped by who or whom we do not know. If this matter does not reach any conclusion and be justified, then the Pakistani constitution and its ministers have to face embarrassment."

Jabir and Chander were both mesmerised and impressed with Sheikh Mujib's long dramatic speech.

"That's what I call, having guts," said Jabir, still staring at Mujib's passport sized picture.

"I must contact my sources, if only I can break who's behind this," replied Chander, turning the page. The coach passed Maulvi-Bazaar. The night grew darker with mist.

Chander's eyes searched for any other news of the leader Mujib. Most of the pages portrayed Iyub Khan with obvious political issues, occurring speech by Iyub Khan caught Chander's attention...

"Jabir, listen to what Khan has to say...

"Orders have been given to the Pakistani Secret Service to solve the case as soon as possible. We regret that we don't have any strong lead to who is doing such an intolerable, inhuman crime.

If there are any witnesses or sources that can help, please khuda-ka-vasta come forward."

"I bet some third party is doing all this," said Jabir as Chander nodded in agreement. The ordeal of Jabir visiting his mother was nearly over, as the coach parked in Sylhet near Zinda-bazaar.

****

Finally it was the seventeenth April. Anwar Khan's landing glowed in the sunshine shadows of coconut and beetlenut trees cast over his tin roof. Shamina, her mother and father were enjoying a traditional Bengali breakfast; Parathas like pancakes, though multi-layered and unsweetened, with Shemai, like noodles but sweeter and finer, boiled with water with added milk.

"When's the flight?" asked Chander. A metallic grey lite-ace (7 seater, smaller than a mini-bus), turned left at Joggonath Road, leaving Bishwanath bazaar behind.

"Quarter to four in the afternoon," replied Jabir, very smartly dressed with a two-piece cream suit.

"Aouch" coughed the three of them as the vehicle went over a large bump.

"You know Jabir, you look like a fresh white rose," complimented Chander.

Jabir expected his brother Rokiv to be at Heathrow when he landed. He almost forgot to visit his aunt and uncle as he promised. Pity. Chander suggested inviting them to Dhaka Airport. He wondered how Shamina would react to his dress sense. Jabir wonders a lot about Shamina lately.

"Left or right?" asked the driver. Jabir gave directions as he combed his hair, the fifth time this morning.

Shamina was walking about on the landing, a frequent digesting walk of hers after breakfast.

"Mama, look who's here," Shamina shouted suddenly, surprised. The lite-ace entered their landing and parked. Jabir and Chander emerged in the sunshine as they leapt out.

"If I'm not mistaken, flying to London today," asked Anwar. Jabir nodded, gazing at Shamina.

Chander spoke;

"Correct, Jabir is a bit shy, he wants all three of you to accompany him to Dhaka Airport."

"Do we have a choice?" said Anwar reluctantly.

"Naa," replied Jabir and Chander at once.

Chander added;

"The flight is at quarter to four this afternoon." Anwar had to make a decision, why not.

Shamina experienced something new. A long journey, more of a guided tour, as Chander had been nattering all the way and the opportunity of seeing magnificent jets. Jabir checked his luggage.

"All passengers for London approach Terminal Seven," was announced. Jabir re-checked his passport, boarding pass and ticket. Inevitably tight for time, Chander requested a uniformed guard to take a family photo, handing his camera over. Finally the friends hugged each other and exchanged a speech of farewell.

"Allah-hafiz," said Shamina as Jabir disappeared through Terminal Seven passageway.

Chapter Three

Mr Larry Sushie Chan's leather coat factory closes at five p.m. every day. Jabir Khan, for the last couple of months, was doing overtime, only an hour, at double time. At six p.m. Jabir and Mr Chan stepped out. Mr Chan closed the shutters of his factory and drove away in his 190E Mercedes.

Jabir stretched himself in the cold breeze. Pity, he thought, his brother Rokiv has a nine to five job. Jabir, in the last twelve hours has sewn forty two lines of nylon interiors, occasionally he feels overactive.

Before it grew dark, Jabir began to walk as he shrugged his shoulders. He took long strides from Whitechapel Road, passed a few streets, then exhaled a deep breath. Soon he arrived at Brick Lane. He regretted not taking Rokiv's advice (*if it gets cold, come home in a black cab.*) Finally Jabir reached Bethnal Green Road. After passing a couple of right turns before a set of lights, Jabir turned right into a side street named Chilton Street.

Mr Rokiv Khan is and has been living at Number Fifteen Chilton Street since he became a high street solicitor after his graduation several years ago. On the other hand he had recently painted the walls stark white and scattered a colourful Chinese oval rug over his timbered lounge floor. The windows faced the street overlooking the fenced balcony. Being a ground floor maisonette, his kitchen and lounge had a partition. There were three bedrooms altogether, and a semi-office built in to the master bedroom. There was a rear garden, a small shed but no garage.

Jabir opened the front door with his yale key, and wiped his shoes on the welcome mat. He walked up two sets of staircases, each with three steps only. He pushed open the entrance to the lounge and stepped inside.

"How was your day, is it not freezing outside?" questioned Rokiv partially.

Rokiv, addicted to Granada News, was listening to news at that moment. Rokiv wondered in this cold weather, why Jabir didn't come home in a cab?

Jabir replied boringly, ignoring the cold outside;

"Today, same as yesterday, worked, worked, and worked." Jabir turned off the gas fire and added;

"Brother, if you don't mind I feel hot." Rokiv expected that, although he found it unusual.

Several minutes later Jabir returned with two mugs of steaming tea and sat beside his elder brother on the velvet settee.

"Any letters for me, baisab?" asked Jabir. As his eyes stared at the Valence Road twins on the fourteen inch colour screen. Jabir had heard of bandits and muggers in East Pakistan, but nothing in comparison to the Krays.

"Yes, only one letter," replied Rokiv, as he handed the letter folded in half, from his shirt breast pocket.

"Isn't that the Krays, baisab?" asked Jabir has he opened the envelope and read.

"Who's the letter from, is it Chander?" questioned Rokiv.

"No, I haven't heard from Chander lately. It's from Uncle Anwar thanking me for the Eid money I sent in May."

Jabir looked around the lounge and added;

"The lounge is sparkling."

"I've been cleaning all day, threw out all the rubbish."

Both of them sipped their tea, and Rokiv added;

"That'll reflect the cold, wait till Christmas, it is worse."

"Baisab, do they always collect bins on Wednesdays. I'm not so sure about Christmas, what is that?"

"Snow, cold white flakes, similar to hail stones but softer. Everything gets covered, and looks white." Rokiv shivered from the thought of snow.

Jabir and Rokiv got on well. For both of them it was a reunion of kinship. Both of them thought about their mother in different ways. There were times Jabir wondered why every time he brought up the issue of their mother, Rokiv avoided it

Sons of Jabir

by saying 'I get *upset, let's not talk about mother.*' Jabir avoids Ayrina's memories, he tends to get depressed. Another question circling around Jabir's mind is why Rokiv is still a bachelor?

On their day off each clean the flat thoroughly. Jabir contributes to all the bills and groceries. The oval wall clock struck ten. Jabir went to bed after filling his stomach. Rokiv stretched himself on the settee. He wrapped himself in a woollen blanket and dozed into the shining cold night watching ITV.

"I know exactly, what I'm gonna say to Uncle Anwar when I return after Christmas. Only four months to go – oh Allah," Jabir sighed, as he counted the months on his left fingers, murmuring to a snapshot that Chander sent him the previous month. Jabir's eyes were glued on Shamina. He felt cold inside his woollen quilt. He replaced the photo where it was, under the pillow, and slept.

According to Jabir's point of view, Bethnal Green Road in the mornings is similar to Zindabazar Road in Sylhet. This morning for Rokiv it would have been freezing.

Jabir sped up. It had become a compulsive ritual to Jabir walking to and from the factory, despite any weather condition so far. He wondered would it be possible at Christmas and shivered. Jabir walked passed the street barrows piled with fresh fruits. For the past five months his eyes couldn't resist staring at the bare, unattractive buildings peak high, abreast with the narrow streets. Very economical he thought. Rokiv told him the Bethnal Green borough encases the history of more than two centuries. It's like paradise here compared to Sylhet in East Pakistan, Jabir judged.

Surprising Jabir's curiosity Rokiv told him extended families used to live in Denby Street. Just like families live in East Pakistan nowadays. Costermongers from Old Ford to Spittalfields. Some say Greenleigh is a better place than Bethnal Green, the flat land of East London.

This morning Jabir, for the first time in England, is disappointed of himself. As he clocked in the factory Mr Chan said to him;

"Jabir it's not the usual you."

"You won't believe me, I-I 'Jabir' overslept."

Days passed along, weeks sailed by, a month was gone. Jabir had saved sufficient money to spend the new year touring East Pakistan. For some reason Jabir hadn't received any letter from Chander for six weeks. It began to worry him, despite his Uncle Anwar's letters cheering him up occasionally. On the other hand Rokiv assured him, Chander could be very busy on an investigation, which reminded Jabir of the abduction story.

Superintendent Leonard Read was waiting impatiently for the Kray Brothers trial to come at the Old Bailey. As Jabir was impatient to hear from his only friend Chander.

"End of the month, has to be a letter from Chander. Hope he is not in trouble," Jabir murmured as he entered their flat at Chilton Street.

"Who you talking to – yourself Jabeer?" said Rokiv. As usual Rokiv was in front of the TV, reluctant to miss any news. Rokiv was a man of awareness of the world's problems. He adored what he practised.

"I'm thinking of Chander," replied Jabir.

"The thirsty have come to the well. Almost forgot."

Rokiv handed a letter to Jabir. Jabir excitedly tore the envelope open and began to read in silence.

CHILTON STREET
BE'NAL GREEN, LONDON
Friend Jabir,

Wish you well. Request not to be very emotional and not to jeopardise your future. What I have to say will be very shocking. The investigation I was on became my nightmare. May Allah help us all, I managed to take a few snaps. When you receive this letter I may be captured, presumably dead.

Your friend Chander.

Jabir's hands felt senseless. *'This is some joke, this is not true, oh Allah it can't be.'* His face turned pale. His eyes blinked over and over again as he re-read the letter again and again. His eyes began to rain...

"What's the matter?" asked Rokiv in sudden panic. He snatched the letter and read it himself. Rokiv gave Jabir a hug for comfort. Rokiv never felt empty hearted and emotional, although Jabir mentioned Ayrina on his arrival in England, since Catherine.

Rokiv booked a mid-week Wednesday flight to Dhaka by British Airways as Jabir insisted and preferred. He helped Jabir pack his suitcase. On the other hand thoughts of cousin Shamina kept Jabir moving.

B.A. 10260 landed at Dhaka International Airport approximately 07.00 hours. The weather was pretty dull, a touch of fog and mist. Gives a cold sweat to the tourists. The air has an unusual odour. Jabir couldn't sneak out of the airport's entrance as beggars crawled to him. To his delight he gave them his remaining English coins. *'I won't be needing them for a while, now that I'm here.'* The early morning made Jabir more depressed. Instead of government transport, he treated himself by hiring a Datsun Sunny with a handsome chauffeur for the journey to Sylhet and then Chansirkapon. The chauffeur took care of his luggage as he sat on the back seat, making himself comfortable. He checked his hair in the driver's windscreen rear-view mirror.

"Clean shave that is, Britain must have sharp razors," said the khaki uniformed chauffeur. He promptly switched on the ignition and began to accelerate. Memories flashed across Jabir's mind. *'Only several months back, Chander complimented – you know Jabir you look just like a white rose.'* Jabir stretched and leaned, resting his back, facing the Datsun's windscreen.

After six hours of steady driving at fifty to sixty kilometres per hour, the Datsun Sunny crossed the Surma Bridge, not to mention the driver never stopped. Jabir was exhausted but the sight of Sylhet cheered him as the town centre glowed in the sunshine.

"Wait please," requested Jabir as the Datsun just drove past his unoccupied house. Jabir searched his house, good thing he has Ayrina's key, no luck, no clues, hopeless Jabir returned.

"Drive to Chansirkapon please."

'Bump ah bump ah bump ah tash ah tush ah bump', and it carried on., Jabir and the chauffeur as if were reciting a poem.

"Hell these roads, one cannot drive, never mind fast." After an hour,

"Turn at the local store, then turn right, please – first right."

Aunt Asia finished hanging washed and rinsed clothes on their washing line, so it would dry overnight in the cool breeze. The washing line goes above and across Anwar's landing supported by wooden poles on each side. Aunt Asia wondered is she dreaming or is this for real, as the Datsun Sunny drove into the landing, stopped and Jabir, very exhausted but not tired, leapt out.

"Assala-mu, alaykum Auntie," greeted Jabir courteously. Jabir paid the chauffeur and gave him a bonus, a razor blade as he carried Jabir's suitcase into the house. He then hurried back to the Datsun, reversed and drove off giving a farewell wave.

"Jabir, what a pleasant surprise. No letter, no telegram. Let's go inside," Aunt Asia was surely dazzled. They walked inside.

"Where's Uncle and Shamina, bazaar probably?" inquired Jabir.

"Yes, they should be here any minute, been over an hour."

Asia gave Jabir a hot cup of tea. Within a few minutes Anwar and his daughter arrived, both hands occupied with carrying groceries. Natural human behaviour and the unexpected visit made Shamina and Anwar stunned. Anwar knew why Jabir had arrived. Anwar wanted to do the right thing before Jabir gets emotional and questioning. Share the

Sons of Jabir

burden of his heart with his nephew. *'After all his only friend Chander is'*...

"Nephew, glad to see you, let's go for a walk, it will relax you."

Jabir didn't question but was afraid of the truth. He wanted to assume the letter was a fake. But how the hell can he mistake Chander's handwriting for someone else.

"Don't be too long," said Asia as she and Shamina started unpacking, settling to cook.

Uncle and nephew walked quite a distance. When they saw nobody was in sight, they sat on an aisle in the middle of the wheat fields.

"My nephew, do not get emotional, you have suffered a nervous breakdown months back." Jabir remained silent and gave Chander's letter to Anwar. Anwar read the crucial sentences and spoke;

"Now I get the picture. He must have written this before he came to see me."

"Uncle, what do you mean?"

Anwar began to explain as Jabir waited for the missing pieces of the jigsaw.

"The night he came to see me, six weeks ago, I noticed he was disturbed. He handed me a camera film, gave me a brief explanation and vanished leaving no trace of him contacting me, for my protection, of course, which I realise now! After I went to see Akbor in Sylhet. Three days later when the film was developed Akbor came to see me. I was shocked as much as he was. We decided to take action, that the time had come to see Sheikh Mujib and Colonel Usmani. Being over-cautious, through Akbor's connections, we arranged to meet the great leader. Keeping everything swift as possible. Despite our discreteness I felt our movements were being watched." Anwar took a deep breath and exhaled to relieve his imagined fear.

"Uncle, kernal Usmani, who's he?"

"Mujib's right hand and B.L.A.'s head. So I went by road and Akbor took the rail to Dhaka, at Sheraton Hotel. At the reception we were given a key to room 112. As we arrived in room 112 two uniformed guards blindfolded us and after an hour we found ourselves in a clean empty cellar. That was when we met Sheikh and Usmani. After an introduction Akbor handed over the snapshots. Sheik and Usmani thanked us. We were blindfolded again and escorted to the railway station. We were relieved the matter was out of our hands, and finally returned to Sylhet." Anwar exhaled.

"Uncle what does B.L.A. stand for?"

"Bangladesh Liberation Army, nephew."

Uncle and nephew felt better, though Jabir wished Chander was all right some place.

They both walked home at sunset.

Friday morning, Jabir had mystic thoughts of Chander. *'Where could he be? Where can I find him?'* He made a decision to marry Shamina, but there is the small *'if.'* Will Uncle and Aunt approve of him as a son-in-law.

Anwar was back from his morning walk. Shamina was helping her mother make breakfast. Jabir quickly had a swim and a shave in the village pool. He wondered how much it would cost to have a swimming pool in the village, like there is in Britain! Jabir got dressed and walked to the kitchen.

"My boy, you look better today," said his Aunt Asia, as she rolled another paratha, giving it to Shamina to fry. Jabir didn't utter a word, only smiled, thinking Chander is so brave. He remembered he has to pay twenty thousand taka, but how? Surely his mind or his heart does not want to accept that Chander is dead. *'He's out there, he's out there, but where.'*

"How was England, is it a nice place?" asked Shamina suddenly, breaking Jabir free from his thoughts.

"It's completely different. Concrete roads, tall buildings, clean environment, and so on, wonderful place."

His Uncle Anwar entered the kitchen. They all had breakfast. It reminded Jabir, it would have been joyous if his mother was with them today, having a family breakfast. She would have said *'There is no other family like the Khan family in Chansirkapon.'* Still in the kitchen, Anwar courteously spoke;

"So what did you work as in London."

"A machinist."

"Good money I suppose."

"Yes not bad, compared to here it's very good." Asia and Shamina listened as well as washed up the dishes.

"How's Rokiv getting on."

"Better off, nine to five job as a solicitor in the capital, a city firm."

"Has he married yet."

"No, not yet."

"Why?"

"Probably hasn't found the right woman." Jabir's mind clicked. *'This is the perfect moment to ask for Shamina's hand in marriage'*, but he hesitated.

"What about you Jabir!" Anwar regretted the moment he said it. Jabir changed the subject;

"I've almost forgotten, I've got gifts and clothes for you all, pity Rokiv had the thought and bought them. I – I was too depressed, just wait." Jabir promptly returned with his suitcase from the living room and placed it on the timber dining table and unzipped it. Shamina returned a smile as Jabir gave her a navy saree and a sky blue blouse to his Aunt Asia. Finally a black pair of cotton trousers, a short sleeve white shirt and a blue tie to his Uncle Anwar. Shamina left the kitchen to try the saree on.

"You shouldn't have spent your money and brought all this" protested Asia. *'This is the moment I've been waiting for.'*

"I have a wish to make from the bottom of my heart with high hopes." Jabir paused, Shamina returned wearing the saree. *'She always seemed prettier to me than Ayrina.'*

"How do I look papa?" asked Shamina.

"Beautiful," complimented both her parents at once.

"Yes Jabir, carry on," said Asia.

"I don't know how to put this in words, suppose you'll understand. I am very much in love with Shamina. I want to marry Shamina." With natural apprehension Shamina blushed and left the kitchen. A silence fell upon them lasting a few minutes. Anwar spoke;

"Jabir my nephew, you have been through a lot and we understand and value your emotions. To tell you the truth, if your auntie agrees I am happy with your wish."

Jabir obviously felt nervous. He felt his forearm veins pumping up and down. In a quick decision Jabir crawled onto his Aunt Asia's feet. Asia felt really embarrassed. Jabir pledged;

"Auntie, my past may doubt you my future. I promise you, Allah witness, I shall never harm Shamina. May Allah punish me if I do. I will keep her the best I can. I'll take her to England with me. Please, please don't say no, please."

"Get up my dear son, don't embarrass me any more. One should be characterised by present and future commitments, not his or her past. Now stand up and give me a hug. I've nothing else to say except, yes."

One week gone, a second week gone and the third week the wedding preparations began. Invitations were given out. Decoration done through the house, Bengali style. Bangladeshi traditional dishes cooked.

On the actual wedding day not very many people turned up. The weather was not very charming. Jabir, for two things, was pretty emotional. One Chander was not around. Two, he wished his mother was cured and there today at his wedding because he is marrying the woman he loves. Shamina was sobbing, why? She will be leaving her parents sooner or later. Now it was time for the engagement to take place.

Jabir remembered to post a wedding greeting card to Rokiv. He would have posted a letter to Ayrina in Srimangal but on second thoughts he didn't.

It was the 2nd October, Imam of Sylhet's great mosque began;

Sons of Jabir

"You Shamina begum daughter of Anwar Khan, do you agree."

Shamina replied; "Kabool.'

Then the Imam walked to a different room and a similar thing was repeated where Jabir said "kabool."

The Islamic lawful and traditional engagement was completed. The reception was nice and quiet with not so many guests. The wedding of Jabir and Shamina was over as the guests left and it grew dark.

Since the wedding night the week floated by in harmony. Jabir didn't mind living with his in-laws, he still seemed as a nephew, not a son-in-law. Jabir took Shamina to Dhaka and visited his mother. Dr. Naidi Hassan told Shamina Mrs Nessa's condition was deteriorating. Shamina didn't know how to tell Jabir but felt sorry for the sad news. She left their present address with Naidi, just in case, for the future. Dr. Naidi wondered about charming Chander!

Shamina did all the things to keep Jabir happy and in a positive mood. For both of them, despite Chander, the days passed in harmony along with the village's atmosphere and friendly environment. Jabir received a congratulations card from Rokiv.

Despite thoughts and nightmares of Chander, Ayrina and his mother, Jabir was trying to build confidence in his concern of Shamina. Jabir was urged to treat Shamina, so they travelled to Kashmir and toured around for two weeks. A month passed by and Rokiv sent Jabir a snapshot of Bethnal Green Road and the shops covered with snow.

"What is all this white stuff? It looks very nice," said Shamina.

"That is called snow." By looking at his wife's lost expression, Jabir realised she hadn't a clue. He added;

"Rokiv bai-sab, told me it drops like flakes, cold and soft. When it melts it becomes icy."

"I see, not so sure," said Shamina. After soft love they both slept as Jabir blew out the lantern.

The Khan family were happy with the union and Shamina's parents were gracious having Jabir as a son-in-law. December flew by entering a new year. January raced along with nothing special. At one time, in several months, Jabir thought of an opportunity to find Chander, *'If there's to be a civil war between the East-West.'* February ran towards the month of Ramadan.

Almost noon, the Khan family were having a feast. It was dull outside but dry. "Shamina how tender, where did you learn to cook like this?," asked Jabir.

"From my beloved mother, of course." Jabir didn't imagine so rapid a change in his solitary life recently. Besides, Chander was still missing and his brother Rokiv was still a bachelor, *'Oh hell, it's his life.'*

Jabir's eyes blinked as at the same moment, the postman cycled on to their landing. He triggered the bell, DRING-DRING.

"Registered letter for Jabir Khan," shouted the khaki uniformed postman.

"Yes, come over here in the kitchen please," Anwar requested in a high tone.

The postman walked past the guest room, through the verandah and entered the kitchen, *'they better give me a tip for this!'*

Jabir washed his hands and signed for the letter. He tipped a taka. The postman thanked him, returned to his bicycle and peddled away.

"You finish eating, I'll read it," offered Shamina. Jabir gave the letter to his wife.

"Who's it from?" inquired Anwar.

"Think it's Dr Naidi from Dhaka." Instinctively Shamina's heart thumped as she replied. She didn't know why. Simultaneously Jabir coughed and began to choke. Shamina placed the opened letter on the dining table. Promptly she and her father massaged Jabir's back so he could regain his breath. Within minutes Jabir calmed himself. On Shamina's

Sons of Jabir 59

insistence Jabir went to bed for a lie down. Shamina picked up the letter and began to read aloud...

Dear Jebir,

I am writing this letter to you in great agony and distress. No one can battle fate. Since you visited your mother with your wife, your mother's condition has dramatically deteriorated day by...

Shamina's voice reduced to a whisper. She read the rest of the letter in silence. When she finished, "Khuda" she sighed and collapsed on a chair, remaining silent.

"What's up Shamina?" said her mother and father, puzzled.

Anwar took the letter from Shamina's hands and read it with Asia. Asia couldn't stop her tears from falling. They both sat beside Shamina. By now Shamina's eyes flooded. Nobody intruded the silence for a few minutes. The day was crispy and bright outside. Shamina reluctantly spoke, softly;

"Pa, Ma, I'm-m scared this n-news could r-result in a shock for Jabir."

"Let's see what he's doing. I'll take the responsibility to tell him. It will have to be later," said Anwar sceptically. Anwar, Asia and Shamina walked towards the guest room. Jabir was leaning against the headboard gazing outside. Shamina sat beside Jabir holding his left hand. Her parents sat opposite her on the edge of the bed. It seemed like visitors visiting a patient that's just gone through heart surgery.

"Well Shamina, did Dr Naidi, I mean Neidi start the letter with Deer rather than Dear, and Jebir than Jabir?" Jabir said and laughed. Shamina smiled with great difficulty.

"As usual he did." It was as if Shamina had put a mask on, so Jabir couldn't read her facial expression. Inevitably Jabir saw tears dripping from his Aunt Asia.

"What's t-the matter?" said Jabir with a sudden worried look. Instantly Anwar held Jabir's right hand.

"My son, what happens is no tragic act of Allah. The Almighty has many ways to show love, but sometimes he asks

Sons of Jabir

for sacrifices," Anwar said in an emotional tone. His eyes were wet, his face affectionate and full of pity. As they all expected Jabir's face became expressionless.

"Uncle, I don't like riddles," said Jabir. His eyes turned cold. Anwar took a deep breath;

"My son, only pray to Allah, that the future be bright for all of us. I hope you understand your mother has passed away." Anwar had to be calm and strong, though he found the words naturally painful. Jabir remained silent as in a trance. He could not believe his fate nor his ears. Shamina broke the silence in fear;

"Say-s-something, say s-something, please." Jabir looked up at Shamina's face, tears streaking down her cheeks.

Instantly he put his arms around Shamina and sobbed on her shoulder. Misery is nothing compared to what Jabir turned into after the shocking news. He couldn't eat much and didn't sleep well. Shamina stayed with him every moment but it made little difference. Jabir cried for two days until his eyes dried up. It was Shamina who encouraged him, that what had happened was what Allah had wanted and now he should build his confidence and eat before he died of malnutrition. Finally Jabir, not for himself but for the sake of Shamina and the thought of Chander, got control over his emotions. Anwar and Asia were helping their daughter to be confident.

Jabir dehydrated, lost more than three stones. Now after seventy two hours Jabir began to eat properly, though he suffered a sleeping disorder. Occasionally, at night Jabir had nightmares. That moment Shamina had doubts about what the future held, despite fate.

The month was coming to an end. Ramadan was due in a few days. Jabir struggled through his depression to recover confidence and composure. Jabir determined for a change, started going to mosque.

It was a Friday afternoon, the second week of March, Jabir came home from Jumma to find Shamina was not in sight. He asked Aunt Asia;

"Where's Shamina?" Before Asia could answer, Shamina entered the guest room. Blushing and a bit embarrassed Shamina remained quiet. Jabir saw happiness written all over his wife's face.

"What is it Shamina and where have you been?" Jabir asked irresistibly. Without speaking Shamina walked across and sat beside Jabir on their bed. She then put her lips on Jabir's left ear and whispered something.

"Honestly," said Jabir in graciousness.

"It is I have just come from Bishwanath with father."

"From when?"

"Four weeks."

Jabir went back to the mosque and gave charity to Imam. He told the Imam to pray for his future child and he wishes it to be a girl. Anwar donated rice, wheat and food to the poor. Asia prepared to look after Shamina's health already.

The Khan family reconciled their bereavement into happiness through Ramadan. They celebrated Eid with glory. They didn't realise it was the end of March because of the thought of the new child entering into their little world. Only months to come.

Jabir heard a demonstration parade, some form of resistance, from the guest room. He didn't bother as he finished writing the letter to Rokiv. Before he put it in an envelope he asked Shamina;

"I haven't written about mother. I think it-be better to tell him later, when we go back to London."

"Whatever you think is suitable."

"I'm off to Bishwanath, you want anything."

"I'd like some raw mangoes," Shamina requested from the bed, relaxed. Jabir still had hope Chander will turn up, *when*? Jabir would wait as long as his hopes are with him. On Shamina's bedside table there were various fresh fruits.

When Jabir arrived at Bishwanath by foot, sweating all over, the first thing he did was post the letter. Jabir searched for raw mangoes. The bazaar was hardly doing any trade. At a distance Jabir saw an army of men marching along the road towards Sylhet and orchestrally shouting slogans. As always Jabir was curious and asked a passer by;

"What are all the slogans for?"

"War-war-war," shouted the passer by, walking in the opposite direction.

'*What war?*' Jabir walked into the centre of the bazaar, where hundreds of people gathered busy listening to an activist. Jabir tapped an old man on the back and asked;

"What is all the fuss about?"

"Shek-Mujeeb has declared war."

"What war? And what for?"

"Bangladesh liberation war – freedom."

Jabir felt and electric current run through his arteries. '*Pity, my only chance to maybe find Chander, joy-bangla*', thought Jabir as he returned home.

Chapter Four

Two weeks flew past and Sylhet's residents were evacuated. Dr. Khashi preferred his surgery to be at Lal-bazaar rather than Bishwanath. Jabir, after a few hours of persuasive debate with Shamina and his in-laws, signed up with the Bangladesh Republican Army with little or no chance but hope to find Chander.

Shamina was reluctant but proud of Jabir's decision. Uncle Anwar felt pity, B.R.A. needed strong hands to operate artillery donated by the Indian government.

Joining the army was the easy part. It took seven weeks for the B.R.A. to reshape Jabir and train him to be the best soldier, which Jabir motivated day and night exercise. Unfortunately for Sylhet's regiment, the captain died of a cardiac arrest. B.R.A. with no choice, had only one option but to appoint Jabir as Captain.

Next morning Captain Khan received orders that his division was to advance over the Surma Bridge and engage the Pakistani soldiers, preventing them from crossing the boundary between Cherrapungi and Sylhet, ten miles north west of Cherrapungi in a forest on the far side of Khasi-hills.

Jabir climbed a beetlenut tree and watched the Third Division cross the Surma Bridge. Thinking it could be blown away at any minute, General Lutfur led his own division behind Jabir's. When Jabir reached the edge of the forest, he and his platoon saw nothing in sight within Khasi-hills, so they decided to go further into the labyrinth of trees. What they didn't anticipate was Pakistani snipers. The going was fast when from above they were suddenly attacked. Shocking and horrific, Jabir's men went down, trying to protect themselves among the trees. In a matter of minutes Jabir had lost half of his soldiers.

Jabir crouched and crawled in the dry undergrowth for a few minutes. Then to his horror he saw General Lutfur's platoon coming through the forest. In fearful indecision Jabir ran from his shelter inbetween the trees to warn them of the ambush. A rifle bullet fired by a sniper hit Jabir in the shoulder. He sank to his knees, "Allah" he screamed in the dry soil and continued to wave, warning his advancing comrades. Another bullet hit him in the elbow. Jabir, half unconscious, lay still on his backside in the hot dry soil and waited for help.

The next thing Jabir knew he was being carried to the Bangladesh Red Cross on a stretcher. They laid him carefully on an operating bed. His mind turned to Shamina and his future child. He wished to heal and go to his family, though he thought the search for Chander may be finished.

****

In Chansirkapon Shamina prayed night and day for Jabir's wellbeing. She wished the war would come to an end soon. Anwar Khan was guarding the village with other men at night, in anticipation of any danger. Asia with the other women, took a commitment to give food to the Bishwanath regiment.

****

In Britain Superintendent Leonard Read had been successful in convicting the Krays. On the other hand, B.R.A. is facing a possible defeat, so the Bengali residents, with others, held a demonstration parade in London near Hyde Park. Amongst them was Rokiv Khan. They marched up and down shouting slogans. They requested the monarchy to help end the civil war. More importantly, bring peace with some sort of mutual truce.

At a later date at a summit meeting, a member of the British Government and Indira Ghandi met with Sheikh Mujib's associates. British and Indian troops were sent to East Pakistan to combat alongside the B.R.A. to win the victory against West Pakistan.

In Chansirkapon months passed like weeks for Shamina. One evening, on the 3rd August 1969, Shamina was faced with pain. Anwar was in Bishwanath getting day to day news of

Sons of Jabir

the war. Asia knew the situation but didn't expect it now. With the aid of another woman they took Shamina as comfortably as possible to Dr. Khashi at Bishwanath. Asia sent a message to Anwar by a soldier.

The young soldier didn't need to look for Anwar, as he knew he would find him at the radio tower. The soldier ran up the flight of stairs, exhausted he spoke;

"Mister Anwar, a mesij for you. Your daughter Shamina bin admit-it to sargery, wife sounded anxious. She wants you there es-ay-pee."

Arriving at the surgery Anwar met his wife. They both found a nurse standing outside the delivery room who informed them that Dr. Khashi was with their daughter. She had lost a considerable amount of blood.

Anwar and Asia both paced up and down the waiting room. Anwar checked his watch each time a nurse came out of the delivery room. Whilst Asia lost patience, minutes turned into hours. Finally Dr. Khashi appeared, his forehead sparkling with tiny beads of sweat. A surgical mask was covering his nose and mouth. Anwar nor Asia could see no expression on the doctor's face until he removed the mask, revealing a large smile.

"Congratulations, you both have a lovely grandson. Shamina is fine but fragile, this being a premature birth."

"Dhanne-ho-Allah," both of them breathed. Anwar shook hands with Dr. Khashi and gave him five hundred taka.

"Can we see Shamina?" both asked, *wishing if only Jabir was here*.

"You can see her in the morning. I've given her a sedative, she's asleep now."

"What about our grandson?"

"You can see him, nothing to worry about. To be safe I've told the nurse to put him in an incubator, just for a few days."

He's got brown eyes, just like Jabir, Anwar and Asia were glad to see their grandson.

At the Bangladesh Red Cross in Sylhet, Jabir was mostly yawning and snoring. It took him fourteen days roughly, to regain full consciousness. His wounds were still pretty raw. He had lost all hope of seeing Chander again. Wondering about Shamina, he thought he would be discharged soon to see his child's birth. He had thought of a name already. If it is a boy then it's Rajah, a girl then it's Naina.

Jabir, lying in bed, made a decision to sell his house, when the war was over. He will donate part of the money, in the name of Chander, to the Ram Mental Hospital. He realised it was a pity but grateful that Dr. Naidi buried his mother as part of their funeral service. He couldn't have borne it at the time.

Jabir detested paracetamols but he had no choice. The duty doctor approached his bedside, promptly checking his temperature with a thermometer.

"What is it? The needle or tablet?" asked the midget doctor. Jabir shrugged at the thought of a two inch needle.

"Painkillers," he replied reluctantly.

In Chansirkapon Shamina had almost recovered from the premature delivery. Asia had been taking care of her newborn son, Rajah. Anwar made sure Shamina was taking the prescribed drugs by Dr. Khashi.

Shamina's only wish is somehow Jabir would come home and see their son. On occasions she laughs. Jabir once said;

"We will have a daughter, she'll just be pretty like you Shamina." Shamina replied;

"No we will have a son, he'll be like his father when he grows up, tall and handsome."

Often in the evenings, Shamina stared at the fields from their patio, again wishing Jabir would come home and surprise her.

"Pa, I wonder which regiment Rajah's father is in?" Shamina asked.

"I'm sure Jabir is in good hands, don't worry just pray," assured Anwar.

Sons of Jabir

Three weeks passed like three years for Jabir at the Bangladesh Red Cross. Today he faced an unusual circumstance, *very strange*, Jabir thought. Just an hour ago the whole ward overcrowded with wounded soldiers. Some were unconscious on stretchers, some had gunshots on their backside, looks awful.

A gentleman beside Jabir, with a gun wound on his left shoulder, leaning against the wall exhaustedly, stood up with great difficulty. Jabir lay on his bed the opposite way, bored, wondered '*victims of an ambush, inevitable.*'

"Hello, may I rest on your bed please?" requested the wounded soldier. He was in great pain with blood dripping off his gruesome wound. Jabir turned around and looked up. For a minute he stared at the middle aged face and concerned, got off the bed.

"You may – sure," said Jabir. He helped the wounded soldier to lie on the bed. Jabir kept staring at the middle aged face.

"Hold on a second," said Jabir. Looking around every nurse and doctor were occupied. Jabir fetched a first aid box and sat beside the soldier, his feet touching the floor.

Jabir did his best. He applied antiseptic on balls of cotton wool and cleaned the gunshot wound, as the soldier naturally screamed. Then he bandaged.

"That will stop the blood, the doctor will take the bullet out later," said Jabir.

"Thank you very much. What's your name?" asked the middle aged gentleman.

"Jabeer – Captain Jabeer," replied Jabir. He felt pleased he could help. Jabir added;

"Iff 'eh you don't mind me asking, how did you get that scar on your cheek?"

"Years ago, from a bandit, why? Why do you ask?"

"Reminds me of my friend Chander," said Jabir.

"Where is he now, gone to the UK, I s'pose."

Jabir didn't want to lie nor accept that Chander is presumed dead, so he changed the subject.

"Have you been to England yourself?" questioned Jabir.

"Yes, used to live in Oldham."

"When was that?" Jabir fired another question. *Oldham up North, colder.*

"When, oh in 1966, after England won the World Cup. I got married and moved to Rochdale," replied the gentleman. Jabir thought '*Rochdale, heard of that.*'

"What is your name, ahh Rosdale has co-operative society doesn't it?" said Jabir, not sure. *He had read it somewhere.*

"Yes the Rochdale Pioneers, by the way my name is Manik Chaudhury."

Chaudhury, reminded Jabir of Ayrina.

"I myself also been to England, before the conflict began. So do you intend to go back when the war is over?" asked Jabir.

"Yes I would very much like to!" replied Manik Chaudhury.

Manik felt a bit eased having the conversation with Jabir. It relieved some of his tension. The doctor approached both of them and was pleased with the effort Jabir took in helping.

"Doctor Mkusa, Mister Manik needs his bullet taken out," said Jabir.

"I'll do that right now," the doctor replied giving a smile and discharged Jabir.

"Captain Jaabir, you are adequately in good health to go home, not fit for combat again." Mkusa gave Jabir some paracetamols and added;

"In case of pain."

Before Jabir left the building, he and Manik exchanged their present UK addresses.

Chapter Five

Srimangal is about forty eight miles south of Sylhet. It is the tea centre of Bangladesh. It has an extensively hilly area, with tea estates, shade trees, lemon orchards and pineapple plantations everywhere. Srimangal is one of the picturesque parts of Bangladesh.

For miles around you can see tea estates forming a perennially green carpet on the sloping hills. It's the one area, besides the Sundarbans, where in certain parts you can look around and not see a soul. This is particularly true of the dense Lowacherra Forest Reserve, three miles out of town.

The town itself is quite small. A single road, the Dhaka Sylhet Road passes from one end to the other with a four-way intersection in the middle. Its bazaar is pretty big consisting of the essentials, including a few banks, one café, two restaurants and a grocery shop.

One of the restaurants was owned by Ayrina Chaudhury, inherited from her family. But Bangladesh has had more than its share of misfortunes. Recently Srimangal had been a victim of a flood, especially its bazaar. It was wiped out by a fierce storm and torrential rain. The locals were glad it wasn't an earthquake but the loss was devastating. Crops were washed away, homes and buildings abandoned and the town deserted.

Amongst others, Ayrina's circumstances had worsened. Because of her twins she had no choice but to become a beggar and for that she had to go to Sylhet. If a miracle happened she may get a job, but with two sons to look after she didn't know how she would manage. In spite that she left Jabir when she was pregnant she had no idea she was carrying twins, Jabir's twins. It's been a whole day since she had eaten anything. The twins had a banana each.

She had to get a passage to Sylhet. There was no hope of surviving in Srimangal for her and her twins. People were dying of contaminated water around her. Ayrina had hope, not for her, for her sons. She had to get to Sylhet somehow. Maybe a lift from a truck driver, whatever. She had to find Jabir Khan.

Chapter Six

Shamina gave her son a quick bath. Every so often for the last two hours her eyes were predating at the openness of the wheat fields.

"Ma, towellia," yelled Shamina from the patio. Asia hurried with a cotton towel and a set of washed clothes for her grandson.

"We clin fresh naw, henna," muttered Shamina, as she withdrew her son from the aluminium tub and wrapped the wet fragile skin with the towel. Then Asia snatched the baby and dressed him. The weather being unusually hot, mother, daughter and grandson were stepping inside. Suddenly a jeep with a noisy engine drove onto their landing. Captain Jabir jumped out. They turned around as the jeep pulled away. It was as though Jabir appeared in a flash. No telegram, no letter whatsoever. Shamina, very surprised, ran towards her husband with outstretched arms. In seconds both were hugging each other in endearment. A feeling of joy never known before.

"Come inside," said Asia as Jabir's son stared at him from his grandmother's cradle. Both walked inside. Jabir wondered, somewhat confused *'that must be my child.'*

"Is that our child?" Jabir questioned foolishly.

"Jabeer, Shamina had a premature delivery. It is your son," replied Asia.

"Wher es uncle?," again Jabir questioned.

"Father is at the radio tower – Bishnath," answered Shamina. Asia went to the kitchen handing her grandson to Shamina. Shamina passed their lovely asset to Jabir. Father couldn't be more prouder, despite his regret at missing the birth.

Aunt Asia prepared dinner and returned;

"Jabir, come to the kitchen, dinner is ready." Jabir placed his son into the pine cot. Shamina accompanied her husband at dinner. As Jabir told his stories in combat, he boasted a little, telling them finally how he ended up at the Red Cross.

"Have you named our son, Shamina?"

"Yes, we have. It's Raja, with H at end."

Soon darkness fell. Outside everyone was attentive and on guard. Anwar arrived home, relieved to see Jabir. Surprised, *'Why is he here now – middle of war.'* Obviously Jabir explained that the doctor discharged him because he was unfit to perform ground combat. Anyway Anwar gave a brief update of Bangladeshi forces advancement.

Jabir and Shamina delighted of their son Rajah's health. Days passed, weeks trembled and months strolled along. Rajah in Hindi means a king of a constitution. The Khans were happy to see Rajah crawling at nine months. Also Rajah grew his first baby tooth. At eleven months he turned over one stone and was vibrant with colour, plus he started to mutter Amma-Aba. The Khans were pleased with his recovery of a premature birth.

Like it or not the war was still on. One occasion Jabir replaced a nurse assisting a surgeon with a minor hernia operation at the Bangladesh Red Cross. Other times Jabir helped with first aid and delivering ammunition to headquarters, central Sylhet. His attributes were becoming known in Bishwanath with appreciation. Flow of the war went along anticipating victory of the East. Home forces took over territories such as Chittogong and Comilla. Jabir, Anwar and others were glad to acknowledge the news by E.P.B.C.

Sheikh Mujib, leader of the Muslim League, quoted on East Pakistan broadcasting channel;

"I Shekh Mujib will not hesitate to sacrifice the last drop of my blood to liberate my Bengalies for the future and of all generations to come."

Uncle and nephew feverishly engaged with the war, that days passed like minutes, weeks like hours, months like days and a year is history.

Sons of Jabir

3rd August 1971, Rajah's second birthday. On his first just Dr. Khashi visited. Today Shamina presented Rajah with a silver necklace with two copper prayer beads attached. She got the beads from a travelling sai-baba (like a psychic.)

At twenty seven months Shamina taught her son the fundamentals of the mother tongue. Jabir had turned somewhat indifferent about life. The influence of war had helped him to build courage and control his emotions about his friend Chander.

In March 1972 Comic Relief fund gave aid to the Bangladesh Red Cross. Every citizen expected the war to be over soon.

Unfortunately on the last day of July Rajah twisted his left ankle when he ran after his father to go to Bishwanath. He tripped over an aisle and ended in a bed screaming. However Dr. Khashi assured Shamina that it was a slight twist. The ankle would be better within a few days by massaging with oil.

On 3rd August Rajah's only regret was that he couldn't walk on his birthday. The Khan family fed the poor in hope and prayed for Rajah's bright future. Shamina assured that Rajah was wearing the prayer beads at all times. Rajah wasn't yet three years old but a lot wiser for his age. He started reading with the help of Asia, his grandmother. He had learnt about why the war was going on between the West and East, from Anwar his grandfather.

After a week, Rajah pleased with himself, his ankle couldn't be more better. He was careful not to repeat the incident out of desperation. More importantly on Sunday evening Jabir and Anwar came home with victorious news. The East won the war. Rajah couldn't make out what all were cheering about. Later Shamina explained now that the war was over things would be much better and different.

"We will have our own schools my son, our parliament and government." Rajah didn't grasp all of it, but understood he would be going to school.

The Republicans (Muslim League) nominated and elected without a ballot, leader, once a political prisoner, Sheikh Mujib, President of East Pakistan, now Bangladesh.

Next morning Rajah and his father were at the Sylhet independence celebration party. Rajah was mesmerised by the crowd. Among the actors there were many impressionists which Rajah found hilarious, but hardly understood any of their jokes. Suddenly there was a deafening Rajah couldn't figure out why? When a gentleman, well dressed, not very tall, stocky, appeared on stage. The silence was broken by a standing ovation. Jabir explained to Rajah that the gentleman was Sheikh Mujib.

Every former army official got a medal of honour according to their rank. The moment Jabir was awarded by the President, Jabir's eyes naturally filled with tears.

"Ababa why are you crying?" Rajah questioned, as Jabir returned to his seat.

Jabir held Rajah on his lap and replied;

"My son I'm not crying, the tears are of joy and happiness." Rajah touched and felt his father's medal time and time again. The only thing Jabir missed was the presence of Chander.

Time flew as everyone enjoyed themselves. One by one they left. Jabir and his son, on their way to Chansirkapon, visited the house he once lived in with Ayrina. It was empty and dusty. Jabir told Rajah he would be selling the house before they flew to England. Later in the evening at Chansirkapon Rajah questioned his mother;

"Mama where England – when we go there?"

"Why?"

"Papa said after selling house – wee go England."

"Oh – ah yes, England – a far away country. You go to sleep now Rajah."

Sons of Jabir

Chapter Seven

President Sheikh Mujib was the heart of the newborn nation. Bangladeshis just loved his speeches at seminars. He was turning his country around like an old locomotive with reconditioned parts. He had managed to get aid from India to reconstruct infrastructures, which were damaged by the inevitable war. He revised the education programme nationwide, plus pursuing many more things.

Jabir was busy with renewing passports and getting visas for his son and wife. He was also on the look-out for prospective buyers for his house in Sylhet. In concern of his wheat fields, he would leave them under the care of his father-in-law.

Rajah was getting distinctive day by day. He certainly didn't like playing with other children in the village because they pushed him around. Oppositely Rajah was excited as he was looking forward to the primary school which was being built twelve yards from the local store. Shamina regretted her son's excitement, she knew they would be on their way to Britain before the school was completed. She didn't worry otherwise as Rajah hadn't made any close friends.

Everytime Rajah came home from the Bazaar with his grandpa, despite the groceries, he had many questions to ask his mother at night. Such as why is the sky blue? Where is heaven? And why does water have no colour? The only thing that worried Shamina is Rajah having too much curiosity for his age.

Jabir was impressed by his son's vocabulary, as Rajah was devoted to reading children's story books. Rajah's parents were amazed by his curiosity and interest in seeking knowledge, at an age of not even four years old. One afternoon Rajah questioned his father, how is London? Jabir explained London has concrete roads, tall buildings and big red buses.

Soon December came, Jabir heard from Rokiv via air mail. Rokiv sent a snapshot of snow as a postcard. Jabir reluctantly hid the photo away from Rajah because he didn't have a commentary explanation for it. Rajah being himself, inspired by curiosity, would ask why is it white? Why doesn't it snow over here? Shamina didn't blame Jabir.

For most children in the village winter is obviously displeasing, despite the rain, thunder and cold. For Rajah the weather doesn't bother him, because he likes reading story books all day long and listening to his grandparents' chit-chat and gossip.

It was mid-week in the first week of January, the new year. Jabir was the victim of a thunderstorm and returned home all soggy and wet. Shamina instantly passed her husband a large towel to dry himself. Rajah was in the kitchen listening to a very exciting bandit story from his grandfather, not fiction at all. Whilst his grandmother lay asleep in one of the bedrooms.

"Rajah-Rajah my son," shouted Jabir as he dried his hair from the rain water with the towel. Shamina didn't get worried as she could visualise Jabir's expression of happiness on his face. Rajah came running from the kitchen, panting. Rajah had to catch his breath;

"Yes abba." Jabir embraced Rajah in sheer endearment with both his arms.

"My son I've got a surprise, in fact for everyone." Jabir handed the towel, now wet, back to Shamina. As he took off his rain coat, still dripping on the floor, Rajah's grandfather came by.

"What abba?" Rajah asked again, still panting.

"I have sold our house for three hundred and forty thousand taka," Jabir announced. Shamina and her father felt great, but Rajah questioned;

"How much money is that, abba?" They all expected a question from Rajah. Jabir ignored his son's question and made another announcement;

"I will be donating fifty thousand taka in the name and memory of my only friend Chander, to the mental hospital

Sons of Jabir

where my dear mother was once a patient." Shamina took the raincoat from the non-carpeted floor and said;

"As you wish Jabeer." Jabir was pleased, no one objected to his donating money, especially Shamina. She did not object to most of the things he's done or does. *I am so lucky that my wife is Shamina.* The next question from Rajah touched Jabir's heart;

"Abba, who is Chander uncle?"

"A good friend of mine. He gave me twenty thousand taka when I first visited England."

Jabir already on his knees, embraced Rajah again but could not assume Chander was dead. Neither of his eyes dropped any tears.

The next day after dawn, after breakfast, Jabir and his son set off to Sylhet to visit the bank manager. Jabir's account was with Sonali Bank. (English meaning of Sonali is Golden.) Jabir wasted no time with the intention of keeping his days schedule on track. He gave instructions to the bank manager to send fifty thousand taka by draft in the name and account of Dr. Naidi Hassan to Dhaka Mental Hospital.

"Mister Alom, also please enclose this letter so Doctor Hassan will know what the money is for." Jabir requested to the bank manager as Rajah handed an A4 piece of paper folded in quarter.

Father and son walked out of the bank and went to the post office for any registered or recorded letters. After a considerable wait the postmaster gave Jabir an A4 sealed brown envelope. In the right hand corner was printed Bangladesh High Commission.

When father and son arrived home in Chansirkapon Jabir was not the only one pleased, not surprised what he revealed inside the envelope. Shamina was pleased too, but Rajah's grandparents were sobbing. Inevitably and obviously Rajah asked;

"Nana-nanee, why crying?" Jabir explained;

"We will be going to England, Rajah my son." Shamina felt a sudden loneliness of the near separation. Rajah was ignorantly impartial of the situation. That night Jabir wrote a letter to Rokiv, that he will be booking the flight for his family the end of January.

The next morning, after posting the letter to the UK, Jabir did exactly what he intended, accompanied by his son. He went to Sylhet International Travel. Jabir felt pity when the operator said they will be flying with British Airways, not the P.I.A. Then father and son went to Sonali Bank. Jabir instructed the manager to transfer and exchange two hundred and fifty thousand taka to his savings account at Barclays Bank in London. Mr Alom replied, after tapping some buttons on a calculator, that it would be approximately five thousand pounds. As they were leaving the bank Jabir withdrew ten thousand taka to do miscellaneous shopping.

Days passed faster than Shamina expected. She wondered was it really essential to go to England, *because we are happy and peaceful here*. Maybe the foreign country does not hold a bright future for Rajah. Above all Shamina was happy, what Jabir wants.

Jabir was busy packing suitcases, obviously he couldn't even mistakenly exclude Rajah's story books. Rajah was counting the days. He was fascinated by the wonders of England (if there is any)? Will they have rickshaws in London? The colour of an English man's skin and so forth.

Rajah's grandparents had come to terms with the near separation, though it's not forever. They would be encouraged for Rajah if their daughter only had a second child. Even Jabir felt the near separation but Rajah was looking forward to the journey on the aeroplane.

It was the end of January 1973. Approximately 300 passengers for the flight to London on Sunday were to board in 45 minutes. The night before Shamina sobbed, inevitably and naturally. So did her parents. Rajah was sound asleep. The Dhaka airport itself had minor changes, except the faces of

Sons of Jabir

the staff around looked different to Shamina. "I thought wrong, there are more people who want to go to England like us," said Shamina standing next to her father.

"It is because the British government wants foreigners like Jabeer from Asia and the Far East for general work, manual labour," replied Shamina's father.

Rajah was stunned by the size of the British jet, which just finished refuelling. He was impatient to get inside. His grandparents waved for the last time for a long time to come. As Jabir, Shamina and Rajah went on board their luggage had been checked in a few hours ago.

"See six A, see six B an see six C, ou kay we sit here," commanded Jabir to his son and his wife as he sat down in between them.

"Amma, did you get my story books?" questioned Rajah, observing the interior of the jet and glad he had a window seat. Shamina looked at Jabir. He nodded;

"Your story books Rajah, we got them."

The next few minutes Rajah was certainly puzzled. He did not have a clue what the air hostess was gibbering, except some up and down nods and body language. The woman looked peculiar to him wearing a skirt with matching blouse. Most women on the plane were in sarees like his mother.

Every passenger fastened their seatbelts as they were told, after the Captain finished speaking and the plane became mobile. Reaching a speed of over 220 mph the aeroplane took off. Rajah felt he was inside a giant eagle as the plane shot into the open air and balanced at several thousand feet off the ground in the sky. Shamina, Jabir and most passengers dozed off. Rajah left his seat, abandoning his belt, and started to explore the interior. He couldn't go past the First Class section, an air hostess stopped him, *there's two of them*! The beautifully smartly dressed woman knelt down and said;

"Now young man, where do you think you are going, that's off limits." Rajah didn't say anything. Instead he circled his eyes, turned around and walked back to his seat. The air hostess followed him and asked;

"Would you like a soft drink?" giving a smile. Rajah nodded up and down, not because he didn't understand English, because he didn't want to be rude to the air hostess. The air hostess returned with a bottle of coke and a glass tumbler.

"This is coca-cola, nice and tasty," she explained. She handed the bottle and glass to Rajah and strode away. Rajah sipped and impersonated;

"Coca-cola." Rajah was impressed that he had learnt something. He then poured, filling the glass to the rim. He drank and uttered;

"Nise," gleaming at his parents very pleased with himself.

Next Rajah was amazed as a film began starring Roger Moore. Mesmerised by the small cinema screen, Rajah leaned back relaxing, drinking his pop. An air hostess passed beside him. He stopped her and asked; *not two, there's three of them*

"What film?" pointing his right forefinger at the screen. The air hostess bluntly replied;

"Live and Let Die."

Rajah mimicked "Live an' die," as the air hostess vanished from sight.

Some passengers were fast asleep, some were busy listening to the radio and others engaged in conversation. Rajah, as he couldn't find anything interesting to do, got his story books out, which he purchased recently when his father and he were shopping on the days before the journey. Shamina and Jabir were still asleep.

After approximately twelve hours BA 1029 landed at Heathrow International at 10.37 hours. Rokiv was waiting among other people. Jabir, Shamina and Rajah checked through passport and customs counters. Jabir collected their luggage and in a few minutes they met with Rokiv.

"Here give me that trolley and follow me, Jabir." Things happened fast with Rokiv. He walked towards a lift pushing the luggage trolley, his guests behind him. They all arrived at the car park where Rokiv's BMW was parked. He opened the boot of the 316 and placed the luggage inside.

"Is this your car baisaab?" questioned Jabir, as Shamina, Rajah and himself sat inside.

"Fasten your seat belt Jabir. Yes I've purchased it recently from a car auction," answered Rokiv. He started the ignition, accelerated and drove out from the car park on to the main road. In a quarter of an hour Rokiv got into London city.

Rajah was staring at double deckers, bill boards, sky scrapers, etc. He found it conventional, not surprising. Rokiv realised Jabir hadn't changed much, except the tan and that Shamina was more beautiful than Jabir explained in his previous letter. Not to mention their cute, charismatic son, *Rajah is it?*

"What did, em-what is your son's name Jabir?" Rokiv bounced the question. He wanted to be sure. Jabir answered; *he must have forgot.*

"Raja with an H at the end." It seemed sudden to Rajah, as Rokiv parked in front of his flat in Chilton Street, Bethnal Green.

"Now have a quick wash all of you and let's eat. I'm very hungry," suggested Rokiv. They all ate soon enough including Rajah. Jabir, not surprised at all, that everything was neat, clean and tidy for them in their bedroom. Shamina appreciated that their bed was prepared. Importantly something was nagging, rather worrying Jabir. That what he has in store to tell Rokiv is just not a possible confrontation at this moment. *When would be the best time to break the tragic news*, thought Jabir. Rajah, very tired, went to sleep mumbling;

"Live an die – Cola cola, live and die ..." taking breaths in between like a broken record playing over and over again.

Jabir woke up alarmingly early in the morning. After he washed his face he trod down the stairs. He passed the lounge into the kitchen. Even after a long gap Jabir was familiar with his brother's flat. His heart had no courage but his mind was obliged to tell Rokiv about their mother. He glanced at his watch, *hour and half he'll be off to work*, made himself a cup of tea and strode out of the kitchen and sat on the settee in front of the 14 inch portable, but didn't switch it on. Jabir began day-dreaming about Chander. The good times they had together, as if his past was flashing through the present, now. Nevertheless he felt content being Rajah's father. *One day he will become a great writer. My son Rajah Khan.* Jabir snapped out as he heard the toilet flush. Rokiv came running down the stairs as if he was going to miss a train.

"Jabir, couldn't you sleep well?" Rokiv inquired, concerned.

"It'll take a few days to adapt" said Jabir sipping his tea. Suddenly they heard a scream. It was Rajah from the landing upstairs. Jabir ran to the scene for rescue.

"Abba pooh-pooh," said Rajah desperately, bottomless. Jabir helped Rajah sit on the pine toilet seat and left saying;

"I'll go and wake your amma." Jabir relieved that his son didn't question about the toilet being different. The scream got Shamina up anyway. Jabir returned to the lounge. Rokiv was in the middle of making breakfast.

"Toast with jam or margarine?" asked Rokiv, as he fried a second omelette.

"Jam," replied Jabir from the settee. This time he switched the TV on.

Ten minutes or so passed. Rajah came down with his mother. Rajah interrupted during their breakfast;

"Abba me see bas-bas me see." Rokiv understood instead and assured;

"Finish breakfast first nephew."

"Are you not going to work bai-saab?" asked Jabir. Shamina felt depressed, thinking about her parents.

"Actually I've got a few days off for the occasion," replied Rokiv. Shamina apprehensive but interrupted;

"How long does a letter take to reach Bangladesh?"

Sons of Jabir

"Now that the war is over, everything is taking its usual course. Should not take more than twelve days," Rokiv paused adding;

"Ah, resenting the fact it's a newborn country. Oh Jabir you should have seen us marching up and down, screaming and shouting near Hyde Park. I guess it helped. By the way the British Royal Mail is the best." Rokiv looked up, Rajah was eagerly waiting for him. Shamina concluded;

"Of course it helped Rokiv baisaheb," still thinking about her parents wellbeing.

Realising the chill outside and the roads would be icy, the snow had just melted by rare sunshine.

"Typical British weather," Rokiv murmured under his breath, as he dialled an East London cab. Not a black cab, they're uneconomical. He requested Shamina to wrap Rajah in warm clothes. Thirty minutes passed. Rajah was anxious. Rokiv was expecting the cab any minute as the morning rush should be just at an end.

"Bai-saab is something wrong with your car?" Jabir questioned puzzled.

"It's not the car Jabir, it's my road tax that's expired and to be honest I don't feel like driving in this depressing weather." Like a flash, a black Ford Cortina braked in front of 27 Chilton Street and sounded the horn continuously. Rokiv picked up Rajah in his arms.

"Let's go nephew." They both sat in the back of the spacious Cortina.

"How things hangin' Roky?" the driver asked.

"Hanging fine Romero," replied Rokiv. Rajah didn't obviously understand a word but assumed it was some kind of grown up greeting.

"Whare-too Roky ain who's tha' little fella," asked Romero.

"It's mey nephew, te tha bus station please Romero." Romero did some right turns, left turns and passing several crossroad traffic lights. The black Cortina halted in front of the East London bus station.

Back in the flat Jabir was discussing with Shamina about when and how should he tell Rokiv. Shamina wondered would it have been better to break the news in Jabir's letter before they arrived here. But that would have been impersonal and may have carried a different impact on Rokiv, because he was living alone until today.

Rokiv handed a five pound note over to Romero for the fare.

"Ya gat ainy chainge Roky aim sho-ort?"

"Afrai-nat Romero." Romero shrugged;

"Ah-kay, wan paun-two paun-threy-paun ain far paun, hare Roky ya chainge."

"Thanks Romero." Uncle and nephew leapt out of the Cortina waving to Romero as he drove to another job. For the next hour Rokiv showed Rajah around showing him the double deckers, then Trafalgar Square and its pigeons. Then the great Buckingham Palace, unfortunately they didn't see the Queen. Then Big Ben and finally London Bridge. Rajah and Rokiv went home exhausted. Rajah was very excited. Later he told his mother about their tour. Shamina had to stop writing her letter to Bangladesh and listen to her son for an hour.

"I'll be back from the post office," said Rokiv as he walked outside towards his BMW. He peeled his expired road tax from inside the windscreen and went off whistling.

"Amma you noh big clock – very big," Rajah tried to explain to his mother. Shamina thought the clock must be very big, because her son didn't stop stretching both his arms around his back, until she stopped Rajah. He may strain himself.

"You will hurt your armpit muscles, Rajah."

Rokiv returned with a year's road tax, he seemed elated. Jabir thought *now*. Shamina, a little depressed, decided to nap. Rajah began reading his native stories.

"Bai-saab I've something to tell you, important," said Jabir reluctantly. Rokiv partially frowned, thinking and replied;

Sons of Jabir

"Important, what could that be? Ah your job recommendation, I'll sort that out. It's just been two days you've arrived."

"Bai-saab it concerns our mother," Jabir said finally. Rokiv blinked a few times as he spoke;

"Jabir listen, you may be wondering in the past why I did not mention or talk in general about our mother to you. That is because I was busy sitting exams to become a solicitor. *Am I being selfish, not really*. After I'd acknowledged she became mentally ill, it used to make me feel depressed thinking about our mother but I was always concerned about you. Several years ago I requested, upon curiosity, a report on her medical status. The hospital rejected you know patient confidentiality. Our mother is all right I hope." Rokiv finished talking as he switched the TV off for more concentration. Jabir slid near Rokiv on the settee. Out of curiosity, Rajah stopped what he was doing and started to take an interest in the conversation.

"Bai-saab I don't know how to say this," Jabir was very agitated now "knowing that how you feel about mother does not help what I am about to say," Jabir paused;

"Our mother is no longer with us bai-saab. Not long ago mother passed away, peace be upon her." Tears dropped from Jabir's eyes as Rokiv grasped the sudden news. *Why is abba crying*, thought Rajah but wise enough not to say a word in this intense moment. Childhood memories, poverty flashed before Rokiv's eyes. He shut his eyes for a few seconds and exhaled. He opened his eyes and began talking;

"Brother Jabir, the day has come to break my promise which was given to me by our mother. God is witness I have been luckiest in a million. Women like Nessa Khan, who had a heart so big, know only to give and give. They don't demand anything. It was God's will, she suffered from a peculiar illness and died. May her soul rest in heaven. (Rokiv in hysteria now.) You may be wondering why I'm talking unusual or that there are no tears in my eyes. That is because all my tears dried up in my miserable childhood. You may be thinking why I'm being rude and saying Nessa Khan. That's because it was Nessa Khan, our great mother, who taught me that there is no duty underrated than duty of being happy. I was only five years old when your mother found me, (Jabir was agape, astonished. Rajah couldn't figure it out), shivering with cold on the corner of a side street near dustbins with too many flies buzzing around. I still vividly remember that thundering cold day, despite. To me it felt that God had come to help me. I was so afraid, very scared with no future. Thinking I was going to starve to death. Many times I asked myself why me? God's will I suppose. Before that day I never knew what a mother really was. I was born an orphan, probably a bastard trying to overcome the inevitable, survive amongst millions of refugees, with no one. But it was Nessa Khan, your mother who felt pity on me – on me. She gave me shelter, food, education and importantly mother love. She taught me to give to others, try not to be selfish. I can never repay her, even if I am reincarnated." Rokiv overcame his hysteria. Naturally teardrops rolled down his cheeks. Jabir's web of thoughts were circling in his mind. His heart enriched with emotions, indescribable stated;

"Rokiv bai-saab. I am truly proud of my mother and you."

The rest of the day passed in a mixture of typical British weather. Shamina, Jabir and Rokiv were all depressed for their own emotions and separate reasons. Oppositely Rajah was reading and writing. He didn't ask any question of his parents, except for one;

"Uncle me want to go school, can I?"

"You will be going to a nursery nephew."

"Nursary," Rajah repeated like a parrot.

"Nursery is where little guys like you go before going to school," Rokiv explained, as Rajah nodded up and down and again repeated like a parrot;

"Little guys."

Sons of Jabir

Chapter Eight

The next morning after breakfast Rokiv went to Seroditch Nursery for admission. It was twenty past eight and he wondered if he was early. Jabir went to visit Mr Larry Chan his former employer, for any vacancies.

Shamina began to get familiar with the flat and the contents of the kitchen cupboards as she was cleaning up. She managed to write a letter confirming they arrived well with Rokiv's help.

Rajah was listening to the nine a.m. morning news despite that he understood very little or nothing at all.

"Mama-mama, come-come," yelled Rajah. Shamina frantically came rushing into the lounge.

"What's the matter my love?"

"Amma look-look, big clock," Rajah said all excited. Shamina could see a political spokesman talking, then she noticed Big Ben behind the gentleman.

"Now Rajah listen to me, do not scream like that again. This is England, you will see lots of funny things. You made me worried."

"Acha Amma."

Shamina returned to the kitchen. Rajah switched channels as soon as the news finished. Instantly his eyes locked on ITV. Now he wondered what kind of creatures were these? In bright colours one looked like a rabbit. Can't be rabbits, certainly rabbits don't talk. Rajah didn't bother to disturb his mother again. He thought these could be magic. Minutes passed by as Rajah became really puzzled, because the creatures could fly, they fall from a cliff and still don't die. They could sing and dance. They could virtually do anything and everything. One thing is for sure, they were not human, Rajah decided. He couldn't tolerate this anymore, so he switched off the television and walked up the stairs. He got his children's story books out that his father bought him and began to read.

The week floated by with a mixture of weather. From splashing rain to heavy showers, with hail storms and light snow, entering into February.

For the Khan's Ramadan was due in a few days. Jabir checked his account at Barclays, satisfied that five thousand pounds was credited by transfer safely.

He was planning for his son's future. Jabir managed to get a packing job this time with his former employer. Rajah's admission to Seroditch Nursery had been accepted via his Uncle Rokiv. Shamina, always religious, was looking forward to Ramadan. Rajah dreamt about how his first day will go at Seroditch. Rokiv told Rajah there would be other Bengali children too, so not to worry. Rajah wasn't nervous when he went to bed, a little over-active. The only thing that worried him was that he didn't know English, except 'live and die' along with a couple of other words.

Ten to eight on Monday morning. Shamina bathed Rajah, despite Rajah could manage himself. She gave her little boy a manicure and dressed Rajah in a white short sleeved shirt and black trousers with black shoes. Rajah stared in the bathroom mirror admiring his cuteness. Shamina, a bit worried and anxious as all mothers are, spoke;

"My son, behave yourself, don't ask too many questions. Be brave and always keep your prayer beads around your neck at all times." Shamina realised her son would not be able to speak English and smiled, *that will stop him asking questions.*

His Uncle Rokiv complemented;

"Handsome as Elvis."

Rajah knew what handsome meant, but tried to figure out who's Elvis. Just then Jabir said;

"Son, don't worry – make friends with other children." Finally Rokiv and Rajah drove to the nursery.

The nursery had a rear playground with fences surrounding its boundary. The front had a concrete drive, surrounded by walls two metres high. There was ample space for a few cars to be parked. The inside comprised of a large hall with a separate cloakroom. A narrow corridor leading to a classroom with a children's library. There was a second classroom full of toys and musical instruments. An office was situated adjacent to the library. The walls and ceilings were decorated with multi-coloured paintings and artistic wallpaper and the floor had square tiles.

Nephew and uncle arrived pretty early, in fact they were first to be at the nursery gate. Minutes later a Volkswagen drove towards them as they shivered because of the cold breeze. The female driver parked next to Rokiv's BMW and leapt out.

Her blonde hair remained stationary as a gust of wind blew her red and white winter dress. She was actually five foot six, but her heels made her look an inch taller. For a moment Rokiv stared at her cream, milky complexion. Sandra Travis locked her car and walked towards Rokiv.

"Gud mornin', I am Miss Travis an' I'm in charge of this little nursery. I believe the young boy is a new admission."

Oh God why don't she be in charge of me, Rokiv imagined for a second and replied;

"Indeed I'm Mr Khan and this young gentleman is my nephew." Rokiv was mesmerised by the sudden beauty. He hadn't met anyone so smooth and irresistible since Catherine. Fabulous he admitted. He added;

"My nephew has recently come to the UK. Matter of fact he is very new, so please take care of him."

Sandra Travis smiled at Rajah. She realised the boy was feeling cold.

"Mister Khaan, so I shall, no need to warry."

Rokiv glanced at his watch, *eight-thirty eight.* Rokiv sensed she sounded a bit aristocratic and uttered;

"Miss Travis I regret I'm a victim of procrastination right *naw*. I shall leave my nephew in your care, wish to see you again – bye."

Sandra thought was he trying to make a pass at me. *Can't believe it, don't even know him – me and my imagination.*

"Well let's go inside, or we'll freeze to death out here, shall we," said Sandra as Rajah nodded, whether he understood or not.

Chapter Nine

If Jabir was finding it difficult to blend in with the cold weather of Britain, then what hope did Shamina and Rajah have. Shamina realised that it would be a long time before she would see her parents again. At least she had Jabir and her son Rajah with her.

She was doing her best to adapt in Rokiv's East End flat. Rokiv's lounge glowed from the sun outside. His lounge had an aroma of artificial fragrance that Shamina just sprayed a minute ago. Jabir twitched his nose as he began reading a letter. It arrived that morning from Sylhet.

Dear Jabir

First of all I would like to apologise. I know you wouldn't forgive me. Importantly I don't have much time. I thought leaving you I would find happiness, but I was wrong. I hope you are well. I thank Allah to give me courage and that I have found you, because you have two sons. They are twins and they are called Bassha and Suna.

Unfortunately I have cancer. It seems Allah is punishing me for my sins. You need to come and take your sons. For they do not have anybody in Bangladesh after me. Jabir please come as soon as possible as I am dying at the Sylhet General Hospital.

Ayrina Chaudhury

Jabir read the letter again. He didn't know how to feel. A brainstorm of emotions was going through his mind. Was he to be happy that he had two more sons? Was he to be sad that Ayrina was dying? Is this some kind of a sick joke from the devil? How can he go to Bangladesh immediately when he has just come from there a few days ago. He has money, but all this seems illogical. What was he going to say to his son Rajah? What was he going to say to Rokiv? Will Shamina let him go? Does he need her permission? YOU HAVE TWO SONS, THEY ARE TWINS AND THEY ARE CALLED BASSHA AND SUNA.

"Jabir what's the matter?" Shamina questioned and took the letter from a motionless Jabir sat on the sofa of Rokiv's lounge. Shamina, having read the letter, sat beside Jabir.

"Shamina, what should I do?" said Jabir. He was having difficulty making a decision.

"Well Ayrina has cancer, so I think you should go and get Bassha and Suna."

Shamina couldn't believe she said that. THEY ARE NOT YOURS, THEY WILL BE NOTHING BUT TROUBLE, YOU DON'T WANT THEM SHARING WITH RAJAH… Shamina shook her head and added;

"Jabir they are your sons, you should go and get them."

"What about Rajah?"

"I'll explain everything to him. He will be happy he has two brothers now," said Shamina suddenly feeling excited about all of this.

"What about Rokiv-baisab?" Jabir still couldn't focus. WHY CAN'T THINGS GO AS PLANNED? HOW OLD ARE THE TWINS? WILL THEY CALL ME ABBA? DO THEY KNOW THEY HAVE A FATHER?

"You stop worrying and go and arrange a return ticket. I'll explain to Rokiv." This indecision of Jabir's was getting Shamina worried. Shamina wouldn't wish her enemies, not that she had any, to get cancer.

"What about the visa for Bassha and Suna. I don't have Chander anymore to help me with these things?"

"You have Rokiv, he will sort the visas," Shamina reminded.

Thanks to Shamina, Jabir made a decision. He will go and get the twins for he is their father. One thing Jabir could never forget was the abandoning letter Ayrina wrote when she left him, which caused his nervous breakdown.

Chapter Ten

Sandra Travis and little Rajah, holding hands, walked together inside the nursery. With a little difficulty and persuasion Sandra managed to take off Rajah's anorak and hung it in the cloakroom with the others. Rajah admired the colourful elephants, giraffes and monkeys on the cloakroom wall.

Once inside, both facing each other, Sandra wondered how she should begin.

"What is your name darling?" asked Sandra.

Rajah was not surprised but puzzled. *Now what is she asking me?* Nevertheless Rajah offered some words in English.

"C-co-cola nice." Sandra misunderstanding, smilingly replied;

"No coca-cola, everyone here gets milk at lunch. Now what is your name?"

I see she wants to talk English, all right then. "Live an' die," Rajah blurted.

It became apparent to Sandra as she realised and remembered Rokiv Khan's words. *My nephew has recently come to UK.* So Sandra tried a different approach. She placed her right palm on her chest and spoke gently;

"My name is Sandra Travis," pausing as she pointed her left forefinger at Rajah and added;

"What is your name?"

Rajah smiled and replied;

"Rajah Khan." *I better learn English quick.*

Afterwards all the children sat in the centre of the large oval oriental rug, including Rajah. He definitely was nervous of the new surroundings. After the register Sandra introduced Rajah to the class.

"Hi everyone, this is Rajah and he is from Pakistan." Rajah couldn't figure it out. What Miss Sandra had said was wrong, but his mind stuck on the word Pakistan. Some looked at him, some were not interested. Once cute and shy little Bengali girl stared at him.

At Unison Street, Mercedes, BMW's and a few other leading foreign makes were parked both sides. A&M (Arthur and Metcalf) and Co, were a firm of solicitors specialising in criminal law. It took Rokiv Khan precisely six years to reach his goal. He first started as a clerk then with tenacity and determination he passed his bar, after graduating from London City University with LLB first class honours.

Rokiv Khan was happy that he had become a criminal solicitor in a city that had a lot to offer. Fair skinned Rokiv at almost 31 was still a bachelor. He didn't have any serious religious convictions. Deep in his heart a scar has healed but the sweet memories are still there. If he believes anything then it is experiencing endurance. His childhood had been terrible. When he was a child Rokiv never dreamed of what he has become today. And for that he thanked Jabir's mother and God.

Lady Freehold, an elegant French lady, walked into Rokiv's small but plush office. His third client that day. She sat facing him as Rokiv explained briefly;

"Ah yes Lady Freehold, your case of dangerous driving has been warded to the Old Bailey from the magistrates. Nothing to worry about ma'am."

"Look they can't take my licence away. It's not my fault I'm driving a Ferrari. I admit I got carried away."

"Being your first time and the fact that you were listening to loud music, a few points and a hefty fine would sort it out ma'am," Rokiv assured.

"Wonderful, goodbye Mister Kaan."

Lady Freehold put her leather thermo-interior gloves on and strode out on her high heels. *That was pretty quick*. Rokiv almost forgot to ring the British High Commission in Dhaka. Since Jabir had come over with his family, it has helped Rokiv's loneliness.

"Amma mee friend Kajol in nursery," said Rajah with tremendous excitement.

Shamina wondered *Kajol – pretty name*. Shamina curiously questioned;

"Your friend Kajol, is she Bengali?"

"Yes amma and she plays with me," said Rajah smiling. Concerned, Shamina checked her son's prayer beads as she hugged him and gave Rajah the motherly love that all mothers give their children. Shamina assured herself the prayer beads were around Rajah's neck tucked under his white vest. She checked them every single day.

First day at nursery Miss Sandra taught Rajah and Kajol (she too having recently come from Bangladesh with her parents) the twenty six letters of the alphabet. What surprised Sandra was Rajah grasped well, except he misses the X sometimes. Kajol staring at Rajah didn't learn much. As Rajah's excitement subsided he asked;

"Amma where's abba?"

"He's gone to Bangladesh, remember."

"Oh yes, abba said he will bring dry fish for me. I love that stuff."

Shamina wanted to tell Rajah about the twins. But the questions that will follow, she doesn't have time for. And so Shamina decided against it.

Rokiv was pleased by Rajah's progress. He just couldn't stop thinking about Sandra Travis. She resembled someone Rokiv used to date a long time ago. The weather outside suddenly turned miserable. Rokiv wanted to take Rajah swimming, so he could show off his cute nephew. Rajah being persistent wrote the alphabet several times. He still omitted the X. Rajah wondered how to spell his name in English.

"Chacha me write my name in English, how?"

Rokiv wrote Rajah Khan in capital letters inside his nephew's squared nursery pad that Miss Travis gave him.

The next morning Rokiv dropped his nephew at the nursery. Rokiv gave a couple of looks at Sandra, which she didn't notice. *Playing hard to get are we, never mind.*

At the nursery Miss Travis was playing 'Simon Says' with all the children.

"And now Simon Says stand up," Rajah and Kajol were copying Steven, an English boy.

"An now Simon Says, hands on head." Steven put his hands on his head, so did Rajah and Kajol.

"And now turn around." An Indian boy standing behind Steven, poked him. Steven turned around, so did Rajah and Kajol. Miss Travis shouted;

"Right Steven, Rajah and Kajol, out of the game." *Now that's what happens if you follow someone else. Can't blame myself. I hardly understand what Miss Travis says, except moving her hands and legs and the occasional shout*, thought Rajah.

Rajah and Kajol began to engage in nursery activities such as drawing, painting and reading. Soon everyone was out, Simon Says was over. Then Miss Travis walked to the piano and sat on a wooden stool.

"Boys and girls, we will learn to sing a song now," said Sandra Travis. Rajah wanted to read, learn to speak English. He thought, *maybe this is a quicker way*. On the other hand Rajah wondered *what good is it learning a word, don't know the meaning. Whisky, casino and Bond still circling around my head because of their meaning*. Sandra placed her fingers on the piano keys;

"Everybody will sing after me."

All the children were sat on the round velvet rug in the centre of the classroom. Sandra played a tune, simultaneously singing;

"Twinkle-twinkle little star."

All the children managed to repeat but some stared at Kajol and began to giggle. Kajol repeated;

"Tinkle-tinkle star," missing the little. Rajah, sitting next to Kajol began to laugh, why? He didn't know himself, because most of the children were. Rajah did realise that Kajol did not pronounce twinkle and omitted the little. Kajol, a very

Sons of Jabir

shy girl, felt embarrassed and began to sob. Immediately Miss Travis came to Kajol's rescue. Sandra picked Kajol up, embracing her within her arms and took Kajol into the nursery's office. She gave her some candy and mopped Kajol's wet cheeks with her personal hanky.

"Good children don't cry," said Sandra. Kajol nodded.

"Say too-inkle, too-inkle little star."

Sandra realised that Kajol was having difficulty.

"Let's try a different song." Kajol naturally smiled. Sandra added;

"Humpty dumpty sat on a wall. Now you say it."

"Humpty dumpty sat on wall," repeated Kajol.

Sandra satisfied of an achievement, they both returned to the classroom.

"Humpty dumpty sat on a wall" sang Sandra as she played the tune on the piano. All the children repeated in chorus, nobody laughed. Rajah figured why the song was changed.

Chapter Eleven

Jabir Khan was looking forward to seeing his two sons and Ayrina. In spite of the Sylhet heatwave Jabir was in a two piece suit, sock, shoes and a full sleeved shirt with a blue tie. Drenched within, he got glances for his smart appearance by passing locals.

"How much?" Jabir said to the gaunt auto-rickshaw driver as the driver parked in front of the newly built Sylhet General Hospital, which had fifty six patients per doctor.

"Fas-teka (five-taka)" replied the swathed driver.

Jabir handed him ten shillings and without saying a word hurried through the hospital's main entrance. Once inside, looking around, having found the reception, Jabir asked the man behind the desk;

"Hello there, my name is Jabir Khan. I have come from London to see Ayrina Chaudhury." (Jabir wanted to say his ex-wife but thought against it.)

The name on its own wasn't enough.

"Do you have a ward number, department, an address?"

Mosquitoes were flying about. Jabir felt like an idiot. The hospital lobby gave off a damp odour. Its interior was half painted. Stretchers were limited. It reminded Jabir of his days in the Bangladesh army. He didn't want to be there, Jabir wanted to get out of this place as soon as possible. He wondered how Shamina was coping with Rajah. At least Rokiv was with them, he assured himself. Chander crossed his mind but he dismissed it.

"Mr Jabir Khan do you have an address, there's two Ayrina Chaudhurys in this hospital. One's in ante-natal and one's in cancer…"

"I've come to see the one in the cancer ward," Jabir interrupted.

"First floor, room one-o-six."

"Dhonyo-baad (thank you)," said Jabir and walked towards the stairs. Recently, Jabir can't figure out, why does he think

Sons of Jabir

of everyone at the same time. Is that normal? *Chander, Ayrina, Rajah, Rokiv, Shamina, mother, father.* Jabir barely remembers his father. How difficult life can be without a father, and a mother. Jabir has experienced it and he was glad his children will have a father.

Jabir reached room 106 after climbing two dozen stairs. His breathing increased, there was a nervous tingling feeling inside his heart. As he was about to knock on the door, he heard a sudden weeping. Reluctantly Jabir barged in by pushing his right palm.

On a single mattress bed with a copper frame with no head rest, Ayrina Chaudhury, his ex-wife, lay motionless. It took Jabir a few seconds to comprehend that Ayrina was dead, not asleep, as the nurse, instructed by a junior doctor covered Ayrina with a white cotton sheet. Jabir wanted to say a few words to his ex-wife. He tried his best coming here as soon as possible. His sons didn't look up, they were still weeping. The doctor and the nurse left the room.

Jabir wanted to reach out. He wanted to grab Ayrina by her shoulder and ask her for forgiveness, despite that she left him. Ask for forgiveness for treating her like a slave, if that's what he did. Automatically Jabir's eyes filled with tears. Jabir hoped the worst was over.

Chapter Twelve

Sandra Travis danced harmoniously out of the condensed shower screen, with a large pink bath towel wrapped from her shoulder blades to her knees.

For the past half hour, Sandra has been deciding whether to wear the red evening dress with the white roses or the black with the white roses. *Red-black-red-black*. Undecided she patiently sat down on her leather dressing table stool. She applied black mascara and used tongs to curl her lashes. Vaguely, she applied crimson lipstick on her dried fragile lips. She smiled at the triple oval mirror as she complimented the red evening dress on her voluptuous body. She put on her leather heels, finally striding down the stairs with her leather mini handbag.

Sandra began pacing left and right as her hair remained uncombed, damp and loose. After a moment she sat on the lounge red leather settee. *Pity mother and father gone away for the week*, Sandra felt relieved. The door bell chimed, her heart began to thump. In control she walked to the front door. Pausing for a second, she instantly glanced at her Accurist, *six fifty nine*, drew her breath and opened the door slowly, but not like a snail crawling.

As the gentle breeze swayed on her medium slim body, her narrow blues eyes stared at the handsome man in black. *Is he flattering or is it my imagination.* The co-ordination of Rokiv's dress sense beat James Bond. The trance between would be Romeo and Juliet broke as Rokiv spoke;

"Are we going to stare at each other while I freeze out here?" Sandra blinked, stepped out with her hand bag, locking the front door behind her.

Rokiv started the ignition, Sandra shuffled as she got comfortable in her seat, simultaneously putting the seat belt on. As Rokiv reached the end of Vallence Road, he opened his refreshing mouth again;

"What do you fancy Miss Travis, Italian, Indian or Chinese? Or anything of your particular interest in regarding your tastebuds."

"Indian would be just fine." Sandra's eyes kept drooling at Rokiv.

"I think I am familiar with an Indian cuisine, known as The Jewel In The Crown, in Sevenoaks. Probably the best Indian in Kent." This evening in particular Rokiv had put a mask on, not to reveal his past and show emotion.

"The evening is in your name Mister Kaan. Take us where you think is best an please call me Sandra."

The BMW raced down the A225. The rest of the journey both of them were occupied with their own thoughts. Sandra glanced casually at her Accurist a few times and Rokiv was humming some lyrics. As they reached their destination Rokiv parked his BMW at the centre of Store Street, in front of The Jewel In The Crown.

"Seems like you have been here before!" said Sandra. She wondered about the non-stop journey. The turns Rokiv took. He never asked a single person for directions.

"Let's go in Sandra my dear," said Rokiv grinning at Sandra. For some reason hesitant, pretending not to notice Sandra's attraction towards him. Both of them entered the glamorous Indian restaurant which was not very busy this evening. A gold and white uniformed waiter approached the multi-racial couple.

"Table for two, alcove please," requested Rokiv. The Bengali waiter nodded and handed them an à-la-carte menu each. They sat themselves at the elegant, spacious lounge. Sandra was mesmerised by the traditional decoration of an Indian restaurant. Scenic paintings of palm trees and beetlenut trees. Chandeliers, crystal of course, and velvet wallpaper.

The bartender approached;

"Would you care for a drink sir-madam, while we prepare your table?"

Rokiv ordered an orange juice, not a cordial this time. Sandra ordered a glass of wine and soda. The bartender acknowledged, wondering as he poured the drinks, if Rokiv is a Bengali. The dark skinned bartender returned and left the drinks in front of them on the oval oak table and fled. Rokiv felt tense, otherwise curious, and a bit nervous of such extravagant company. Sandra persistently questioned;

"Mister Kaan, the bartender looked at you as if you have been here before, have you? I am just curious."

"I have, and it brings sad memories, unfortunately," replied Rokiv.

Just then a waiter took their order and placed them in an alcove which was in the centre of the restaurant almost. Classical Indian music was playing in the background. Sandra was very curious but didn't want to be rude. She asked Rokiv anyway;

"What do you mean? Sad memories Mister Kaan."

"Sandra, please just call me Rokiv. It's been five or six years that she left me but it wasn't her fault. I haven't told anyone before, shared my grief. Now that you ask me. We used to come here every fortnight. She was a pretty woman with a humorous personality. She died of breast cancer, it was fate," said Rokiv in remorse.

Sandra suddenly in obvious typical circumstance, like in the movies, didn't know what to say.

"A' I'm terribly sorry, I shouldn't have asked. It's our first date, gosh."

"It's all right, I feel relieved in a way by telling you Sandra."

"So you haven't dated anybody since, until today?" Sandra did not have the heart to ask about Rokiv's late girlfriend's name.

"That's correct. To be honest you look just like her. Slim and tall, your eyes."

Sandra, flattered by the compliment, changed the subject;

Sons of Jabir

"Rokiv, that song playing! I assume it's Bengali, could you interpret."

"It's not Bengali, it's Indian. I think I can, just let me hear the verse again."

Whilst Rokiv listened and drummed his fingers on the table along with the rhythm, the aroma of Indian cooking from the open kitchen made Sandra famished.

PYAR KIYA THO DARNA. PYAR KIYA CHORI NAHIN, DARNA KYA… Rokiv mumbled, as Sandra waited patiently for the interpretation. Rokiv recited in English;

"I loved so why should I fear, I loved I didn't steal."

"That is the most romantic thing I've heard in years," said Sandra, all fluttery and blushing. Their enchanted evening had just begun.

See Rokiv it's a good thing you asked her out.

Chapter Thirteen

It's been only a day since Jabir had returned from Bangladesh. It was a mission impossible getting Bassha and Suna over here. After their mother's funeral they cried for six hours. At last they were in Rokiv's flat. Jabir has realised stress has become a part of his life as he left for work that morning.

"Ammaaaaaaaaa …" screamed Rajah. Shamina in sudden anxiety from Rajah's scream, *my baby*, came running from the kitchen.

"What happened son?"

"He took my water pistol, the one Rokiv uncle gave me yesterday." Rajah was angry and was pointing at the taller of Ayrina's twins.

Shamina was a bit disappointed when she noticed the twins weren't identical when she saw them for the first time yesterday.

"Bassha give your little brother the pistol back. I'll tell your father, he'll get you a new one tomorrow" said Shamina, a curry stirrer in her right hand. She was impressed by the names that Ayrina kept for her twins. The taller one and five minutes older, with black hair, dark brown eyes is Bassha. The shorter one, the same height as Rajah but older, again with black hair but light brown eyes is Suna. Bassha hesitated as Suna pushed Rajah onto Rokiv's lounge carpet. Shamina was puzzled by the sudden aggression in Suna. *Children aren't supposed to be like this, are they*?

"He's not our brother" Suna blurted, standing upright pointing his right forefinger at Rajah. Rajah got up and Suna pushed him again. This time he fell face forward and began to cry. Shamina was boiling with anger inside. For a moment she forgot Suna was Jabir's son. *Rajah, hit him back, get up and hit him back.*

"Suna he is our brother, so stop pushing him around" said Bassha, the full green transparent water pistol in his left hand.

Sons of Jabir

A black cab parked up. Jabir, due to a headache, had returned home early. He had already taken two 500 mg of paracetamol. Rajah's cry subsided as soon as he saw his father walk into the lounge.

"What is going on?" Jabir demanded. Before Shamina could say anything Bassha told on Suna.

"Abba you said Rajah is our brother, but Suna says he is not and he pushed him as well."

Everyone forgot the fact that what started all this was the water pistol. Jabir glanced at Suna, thinking of what to say, but Suna looking at Bassha blurted;

"Bassha you idiot, how could he be our brother if she's not our mother."

Shamina was surely surprised.

"That's it both of you, go to your room. I've had enough of this, no more sweets for you Suna." Jabir didn't need this with the headache he's got. And now his stomach was grumbling. Shamina wanted to protest this punishment. *They're only children*. But looking at Jabir's face, second thoughts, *no*. She just walked back to the kitchen.

Chapter Fourteen

After a long time Rokiv felt happy but at the same time alone. He remained humble of what to expect, things to believe or what to choose. His love for beauty has never decreased, that he felt today, since his adorable Catherine died six years ago.

Moments passed with considerable thought. Rokiv dialled the operator.

"Good afternoon, this is directory…"

"Please give me the number of Seroditch Nursery."

The sweet greeting of the female voice deepened his thoughts for Sandra as it left him with the answer machine. Rokiv jotted down the number and considered what to do next. He called in his secretary;

"How many appointments do I have for the afternoon?"

Lewis turned the pages of his appointment book to February.

"Mister Tony Bregaano at one, Mister Jenson Slavina at quarter to two. Lady Freehold half two and Mister Chec-novak at three."

Rokiv frowned;

"Lady Freehold, why?"

"Aye dunno," replied Lewis.

"Thanks Lewees, may leave."

Rokiv glanced at his Rotary, *twelve forty nine*. Lewis curious, wondered why Rokiv hadn't asked for any coffee for the last few hours. What she didn't know was Rokiv's mind was elsewhere.

It was the end of lunch hour at the nursery. Rajah remained brave, miraculously strong, and gave his milk carton to Kajol. Kajol drank half the carton without asking why. She was already full with her own carton.

Sandra's thoughts were in The Jewel In The Crown. She had learnt a verse from the song after Rokiv gave her some practice.

Sons of Jabir

"Pyar kiya koi chori nahin" she hummed. Sandra sat in front of the piano wondering if she could play the tune. *It's good to learn things if you know the meaning.* An Indian infant called Dipon snatched the remaining half carton from Kajol. Kajol pyschologically didn't like it a bit, naturally being a kid. She spread her tiny legs, threw her head back and gave a scream, getting the attention of Miss Travis who came running;

"Kajol sweetheart," Sandra picked her up and asked;
"What happened, dear?"

Kajol stopped screaming. Rajah was in the library reading, he saw everything. Kajol panting started to explain;

"He Di-di-dipon snatch," got interrupted by Dipon.

"I did, no snatch milk, you Paki you – you liar!" shouted the little Indian, showing his tiny fist at Kajol. No children moved nor Kajol or Miss Travis. All astonished by the bullying bravery. Unfortunately Rajah didn't like the sound of the word Paki. Maybe because looking at the little Hindu face, Rajah can smell hatred. Whatever the reason, Rajah got aggressive. His face turned like a raging chicken. Before Dipon realised he got punched by Rajah right across his face. *Serves him right*, thought Miss Travis. Feeling guilty she had not done the right thing. She should have stopped Rajah.

Kajol and all others were taken aback. Kajol especially pleased as she was sneering at now sullen Dipon. One thing Rajah was sure of, Dipon will never say Paki again. Afterwards Miss Travis cautioned Rajah and warned him not to punch anybody in the future. Rajah reluctantly apologised, he wasn't regretful. Miss Sandra Travis questioned Rajah;

"Why did you give milk to Kajol?"

"Mee fasting," answered Rajah.

Sandra knew little but enough about Islam. She was sure Rajah was very young to fast. What she didn't know was Shamina explained to her son about Ramadan well in advance because surely Rajah would question why aren't Amma (mother) and Abba (father) not eating, drinking tea in the morning? Instead Rajah persuaded his mother, can he keep a fast. At least half of the first one. The Khan's were proud of Rajah. He was already following the religion.

Two in the afternoon, Sandra expected Rokiv to turn up, but Jabir arrived to pick Rajah up. All the children left with either their mother or father. Sandra elated remained in the nursery. She placed herself in front of the piano. The phone rang suddenly. Immediately Sandra ran to the office and grabbed the receiver.

"Hello there, is this Sandra?" the coarse voice questioned.

"Who is this?"

"We have forgotten already!."

"We, who?"

"I mean you Sandra, it's Rokiv." Sandra felt an idiot.

"Oh Rokiv, how sweet. I'm still in thoughts of yesterday." Sandra was smiling.

"Sandra how about you an me go pictures tonight."

"To watch what?" Sandra asked. She has to admit she does like Rokiv Khan.

"Marlon Brando." Sandra couldn't say no. *That man is irresistible.*

"Listen Sandra, I'll pick you up at six pm" concluded Rokiv.

The fact that Bassha and Suna weren't getting along with Rajah left Jabir slightly hurt. But Shamina assured Jabir, time would consolidate relationship between Ayrina's twins and Rajah. In spite they were half-brothers. Shamina too was sure of that.

About the other day's incident, at night. Shamina explained to Jabir. Bassha and Suna aren't bad mannered kids and you can't blame them, because when they were born they didn't see their father and recently they have lost their mother, at such an early age. Jabir understood very well and promised Shamina. From now on he will love them more and more importantly he loves her more than ever stating, 'I have got the best wife in the world', because Jabir inspite he is surprised.

Sons of Jabir

He is happy and couldn't ask for more to Allah, because Shamina loves the twins much more than him acknowledging the fact that she isn't their mother.

On occasion Shamina had been upset by Bassha and Suna, calling her 'thui' (you), 'eh-beti' (you-woman...) instead of calling her mother, which she wants to hear. Shamina was adamant, she will change Bassha and Suna's attitudes soon. She has promised herself that she will give them so much love that they will not only think but feel that she is their mother, because she loves Jabir and Jabir loves his three sons.

Rajah couldn't wait. Once he was home he told his mother about the nursery incident. Shamina was shocked. Jabir understood Rajah about the Paki thing. Bassha and Suna apparently liked the part, Rajah punching Dipon right across the face. That Shamina didn't approve, *aggression*. When Rokiv arrived at ten past five, the family were waiting for him at the dining table. Rokiv was overwhelmed for the respect from Jabir, his sons and Shamina. Not to mention all these delicious dishes that Shamina has cooked. But Rokiv again ate usually less. Rajah, Bassha and Suna nibbling away with their fingers of the right hand. Shamina was curious but didn't speak as she glanced at Rokiv. She finished eating before he started. (There's a saying back home, 'if you don't fill your stomach, then there's no point dirtying your hand.') But Jabir hesitantly asked;

"Rokiv-baisab is something wrong with the food?"

"No, no, not at all," said Rokiv moving his head sideways and added;

"The food is absolutely fine, I'm on a diet."

Rokiv couldn't wait to see Sandra that evening. When Rajah recited the story to his uncle, Bassha and Suna had become bored of it but still listened. Rokiv found it humorous and couldn't stop laughing and laughter being contagious they all joined him. *Paki*, Rokiv wondered what will Rajah do if someone called him or one of his brothers a Bungi.

Jabir hadn't forgotten his friend Chander Ali. He believed Chander is alive and well somewhere in Bangladesh. And one day he will find his friend or his friend will find him. Jabir loves his friend in the same way he loved all the members of his family.

Twilight passed. Rokiv got dressed in his casual best. On the way out Rajah asked;

"Uncle where going?" it was more of a question. Rokiv's face radiant, his eyes glittered as if the cat has got the cream. He glanced at Bassha and Suna behind his lounge sofa. They were busy playing snakes and ladders. Inspite of him being late he felt like hugging everyone.

"It's a secret" Rokiv said and left. *Now what does that mean*, Rajah wondered.

Jabir sat with his sons on the sofa watching television, nothing in particular. Shamina was cleaning the dishes in the kitchen and thinking of what to cook for tomorrow.

"You lost" Suna said to Bassha.

"Yes, because you cheated" replied Bassha.

"Lost what futh (son)?" Jabir questioned looking at his son Suna, smiling.

"Bassha baisab lost playing snakes and ladders abba," Rajah interrupted.

"Because he cheated abba" said Bassha.

"No I didn't abba" replied Suna.

Rajah didn't want to get involved. He pretented to watch TV. Shamina walked in the lounge from the kitchen as she finished the washing up and interjected;

"Suna it's okay, Bassha it's okay, it's just a game."

Jabir changing the subject asked, *kids being kids*;

"Shamina has any letter come this morning?"

"Yes, I forgot all about it. One from amma-abba."

"How are they?" Shamina joined her family on the sofa.

"They miss us a lot, their health is fine. They'd hoped you'd stayed longer when you went to pick Bassha and Suna up."

Sons of Jabir

Shamina fidgeting with her hair, Rajah picking his nose, Bassha and Suna dozed off.

"I'd hoped too but I had to come back soon as possible or else I would have lost my job in the factory. They're laying people off you know. By the way Rajah doesn't talk about his nana-nanee much. Isn't that a bit strange Shamina?"

I have never thought of that. Shamina changed the subject;

"Let's put Bassha and Suna to bed. You grab one and I'll grab the other."

It was almost dark outside. Rajah stayed downstairs because he wanted to read. Having tucked Ayrina's twins into bed Shamina felt tired from menstrual burden that every woman endures so she went to bed. Jabir watched soaps and documentaries till half nine and joined Shamina. Rajah dozed to sleep with a story book on his chest. Rokiv returned at eleven, exhausted. He went straight to bed with love bites all over his body.

Chapter Fifteen

NO WONDER YOU TURNING INTO ONE. JABIR YOUR FATHER WILL COME BACK YOU PSYCHO YOU CRAZY MY FATHER'S PROMISE PROMISE JABIR HELP HELP HELP HELP…

"Ahhhhhhhhhhhhhhh…" Jabir screamed ferociously, as he broke free from the nightmare. It was not the first time. Both of his hands on the side of his head above his ears. Unusually Jabir felt cold. Shamina controlling her anxiety, asked;

"What happened? What happened?"

Bassha and Suna were in a deep sleep, Rokiv and Rajah came running.

"Abba, abba kitha oyse (what's happened?)" Rajah asked.

Rokiv picked up his nephew in his arms and whispered;

"Rajah, it's all right. I think he had a bad dream."

Jabir's mind balanced to its senses, still drowsy. Shamina offered the glass of cold water from the bedside cabinet. Jabir drained the glass to the last drop.

"Ah, I feel better now. All go back to bed," Jabir requested. He was glad, his headache had vanished since that morning. Lately he'd been suffering from a lot of headaches.

"Are you sure Jabir, if not, take the day off. I'll ring Mr Chan for you, if you want," Rokiv suggested as he gently put Rajah down. Jabir looked at Shamina, as if for approval.

"I think you should take the day off and just relax" Shamina insisted.

Whilst Bassha and Suna slept like angels, Rajah through the night couldn't sleep well. His father's sudden nightmares left him scared and worried. At times Bassha and Suna were ganging up on him. But he didn't worry about that because his father protected him from them. And his father bought him a new water pistol, a red one. As for Shamina it reminded her of a similar past incident, which happened soon after her marriage with Jabir, at the time when her mother-in-law passed away.

Sons of Jabir 113

It was six a.m. Bassha and Suna were weeping in silence. They were grieving for their mother in their beds, wrapped in white quilts. Their mother loved them dearly, they missed their mother so much, in spite of her occasional black moods. *I really didn't love your father that's why I left him*, now they have their father but no mother. Allah had played a cruel joke on them. Their father didn't like them so they thought. How are they supposed to call a stranger, mother. Can Shamina ever love them as she loves Rajah, they question themselves. Their father loves them, no doubt about that, or else they wouldn't be here today. Probably rotting away somewhere in Sylhet, with no food, no clothes and no shelter. They wept some more in silence and dozed off.

An hour later Rokiv woke up, a bit early for him. Apparently he felt elated. First thing, he rang Sandra massaging his stub.

"Hello" came the whisper from the other end, sweet as usual, and a bit groggy.

"Last Tango in Paris" rhymed Rokiv.

"Rokiv darling what time did you sneak away last night?"

"While you were sleeping, see you at the nursery." Rokiv hung up. He felt like a sixteen year old in love. *You love her, admit it*. Then Rokiv dialled Jabir's factory.

Rajah came down scrubbing his eyes with the back of his hands. He managed to sleep an hour or two. Rokiv shaved, then Rajah showered as Shamina prepared the breakfast. Bassha and Suna were still snoring as they didn't have a nursery to go to. Rokiv was trying his best to get them a place, perhaps at the one that Rajah goes to. It would be convenient for the family. Jabir was relaxing his muscles in bed.

Shamina in the kitchen, realised anxiety had become a part of her present life. Alternatively she wondered, when will the day come, Bassha and Suna will call her mother. She felt horrible about the other day, she really wanted to hit Suna. Only because he pushed Rajah. *Children are like that*. Shamina doesn't want them to be deprived of motherly love. She acknowledged Suna was aggravating at times. Oppositely, Bassha is nice to talk to, *that one is calm, how come?*

Despite Shamina missing her parents, she was fortunate, somewhat lucky to have both of her parents alive and well. Shamina couldn't even contemplate living a life knowing your mother or father have passed away. And for those indescribable emotions only she can imagine not experience, she understands what Bassha and Suna are going through. But if they ignore her, she can't help them, though she will try.

It's all right for Rajah because he has both his parents with him. And Rokiv adored him too.

Uncle and nephew got dressed, and had a hearty breakfast. They set off to the nursery ten minutes early. Rajah and Shamina wondered why.

As the Royal Mail postman knocked with his bare knuckles on Rokiv's new varnished front door, Big Ben struck nine. Shamina had just finished her breakfast. She hurried to open the door and managed to babble;

"Yes-sar."

"I have a recorded letter for Zabir Khan" said the postman.

"He's sleeping" replied Shamina.

The postman handed the letter as Shamina signed for it.

Shamina shuffled on the settee making herself comfortable. There was no sender's name on the white envelope. Her husband's name was misspelt but the address was correct. After a minute or two thinking Shamina tore open the envelope. She unfolded the letter and began to read.

Dear Zabir Khan

A person like you I find hardly or met very rare in everyday life. It's been few years or more I am not sure I hope you are living at the same address. I still remember when you sympathised at the Bangladesh Red Cross at time of liberation. It was the first time we met and may be the last time, I hope not. I am sure you have guessed who I am by now.

Sons of Jabir

It's been about seven months I have come back to England. Living in Rochdale. I would have written earlier, never seemed to get the time. In the near future I'm coming to London on business. Was wondering to get in contact, if you would like that too. Phone no: 0706-372127.

IF THIS LETTER HAS NOT REACHED THE ADDRESSEE. THEN PLEASE PASS IT ON. IF THE ADDRESS IS UNKNOWN. PLEASE SEND IT BACK. TO WHOM THANK YOU VERY MUCH.

Shamina replaced the letter in the envelope. She heard the toilet flush. Jabir came down steadily. Shamina handed the letter to Jabir, feeling proud of her husband.

Chapter Sixteen

"Recco-mend a good film Mister Chaudri."

"Comedy, thriller, western orr luvvh stoo-ry Danny."

Teenage Danny skipped school, which Manik Chaudhury didn't know about. Danny convinced Manik that he'd got a toothache, and always complimented Manik on his scar.

"You know Mister Chaudri you just remind me of Al-Capone. It's a pity you're not."

Manik was observing Danny with his shabby clothes and dirty fingers, as Danny gazed through the dusty shelves, spoilt for choice.

"Danny m'boy have you seen *Butch Cassidy the Sundance Kid?*"

"I haven an I dunno like cowboys."

"You like Dustin Hoffman."

"Very much."

"Then take *Midnight Cowboy*. You will luvh it."

"O-kay" Danny agreed reluctantly. *I dunno like cowboys*.

"Paying now or tomorrow?"

"Tomorrow."

That boy is too much, funny though. Danny hurried because his friends were waiting around the corner. Manik couldn't hide his humour, as the telephone rang besides him. He mumbled;

"I dunno like cowboys." Manik paused picked the receiver up and said;

"Hello, Bombay Video Vision."

"Iss these o seben o six, tree seben two wan two seben?" asked Jabir from the other end, two hundred and twenty miles away.

"I don't believe my ears, Zabeer Khan is that you. Thank Allah you have received my letter" said Manik.

"I have and how are you Manik" said Jabir. Manik Chaudhury reminded Jabir of his lost friend Chander Ali.

Sons of Jabir

"Oh hamidor maa huvaar ta ektu shomoil la-gi bondo koro, amee telifonno" Manik requested to his wife. She switched the vacuum off and started dusting the window sill.

"Oh Manik Choddry, are you there?"

"Sorry Zabir, you were saying. Emm, you live at the same address, that's good – good."

"What about you Manik? By the way which town are you from – from Bangladesh. I meant to ask you that before, but…"

"Oh-wee moved, my family and I moved to Rochdale now. And in Bangladesh I am from, Sharfara-sunamgong. Lower parts of the country, unlike yourself."

"Never mind (Jabir changed the subject), so when are you coming to London – says on your letter."

"Friday-weekend."

"Bala (good) I invite you come my house, meet my wife and my brother. Manik can your wife come too?"

"No Zabir, she look after my son Hamid. I have to go, customer coming. See-you-Friday." Manik hung up. A Mr Lawrence, local, walked in and up to the counter. Manik's wife closed the door in between the shop and their dining room. She re-started hoovering. Outside lightning suddenly struck.

"Dammit it's gonna rain, how are you Mister Chaudreh?"

"I'm fine, how'se yourself. By the way how is Danny's toothache coming along?" Manik asked casually.

Mr Lawrence's face seemed as it would explode with rage.

"Has-has Danny-Danny, been-in-here?" Mr Lawrence said furious.

It was not the first time Manik had encountered that sort of thing.

"I'm afraid yes, he tricked me. He has rented *Midnight Cowboy.*"

"I'll make sure he becomes one." Mr Lawrence left.

Back in Chilton Street, East London, even though Rajah came down with the flu, on his insistence and stubbornness, Rokiv had to drive him to the nursery, when he went to his office. But Sandra drove Rajah (explaining to him, his flu will

Sons of Jabir

make the class ill) back home. Shamina appreciated it, as Sandra returned to the class.

Chapter Seventeen

Bassha and Suna were fascinated by Petticoat Lane as Rokiv gave them a tour of London's most famous street markets yesterday lunch time. Rokiv had managed to find a place for the twins in a good nursery in Mile End. Rajah had overcome his flu with the help of antibiotics, but didn't feel like going to the nursery today. As Sandra walked into Rokiv's life, he is having a time of his life. His decision was final, he wanted to marry Sandra. Irrespective of what the community people think, Rokiv wants Sandra in his life for eternity. He definitely wanted Jabir to be the Best Man.

"You look happy today, what is it Shamina" asked Jabir cutting his nails.

"I'm always happy" replied Shamina combing her greasy hair. Both of them sat comfortably on Rokiv's lounge sofa, having had breakfast.

"I know why you're happy, you have received a letter from your parents" guessed Jabir.

"That and, well it was a surprise. My mother had a best friend. I only saw her when I was ten or eleven"... Shamina paused.

"Carry on I'm listening."

"So my auntie somehow managed to find me and called me when you went out with Rajah to the markets to get some vegetables. By the way the cauliflower doesn't look too good. I'll probably have to throw half of it away. Take your time shopping next time and be careful.

"Is that the auntie uncle gave a proposal before he married your mother, and the proposal fell through because she ran away with someone she fell in love. And about the cauliflower, that was the only one left," Jabir asked, now cutting his left hand nails.

"Yes father did give a proposal but she didn't want an arranged marriage, also she was in love with someone else."

Sons of Jabir

Shamina finished combing her hair. She hated combing to get rid of the knots every morning.

"So where does your mother's best friend live?" asked Jabir.

He was having difficulty with the blunt nail cutter.

"Coincidentally she, my auntie lives in Rochdale too." Shamina was waiting for the nail cutter.

"That is convenient, remember to get her address, we'll visit her when we visit Manik Chaudhury" … Jabir paused, annoyed.

"Shamina I'm going out to get a new nail cutter. This one is a waste of time."

"That's all right," replied Shamina and walked to the kitchen to wash the dirty dishes from that morning's breakfast.

Rajah came down and walked into the kitchen.

"Amma, where's abba?"

"Why?" Shamina realised the flat had become a lot quieter as Bassha and Suna have gone to the nursery. They were a bit old for nursery, but Rokiv insisted, as the change of environment will help them adapt to other people. And it will be a help when they go to school. Nursery will help them be children, because especially Suna's mind seems to be growing faster than his age.

"Abba promised to tell me a story" said Rajah scratching his nose.

"Go and put the TV on, he should be back soon." Shamina finished rinsing the dishes. She was thankful to Rokiv as he bought her a pair of pink rubber washing gloves yesterday coming from work.

Sons of Jabir

Chapter Eighteen

"Suna-Suna dekh ayya (come-see) bagh-bagh" shouted Bassha. He wished he stayed at home. A bug must be going around or probably he had caught Rajah's flu. He just came because Suna insisted. Suna came running from the other end of the cage, as he was gawking at the wild bears inside their cages.

"Where, where" Suna asked panting and added;

"Where's the tiger Bash."

Bassha and Suna were lucky to be on this trip as they were new admittances. Jabir mentioned an uncle from Rochdale was coming to dinner. He couldn't persuade the twins not to go on the trip, when the teacher, Mrs Pentolow mentioned tigers, giraffes and monkeys, Suna got excited and so they were there. Suna loved animals, he had a dog in Srimangal, he had it for good few years. Unfortunately he lost it when the flood hit the town. It was getting cold and dark.

Having seen all the animals a few times over, Suna wasn't fed up. He wanted to see the giraffes again and the monkeys. The Mile End Nursery teacher took everyone to the Chester Zoo café, as it was just about to close. Mrs Pentolow assured the manager, they'd be gone in half an hour. Bassha and Suna began to nibble on Shamina's cheese and tomato sandwiches. Bassha couldn't wait to get back home.

"You know Bash I miss amma" Suna said. Tears in his eyes.

"Hey I miss her too, what can we do she's gone to heaven. Now don't you start crying again. Hey look at the bright side, we have a father and a mother now" Bassha on his second sandwich.

"Shamina is not our mother," Suna protested.

"Hey calm down whatever." They both finished eating all the sandwiches. Washed it down with milk given by Mrs Pentolow purchased from the Chester Zoo café.

"All right everyone, time to go home" shouted Mrs Pentolow.

Rajah was happy that it was the end of the week, Friday. Tomorrow his Uncle Rokiv promised to take him out touring London. One thing bothered Rajah. That, his uncle and Miss Travis, chatting at lunch time in the nursery yard in the past couple of days.

Another exciting thing his father mentioned, that his father's friend was coming to dinner tonight. Rajah was watching Blue Peter when Shamina shouted;

"Dinner's ready, Rajah my son." Lately Shamina was intrigued by Coronation Street, which she hardly comprehends. Rokiv was more happy than usual. A lion couldn't kill its prey faster as Rajah finished eating his rice and fish. Persuaded by Shamina Rajah took a short nap.

Jabir arrived from the factory at half five. Rokiv came from Sandra's house just after. Rokiv felt satisfied that he had met Sandra's parents and vice versa. Rokiv had made a decision but waiting for the perfect moment.

"What time did he say he's coming?" asked Rokiv.

"He didn't give precise time. Evening suppose seven-eight."

Shamina prepared a variety of dishes for the guest. From Aloo gobi to lamb bhuna along with fish delicacies. Pilau rice cooked with cubed chicken pieces and freshly cooked vegetables. (Chicken and vegetable biryani with no omelette on top.)

Rajah couldn't sleep any longer because of the anticipation. He missed his grandparents but didn't show it. Camouflaged by infrastructural change and clean environment. He was already capable of having a shower, wearing his own clothes. The day broke into darkness and frost. The Khan's waited for Mr Chaudhury in patience. Every time a car passed Chilton Street Rajah would glance out of the window. The lounge wall clock struck eight. Finally there was a knock. Jabir promptly opened the door. Rajah saw the parked Volvo Estate. Manik Chaudhury in the flesh stood in front of Jabir.

Five-nine, no facial hair, forlorn scar on his cheek, dark brown eyes, oval face which complements his medium body.

"Assala malaykum Zabir" said Manik.

"Alikum salam" replied Jabir. (Religious greeting was exchanged.) Manik brought gifts out of generosity. He handed them to Rajah as he reflected Rajah's smile.

Shamina took the carrier and stored it in the kitchen. Jabir gave a brief introduction with Rokiv, then the three of them sat around the dining table.

"I hope you had no problem finding us Manik baisab" said Rokiv. His subconscious was elsewhere.

"I expected to arrive earlier but traffic you know! So (former) Captain Zabir, how do you find London second time round" Manik answered Rokiv's question indirectly.

"Manik it's Jabir with J an' don' be sorry about it. I'm glad you remembered the war years and me especially after it." Jabir tempting to talk about wartimes and B.R.A., second thoughts (no because of Chander.)

In the kitchen Rajah was examining the carrier which contained chocolates. Shamina walked towards the dining table with a tray of pot of tea and plate of triangular pastries stuffed with spicy minced meat.

"How many hours do you work Zab-Jabir" said Manik.

"Ten hours, six to five, one hour for lunch. I don't take breaks, cos I don' smoke. In sixty eight did thirteen hours a day" intoned Jabir. In the kitchen Shamina began to reheat the dishes.

"Rokiv baisaab, what do you do?" asked Manik. Rokiv was in deep thoughts of Sandra. *Does she feel the same about me, oh God I very much hope so.*

"Beg your pardon Manik?"

"What do you do for a living?"

"I'm a solicitor."

"Specialising in?"

Sons of Jabir

"Criminal law. Now let's eat these samosas, not very nice when they're cold. And yes what type of business you have Manik baisab?" questioned Rokiv.

"It's a video store. I come London every three months to buy the latest Hindi and American films," Manik explained.

Rajah sitting besides his Uncle Rokiv was observing the conversation. He remained silent understanding them well. Manik knew why Jabir's son was looking at him every two minutes, because of his scar. Manik only wished he didn't detest cosmetic surgery. Then his right cheek would look no different from his left.

Half an hour passed in general gossip. Jabir hesitant at the same time very curious. If only Manik would pop the question, 'Rokiv why aren't you married yet.' Jabir and Shamina wouldn't have minded knowing.

Shamina decorated the dining table with the dishes she had prepared. Jabir served Manik, Rokiv and himself. Shamina will eat afterwards, whilst Rajah ate separately in the kitchen. Manik forgot all about the twins. As he remembered he questioned;

"Where are the twins Zabeer?"

"They've gone to Chester Zoo, they should be back any moment now, must be traffic," replied Rokiv. Jabir and Shamina became anxious, but remained calm.

"Must be traffic," Manik assured and added,

"Well I'll see them next time."

Rajah wished the twins don't come back, because they always take his stuff and pick on him. After the meal, everyone having stuffed themselves, except Shamina, Manik was pressed for time;

"Thanks for everything, Shamina bhabi (sister-in-law.) I'm afraid I have to leave now. Rokiv and Jabir please come and visit me sometime, and definitely bring the twins along."

"Have a cup of tea before you go Manik" insisted Rokiv.

"I can't really, I have to go."

Sons of Jabir

"We will come and visit you at our earliest opportunity Manik" concluded Jabir, as Manik drove off switching the headlights on, waving at Rajah and the family.

The Mile End Nursery turbo diesel mini-bus dropped, tired and exhausted Bassha and Suna off in front of Rokiv's flat. Rajah became miserable, Rokiv, Jabir and Shamina were relieved from their anxiety.

Chapter Nineteen

Before until now Rokiv used to think often, his name and he himself was unlucky. A part of his heart was unfulfilled, growing without real parents. He can't even remember who gave him the name Rokiv, and he didn't care. Does Rokiv sound like it has a purpose or a meaning? When Catherine died, he did promise himself that her memories will be treasured in his heart forever.

Little did he know, as science makes a breakthrough in an incurable disease. Rokiv feels the same, letting go of his past as Sandra walked into his life. Sandra has made him realise, there was more in life than one's treasured love. Valentine Day, Rokiv once again encouraged Sandra to have dinner with him at The Jewel In The Crown. On the occasion Rokiv made acquaintance with Sandra's workaholic parents.

Dating was all right, eating out was all right, but it wasn't enough. What Rokiv wanted was to see Sandra every morning when he goes to work. To have Sandra close to him every night when he goes to sleep. Eventually when Rokiv summoned all his emotions, joy, sorrow, anger and loneliness, his heart and mind indicated that he was in love, deeply in love with Sandra Travis.

His belief was Sandra's parents found him auspicious and ostentatious, therefore accepted him as their future son-in-law, despite his colour and origin. He is awaiting a hint from Sandra. Hoping God was on his side. And whenever the moment is perfect Rokiv hoped to propose. Days passed with Sandra's sweet thoughts and Catherine's vague memories.

After work Rokiv drove straight to Sandra's house and took her to the movies. Afterwards he had dinner with her parents. At that moment, *Rokiv now is the time* in front of Sandra's mother and father, at the dining table a slightly nervous Rokiv took Sandra's elegant right hand in his and looking into her eyes he proposed without a ring. Sandra blushed and ran to her room, unusual of her culture. Rokiv felt a bit awkward, for a moment he didn't know what to do. His future in-laws assured him 'she got embarrassed, you know when she was a little girl, she used to be really shy.' Rokiv realised as it was a surprise, his proposal to marry her, she must have felt embarrassed. Rokiv regained his confidence and slowly walked upstairs. Thinking of what to say, *will she break my heart, I hope not. What if she says no, because of me being a Bengali. Stop it, you know she loves you.*

Inside the Victorian furnished bedroom, peach fragranced Sandra was sat on her grand bed, instead of sitting in front of her dressing table. As the door was wide open, Rokiv walked in and said;

"Sandra darling, I hope I haven't misunderstood our relationship, we do love each other right."

Sandra looked up as her eyes matched with Rokiv Khan. And for the first she realised, how much she loved this Bengali man. This handsome Bengali man. And that fact that she wanted him to be the father of her children, she had already decided how many children she wants, *three.*

"Come and sit down near me Rokiv" requested Sandra. Already thinking of what type of wedding dress will suit her. Who will be the Maid of Honour? The Best Man? What about her parents? Are they all right she is marrying Rokiv Khan? She doesn't care.

"We do love each other," added Sandra.

They embraced each other and kissed. Rokiv felt relieved and deeply happy. He will be marrying the woman he loves. A surge of overwhelming lust and desire rushed through his body as it trembled slightly. He wanted to make love to Sandra right now, but he knew better.

"Are you all right darling?" said Sandra as she felt the slight shudder from Rokiv's upper body.

"I'm fine." Rokiv kissed Sandra again. She pulled herself free and said;

"You took your time. I may not be like Catherine, but I will try my best to be a decent wife to you. I'll make your breakfast and iron your clothes, gosh I thought you'd never propose."

"I am very happy. I would like to introduce you to Rajah's parents. You will he having a feast with the Khan's tomorrow" said Rokiv.

This time Sandra kissed Rokiv. It lasted about a minute as they parted. *Now Rajah will call me auntie*, Sandra was already thinking of the near future.

When Rokiv arrived home, he was already thinking of how to plan his wedding. First thing he had to buy was a diamond ring. As everyone was asleep, apparently the excitement had made him tired, he too went straight to bed after a cold shower. Soon Muslims will be celebrating Eid. Jabir, especially, was looking forward to that.

It was Wednesday and Rokiv was free. He always had been since he joined the firm, unless otherwise. It was the only perk he requested. It helped with the stress of being a solicitor. That morning Rokiv was elated as he drove his nephews to their nurseries. Rokiv wondered what Rajah would make of him and Sandra. Rajah had seen them together kissing in the nursery playground. Oppositely Bassha and Suna didn't have a clue.

Afterwards Rokiv discussed some dates with Sandra's parents and visited the East End marriage bureau. Luckily he persuaded the receptionist to book them on a Wednesday. The last Wednesday of next month.

As noon passed after three cups of coffee and tuna and cucumber sandwiches. Soon it was two in the afternoon. Rokiv picked Bassha, Suna and Rajah from their nurseries. Mrs Pentolow told Rokiv, Bassha was trying very hard to learn, but Suna didn't seem bothered, and was afraid to play with other children in the nursery playground. Sandra told Rokiv proudly, Rajah's observation of the English Language is getting better day by day. Rokiv dropped his nephews home to Shamina, as it has become one of his chores. Rokiv rushed to Vallence Road as Sandra his future wife patiently awaited him.

"Rokiv did you know…?"

"Did I know what."

"Stop interrupting me an I'll tell you a bit of East End history."

Rokiv was playing with Sandra's recently washed hair;

"Sorry, go on."

"End of the nineteenth century, Charles Booth, social reformer described the area of Whitechapel and Bethnal Green as the Eldorado of the east."

"Charles Booth, I've read about him somewhere…" Rokiv paused and added;

"I better be off." Rokiv left to shop for some groceries, including lamb and chicken. The African butcher- shop owner assured him it was halal.

When Rokiv arrived home he requested Shamina to prepare a light feast. Shamina didn't ask him why but Rokiv told Rajah. One thing bothered Rokiv. How should he approach to break the news to Jabir and Shamina. Unusually Rokiv helped Shamina in the kitchen. Shamina never spoke to him once. She had nothing to talk about. Rajah was waffling to Rokiv about the things he and Kajol did at the nursery today which made Rokiv smile. That Sandra has taught Rajah the verse of that Indian song she learnt at The Jewel In The Crown.

Bassha and Suna were playing Snakes and Ladders in Jabir's bedroom, as they have eaten. Jabir came home late just after five, he was unaware of the time, he didn't feel tired after a hard day's manual labour.

"Jabeer, Manik Chaudhury phoned. He pleaded us to go and visit him in Rochdale. I couldn't talk him out of it. So I said I'll let him know, I mean I don't mind driving to Rochdale for the weekend, if you seem happy with it" Rokiv reported.

Shamina hoped Jabir would say yes so she could visit her auntie, her mother's best friend. Jabir thought for a few seconds;

"Weekend is not very busy in the factory…" Jabir paused and concluded;

Sons of Jabir

"Yes, I'm all right with that."

Shamina felt good. She wondered what her auntie would look like now.

"By the way, I have invited Rajah's nursery teacher for a light feast (Rokiv wanted to say 'Sandra', Jabir wondered 'what about Bassha and Suna's nursery teacher) this evening."

"You have, Rajah does talk about her a lot" replied Jabir.

For Rokiv time passed slowly in wait of Sandra. She had promised to come, she wouldn't let him down.

Eventually Rokiv's future wife parked up on Chilton Street and walked to Rokiv's flat for the first time without a handbag. Sandra Travis looked elegant in an evening dress. Her hair blow dried. She could have done with a bit more make-up on. Jabir wondered why Rokiv looked so happy, Shamina figured.

"Hello Rajah, how are you" Sandra said as she chuckled.

Rajah being a good boy just smiled, as Sandra pecked Rajah on the forehead and added;

"Where are the twins?"

"They are upstairs playing, shall I go and get them" answered Shamina.

Shamina wondered how she would look in an evening dress.

"No leave them. I'll see them some other time" replied Sandra.

As Rokiv was always complimenting on Shamina's cooking Sandra couldn't wait to try it. Looking at Rajah, *I'll have a child like that soon*, dreamt Sandra.

Wasting no time as Jabir was starving, they all sat around the dining table decorated with pilau rice, boiled rice, lamb bhuna, chicken jalfrezi and mixed vegetable bhaji. Not to forget the glasses of sweet lassi.

Shamina reluctantly asked;

"Do you like our home, miss?"

"Call me Sandra please, it's nice." O*vercrowded really.* Sandra was impressed by Shamina's English despite the accent.

"Where have you learnt English, you speak well Shamina."

The Khan's ate with their right hands and fingers, scrubbed and washed, *of course,* thought Sandra. She was using a silver table spoon.

"Class eight, Bishwanath High School, Bangladesh," Shamina said proudly.

Sandra felt at home in spite this being her first time in Rokiv's flat.

"Miss, you like Uncle Rokiv?" Rajah questioned suddenly. That took all of them by surprise except Sandra.

"Well your Uncle Rokiv is a nice person."

Rokiv felt this may be a good time to expose his plans to Jabir.

"What is your religion?" Shamina questioned.

Sandra wondered why Jabir was so quiet.

"I'm a Catholic," answered Sandra, wondering why Rokiv was so quiet as well.

They were all eating in silence for a moment. Shamina thought of breaking into some interesting conversation. She hesitantly questioned;

"Sandra nothing personal, when you plan getting married?"

"Soon, Shamina," Sandra said frankly. Sandra realised Rokiv has not yet mentioned.

"Will we be invited?"

"I guess you, Jabir will be first to know," Sandra said. This is anticipating. Rokiv prayed Shamina changed the subject. Curiously Jabir spoke;

"Me, Shamina first to know. I not understand what you mean Miss Sandra. No get me wrong I respect my son teacher. But we hardly know you."

Sandra a little nervous looked at Rokiv. He nodded and assured, hoping that Sandra would expose them now. Sandra understood the nod and said;

Sons of Jabir

"Jabir, I thought you knew about Rokiv and me. We love each other." The last four words Sandra said quickly.

Jabir became all confused, lost his colour. His eyes blinked as he tried to reply;

"Rokiv baisab I no understand Sandra."

Shamina did not hope for this but had a good idea what the evening may turn out to be. An embarrassing one. Not that Jabir was against love marriages. It's Sandra's religion and colour what's bothering Jabir. Rokiv didn't say anything for the moment. As Sandra spoke;

"I'm sorry if this is shocking to you Jabir. But we plan to get married next month."

Surprised and shocked, Jabir couldn't believe his ears. Sandra my – my sister-in-law, this can't be true, oh Allah. Instantaneously Jabir began to choke. Shamina promptly patted Jabir's back and massaged his spine. Whatever it was, went down Jabir's chest. Sandra felt uncomfortable and Rokiv got worried.

"He chokes now an' then, he be aright," Shamina assured.

"Amma what happened to abba" Rajah asked.

"Nothing son abba oright."

"Escuse me I like to rest. Shamina help me please," Jabir said as he stopped coughing.

Rokiv sensed Jabir disapproved already. Him marrying Sandra. Shamina helped Jabir to their bedroom. Rajah finished his meal and started to play with his double decker bus.

"Sandra you must be wondering why I haven't told them about us. I was just waiting for a convenient moment," Rokiv tried to explain.

"It's all right Rokiv," Sandra said bluntly.

She was a bit disappointed by Jabir's manner of behaviour in front of a guest. Not just tolerable. If one does not know someone, then one should not judge someone. Shamina returned to apologise.

"I am sorry about what just happened and Jabir going to bed suddenly."

Sons of Jabir

"Sah-mina it is all right, really," Sandra said dramatically.

Dinner was over for Sandra. She wasn't in the mood for dessert. Rokiv escorted Sandra to her home.

"Shamina take care, I'll be late," Rokiv said on his way out. Shamina just nodded.

Shamina sat down on the settee after cleaning the greasy dishes with Fairy. She began to think, actually worry about the consequences of Rokiv's marriage from her husband's point of view. After a while Jabir came down, Sandra nagging in his mind. He sat besides his wife, raking in the scent from Shamina's hair.

"Shamina I cannot believe this, tell me it's not true. How could Rokiv baisab marry Sandra? There are beautiful women in Bangladesh," Jabir said.

"Rokiv bai is very much westernised. He is in love with Sandra and he can't help it. If she was an African he'd still marry her. You understand, Jabir."

"I understand love, but love outside your culture, that's what I don't understand."

"You mean it's not common sense."

Shamina and Jabir discussed but came up with no conclusions. After all it was Rokiv's decision. Rajah went to bed and read himself to sleep, his usual way. Shamina exhausted, retired to bed at ten after a cup of tea. Jabir waited for Rokiv as he watched TV. Ignorant Bassha and Suna had gone to bed too after drinking some milk.

In Sandra's house at Vallance Road Rokiv felt hollow for some reason.

"Oh Rokiv, whatever you do, don't spoil our wedding. Okay honey" Sandra said, a bit possessive of Rokiv.

"Of course not. Jabir is old-fashioned and narrow-minded. Look I don't want to sacrifice you at any cost. I'll make him understand, darling." The would-be Mr and Mrs embraced, kissing each other for a few minutes.

"I can't wait for our honeymoon" Sandra shouted as Rokiv drove home.

Sons of Jabir

It was just past midnight. Rokiv entered his flat. He saw Jabir awake on the settee. It surprised Rokiv not because Jabir was awake but Jabir didn't look tired.

"Jabir shouldn't you be sleeping?" Rokiv said.

"Waiting for you baisab," Jabir replied sullenly. Rokiv sensed what was coming. Pity Rokiv didn't take psychology for his career. Rokiv can already imagine, *why, why marry someone different from your own race. How can I tell him! Even my first love was Jewish, Catherine.*

"Do I have to guess what for Jabir? You are still awake."

"Baisab there's no doubt me not respecting you. I can never imagine in my dreams my brother marry non-Muslim." Rokiv was surely gobsmacked.

"Jabir I understand I am bit distant. I respect your feelings but you ought to understand I love Sandra very much. Years I was lonely. I've found someone special to me I can marry and spend my life with." It was as though Jabir wasn't listening to Rokiv.

"Baisab it is embarrassment. What will I say when I go Jumma. Society will detest us. Love I understand, why not go Bangladesh find someone there."

"Jabir you don't care about my feelings. You only care about the society. This love or any other is given by God. It is a religion in itself."

"Is that your final decision baisab?"

"Jabir this is not about making decisions. It's a matter of my life, my loneli . . ."

Rokiv's voice trailed off in Jabir's ears as he interrupted;

"I ask again, is that your final decision," Jabir metaphorically turned unconcerned. His tone arrogant. Rokiv remained calm, he comprehended it may take time to reason with Jabir. *Love I understand yeh sure you do Jabir.*

"Am afraid that is my final decision" Rokiv said reassuring himself. After a moment of silence Jabir spoke in disrespect, oblivious to Rokiv's past.

Sons of Jabir

"Rokiv Khan I'm afraid we cannot live under the same roof the day you marry Sandra" Jabir paused. If that wasn't shocking enough for Rokiv. Jabir added;

"I shall soon as possible buy my own house and move out with my family. I cannot live with a non-Muslim." Rokiv was now entitled to be angry. So;

"Listen Jabir, you are nothing but a stubborn person. Dignity and pride does not put food on the table. Important of all I believe in God. If I didn't help you, you would still be in Bangladesh." Jabir was taken aback but not surprised. There was obvious tension between both brothers. Pity everyone is asleep.

"You did no favour to me Rokiv. My mother adopted you or else you would have been in some side street begging for money to eat."

What they weren't aware of, they were stabbing one another with their words. Rokiv was hurt but didn't reveal it. He shut his mouth, sat down on the settee as Jabir's standing shadow towered over him. Jabir wasn't finished;

"What's the matter now, the truth stinks doesn't it? Why? Don't you speak now Rokiv. They say it's true, cheap blood is cheap after all. No matter how you cherish and adore it. You marry Sandra like I care. You call yourself Muslim or not like I care. I hope you sleep well, damn you Rokiv, I'm going to bed." Jabir very drunk in his pride, principles and religion, above all being a Khan. He did not realise that Rokiv began weeping when he left for bed. Every word spoken out of Jabir's mouth felt like a knife wound in Rokiv's back. Rokiv although he was deeply hurt, he didn't take it personally. It reminded Rokiv of Jabir's mother. Rokiv promised his late adopted mother he will never hurt Jabir in any way, though he almost did. One can't be too careful Rokiv thought. As he sobbed in silence.

Jabir in bed hated to admit that he had no right to dig up Rokiv's past and throw the dirt all over him. Forlornly Rokiv

Sons of Jabir

finally slept after a warm shower, hoping the dawn may help to reconcile things. Jabir's agitation woke Shamina.

"What's the matter?" Shamina asked, still half asleep.

"I said some nasty things to Rokiv. I feel bad about it."

"Well the damage is done. Try to sleep and apologise in the morning, whatever," Shamina suggested.

Dawn broke, Jabir was filled with guilt and remorse. He can't imagine what happened a few hours ago, actually took place. Rokiv was already in the kitchen, fresh tea in his hand. He walked out into the lounge, switched the TV on and sat facing it as usual. Jabir and Shamina came down together. Jabir couldn't look at Rokiv, although he wanted to. Rajah was still snoring. So were Bassha and Suna.

"Jabir have you slept well" Rokiv said reluctantly. Jabir thought Rokiv may not speak to him for a while but he was wrong. *Pity.*

"Not really, what about you ba-baisab?" Jabir replied. (The word baisab, calling your elder brother with respect.) What Rokiv anticipated, he sensed it coming, reconciliation. Jabir disappeared into the kitchen. Shamina found the opportunity to talk about last night.

"Rokiv baisab. Jabir didn't mean what he said last night. You got to understand it's his temper. He is very ashamed of himself. An apology to you would occur as an insult he thinks. Please forgive him. Long before we were married Ayrina may have cursed him for his temper. In result he suffered nervous breakdown," Shamina said.

Jabir eavesdropped from the kitchen.

"Shamina I understand Jabir is a sensitive person. I respect you as a little sister. What happened last night was coincidentally circumstantial. Tell Jabir I have forgiven him, mistakes happen. One thing you and Jabir should understand. That how unreasonable it may seem, I love Sandra."

At that point Jabir came from the kitchen. He knelt down in front of Rokiv like a child and said;

"Baisab I thought you never forgive me."

Sons of Jabir

"It's all right, now get up and sit besides me Jabir."

"Amma amma," shouted Rajah from the bathroom.

"I told you things will be all right," Shamina said as she ran to the bathroom. Rokiv handed an opened envelope to Jabir.

"Jabir, I opened it by mistake. They made an error when printing. It should be initial J not R. It seems you have good money in your account."

"Oh it's from selling the house in Bangladesh baisab."

Jabir and Rokiv to themselves promised they would not hurt one another again. Bassha and Suna didn't feel like going to the nursery today. They went back to sleep.

Chapter Twenty

The last days of fasting struggled past. Ramadan was eventually over on Eid, the big day for Jabir and of course other devoted believers of the Islam religion. Jabir's influence took Rokiv to Jamaat. He had seldom been in the past. The mosque was small and crowded. Jabir and Rokiv celebrated Eid with great passion, amongst hundreds of others.

After, Rokiv drove his adorable nephew to a fair near Hounslow, then toured Rajah around London, except Wembley. Rajah felt the world, memories for life. Bassha and Suna were shopping with Jabir and Shamina. The Khan family made a duty of being happy on Eid.

At six in the evening, Rokiv went to visit his future wife. He spent a few hours embracing and kissing her. Too bad she was on her period.

Around about ten Manik Chaudhury rang from Rochdale with greetings of Eid. After confirmation from Jabir, Rokiv informed Manik they would hopefully visit him and his family at the weekend. Rokiv got directions of Manik's address as he replaced the receiver.

Jabir and Shamina understood about Rokiv's love but despised Sandra. Jabir had made up his mind of moving out. But it was not as easy as it sounded, 'moving out.' Jabir, being a devoted Muslim, does not help Rokiv. The bottom line was Rokiv didn't mind as long as Jabir nor Shamina hold any grudges against him. Sad thing, Rajah was the victim in all this. How does one sacrifice love for religion, that he hadn't practised for years but has respect for (ISLAM.) Gladly Rokiv will help Jabir, as it was clear Jabir did not want to stay under the same roof, once Sandra became Rokiv's wife. Shamina did not have a say in Jabir's decision. On the other hand Rokiv's affection for Rajah increased. Rajah was becoming a bookworm at the age of, not even four. May be somewhat indifferent, perhaps.

Sons of Jabir

As promised and therefore planned they were all ready and dressed. Rokiv set off for Rochdale. The day before he had his BMW serviced. One could not know, what may happen on the motorway, if a breakdown occurs. City traffic was steady. In fact too slow, it took Rokiv more than quarter of an hour to get on the motorway following North.

Rokiv managed to pass Birmingham in an hour and forty minutes. He felt a bit tired so the Khans took a break at a service station with BP insignias all around.

Although Rokiv had half a tank, he still topped his BMW with four star and paid cash. Out straight onto M6 driving towards Manchester, Rokiv increased his speed by ten miles. Rokiv kept his eyes wide open for police cars as he broke the speed limit but was in full control. Approximately after an hour and fifteen minutes the Khan's entered the town of co-ops and cotton mills, Rochdale. It wasn't too difficult to find Yorkshire Street, after asking a police patrol constable on Manchester Road.

"Hundred and one, ninety-nine, ninety-seven, ninety-five and ninety-three" Rokiv recited as he parked his BMW in front of Manik's front door. He turned the ignition off. The stillness woke Rajah up from his nap.

"Chacha are we here" Rajah asked. The twins woke up from their nap too.

"That's right Batija," Rokiv replied.

The time was nine forty eight. Manik must have heard Rokiv's engine. Instinctively he and his son came out to receive the Khans, who walked in abreast with Manik and his son, with their adequate belongings for a weekend stay. From Manik's kitchen the aroma of his wife's cooking started to make Rokiv's stomach grumble. Rokiv enjoyed good food.

Once inside, stretched, shuffled and comfortably seated, Manik introduced Shamina to his wife.

"Oh bha-bi, this is Hamid's mother, my wife Afia," Manik said.

Shamina acknowledged. It may have been the atmosphere of Manik's home that Shamina became familiar with, as in no time she began to help Manik's wife prepare dinner. They chatted about the infrastructures in Britain, compared to Far East countries. (Shamina had spoken to Afia once before, on Eid-day on the telephone.) To Shamina it seemed as though she knew Afia for more than a decade. Obviously nothing to do with reincarnation. They both felt they're in the same boat, lonely housewives in Britain and partly alienated. Shamina couldn't wait to visit her auntie.

Manik's living room was twice as big as Rokiv's lounge in East London. Manik's son was no bigger than Rajah, but with a dark skin complexion. Afia looked nothing like Shamina, though she was very friendly.

"So Rokiv baisab the journey wasn't frustrating was it?" Manik said, making conversation. Manik noticed the twins were not identical.

"Couldn't have been better" Rokiv replied as though he had rehearsed it.

"I'm very happy you've all come as promised. Round here there're not a lot of Bengalis. A few houses compared to East London."

The journey had made Jabir pretty tired. He wasn't in the mood to interact in the conversation. Instead, surprisingly his son Rajah did;

"Uncle Manik, what your son name?"

"Hamid," Manik said taken slightly aback.

On the mahogany dining table Jabir's appearance looked better. After dinner Rajah made friends with Hamid. He mentioned Kajol. Hamid was not old enough to be envious. Bassha and Suna watched TV with interest.

The grown ups enjoyed British tea with home made pastries, gossiping along. Rajah and Hamid were snoring already. Manik's wife prepared the beds for the guests. Jabir was very pleased with the hospitality. Rokiv was inevitably thinking of Sandra.

Sons of Jabir

Saturday morning after a stormy rainfall. It was being unseasonal but really it was British weather. A while after dawn, the day glowed in tremendous sunshine. Rokiv was thinking of wedding preparations. Who's going to be the best man?

Manik and his dear wife had prepared breakfast, consisting of sheemai and paratha with slices of fresh mangoes, bananas, apples, and pineapples. They ate as though being one family. Everyone had a go at everything, except Rajah didn't like the smell of bananas and mangoes.

Jabir, the moment he set foot in Rochdale, had wanted to ask Manik about prices of houses. Instead he blurted;

"Manik what about your shop today, is it open?"

"Danny a teenager, he's looking after the shop for me. Honest boy not very keen."

"Who's not keen?" Rokiv said out of nowhere, figuring everything out for his wedding.

"Danny a…" Jabir interrupted.

"Manik what are the price ranges of two to three bedroom terraced houses in this town." It came out exactly Jabir had rehearsed.

Jabir glanced at Rokiv without eye contact. For a few seconds Rokiv couldn't believe his ears. Rokiv realised it was obvious Jabir was depending on lost and found friendship. He wanted to move to Rochdale. Why not? The living standard in this town would be cheap compared to the capital. For Jabir he'll be free of what may be an embarrassment and a scandal for only him because of Rokiv marrying Sandra. Whatever Jabir wanted, Rokiv as promised would always help.

"Is this just a curiosity" Manik said.

"Not really" Jabir replied.

"From three to six thousand you can get a two bedroom terraced in good condition. It's a good investment…"

"By the way what is there to see in Rochdale. Actually near yourself?" Rokiv suddenly interrupted, which made Manik more curious. But Jabir didn't object.

Sons of Jabir

Manik felt there was an understanding about this between Rokiv and Jabir. Despite being surprised, Manik would definitely like Jabir to live near him. *Let's show him Rochdale first*, Manik thought.

"This being the town of co-ops, there are things of interest to see. Example Toad Lane museum. Tell you what finish drinking tea an' we'll go for a tour."

Typically or not Manik took Jabir and Rokiv to the museum. Rokiv found it boring but Jabir took the liberty to learn about the co-operative movement. One thing Rokiv acknowledged, John Bright a campaigner for corn laws, a century ago.

After the Toad Lane visit, whilst they drove around, Jabir was interested, so he asked about the Rochdale textile industry. At that instance, Rokiv figured out part of Jabir's future plans, *not bad*. Rokiv realised Jabir, his sons and Shamina would be moving out a lot sooner than he expected. If only it didn't hurt so much. He will miss Shamina's cooking. Maybe he will move to Rochdale some day, Rokiv thought.

Rochdale was pretty intriguing. Although all gentlemen may not wear mackintoshes Rokiv learned from Manik. The Town Hall has great colourful decorated windows of kings and queens. Victoria was one of them.

In the evening Rokiv and Manik entertained themselves with James Bond. Jabir felt abnormally tired. He was busy snoring. Rokiv anticipating but not sure when, as Manik uttered some unexpected but true words, reluctantly.

"Rokiv baisab, please don't get me wrong but Zabir seems very keen suddenly in moving Rochdale. It hasn't been long he's returned from Bangladesh."

Rokiv frankly replied;

"Manik bai, there's nothing to hide. Except I will be getting married shortly. Jabir and Shamina understandably think we will be overcrowded. I am a bit embarrassed to admit the woman I am marrying is a Christian. The thing is I love her …" Rokiv trailed as he was stuck for words, simultaneously interrupted by Manik;

Sons of Jabir

"Please stop, I understand," Manik paused. He added;

"Now that I understand, there's one thing. There is a two bed terraced, actually next door for sale. Jabir already asked me to help him buy a house. I know this is hurtful but as you said stubborn, and I must say insensitive, but a good person at heart." Rokiv more than surprised, despite his hurt replied;

"Suddenly all this so soon." *Pity.*

"Zabir sounded serious," Manik said.

Rokiv couldn't be bothered. It's not that he didn't care. He'd like to help Jabir.

"If that's what Jabir wants, any idea of the value of the property," Rokiv asked.

"Round about seven thousand asking price, I'm not sure" Manik answered.

"If I can recall I'm sure Jabir can put good deposit down. Find out the details as you said and I know Jabir is serious. I'll do all his conveyancing and help him move out."

"First thing Monday morning I'll do that" Manik said.

Entertained by Sean Connery and Roger Moore time flew. Just past seven and Rokiv and Manik had drunk a dozen cups of coffee. Manik's wife disturbed them and called him because, Hamid his son wouldn't go to sleep without him. Just then Jabir entered the lounge joining Rokiv, his face washed but still yawning. Rokiv told Jabir what he had instructed Manik to do but questioned him patiently.

"Why Rochdale, why not near me?"

Jabir seemed a bit surprised.

"If I live near yourself, Bengalis will criticise you an'…"

Rokiv abruptly interrupted;

"Please stop, as long as you are happy with Shamina and your sons, it's all right with me."

Saturday evening it began to rain. Manik offered to take Jabir and Shamina to visit her auntie.

"What street was it Shamina bhabi (sister-in-law)" asked Manik for the second time from the driver's seat of his car.

"Brunswick Street," replied Shamina excitedly.

Manik just turned into South Street. There was sudden lightning and the rain increased.

"Oh yes Brunswick Street, I know where it is. What number bhabi?"

"Number twenty-five," replied Shamina.

She and Jabir sat on the back seat. Jabir offered to take Rokiv along, to be sociable but Rokiv insisted they should go as he will be taking care of his nephews. Rokiv was already getting bored. He wanted to go back to London.

Manik parked in front of number twenty-five Brunswick Street, facing his car downwards as it was a slanted street abreast with Buckingham, Bulwer, and Trafalgar Street. From the bottom they join Ramsey Street, from the top they joined South Street. Number twenty-five was an end terraced house. The rain subsided.

Shamina was hoping her auntie would be in, as she hadn't considered calling in advance. Jabir and Shamina leapt out, Manik followed after he locked his car. Jabir knocked on the front door, a plastic carrier bag in the grip of his left hand was swaying side to side because of the wind. He bought some biscuits from the Yorkshire Street newsagent.

The door was opened by a six year old pretty girl, called Jazzi Bi by her friends, wearing a washed, worn out pink dress. Behind was Shamina's auntie Somrun Bibi in a sky blue saree.

"What a surprise. Shamina it's you isn't it come in, please come in."

Shamina couldn't believe her mother's best friend recognised her after all those years. They walked into the lounge. Jabir and Manik sat down on the settee. Jazzy Bi took the carrier bag off Jabir. Shamina walked to the kitchen with her auntie.

"You know Shamina I didn't think you would be visiting me so soon" said her auntie.

Suddenly Shamina was anxious to go home. She noticed her auntie's kitchen didn't smell of Bangladeshi cuisine. She thought her auntie probably ate fish and chips all the time.

Sons of Jabir

"What it is afnar damand (son-in-law) has come to visit a friend, Manik Chaudhury. They know each other from the East and West civil war."

"I see, anyway why haven't you brought the children along?"

Somrun Bibi was making Bangladeshi tea. It's like how you make Cappuccino, but it's not.

"I wasn't sure if I'd find you at home." Shamina wanted to ask where her uncle was but decided against it. *Must be at work.* Shamina understood, you can't just bombard someone with questions, as if there wasn't a fifteen-sixteen year communication gap. One thing Shamina was glad about, was seeing Jazzy Bi, because if she can remember her mother did say her auntie couldn't have any children due to infertility.

"Here have a cup of tea, I'll be right back."

Shamina noticed her auntie had put on some weight and talked with a Mancunian accent. *Well she has been living here fore the last, Allah knows how many years*, thought Shamina. Somrun Bibi returned from the lounge, after serving Jabir and Manik with tea and biscuits. Shamina took a gulp of her tea, and wondered what Bassha, Suna and Rajah were up to.

Outside the rain had stopped completely, but it was windier and cold.

After another ten minutes, after finishing their tea, Jabir and Shamina with Manik Chaudhury went back to Manik's house.

Sunday morning, Shamina and Afia were chatting in the kitchen about Bangladesh and its new found independence. That it would take time to regain political confidence building public relations to help rebuild infrastructures. Hamid and Rajah were busy playing Snakes and Ladders. Bassha and Suna were watching television.

Jabir, Manik and Rokiv went to view next door, ninety-one Yorkshire Street, without an appointment.

"I dun't maind loong as you dun't tell the estaite ejaint that yuv seen the house without maiking an appointment thru them," growled the owner occupier, an old shrewd woman.

"We promise not to" they replied in unison.

The woman gladly showed them in. No matter how hard Rokiv tried he couldn't imagine this was actually happening. A social visit turned into something entirely different. If only Rokiv could have seen through Jabir. Earlier Rokiv mentioned to Shamina about Jabir's decision. Shamina had been informed by Manik but having no say in the matter, looked impartial.

The old woman, told them she had been offered a pensioner's apartment from the council, where there will be lovely nurses to look after her. She was willing to bargain at a reasonable level for a quick sale. The house has a double and single bedroom, two bathrooms, up and down, lounge, dining area apparently with a rectangular giant yard after the squared kitchen. One thing very attractive was the colours, blue, pink, yellow and red, used to decorate the house, co-ordinated. Rokiv wondered what would a similar refurbishment seem like in his small city office and flat.

After negotiating and bargaining buyer and seller agreed on six thousand pounds. Jabir was very pleased. Later in the early afternoon the Khan's set off to London. At a constant ninety miles per hour, it took Rokiv two hours and forty five minutes roughly to get back in East End. Later he had to go and see Sandra. Bassha, Suna and Rajah enjoyed the weekend vacation. Rajah has a friend now, Hamid Chaudhury.

Sons of Jabir

Chapter Twenty One

Rokiv wondered was this real, was he day-dreaming or imagining things. Was it really twenty eighth March, his wedding. Sandra and her parents wanted a huge wedding, the decorations, celebrations, big wedding cake, everything.

Rokiv suggested a modest wedding, not to save money. He just wasn't comfortable with the idea of an enormous wedding. He wished his nephews, Shamina and Jabir were present today. It hurt Rokiv that Jabir moved out so quickly. Sandra wouldn't have minded a few days of being overcrowded. One thing struck Rokiv every moment his mind was unoccupied, Jabir would never accept Sandra as his sister-in-law. *We'll see about that.*

Far distant relatives of Sandra's parents and friends amongst Rokiv's colleagues were there to add a bit of rainbow to the occasion. Rokiv really wanted Jabir to be the Best Man. Sandra wouldn't have minded Shamina being her bridesmaid. Fortunately it was a sunny day, Sandra regretted not seeing Jabir's twins.

Inside the marriage bureau the guests applauded as Rokiv kissed (after the formalities) his beloved bride. Rokiv felt relieved and excited now that he was married to the person he loves dearly. *I missed my period, now don't jump to any conclusions, it's still early* Sandra had said to him last night.

A reception for seventy people was arranged by Rokiv and Sandra's parents in a luxurious Italian restaurant at Charing Cross Road in the West End. Sandra was filled with excitement almost impossible to contain. Part of the expenses were paid by Rokiv's employers as a wedding gift.

As the newly wed couple posed in various corners of Hyde Park, the professional wedding photographer was snapping along. As time flew and the day became sullen, guests began to depart. Few of the guests were surprised to acknowledge Rokiv is an Asian (a Bengali.) Sandra's parents told him to ignore silly remarks and requested him to look after their only daughter.

"I will, I promise, as long as I live," Rokiv assured his in-laws.

Rokiv with clenched teeth was ignoring remarks such as;

"I can't believe he's a solicitor. He looks like a janitor to me." "He's a gold digger. I'm telling you, poor Sandra." "She could have got married to Prince Charles."

Hopefully all the guests were gone. Sandra felt embarrassed in front of Rokiv.

Rokiv assured Sandra not to worry about all that;

"Long as I've got you I don't care."

Rokiv was glad Jabir's mortgage was plain sailing. It was easier as Jabir had a lump sum, part of it as deposit. With a fifty-five percent repayment mortgage for twenty years, the monthly repayment was two pounds twenty. Jabir was happy about that. Rokiv was happy to do the conveyancing. His firm charged Jabir half the cost. Rokiv reminded Jabir and Shamina to keep in touch.

Finally the husband and wife opened their presents. After reading all the wedding cards and revealing their merry messages.

"Guess what?" said Sandra looking as if she'd won the lottery or something.

"What's up darling?" replied Rokiv.

"Mum and Dad have given us First Class tickets to Hawaii for our honeymoon. Including five-star accommodation and two hundred pounds in cash for spending."

Sandra couldn't imagine being any happier. Rokiv felt the same.

"That's great, we are going to have a wonderful honeymoon, darling."

Chapter Twenty Two

It is unusual how a particular incident can stick in one's mind, unforgettable nor unforgiven. It must have been embarrassing, even though it was an act by a close friend.

Was Rajah a fool to believe his friend Hamid Chaudhury. If only he hadn't had the disadvantage of being new in Britain. Also inauspicious or not, very new in Rochdale. The birth of the co-op, that what folks say around there.

On the other hand, Hamid (Hammer nicknamed in school) sure was a bully. He had an advantage over Rajah as he was accustomed to British ceremonies and traditions. Rajah, his mother and father had just about been a year in Britain from Bangladesh (which was East Pakistan.) Besides Rajah's beloved Uncle Rokiv was not with him. Never mind doesn't matter today.

Rajah must admit Hamid was surely convincing. Hurrying home (last year) from school, flinging his work of basic drawing on their home lounge settee, picking the telephone receiver and shouting, excitingly and vigorously;

"Uncle Rokiv, Uncle Rokiv."

For a moment it seemed imaginary to Rajah. Unfortunately it was.

Incredible it was, what Rajah had planned and waited patiently for this particular day. Hamid could never imagine, even in his dreams. Now that would be frightening. To scare someone like Hamid one needed his dad's co-operation. Obviously Uncle Manik not as admirable as Uncle Rokiv, would agree when Rajah explains for what purpose and why?

Almost three in the afternoon and Rajah had come up with a brilliant procedure. The idea inspired the third time Rajah saw a horror movie. His teacher Miss Manchester, short legs, over fifty and a spinster, not devoted to celibacy, gave Rajah just the apparatus he needed. Not only did Rajah persuade Miss Manchester to let him go early, but unexpectedly she cautioned him.

"Rajah dear be careful, go easy on that child. Dun frighten Hamid to death. An' yes thank your mama for the somosas on Eid."

Rajah replied in a hurry, holding his breath;

"Sure – I will – Miss Manchester."

The sky seemed to distaste the clouds. Home time was at half past three. Before Rajah mistakenly forgot he placed the paintbrush and jar of red paint into his blue acrylic squared lunch box. He then sneaked out of the Victorian building and walked home in the act of feeling sick. so Hamid wouldn't suspect anything of his reason for early departure.

Their house was not far from Heybrook Primary, probably a hundred metres. Rajah's mother asked him why he was home so early. So he explained to Shamina that his teacher had thanked her for the somosas.

"Where's abba?" the words slipped from Rajah's mouth as he already knew the answer. *Bassha and Suna aren't here yet, good.*

"Sleep," *as usual*, Shamina replied. Jabir slept longer nowadays. Rajah found it upsetting at times. Today the excitement of scaring Hamid withdrew Rajah's disappointment from his mind, which is far more intelligent than his body and age. With his art apparatus, Rajah strode to Hamid's dad's video shop. Rajah acknowledged. Hamid enters his father's shop before he goes home. It's an habitual son and father hug routine.

"Hiya Daney, *live and let die* Bond James-Bond. Yu'll love it," said Hamid's dad. The words echoed as Rajah entered. Danny left with a sneer. Uncle Manik had knowledge of half of Rajah's plan. Quickly Rajah explained to Manik the other half. They both checked the calendar and reassured it was the first of the month.

Hamid's dad closed his shop early, only for today, giving Rajah a chance to get even with his son. Rajah and Uncle Manik went into action as the wall clock struck three thirty. Rajah managed to paint Uncle Manik's face to look like scars as realistically with the little talent he had. Next, Rajah drenched a butterknife with red paint. The complete preparation of this drama was not yet done. Until Hamid steps in! Rajah finished painting half inch slash on Manik's neck as he lay flat facing the suspended squared ceiling. As Manik has a scar on his face already the whole situation seems very scary.

Rajah's heart began to pound as he waited anxiously, behind Manik's counter. Manik lay flat and motionless as requested by Rajah. This beats any horror movie Rajah ever saw and Hamid was about to encounter.

The waiting was over, as Hamid stepped in by pushing the shop's entrance door with his right shoulder. His school lunch box dangling by its handle on his left fingers. Rajah quickly lowered his head completely out of Hamid's sight. As Rajah couldn't see anything, so he tiptoed to the right. Rajah peeped through slits in-between video cassette cases on dusty shelves.

Hamid's lunch box hit the floor and split open. Hamid was only inches away from what looks like his dead father, murdered. He picked the artificially bloodied butterknife subconsciously with both his shivering hands. His pupils began bulging. He broke into instant perspiration, with his mouth agape and a very scared face.

"April fool," Rajah and Hamid's father simultaneously shouted.

Hamid regained into a relieving sweat, he was still too scared to talk.

"Raj, Raj" shouts came from outside Manik's shop window. The three of them turned to see who it was.

"Raj, amma wants yah," Suna shouted as he walked off with Bassha.

Manik couldn't get them a place in Heybrook, but he managed to get them a place in Greenback Primary. Bassha had put some inches on, Suna had put some weight on like Rajah and Hamid. It had to be the fish and chips.

Sons of Jabir

Rajah was proud to boast about his brothers, at playtime in school. He wished he had a sister. Only Hamid knows, and has promised not to tell anyone, that Bassha and Suna are his half brothers.

Chapter Twenty Three

"I don't understand why are we arguing. I'm telling you she was conceived before you married me" Sandra said, resting her back on their new leather sofa, sneering at Rokiv.

"I thought our daughter was conceived on our honeymoon in Hawaii" intoned Rokiv, a little confused.

"Honey are you going to ring Shamina or shall I break the wonderful news."

Despite Rokiv fortunate of being a father of a lovely baby girl and over the moon with joy. The headline of The Independent, had been nagging him since this morning. It read;

INVOLUNTARY BUT SURELY HOMICIDE. Anxious to read the lead story, he dismissed it due to being victim of procrastination.

Out of impatience Sandra lifted herself off the sofa to reach the telephone on top of their twenty one inch new colour television, three metres away, as Rokiv shouted;

"Dar-lingg, the doctor advised you to rest. It's been less than a day yuv come from maternity."

Sandra, excited, feeling silly sat herself back. Rokiv added;

"I'm going to call Jabir right now, right now."

Rokiv dialled without hesitation but he couldn't get through as the line was engaged.

"I did not, did not try to scare you to death. I tried to frighten you to death" Rajah said into the telephone receiver as he broke out laughing.

"Not much of a difference is it, dickhead. I'm never going to mess with the likes of you again. That's for sure," Hamid replied from the other end.

"Rajah put that phone down right now. You been on it for the last fifteen minits" Shamina shouted from the curry smelling kitchen.

Rajah shuddered as it was unexpected. He did as he was told. As he was about to turn for his afternoon snack, the phone rang. Returning to his original position, he picked up the receiver as Shamina shouted again;

"Better not be Hameed." She was cooking ayre fish curry with ripened tomatoes and boiled rice, which Jabir loved very much, and Bassha. Suna had become obsessed with ice cream.

"Assala-mu-alay kum," Rajah said. The one thing he learnt from his father.

"Hello there, nephew" came the half flat voice from the other end, two hundred and twenty miles away.

Rokiv missed Rajah's cheekiness, his questions and his cute face. Naturally Rajah's face glowed. His voice filled with excitement.

"Uncle Rokiv I miss you." Those are the five words he always expressed to Rokiv.

"Likewise nephew. Now is your father about."

"He's asleep uncle." *Always.*

"Give it to your mother, I'm in a hurry nephew!"

"One-sec, uncle" Rajah said. Placing his right palm over the mouthpiece he screamed;

"Amma-go-amma!"

Shamina reduced the heat under the fish curry pot and came running as her heartbeat increased.

"What?"

"Uncle Rokiv on the phone." Rajah handed the receiver to his mother. Shamina wiped her wet hands on the edge of her cotton saree before she spoke;

"Assala malaykum, bai-saheb."

"Walla kum salam. Good news Sandra has given birth to a beautiful daughter. I'm a father now." (Shamina could detect the excitement.)

"That is wonderful!" exclaimed Shamina.

"I'm in a hurry, do tell Jabir and Rajah, bye."

Shamina didn't mind the abruptness and the suddenness. Rokiv is who he is. Shamina respected Rokiv because of the adopted element. *He doesn't have to phone us if he doesn't want to.* Eventually Shamina replaced the receiver, but couldn't hide her excitement. Rajah curious as always and had the right to know.

"Is Uncle Rokiv coming in Eid?" he asked.

"No" Shamina said smiling.

"Then what are you so happy about amma?"

Shamina remembering her curry over the heat.

"You have a first cousin, that's why" she said and ran to the kitchen. Rajah was about to express his euphoria when the phone rang again.

"Hello."

"Raj, its Hammer. Do you wanna go to the fair?"

"Who's goin?"

"Bassha and Suna already have. I'm going with abba." *I'm going with abba*, that's what struck Rajah. He wanted to go with his father too, in spite that his brothers didn't take him with them. But his father was asleep. Shamina must have given money to Bassha and Suna to go to the fair in Rochdale town centre. Bassha and Suna come first for Shamina as she was not their mother. Besides the fact that she is their stepmother, she wanted them to feel they are treated as their own mother would have treated them if she was alive.

"Yow Raj are you there."

Rajah shook his head and replied;

"I'm not in the mood," and hung up.

Jabir was sleeping more than normal. He was missing a lot of work lately, neglecting not only Shamina but his sons as well. Shamina was a bit worried about Jabir's health.

Chapter Twenty Four

Rokiv had become a partner at A.M & Co. Hundred hours work a week had paid off. What would make Rokiv happier than this, is if he could father a son. He loves his daughter Hasina very much, their first born.

He had named their daughter after agreeing with Sandra, because Sandra wanted the name Sarah. At the end Sandra gave in saying;

"Whatever makes you happy darling."

Poor Sandra's parents had passed away recently. Her husband helped her through her bereavement. Shamina did ring and give her condolences. Sandra had stopped visiting her friends and relatives, because they disapproved of Rokiv. She had assured them Rokiv loved her very much and that is all she needs.

Things were getting expensive in London. Petrol prices were going up. Cars were increasing on the road. Rokiv was considering a move to Rochdale. He missed Shamina's curries. Sandra can cook but it's not the same. But Rokiv had become accustomed to living in the East End. He missed Jabir's sons, especially Rajah.

Rokiv wondered if Shamina could teach Sandra how to cook Bangladeshi food, especially dry fish jalfrezi. Rokiv loved Sandra, there's no doubt about that, but he felt he was losing his roots. Jabir seldom rang. More importantly Rokiv wanted a son as he intended to build an empire.

Shamina told him a few days ago, Jabir was thinking of signing on. He reassured Shamina;

"Maybe he wants to go back to education. This country has a lot to offer."

And why not. If Jabir can get a degree he will be a role model for his sons.

Chapter Twenty Five

"Abba can I have a five penny?" said Suna. It was more of a demand.

He finished picking his nose. The weather outside was damp. At least it's not raining Jabir sighed.

"What ffh…"

"Abba I want a five penny too" Bassha interrupted.

Jabir was getting late for work, waiting for Shamina to give him his fish and rice tiffen carrier as he had a twelve hour shift today.

"Go and ask your mother."

Jabir didn't ask why they needed the money. He finished putting on his socks and shoes, stood up from their lounge sofa and shouted;

"Shamina…"

"Coming…" Shamina having corresponded and happy that Jabir was going back to work, ran from the kitchen with Jabir's stuffed silver tiffen carrier. Jabir took his tiffen carrier off a half panting Shamina and said;

"Give them some money, I'm going, I'm late."

Jabir put his anorak on, grabbed his umbrella and stormed out. Jabir was finding Rochdale colder than the East End. He still hadn't forgiven Rokiv for marrying Sandra.

Rajah came running down the stairs and hopped into their lounge. Their lounge carpet needed cleaning.

"Mission Impossible, Mission Impossible's on you guys," Rajah announced excitedly. He wished they could get a colour TV. If only Shamina would stop sending money to her parents in Bangladesh. Shamina gave Bassha and Suna five pennies each, and didn't even question what for. But she found out soon as both of them handed her their letter from Greenbank School which stated the money was for a day trip to Hollingworth Lake, including lunch.

"You guys *Mission Impossible's* on, you watching or what?" Rajah shouted again.

Sons of Jabir

"Yeh, yeh, we can't miss that. It's the best action series going" said Bassha, as he sat next to Rajah, and Suna sat next to him. Shamina was delighted witnessing this harmony amongst Jabir's sons.

After dinner, Rajah asked his mum for some money. He wanted a pair of new trainers. His mother replied;

"Next month futh (son), money's tight."

The few weeks Jabir wasn't working in spite of the job being only a year old, not to forget it was his third job in a different textile factory, because of his temper. He had been sacked from the previous two places. The savings in the bank were reducing.

Rajah walked to his bedroom sulking. Bassha and Suna ignored him. *Yeh sure Bassha and Suna can go to Hollingworth Lake, next month futh money's tight. They always go out with abba on Saturdays. Whenever I want something, no money, next month, 'why do you want new trainers, the ones you've got will do for now futh.'* Rajah didn't want to go down memory lane. He wished his Uncle Rokiv was with him. Then he could get whatever he wanted. The late evening grew darker. Rajah dozed off after reading a school story book. He slept like an angel, but had a series of peculiar dreams. *I'm not even six yet!*

One cannot fall in love at an age of six. It has to be impossible, because a six year old would not comprehend what love is. But for reasons unknown Rajah saw his nursery friend Kajol in his dreams.

"Preposterous!" Rajah screamed silently shaking his head, his body smelling of sweat. He had picked the word up randomly from his Oxford Pocket Dictionary, that Jabir bought him from WHS last week. But understood the meaning of it now. He lay in bed lazily missing school. There won't be any sweets for him today.

On occasions Shamina noticed that Rajah rather than playing with his toys in the usual ways would just spin his double decker buses wheels over and over again. Apart from that Rajah developed an unusual interest in liquids. Lemonade, coca-cola, milk and water. Pouring them out instead of drinking, at every opportunity. This lead to many precarious situations and a great deal of anxiety for Shamina and Jabir. Bassha and Suna found it amusing.

Jabir thought it must be something to do with childhood. Shamina concerned, curious and uncomfortable decided to search for answers. Jabir slept more than working in the Rochdale cotton mill, nowadays. Could be an early mid-life crisis.

Since Jabir moved to Rochdale, Bassha and Suna hadn't missed a day of school. Shamina was concerned for Rajah and Jabir. Why is Jabir sleeping more than usual?

Why is Rajah acting abnormal at times? Why is Jabir's aggression evident as each day passes? These were some of the questions going through Shamina's mind. And Bassha and Suna always demanding money for this, for that, was not helping.

Chapter Twenty Six

"Rajah let me see" Shamina ordered as she pulled Rajah's Batman sweater by its neck, checking whether Rajah had got his prayer beads on. Shamina was very strict on Rajah wearing them at all times. She had called a taxi ten minutes ago.

"Amma where are we going, swimming?" Rajah questioned, tying his shoe laces.

"No Birch Hill hospital," replied his mother. Shamina checked her purse. She missed her parents a lot back home.

"Again" Rajah uttered, not very pleased. The doctors did some tests on Rajah last week. Today Shamina was hoping for some good news. Having called the taxi for the second time, Shamina explained;

"To find out why do I sometimes find you asleep downstairs on the lounge carpet."

Rajah looked at his mother with contradiction. He had no recollection of what Shamina alleged, just now. Because his mother put him back to bed on the occasions, which only occurred twice in the past three weeks. Shamina was referred to a specialist after she had explained what the problem was to her GP. She was impressed by the efficiency of the NHS.

Just yesterday MENSA phoned Shamina and told her from Rajah's school reports they have come to conclusion that Rajah is a brainbox. His IQ (Intelligence Quotient) is in the top five percent. They are happy to take him on. Shamina delighted, wasn't sure about that yet.

An X reg Datsun Sunny pipped the horn outside. Shamina shook herself from the daze.

"Taxi's here, let's go Rajah."

It took the taxi, an Italian driver, ten minutes to cover just two miles from their house to the hospital, on a Monday afternoon in the November windy breeze. Shamina paid the taxi driver the correct amount.

"Thank you madam."

Shamina felt good for a housewife. Rajah remained silent and sullen. Mother and son leapt out and hurried through the entrance. They came to a halt in front of the reception and the adjacent waiting area, as it began to drizzle outside. Rajah was surprised there were no other outpatients, except them. After Shamina had produced the appointment card, within a minute they were ushered into Dr. Rimmer's chambers by his secretary.

"Good afternoon Shamina" Dr Rimmer having said that, smiled at Rajah. But he remained still miserable and quiet. Mother and son sat down next to each other opposite the doctor.

"Now Shamina, I have to be to the point and make sure you tell your husband as well. Either diagnosis is not a grave matter. As time passes by Rajah will get cured, not hundred percent though"… Dr Rimmer paused.

"Your son Rajah suffers from two different conditions. First one, what known as non-insane automatism, basically sleepwalking. Can be very dangerous if he falls down the stairs" Dr Rimmer paused. He could feel Shamina had tensed up but strangely Rajah was staring at him. Shamina having comprehended, managed to hold her tears back for the second bad news. Dr Rimmer wasn't sure how to carry on. Shamina said;

"You said two conditions."

"Ah yes, second condition is autism."

"What's that, sleeptalking?" Shamina snapped. She was angry, not with Dr Rimmer or anyone in particular. Because a child as young as Rajah was suffering. It doesn't help the fact that the child was hers.

"Shamina, like I said as time passes by…"

"I'm sorry," she interruptingly apologised. *How could this be?*

"It's o-kay Shamina. It's not known what causes it. People with autism are affected in different ways. Some need constant help. Others may have a higher than average IQ and be able to carry out extremely complex work." Dr Rimmer finished explaining. *Ya Allah please spare my Rajah.*

"Amma I wanna go home," Rajah requested.

Chapter Twenty Seven

Matthew Moss Secondary School. Mr Kershaw has a reputation of punishing a pupil with no less than the capital punishment comparably, the cane. And yet children do silly things, be naughty, swear at teachers and so on.

It was the break before home time in the afternoon. Seventy or so students were in the school front yard. Some playing tag, some playing hopscotch, some playing five-a-side football. It was a dry day but it rained earlier. Bassha was the tallest in the school.

"Sunna why are you crying?" demanded Bassha in a rage, as he was playing football with his mates.

"Well who's hit yeh?" Bassha asked again.

"Her over there," said Suna pointing his right forefinger at a girl. Bassha turned around and walked over.

"Hey you!" shouted Bassha.

"Jazzy Bi, I think that boy is calling yah," said one of her friends, as she stopped skipping and turned around with her fine bobcut hair.

"What?" she said.

Bassha felt a bit embarrassed asking a girl, *have you hit my brother*, but he had to ask, because Shamina and his father told him to look out for Suna.

"Is it true you hit my brother Suna?"

Jazzy Bi and her friends broke out laughing.

"What it is, Suna was playing tag with us, he tripped on his laces and fell. Nobody hit him."

Bassha walked back to Suna feeling an idiot.

"Stop crying, you wimp."

What Jazzy Bi didn't reveal to Bassha was, she was the one to untie Suna's laces, when he was talking to one of her friends.

Was it coincidence Manik couldn't get Bassha and Suna into Haworth Cross. Shamina wondered, or was it Bassha and Suna didn't want to go to the same school, because of Rajah

Sons of Jabir

having unusual health conditions. That is what was worrying Shamina. Jabir and Manik assured, it's nothing like that. They didn't get a place at Haworth Cross, that's all.

Haworth Cross Secondary School. The Cross was nothing to do with Jesus Christ. However the symbol of the cross was worn by the pupils of the school on their maroon v-neck full sleeve jumpers. The school overall was unattractive but very clean and tidy. Last year Greenpeace awarded Haworth Cross the cleanest public secondary school in Rochdale Borough.

It was not far from Heybrook Primary, ten to fifteen minutes walk. A mile from where Rajah and Hamid lived. It was their fifth day at new surroundings since induction. They were happy and sad leaving Heybrook Primary behind due to growing up. Happy because they were secondary school pupils. Now they were referred to as boys rather than kids. Sad because the teachers of Haworth Cross were much more strict.

The school had four academic divisions. It was a way of keeping all the pupils fit and encouraging them to compete with each other as well as with outside secondary schools within the borough, in sports, tournaments and drama. The divisions were named, Buckley, Hamer, Belfield and Entwistle. Green represented Buckley, Yellow – Hamer, Blue – Belfield and Green – Entwistle. Rajah and Hamid were Buckley.

Rajah and Hamid had five minutes to go of their Humanities lesson with Miss Manchester. She got a place there after her post graduation last year. She was Rajah's tutor. That made Rajah a little comfortable in the new school. Rajah and Hamid had P.E. and Humanities together. Hamid was sitting in front of Rajah at a desk among other twelve pupils in the annexe of H.C. Rajah was playing noughts and crosses with his pen on Hamid's back whilst everybody else was reading about famine.

"Stop that now and where's your text book" shouted Miss Manchester. She'd been observing Rajah for the past half hour. He'd been fidgeting practically through all the lesson.

Sons of Jabir

"Ummh a-a-a, I forget it home," replied Rajah. He was still poking Hamid with his pen.

"Rajah get up and get out of this classroom" Miss Manchester said. That caught Rajah's attention. Blankly he asked;

"But why?" as if he really didn't know what he's done wrong. The whole class was staring at him, except Hamid.

"That's it, you are in detention son, an' don't talk back to me."

Although Miss Manchester found it a bit extreme saying that she assured herself that Rajah needed some discipline. The home time bell rang. The class shuffling got their school bags and packed lunch boxes and walked out peacefully, except Rajah.

"Told you to pack it in" Hamid whispered as he left the classroom with noughts and crosses and tiny dots all over on the back of his white school shirt. It looked like a contemporary designer shirt.

"You will write, 'I will not be naughty in class again', hundred times in your rough book, while I supervise you" before Rajah could protest.

"An' please don't say no because it will be the cane" Miss Manchester added.

As she widened her eyes and shook her head up and down, an indication of her seriousness made Rajah write probably faster than a freelance journalist. Outside Hamid explained to his father, so they waited for Rajah as it began to rain.

"Damn British weather" Manik murmured. Hamid was looking forward to watching *Blue Peter*.

Ten minutes passed, Rajah finished his hundred identical sentences, which covered three and a quarter sides of his rough book. He stood up, walked over and showed it to the teacher, as she was reading *'Not A Penny More, Not A Penny Less'* by Jeffrey Archer.

"What is this, Rajah?" Miss Manchester asked referring to the lines of scribble.

Sons of Jabir

"What do you mean? Av done it. I will not be naughty in class again" Rajah said pleadingly.

"All right Rajah I will let you off this time. Now go home." Miss Manchester noticed the boy was anxious to go home.

Manik started the ignition and drove out of the school's car park.

"I'm sorry Uncle about Hamid's shirt," Rajah apologised because he didn't want Hamid to get bollocked for it. He got his school yellow and red tie off, shoved it in his knapsack and unbuttoned his collar.

"Sorry not good enough Rajah my nephew" Manik intoned and waited.

"Hamid take your shirt off give it me. I'll wash it an' give it to you tomorrow" Rajah offered, wondering what's in store for him at home.

"Nephew I'm only joking" Manik replied. Rajah exhaled in relief.

"Far as I'm concerned his been punished for it baba (dad)" Hamid said from the front passenger seat. It took Manik seven minutes to park up in front of his video shop from Haworth Cross.

"Hammer see you around and see you Monday," Rajah said and leapt out of Manik's Ford Escort Estate. Rajah longed for a father like Hamid's father. If his father could pick him up from school now and then. The rain had subsided.

"I'll call you later" Hamid replied. Rajah just now nodded and strode home. Rajah knocked on his front door thinking of how to explain his lateness. As nobody answered their front door he naturally knocked on it again, a little harder. Still no answer. Rajah knocked vigorously with both his palms in anger. Shamina finally opened the door. She didn't utter a word as Rajah stepped inside, partially shivering from the cold outside. Rajah closed the door behind him and faced his mother. Furiously he said; (a little over the top for a ten year old):

"I've been knocking and knocking, where were you amma" Rajah looked at his mother a little closer. Both of Shamina's cheeks were orange. Rajah's tone changed immediately, concern in his voice.

"What happen amma, what happen amma? Abba hit you again hasn't he. Why does he do that?" Rajah couldn't feel his heartbeat, but it was thumping regular. Shamina without offering any words knelt down and embraced Rajah with both her arms, holding him to her chest and wept silently behind Rajah's back. Rajah tried to shed some tears but couldn't as he stood motionless.

Since Rajah's condition surfaced things between Shamina and Jabir were somewhat abnormal. Partly it was Shamina to blame. At times she would not stop weeping over Rajah's illnesses. Her emotions took over in love for Rajah and she was becoming incapable of self control.

A few days ago Shamina was crying when Rajah was in school. As Jabir came from work he had said to her, 'What happens, happens for the best, now where's my rice an fish?' Shamina couldn't control her flow of tears. Suddenly Jabir slapped her right across the face and went to bed. That didn't frighten her but surprised her. Shamina assured herself she needed to regain self awareness.

After half an hour when Rajah had had his tea, Hamid phoned him to see if he was interested in rolling the dice with Snakes or Ladders or watch an American movie. Rajah declined saying 'promise, tomorrow morning'. Rajah felt like reading poetry that evening in particular. A surge of overwhelming feelings of emotions travelled through his mind and body, when his mother embraced him, that he couldn't comprehend.

In the capital congestion and traffic was polluting the air. The very carbon we take for granted. Another twenty five years and it probably would affect global warming. In the East End Kray's were prospering. But Rokiv Khan was fed up of bacon and eggs for breakfast. It wasn't the end of the world for him,

Sons of Jabir

though he missed very much Shamina's home made parathas, and was wondering when would he have the opportunity next for such a treat, even if it cost him twenty pounds in petrol. One thing he was very proud of, was being Hasina's father. His wife Sandra was phenomenal in bed, no doubt about that, but she lacked skills in home cooking, except the basics, beans on toast and bacon and eggs. Rokiv and his wife were trying for another baby. No success as yet.

Chapter Twenty Eight

Week on Monday, four days left till half term. The classroom wall clock reached eight fifty nine. 'She's gonna be late', Rajah thought. The fire door (all school doors, standard health and safety) opened and Miss Manchester walked in, *damn*. The clatter of noise subsided. Rajah came to a complete hush. Miss Manchester seated herself behind her desk and in front of the blackboard. She got comfortable and opened her class register. Wasting no time she began calling;

"Aaliah." The pen she got out from her handbag was cold and did not write despite being a new biro, so she used a HB pencil instead.

"Yes Miss Manchester."

"Benjamin."

"Here Miss Manchester."

"Boby."

There was no answer. Then she remembered his father had rang and explained the absence, that he'd come down with the flu this morning.

"Brown, Tiffany Brown" (there were two Brown's in the class.)

"Here Miss Manchester."

"William Brown."

There was no answer and no explanation.

"Kaan"

"Here Miss…" before Rajah could finish he was interrupted.

"Rajah my dear, you are to go to the headmistress's office right now. An' please come back straight here."

Rajah made his way out of the classroom as quietly as possible.

"Leeroy…"

Curiosity is nothing compared to what Rajah's mind was going through. What could the headmistress possibly want

Sons of Jabir

with him. ('Abba please don't hit amma, please don't. Jabir then froze his hand in the air, inches away from Shamina's tearful sullen face as Rajah pleaded. That had taken place yesterday evening.)

His parents were having problems, which was affecting his school homework and partially had made his life inconvenient. *I hope abba hasn't beaten amma up.*

"I guess al find out" Rajah murmured as he joined the queue in front of a freckle faced girl, that he had probably come across at the school assemblies.

"Say what handsome" she blurted turning around facing Rajah. She showed attraction towards him.

"Oh nothing, nothing I was jus... Are you seeing the headmistress as well?" Rajah asked, picking his nose. "Do you know what's it about?" Rajah added.

"Av no aydeah" she replied pinching his bum.

"Auch." Rajah uttered, very surprised.

"Next please" a coarse shout came from the headmistresses office. Rajah sighed;

"Thank Allah (God) for that."

"Hey Hammer, what time is it, we shouldn't be here you know" Rajah asked. Both of them staring at Burton's window display. Hamid glanced at his Casio and replied;

"Three fifty nine."

"Shit, enough of window shopping. Let's go home or else your dad will be out looking for us," Rajah implied, rubbing his bare hands together and exhaling, trying not to shiver from the breeze and the drizzle. Maybe because of the moors and the Pennines, Rochdale probably gets more rain (unseasonal) than any other town in Lancashire. One thing Rochdale is proud of is Gracie Fields.

Hamid couldn't agree more. He didn't want his baba to get anxious, because he and Rajah had wandered off like this, once in a blue moon, especially. Not to mention paedophiles could be lurking about and around. Immediately they both set off for home. As they already sneaked past home ten minutes ago, to visit the town centre. They had checked there were no movies of interest to them running at the pictures that evening.

"So what did the witch exactly want from you?" Hamid asked. Suddenly remembering when Rajah mentioned it at dinner time. Even Rajah had forgotten all about that. Not to mention pinching his bum dilemma.

"Oh you mean the headmistress."

"Aha."

"I've been moved up to top band. From now on my tutor will be a Miss Pentolow. I've heard rumours that she's more stricter than Miss Manchester ever could be."

"You lucky bastard, Raj," Hamid commented, pulling a grin, and added;

"Look at the bright side. You won't be seeing Manchester anymore. An' it shows that your brain's a lot better than mine." They increased their pace as the drizzle turned into rain. Rajah knew there was no need for modesty. It was a fact that he was more talented than Hamid.

"I guess so, but it's nothing to do with luck. On my tests I got distinction and merits," explained Rajah. '*Stuck up bastard,*' Hamid murmured.

"Shit am gonna catch a cold, an' don't call me a bastard. Do you know what a bastard means, an illegitimate child" Rajah added. He lost Hamid there. Despite;

"Hey I'm sorry now don't go all smart on me, mista" replied Hamid as he widened his grin, showing a bit of his sarcasm. Rajah realised this could go forever. So he changed the subject.

"Hey Hammer, an unusual thing happened. This girl she let me go in front of her. Next thing you know…"

"Know I don't know."

"Stop interrupting me an' I'll tell you, you dufus. Ah yeh next thing you know she pinched me on me buttocks. It felt embarrassing."

Sons of Jabir 171

Traffic noise increased because of the wet roads. Both of them were five metres (and a pelican crossing) from their homes.

"It means she fancies ye, you idiot" Hamid replied. Thunder struck, it made them run to the lights. Rajah pressed the button for green and was picking his nose. Rain had drenched both of them through.

"Why would a girl fancy me, me. Anyhow I feel dead nervous around them" Rajah having said that, the lights changed. Both legged it home, as Manik and Shamina stood by their front doors awaiting with opened umbrellas.

After, Shamina bollocked Rajah for being late. He did not lie, saying he was in detention. But she was pleased to hear that he'd been moved up to top band in school. She did not forget to check Rajah's prayer beads. Rajah finishing his tea, asked his mother frankly;

"Amma why does father say silly things now an' then?"

Shamina surprisingly not unexpected, questioned back;

"Like what Rajah?"

Shamina was on her Brother sewing machine, sewing summer skirts. Bassha and Suna were out playing football with Danny already. Apparently last Saturday Jabir didn't take them out.

"Marilaw-katilaw (stab-kill)" Rajah said.

Shamina had to change the subject of only being too aware of Jabir's indifference lately, but even she didn't know why yet. Shamina hoped it was nothing serious.

"I don't know Rajah but I will sure find out" Shamina assured, but it wasn't as assuring to herself. Rajah just couldn't bottle it up anymore. So he spluttered his kind of childlike agony, shaking his head as if in resentment towards his own childhood crisis.

"You noh amma, abba don't take me swimming, hardly picks me up from school, parents evening, don't take me to fair like Hamid abba and most of the time he's sleeping."

Sons of Jabir

Rajah's tiny droplet of tears inevitably rolled in the circumstances. Shamina found it extremely difficult to explain to an eleven year old that it could be the cause of Jabir being in war and losing a dear friend before, not to mention his first wife Ayrina's heartless rejection. Shamina stopped her Brother machine and called Rajah;

"Come to amma, come here futh (son)" Shamina comforted Rajah within her arms resting her son's head on her chest. *Ya Allah, what am I going to do?*

In bed Rajah wondered how his mother managed to sleep with his father, as his bedroom was adjacent to theirs. Despite it being one o'clock in the morning, Jabir suddenly came out of their bedroom, stopped on top of the landing and turned ninety degrees to his left, facing the wall in-between his terraced house and next door's with the unseen insulation in the middle, and began talking gibberish in his pyjamas, as if someone was standing in front of him.

"Cut it throat, cut it throat, kaafir, you kaafir, marilaw katilaw......"

Chapter Twenty Nine

In sceptical reasoning no one can guarantee a controlled and planned way of living, because matter of chance for chance exists in everyday life within the twenty four hour time frame around the environment built by man (women) after God has created the earth and the universe. Incidents happen by accidents (most of them) so does the changing occur. Anyone can die at any time and place, age does not matter. Life after death is there one? If there is, no one is sure, what is in store?

Some stories are told. Some are untold, depending on how famous one . . .

"Chacha (uncle) look what she done. She weed on me." Hasina's urine stank of chlorine. Rokiv couldn't read on due to the complaint by Rajah of his daughter being very naughty. It didn't bother Rokiv as it was an article by some undergraduate philosopher, he was reading at random in *The Times* magazine. It doesn't have to be your own blood to get close to someone. And love someone. Rokiv adored Rajah. He wanted a son like Rajah. Having heard of Rajah's conditions, he was devastated at first. He couldn't believe it. How could that happen suddenly?

"Sandra, Sandra, come over here please," Rokiv called sipping his coffee. Hasina was not suffering from child incontinence. She was just a spoilt, dad pampered kid, somewhat dirty at times. A few days ago she managed to get Heinz tomato ketchup all over her new clothes and her cute face. She wanted to be a clown and work in a circus. That was her explanation to her parents at the time. Hasina was pretty tall for a five year old, turning six soon, with bluish brown eyes, sensitive fair skin and light sandy hair.

Sandra was in the kitchen talking to Shamina, generally gossiping.

"Sandra!" Rokiv shouted.

"Yes darling, you called?" said Sandra, leaving Shamina as she offered to make some parathas and Keema Madras curry for all of them, except Jabir, Bassha and Suna. Jabir stayed behind because Bassha and Suna had a five-a-side football tournament. And Jabir did say "Rokiv there is a lot of burglaries going on, I'll stay behind. Bassha and Suna wouldn't miss football for the world."

The tournament had been organised by Danny. There were nine teams competing, eighteen games to play within eight days. The winning team would get a silver trophy from Manik Chaudhury, as he was the leading sponsor. Jabir and Hamid would be amongst the spectators. Danny was the Captain of Bassha and Suna's team. Rajah felt sad because Jabir hadn't come along. He wasn't bothered about his brothers. Rajah had brought his story books with him, just in case he got bored.

"Look what our daughter's done. She has urinated on Rajah. Take both of them and clean them up honey please," Rokiv requested.

He finished drinking his coffee.

"Sure darling. Hasina you naughty – naughty girl," Sandra intoned.

She picked her daughter up with no knickers on and gestured Rajah to follow her to their bathroom. Rajah wasn't annoyed, but Sandra was, *one of the disadvantages of school holidays.*

After lunch Rokiv drove to his office. He wondered how would life be if he was a homicide detective. Sandra left Hasina with Shamina and Rajah. She had domestic and personal shopping to do. Recently she had had a miscarriage. On her way back she will be seeing their family GP for some painkillers, preferably paracetamols. Regrettably Rokiv had been so happy as soon they would have had a son. Now Sandra felt she had failed Rokiv.

"Raja-fasta, fasta-fasta" Hasina said. She was having a piggyback around the flat on Rajah's back. In the last half hour both of them, had an energetic water pistol fight with Shamina in the middle trying to stop them. Then with coloured felt tip pens, coloured each other's toes and Shamina's face leaving her looking like a clown from the sixties. It took Shamina plenty of soap and warm water to clean it all off. She was glad that Rajah was having a good time. The soap left her face very dry.

Later Shamina was watching *Coronation Street* with interest. Rajah and Hasina had calmed down. They both sat besides Shamina.

"Auntie can I have some ice cream" Hasina requested, chewing her left thumb.

"Give me two minutes, I'll get you some" replied Shamina. Rajah felt a bit dizzy from going around in circles earlier. Rajah asked hesitatingly;

"Amma, was my grandfather a slave? What is our Zaath?" just curious.

Coronation Street finished, Shamina switched the TV off.

"No your dha-dha (grandfather) wasn't a slave. He was a owner occupied agricultural very hardworking farmer. Like your nana is now (Shamina's father.) I can't recollect your dha-dha, he passed away when I was very little. Our Zaath (caste/origin) is above middle class of whole of Bishwanath town. We have ancestral land inherited of course from generation to generation. (Probably where Jabir gets his arrogance and stubbornness from, Shamina wondered.) Shamina was pleased to explain a little family history to Rajah. Whilst Hasina got anxious for ice cream.

"Auntie, ice cream now!" Hasina demanded, now chewing her right thumb.

Chapter Thirty

The buzzer inside the East Street Surgery for the next awaiting patient to go in, went off. The flashing light connected above the counter on the adjacent wall came on and off. Next to it, the name plate read DR N GHOSH. The receptionist called;

"Shamina Begum of Yorkshire Street. Dr Ghosh – thank you."

The surgery wasn't very busy for a Tuesday afternoon. Still Shamina waited an hour. She got up and walked to the doctor's chamber. Rajah was probably watching *Blue Peter* and Jabir was asleep. Bassha and Suna were playing football with Danny as usual.

Shamina sat in front of Dr Ghosh trying not to be anxious, as she waited for the doctor to explain Jabir's recent unusual behaviour. The diagnosis on Jabir by Dr Rimmer came through the post to East Street Surgery that morning.

"Considering the clinical symptoms and eliminating other forms of possible mental illness, Shamina I'm afraid your husband Jabir is suffering from what is known as schizophrenia," said Dr Ghosh. He was a Bengali not from Bangladesh but from India.

The doctor's last word took Shamina to her recent past. YOUR SON IS SUFFERING FROM AUTISM, because she had no idea what schizophrenia was.

Shamina asked;

"Dactar babu, what is sizo-prena." Shamina found it difficult to pronounce. She wondered how she would cope with (Jabir) it. Dr Ghosh wasn't sure how to go about explaining it so he answered;

"Schizophrenia is like dreaming when you are wide awake."

"What else, is there a cure, I hope so, medication, treatment?" Shamina bombarded the doctor with questions. THAT KIND OF EXPLAINS JABIR TALKING TO THE WALLS.

Sons of Jabir

Shamina could imagine not having a social life any more. Not to mention Rajah's frustration about Jabir's compulsive rituals. Dr Ghosh wondered what Shamina would look like in a business suit. *Modelling perhaps.*

"Well is there any treatment dactar babu?" Shamina asked again. She was wearing a navy saree over a sky blue blouse and petticoat, with no make up. There were some faint lines showing above her eyes. Nevertheless, she'll still be good for contemporary modelling material if she had a classic bob hair cut.

"Jabir may have hallucinations of all forms, smelling, seeing, and possibly hearing. What exactly goes wrong with the chemicals inside the brain is not clear. There is a medication and it is called Chlorpromazine. I am going to prescribe that for Jabir to be taken twice a day, noon and night. That should calm him down and prevent relapses," Dr Ghosh concluded. He pretended not to feel Shamina's anxiety but thought Shamina could do with some Oil of Ulay.

It can't get any worse Shamina thought. She just couldn't understand why Allah had come down on her so heavily. She prayed five times a day, kept all the fasts on Ramadan, except if she was ill, and one day hoped to go on a pilgrimage. What possible sins may she have committed for all this injustice. Silent tears but painful, trickled down her non-moisturised cheeks. In fear of embarrassment she snatched the prescription from Dr Ghosh and swiftly walked out of his chamber. Whatever her circumstances may have become she would not let vulnerability take her courage away in front of strangers. Even if it was the family GP.

As soon as Shamina stepped into her home she unleashed a silent cry in their bedroom making sure not to disturb Jabir in his sleep. Rajah was reading poetry in the lounge. Her life won't be the same again. Divorce had crossed her mind but that would leave Jabir in despair, and Rajah may end up with a stepfather. Which he may not tolerate and abandon Shamina. No matter how many obstacles, for better or worse, Shamina was willing to go through this test of sacrificing her adulthood, her sensuality, her emotions, and she had to admit she did love Jabir. Like many housewives take for granted, doing the shopping, doing the laundry, helping with the ironing, dropping children to school and picking them up. But for Shamina unfortunately and perhaps it was fate, all those things are unachievable for her. No women would sacrifice the rest of their lives, especially when you're in your late twenties, for their children. But Shamina will only do that for Rajah as she adored him very much. Because she didn't want Rajah to have a stepfather and didn't want to take Rajah away from Jabir. Allah may become angry. For a moment she became selfish, only thinking about herself and her son Rajah. She forgot all about Bassha and Suna. In the last few minutes they didn't even exist for her. *Allah please forgive me.* In thought of freedom of living and personal independence Shamina was almost going to leave Jabir and his non-identical twins.

Weeping was over. Shamina accepted Rajah's conditions and Jabir's schizophrenia as her fate. She will experience endurance that no woman will tolerate. Yes, she had a choice but she has made the decision of staying as Jabir's wife. Her belief in superstition told her not to leave Jabir, as she may end up like Ayrina, deceased. Shamina wondered did Allah punish Ayrina for leaving Jabir and being the cause of his nervous breakdown. *Why am I comparing myself with her? I am not a selfish person.*

Shamina reasoned, made some sense of this. Her life can carry on watching Bassha, Suna and Rajah grow into men. She will try her best to keep Jabir as stable as possible. Shamina had convinced herself it's not the end of the world. Eventually Shamina came down, after she had washed her face with warm water, and massaged some Johnson's Baby Oil on her face and lower arms.

"Amma can I have some hot chocolate?" requested Rajah, now doing his mathematics homework, algebra. Shamina hoped Bassha and Suna would become professional football players as they play and practise almost everyday after school.

"Of course futh (son)," replied Shamina.

It took her five minutes to give Rajah a mug of Cadbury's hot chocolate. Then she sat down and wrote a letter addressed to her father.

She wrote that there are no mosquitoes to be seen in Rochdale, in fact there are no mosquitoes in Britain because of its cold weather. Bassha, Suna and Rajah are growing from strength to strength, and Jabir loves her and is taking care of her as promised. This was a lie but a good lie. She definitely didn't want her parents to worry about her at their old age. She also mentioned now and then she visits Somrun auntie and above all she misses them very much, and she is saving money for a holiday in Bangladesh. And to let her know if they have received the giro she sent last month.

Chapter Thirty One

Shamina had to stop her Brother sewing machine temporarily. She wished the company that employed her part time paid more. She will have a break after another two hours.

"Amma, we have something to say" said Bassha, a football in his right hand. Suna was standing beside him. Both of them were wearing Man Utd. jerseys and Adidas football boots. Shamina noticed both of them needed a haircut and wondered what on earth they have to say to her.

"What?" Shamina asked, anxious to switch her sewing machine on again. She had a slight headache with a temperature, nothing to worry about she assured herself. Rajah, apparently was in the bathroom combing his hair. Recently he had become obsessed with his appearance, to look good. He was still shy of girls. At least Jabir's sons had not become teenage rebels, that Shamina was proud of.

"Amma we are sorry about Rajah's illnesses and that abba at times be horrible with yourself," said Suna.

Bassha and Suna had become partially ignorant of Jabir's condition, and Rajah's conditions until now, because of their obsession with football. Danny had become their role model as his dream shattered, because he couldn't make it into premiership football. Shamina was taken aback at Bassha and Suna's sudden concern. And that everytime they call her "amma" (mother) her heart filled up with glory. At times she wished she had given birth to both of them.

"Don't you boys worry about it. Allah will make everything all right. Now you go and practice, now go on. It's already late. And come home as soon as you finish."

"We will, amma," replied both of them as they stormed out.

Shamina was glad at least Bassha and Suna had no problems with their health. She tried to read all her namaaz (daily prayers) in the hope that Allah will cure Jabir and Rajah.

Sons of Jabir

"Shit-shit, amma would kill – kill me" Rajah gasped. He tried to look at himself in the bathroom mirror but couldn't see the cut he just received on his lower chin from shaving with his father's Wilkinsons razor, because of the condensation from his breath.

"Idea" Rajah murmured. He opened the top of his father's aftershave (Old Spice) bottle, poured some on his palms and applied it on his sensitive, shaved, young cut skin. What followed was a very painful experience.

"Owh-Gawdhhhhhhhhhhhhhhh" screamed Rajah, *shit-shit*.

Shamina came running from her Brother sewing machine, as she left its motor running. Sewing served the purpose of filling Shamina's spare time, staying occupied and earning some extra pounds. Not to mention she was trying very hard to save to go to Bangladesh hopefully in a couple of years. Chlorpromazine had taken its course on Jabir, and now he was sleeping more than ever.

"Rajjahh, you silly-silly boy. (She had smelt the aftershave and grasped Rajah's foolishness.) You too young to shave. It has to be Hameed who gave you idea" Shamina said.

Rajah protested;

"Noh amma it's my own idea."

Shamina got angry;

"You have eaten, go bed now. I have work to finish."

Shamina having said that returned to her sewing machine. Rajah could still feel his skin sizzling from the aftershave.

That evening, Rajah looked forward to going to bed. It was going to be a new and pleasurable experience for him. His first encounter, hoping not his last. He's having doubts if he'd catch AIDS by doing it.

Chapter Thirty Two

"Open your present then," said Hamid giving Rajah clowny looks. As both of them were in his bedroom seated on his bed. Rajah opened it steadily, curious what it might be, but was stunned and excited in a way when he revealed what it is.

"Wow, a pulsating vibrator. How on earth did you get hold of this? I mean don't you have to be eighteen or something?" Rajah said. Rajah was mesmerised by the artificial sex tool.

"I ordered it through one of me dad's porno mags, using his name and sending a postal order…" Rajah didn't want to hear the rest.

"It's funny you gave me this present. Let me tell you how I accidentally wanked for the very first time." (On the word wank Hamid got very interested.) "It was last year, yeh it was. I turned thirteen so I thought I'd treat myself. Somehow I managed a bluey, got it from you dad's shop using Danny…"

Danny interrupted;

"Did you sneaky bastard."

"Hear me out will ya. Right, so late at night when amma, abba, Suna and Bassha gone to bed I put the bluey on, on loaned VCR despite our black and white TV (Rajah was more weary about his conditions now than before), you know it was lousy, a lousy blue movie. All it had was sagging and oversized breasts. So I couldn't be asked to finish the film…"

Hamid interrupted again;

"I can't believe you watched that blue movie without me Raj."

"I promise next time I rent one, and a good one too, we'll watch it together. Now where was I?" pause.

"Sagging breasts you did not bother to finish…"

"Yeh got it, so I went to bed. Now comes the interesting part. You know I think breast is fascinating (Hamid nodded up and down in agreement) so fantasising about naked women in general or it could be the bluey, I got an erection. So even at

Sons of Jabir 183

the age of thirteen I couldn't figure out where the penis suppose to get its pleasure from. So I began to massage my penis, ten seconds or so, I jumped out my bed because at the time I thought I urinated in bed. Funny thing the piss felt thick and sluggish. So I got really worried over a fucking fastest lousy wank, that probably no one can ever beat."

It wasn't a joke, but Hamid couldn't stop laughing.

"So ayy got warried ovah a lausy wank" Hamid mimicked.

"O-kay, o-kay will you just stop laughing please," replied Rajah (regretting he had told his secret.) He changed the subject, adding;

"What options are you going to choose at Greenhill High coming September?"

"Is it September already, damn," replied Hamid, his laughter subsided.

"Just few days left," Rajah reminded.

"I haven't decided yet, have you?"

"I have." Rajah paused as his mind wandered.

"Let's hear it then?"

"Well English and Maths are compulsory..."

"Yes, they are," Hamid interrupted sarcastically.

"Sociology, psychology, commerce, chemistry and history."

"Some combination eh."

"I guess..."

"Hey how come you're doing psychology, commerce I understand."

"It's an interesting area of study, if your own father has mental problems. Hammer, I have to go to the bathroom, try my new fourteenth birthday present out, see ya." Rajah having said that dashed home.

LONDON GENERAL HOSPITAL

Please God, please God, please. Rokiv was not only praying to the Almighty, all-powerful and all-merciful. As Sandra was in labour, his anxiety was making him walk around the hospital's half full waiting room, unaware of what other people may be thinking about him. It's been two hours Rokiv couldn't wait to see his son.

Hearing about Jabir's diagnosis from Shamina only yesterday was an upsetting moment, but Sandra carrying this baby full term was a miracle for Rokiv. Rokiv wondered as once Shamina mentioned Rajah was born prematurely, and so his second child will be a premature baby. *Some coincidence.*

Rokiv had called Shamina earlier, notifying her of their circumstances. Shamina said "She'll pray to Allah for a successful and normal delivery." Hasina was home with a babysitter, though she was not a toddler any more but she can be very stupid at times. Like opening the door to strangers.

Rokiv stopped pacing and relaxed and began to study Claude Monet paintings on the wall of the hospital waiting room, to eliminate boredom. He could never thank Sandra for the endurance she went through of them having this second child. After a minute or two, Rokiv walked out of the waiting room to get an update on Sandra. Suddenly he heard a new born baby cry, turned around and as if out of nowhere a midwife appeared.

"Are you Mr Khan?"

"Yes I am Rokiv Khan" replied Rokiv. He didn't hear a new born cry it was his imagination.

"Congratulations, your wife has given birth to a lovely and healthy daughter... *daughter-daughter-daughter.* Rokiv felt his life has just turned upside down.

"Mr Kaan, are you all right?" asked the green uniformed midwife.

"Can I have a glass of water please. Is my wife all right?"

"Yes, she's fine, the baby's fine. I'll get you some water."

The midwife disappeared.

Rokiv wished all this was a dream. He wished if he could get another chance, if they could get another chance of having a son. But there weren't any more chances. They just had to accept their fate. His life would be without a son and only daughters.

Sons of Jabir

Chapter Thirty Three

Bethnal Green Road was pretty wide and stretched rather long. On Milton Street, not far from Chilton Street where Rokiv resided, an illiterate Bengali family (parents only) lived. Their flat resembled Rokiv's flat but not his interior plushness. It was built by the East End Council approved via Tower Hamlets, and probably they used the same architect.

Athiqul Haque had brown eyes, black hair and a white beard. He is five-ten and dark skinned with a belly protruding from his medium sized body. He did not know his actual date of birth because when he came with another family (through immigration his official parents in England, he did not have any contact now, he didn't know where they lived, were they alive or dead) in 1959, he had to make up his DOB on the Bangladesh passport application form.

Janaab (Mister) Athiqul was anxious, pacing up and down, waiting for his only daughter to come from school. His lounge wall clock (from Poundstretchers) struck ten past four. He was chewing away on beetlenut and paan, as he just had his afternoon dinner. His wife, Sufia Begum, not a discontented housewife, was preparing to cook for the late evening meal, in their small tatty and battered unit kitchen.

Their home in Bangladesh was a village called Sharparah, in the district of Sunamgonge, the lower parts of the country. When he was a boy, he and other members of the family in Sharparah used to have maar (when boiled rice is cooked, the afters that most people throw away, form soup with no flavour in particular) at breakfast.

He had forgotten those poverty days, now that he was in London. From DHSS he received Income Support with some Incapacity Benefit. He had proved to his GP he has arthritis and a sick note was not a problem. He wished to claim Disability Living Allowance soon. He spent most of his time at the East End mosque discussing community politics. He'd very much like to be the treasurer of the mosque one day. He and his wife, including his daughter Gulshana, had been to pilgrimage last year. All he could hear was the ticking of the clock but no knocks. Instead his phone rang, it startled him as it was unexpected.

"Assalamalaykum" Athiqul greeted. Pause. *Manik Chaudhury from Rochdale*.

"Manik Baishaheb, how are you?" Pause. It was a surprise.

"I don't have time to ring anyone, am afraid Manik bai. But I promise probably will come and visit you and your Rochdale that you are so proud of, one day, Assalamalaykum."

The conversation was over, they spoke once in a blue moon. As he replaced the receiver the doorbell rang. He reached and opened the door immediately. Gulshana stepped in wearing a hijaab (a black overall in polyester covering from neck to the ankles, above her school uniform.) As soon as he closed the door behind him, his mood changed to rage.

"Do you know what time it is eh, eh. Now don't speak back to me, I'm your father. You are thirteen, almost fourteen years old. Not a child anymore. If this was Bangladesh I'd make sure no school and you start cooking at home. That's what my mother and auntie did until they got married off. Not stroll East End streets after school." (Gulshana had become a statue, too frightened even to cry.)

"If you ever be late again, I'll slap you silly. Now go to your bedroom, no dinner for you, Kajol."

Athiqul Haque wondered was he rude with Manik Chaudhury over the phone, when he said, 'I don't have time to ring anyone.' It was the mosque politics. *He'll understand, gaour beta* (back home neighbour.)

Sons of Jabir

Chapter Thirty Four

Sunamganj was approximately sixty nine kilometres west of Sylhet. The town offered little for tourists but the local haors (wetlands) were rife with birdlife, especially during mid-winter through to the end of April.

Near the wetland's terrain, terrapins, raptors and ducks congregate. To get to the three famous wetlands, that seem to be the best for birdwatching and hang-gliding, will take one several hours up river from Sunamganj town centre.

Chander Chaudhury, former Chander Ali, was returning from Sylhet. He has a full trimmed beard now, especially to conceal his scar. He loves the wetlands on his own. It helped him forget his horrifying past. His dream of becoming a leading reporter of a British national paper was no more.

Frustrated Chander wanted to go to Bishwanath, Chansirkapon to get his friends London address from Anwar Khan, Jabir's father-in-law. On second thoughts he decided against it, because Pakistan's Intelligence Agency was still searching for him. His life miraculously has become better. There was a time, he was convinced, journey of his life had come to an end. Now if he wanted to stay safe, alive, well and happy then he had to forget his friend Jabir, *may be someday I'll see him again.*

They say brains are better than muscles, and that is exactly what Chander had proved to himself. After he had managed to get a Masters of Arts Degree from Dhaka University, which cost him only a thousand taka, he married the daughter of Ansarul Shah Chaudhury and changed his surname. Luckily the old man passed away soon, and now he was the proud owner of two Three Star hotels in central Sylhet, ten autorickshaws, fifty rickshaws and three speedboats. Most important of all, Allah has blessed him a daughter. He had kept her nickname Bebby.

Chapter Thirty Five

"Imam-saab, my husband was never like this. Day-dreaming a lot, talking to himself a lot. I was wondering if you give, show me some light. May be there is hope that he will become normal, and since the doctors give him tablets, he sleeps more" Shamina explained calmly.

"Have your husband's parents suffered from similar abnormalities?" asked the great Imam of Jalalia Bradford Mosque, not far from the Bombay store. Shamina, her son and Manik arrived early. Shamina was hoping, by the time they got back, Jabir hopefully would still be sleeping. She and her son had to wait two hours for a ten minute session with the Imam. There are visitors from Birmingham and London, Bengalis and Pakistanis, probably have to wait longer.

Imam Al-baraque was wearing a punjabi (similar to pyjamas, the top longer, falls beneath the knees.)

"His mother suffered some mental problems before she died, years ago" replied Shamina.

Imam Al-baraque was no sai-baba. He had a Masters in philosophy from UMIST. He knew the Koran by heart and was a great public speaker (when given, mainly on hadith/ revelations of Mohammed P.b.u.h.) He was single, a Pakistani and had a beard seven inches long.

"Allah's child, so is everyone and I. There is hope as long as you pray. Pray only to Allah. Here are some written thabease (small prayers written preferably with a fountain pen on small squared paper) for your husband. Mix them with water and he should drink half a glass every night," Imam explained.

His chambers inside the mosque smelled of incense sticks. What people didn't understand was at the end of the day he was only a man, maybe extraordinary. They expected him to make miracles happen.

As Rajah sat besides Shamina in front of the Imam, Manik was outside waiting in the car.

"Imam-saab, one more thing, my son here walks in his sleep and has autism," Shamina said with little hope.

Imam Al-baraque closed his eyes, tensed his mind and whispered a minute prayer probably from the Koran. He then leaned forward, opened his eyes and blessed Rajah by blowing air from his mouth on Rajah's forehead finishing with;

"Chu-chu-chu."

Rajah remained quiet during the session as he was told so.

"Shamina pray to Allah, the Almighty-all powerful. Don't give up hope. Allah's child, so is everyone and I," concluded the Imam.

Shamina opened her handbag, retrieved a ten pound note and slotted it into Al-baraques donation box, next to him.

"Thank you Imamsab, thank you very much. I will pray to Allah more" Shamina said and left with Rajah.

"Go on try it, it's just a cigarette. It won't kill yah" Danny said as he handed the lit filtered Benson and Hedges over to Bassha.

Danny (Daniel Lawrence) had decided to pursue a hairdressing career. They were in the public lavatory at the bottom of Drake Street. It was after dinner time, Suna was still in school. Bassha was playing truant, his first time, Integrated Humanities, he couldn't be bothered.

Bassha was hesitant, but curiously took a puff.

"Ah-he, ah-he, ah-he!" inevitably he choked.

"Here, give it here. Let me show yeh Bassh."

Danny having snatched the cigarette off Bassha, took long puffs and exhaled through his nostrils.

"You see, try to breath with your nose. You won't choke."

Bassha tried again.

"Hello" said Shamina as she picked up their telephone receiver. She was expecting Bassha, Suna and Rajah from school soon. Jabir was sleeping due to the Chlorpromazine.

"Sandra how are you? Are you all right?" Shamina having recognised the voice bombarded Sandra with concerned questions.

Sons of Jabir

"How's the baby. Is she all right? I forgot her name, what? Hali-what? Halina Khan, okay goodbye." *Hasina and Halina, similar names*, Shamina thought. Shamina was happy, Rajah was a dedicated student because he went to school at dinner time unlike Hamid, as soon as they arrived back from Bradford.

"Hammer have you seen *'Trading Places.'* Anyway this African actor, he is really really funny. I didn't get his name though."

Hamid changed the subject as he remembered something important.

"By the way, there's something come up, don't get mad at me cos you are my best friend, Raj. Jus' hear me out. (Rajah was wondering if this could be one of Hamid's many tricks, but it was not April Fool.) I have a cousin brother, they live on the other side of Rochdale. There's been a feud goin' on between us for a long time but recently there's been a reconciliation. That's why last week I was given yah sickness excuses and did'n' come out but you know…"

"Carry on Hammer" Rajah gestured, thinking where was this leading, interestingly.

"Right, cut the story short, he's getting married soon and you being my best friend, as I mentioned your name…"

"Thank-you, thank-you" Rajah interrupted sarcastically.

"You probably will get a wedding invitation card Raj."

Rajah wasn't bothered.

"Is that it, that's it Eddie Murphy…"

"Eddie what?"

"You know *Trading Places,* that black actor."

They reached home.

"Oh – right Eddie Murphy. See yah later, Raj," Hamid said as he disappeared through his front door.

Sons of Jabir

Chapter Thirty Six

Recently Rajah and Hamid had become American movie fanatics. They had both become the local newsround boys. Rajah was trying to get a part time job at a local Indian or Italian restaurant.

At times Rajah wanted to become an FBI Agent or a CIA agent or maybe KGB. At times he wanted to become a British police constable. Hamid once said to him "Raj, you have to stop dreaming or you sure will go crazy."

Bassha and Suna went to football practice regularly. Their dream was bigger than Rajah's. They were sure they will become professional football players. At times over-confident. On one occasion, Shamina caught Bassha smoking in the bathroom. Before she could utter, he promised, he would not smoke again, ever. That was a lie. At night in bed, Bassha and Suna dreamt of fast cars and beautiful girls. And sleeping on money, eating money. They had become theoretically obsessed with their dream and were not bothered with sitting O-levels. Allah help them.

"Here, hot chocolate and omelette toast sandwich. I'm going to the doctor's to get your abba's tablets" Shamina said as she disappeared.

"Okay" replied Rajah.

He was too busy completing a questionnaire for Cover Shot's International in the hope of winning a make-over session, their first prize, that he doesn't require. His features had developed into smoother than a snowman. He wished his brown eyes were blue and his black hair was blonde. In fact he was jealous of Bassha's height, six feet tall. The semi-oval face with wide dark brown eyes, black hair and a symmetrical nose.

Suna wasn't better looking than him, but he had this invisible charm, which made the girls more attracted to him.

Rajah came across the Cover Shot competition in the Rochdale Observer. He was on his own in the kitchen. Recently he'd been dreaming about his nursery friend Kajol but the weird thing was he didn't know what she looked like, *how could that be*, Rajah racked his brain and let it go.

Even now, Rajah wished he could have a sister. Maybe next year. He was glad Christmas was over and it was the beginning of a new year, 1985. Hamid and him both reached sixteen and were proud of it. Bassha and Suna had had a change of heart suddenly. Now they wanted to become boxers. As Rajah expected they were re-sitting their O-Levels, because Jabir and Shamina had said so.

"Trrring, trrring, trrring, trrring, trrring…"

"Hello," said Rajah panting, as he had to run from the kitchen into their lounge.

"Raj, it's Hammer you wanna snowfight," Hamid blurted from the other end.

Rajah seemed disappointed as if he was expecting some one else.

"No Hammer, it's cold and totally unromantic" replied Rajah.

"Since when have you become Romeo?"

"Since listening to the Beatles, you Casanova" Rajah hung up and got his new pocket diary out from his school trousers. Having opened it he dialled a residential London number. Greeted with an annoying engaged tone, he replaced the receiver promptly and was about to walk back to the kitchen when the phone rang again, *Dammit-Hammer*, he picked the receiver and shouted;

"Look I don't wanna snowfight Hammer…"

"Hey calm down cousin" Hasina interrupted from London. *At least I have a cousin sister, sisters*, Rajah thought.

"Oh Hasina I've been trying to ring you."

"What for?"

"I have a poem for you."

"You would wouldn't you Mister Romeo." *Why is everyone calling me Romeo today?*

"How is Uncle Rokiv, Sandra Auntie and my kid sister Halina?"

"They're fine." Hasina paused for something and added;

"Now don't sidetrack me, tell me that poem". It was a command.

"Here we go then.

> *Love is magical, love is mystical, it's a feeling that beats every emotion. In deep oceans there're a million waves. In life there're many obstacles. He or she who manages across finds true love. He or she who doesn't find true love, falls in despair and becomes abandoned from everyday life.*"

Rajah exhaled.

"Wow, that's something. Are you in love with someone? You definitely sound like it."

"The thing is, it's a bit silly, I haven't seen her in ages since…"

"Who?"

"Kajol."

"Who's she?"

"We use to go to nursery together," Rajah giggled, feeling slightly embarrassed.

"What?"

"Used to go to nursery together."

"Raj, you are pathetic. You are trying to tell me, you fell in love with this Kajol, when you were what? Two, no, three" Hasina exclaimed. Paused;

"You know Raj, even Romeo was better than you."

"What is that supposed to mean?" asked Rajah. He felt a bit stupid.

"I don't know." Hasina laughed having said that, and hung up.

At least it changed Rajah's mood into snowfighting. Will he ever see Kajol again, Rajah wondered. Probably not, one in a million chances. *If that's the case, why am I making a fuss about it?*

Shamina was very worried about two things. How to answer Rajah's 'why his father becoming a mental outpatient.' Secondly, because Rajah being Jabir's son, 'will son end up like father'? Could this illness be hereditary? These questions in her own mind had become a regular nightmare. Not to forget Bassha and Suna, now that they hadn't made it into premiership football.

It was not easy for Shamina to explain to Rajah. Not that she didn't want to but because as Rajah himself suffered from neurological illnesses, it may affect him. Maybe some explanation of the past, may justify to Rajah his father's behaviour.

Jabir lost his one and only best friend Chander in the East/West 1971 Pakistan Civil War, Shamina remembered. Not to mention Ayrina left him, his first wife. Shamina decided very hard to not be anxious. She would be patient. Good things come to those who wait. But at times her youth recalled, exploration and flexibility, her mind broadening horizon. That moment her emotions tell her heart to leave Jabir. Her mind fights back, how could she. Jabir was so vulnerable, so dependent on her. A person after all who has done her no wrong.

Jabir was a lucky man. How many other women in Shamina's situation would have put their husband's needs before their own desires. Shamina's upbringing would not set her free to make others suffer, so that she could be happy. Shamina realised things may get worse before they get better, as some weeks she struggled to make ends meet. Now that Rajah had got himself a weekend late night part time job at an Indian restaurant, things should look up, at least for Rajah. He could buy most of the materials he desired, that Hamid took for granted.

Bassha and Suna were thinking of moving out, so they could explore their youth more freely. Bassha was always taking money from Shamina. Suna at times was sensible.

Sons of Jabir

Chapter Thirty Seven

"Take a sip, go on it's only beer," said Danny.

Bassha was on a date, a pretty Caucasian he pulled last week from Xanadu's Nightclub in Rochdale. They were in the Golden Lion Pub on Whitworth Road. Everyone there loved Tetley's Bitter. It was early yet for the pub to be full.

"It's probably crap," replied Suna sipping his iced coca-cola. *Does everything justify itself? Is there any justification for the things we do, that we don't have a clue about?* Suna wondered.

Suna wasn't devastated as much as Bassha, of them not making it into premiership football. The reality was it was the hardest profession probably in the world to get into. And now, why do they want to become boxers? Probably "It's the next best thing" Bassha had said a few days ago. Above all Suna still missed his mother Ayrina.

The pub wasn't grand but it was clean and tidy. The aroma of freshly cooked battered fish and chips made Suna's stomach grumble.

"Have you ever tried it?" asked Danny. Last week he got caught driving an XR3i with no licence or insurance. Danny had become a small time crook. Shoplifting at supermarkets, mugging old women, stealing car stereos and so on.

"No."

"Then how do you know it's crap?"

"All right then, pass it here," demanded Suna. *What the hell.*

"Who could that be making me late for work, on my first day at Omar Khayam" Rajah greeted.

"It's your cousin Hasina, you dufus" replied Hasina from London.

Rajah with his right palm, felt his clean shaven cheeks. He wasn't too pleased wearing Lynx deodorant and his ironed black trousers and a dickie bow over a former white school shirt.

"What do you want cousin? By the way how is my kid sister Halina? Rajah asked. *Shit I'm going to be late.*

"Halina's fine, she's very naughty though, I mean…"

"Look Hasina I have to go to work, I'm late. Sorry-bye. And yes will you stop wasting my Uncle Rokiv's money on irrelevant telephone calls." Rajah hung up and left for work. *She can be annoying at times.*

Omar Khayam. Saturday morning.

All the customers left except one stocky English male.

"Rajja-Rajja" said Karen, sipping coffee at four a.m. He switched off the vacuum and looked up at her.

"Make sure you get all the bits an' poppadums under the table, right!" reminded Karen.

Rajah nodded and switched the vacuum back on. He approached the lone customer.

"Excuse me would you mind stepping aside so I can hoover underneath" requested Rajah. There was no answer. The man seemed to be snoring.

"Aaaaaaaaah!" Rajah screamed.

He realised despite the excruciating pain, his feet were not touching the carpet. Hanging from the grip on his hair, by the customer's right fingers, palm and forearm. In a matter of seconds workmates, now friends, dashed over, stopping whatever they were cleaning and pounced on the drunk and disorderly man. Rajah was relieved of his pain.

"Stop it!" screamed Karen. It was too late. The paramedics later took the black-eyed, broken nose and bruised up, now banned customer to the hospital. Police had cautioned the staff, excluding Rajah. Next time there would probably be charges of Grievous Bodily Harm.

Rajah got paid fifteen pounds and had been told, he would get twenty pounds for Saturday, as he was only a poppadums waiter. Karen, the manager and bar lady, Saddique's girlfriend (owner of Omar Khayam) gave Rajah a lift home, out of pity.

Rajah had to rest about twelve hours after his first two nights waiting on customers. It was probably the busiest and roughest (rowdy) Indian restaurant in Rochdale. When he had told Hamid about his ordeal, they both laughed.

"It wasn't funny at the time you know, you should have seen the guy all mashed up."

Mid-March and the snow had stopped. After-effects were still lingering, such as icy pavements and frosted windows. The occasional sun was not helping. Rajah didn't normally wake up at nine a.m., Monday mornings, especially when it was Easter holidays. His feet were killing him, for all that running around over the weekend. Nevertheless, he half slept overnight. Definitely not insomnia, why? Wondering about Cover Shots. Company correspondence rang him and informed he had won a prize four days ago. He hoped his prize would be beneath the letter box today. So he had his usual masturbation, the morning one. It got rid of all his yawning. He was out of bed and ready for (if appropriate) S, S, and S. Shit, shave and shower. Rajah was almost sixteen and a virgin. Lately it had been nagging him, even though it was on the back burner of his mind.

Rajah dressed in an Adidas tracksuit and went to greet the letter box. There were several letters, most of them utility bills, on top of one another lying on the hall carpet. From those only one was addressed to Rajah. The contents of the envelope felt more like a card. *This has to be it*. In opening the Manila A5 sized envelope, Rajah went pale in disappointment. It revealed a wedding card. *Damn*. Having no choice, Rajah disclosed.

<u>WEDDING INVITATION</u>.

<u>GROOM</u>
Shantu Chaudry
S/O Faizal Chaudry
111 Hiltop Drive
Kirkholt
Rochdale

<u>BRIDE</u>
Syeda Anjali Begum
D/O Anwar Ali
29 Brixton Court
Chapeltown Leeds

> We, Mr & Mrs Chaudry invite you
> to solemnise our son's wedding
> on: Friday 29th March 1985
> **Mr. Rajah Khan**

BANGLADESH ADDRESS
Sharparah   Karikuna
Sunamgong   Bishwanath
Sylhet   Sylhet

> RECEPTION
> Sunday 31st March at 1 pm
> Kirkholt Community Centre

Having read the unexpected wedding card, Rajah felt stupid. Hamid had mentioned it, though in an apologetic sense. *Of course he did.* For the moment Rajah held his thought, he was disappointed with Cover Shot's customer service.

29th Friday, ssh, I'm at work. He had to explain this to Hamid. It's not good. This guy out of the blue gives him a wedding invitation, and he can't even sacrifice one day. *I hate dilemmas.* But he needed the money for the black Adidas trainers he saw at JJB Sports in town. *Dammit if only Bassha and Suna stopped dreaming and started working part time. It's amma, she's given them too much freedom. She loves them more than me. And I've told her to stop that part time sewing of hers. It's going to give her a heart attack some day. And does she have to send money to Bangladesh every month? Whatever there's a few days to think.*

Sons of Jabir

Chapter Thirty Eight

In anticipation of going to work and deciding against going to the wedding Rajah missed school. He was regretting both. Not going to Leeds with Hamid, as it was today Hamid's cousin's wedding. And missing physical education, afternoon class. Swimming he very much enjoyed. Besides what Bassha and Suna are up to is affecting him psychologically. Now he was in no mood for going to work. But he definitely wanted the Adidas trainers.

Shamina was not very happy of Rajah working at Omar Khayam, after what Rajah told her.

"Amma you know it's so, so busy, very busy. Everybody running and this Billy, owner's brother, he keeps not just at me. To everyone penchodd (sister-fucker) maachodd (motherfucker), swears busy time."

Jabir was impartial and trying to balance his thoughts. Shamina couldn't distinguish if it was the Imam's thabease or Chlorpromazine that was keeping Jabir stable.

The teenage years are undoubtedly over. Not Hamid, especially Rajah feels that way. Adulthood yet away, his natural instinct was to break free from parental control. (In Rajah's case only his mother. His father had no influence over him because Jabir lived in a world of his own), to express youth. Wear baggy jeans, Carbrini sportswear, Joe Bloggs or Chinos. Whatever the latest fashion trend was, if only he could afford it.

Shamina was equally a strong woman, and because she was brought up in the tradition that you ate what you were given, you didn't get the nicest things until you had dealt with the nastiness. So for Rajah, when there was lamb bhuna Friday afternoons, after school, there was no lamb bhuna until all the vegetables had been eaten up. Rajah snapped out of his day dream of his unpleasant past. He decided to ring Hamid and tell him, he would not miss the reception at least. *There is no duty underrated than duty of being self happy.* Rajah was glad people from the outset couldn't tell he suffered from autism and automatism, except Hamid and his brothers. *Raj if you want them Adidas trainers, then go to work* Rajah had to command himself.

It was Saturday night, late but not yet midnight. Hamid was partially sullen, because Rajah had called him a 'silverspoon', in an argument. Nothing much to do, Rajah being at work. *How the hell does he work like a dog from six to four o'clock in the morning.* He was watching *'Never Say Never Again'* on video. One of the freebies with his father owning a movie rental shop. What really pissed Hamid off was when his mother said, on behalf of his father;

"Hameed, son you have to sleep in that single bed in our bedroom."

"Ce-ne (why)?" that was loud when he said it, at the time.

"Some relatives are coming from London for tomorrow's reception, that's why."

"O-kay." *Why have I got so many relatives.* Hamid had reason to think like that especially when he hadn't seen them for ages. He didn't even remember what they looked like or if he ever saw them before.

Hamid was disappointed with Rajah, because he didn't enjoy flirting with the girls. He was on his own at the wedding in Leeds, though Rajah rang from Omar Khayam, and promised he'd make the reception tomorrow noon.

"Hameed, open the door please," his mother shouted from the kitchen. His father had an early night, he had to be up at nine, unusually for Sunday morning. It was to help with the preparation of the grand reception at Kirkholt Community Centre. There were two hundred and fifty guests expected.

Hamid yawning opened their front door as the knocking subsided, when he had said "coming, coming." Just then he took the liberty to fart. A teenage face smiled at him and stepped inside their porch sideways, facing him, revealing almost all of her front upper teeth. Her face like the border of a peach only from both ears. Enclosing coming down to her jaw, emphasising her chin. Not to mention the beige skin complexion. The porch stank of boiled eggs. Hamid felt very embarrassed, as Kajol and her parents squeezed past him into the house.

Sunday noon. The reception of Hamid's cousin. Manik assured the groom that little or nothing will go wrong today. Everything is looked into and will be well catered for. Hamid found it difficult to believe. A change in set of clothing can add modesty. Kajol probably was a down to earth person. She looked mature and very attractive, wearing a paisley patterned white embroidered, black background saree made of satin, over a golden silk blouse and a navy silk petticoat. She wore non-gloss pink lipstick. Her eyes and brows black and shiny without mascara. Her natural black hair, shampooed, washed and blow dried by her mother, down straight, falling beneath her shoulders, very smooth. Her sky blue eyes dazzled like fresh ocean water. Kajol, her physique so ripe, may have just snapped from the vine, as if a sweet mango fallen from a branch.

Every man passing her, inevitably gave her a second look. She was sitting on the last row in the middle of the long tables, amongst other decoratively dressed girls and women.

Rajah was resplendent after a shower and a shave. His dress sense beat every male, including the groom, that particular day, in the community centre. He was wearing cream silk pleated trousers (borrowed from a work mate.) No thanks to the bright but windy weather outside. Matching wing collar shirt with a black and white checked cummerbund around his waist. A beige single breasted blazer over and black dickie bow with white border complimented his outfit. His hair was combed back with Goldwell wet look gel. On his feet, a pair of hush puppies in black with leather uppers (Shamina gave him last Eid.) It was a pity he was not wearing any deodorant.

Despite all the commotion and hired waiters/waitresses serving the invited guests almost impeccably, Rajah suffered an on the spot temporary light shock when Hamid introduced him to ravishing Kajol from a distance. Staring a while at Kajol's eyes it seemed he had seen them before. Not many Bengali girls had blue eyes, only probably if you're half German. What was going through Rajah's mind, some sensation. An exhilarating feeling, as if a supernatural invisible force told him. *This is your Kajol from the nursery. Ridiculous, yeh but it could be.*

The starter was served ten minutes ago. The bride and groom were on a man-made stage, built that morning for the occasion. The bride wore a red satin saree and gold jewellery, the groom a brown striped single breasted two piece suit. Many guests had cameras and Rajah was one of them (the Fuji camera given by Uncle Rokiv last Christmas.) Rajah took a few snaps of the newlyweds. Amongst the two hundred and fifty guests from home and away, seventy percent were Asian and the rest Caucasian. As bees buzz in their hive, so were the guests sounding like an army of ants talking at once. Rajah, maybe being a male, couldn't resist walking past, strolling the last row. As he approached, his feet trembled slightly, when he stopped beside Kajol.

Kajol was busy nibbling her chicken tikka starter. Others started on their main course. The chicken tikka smudged Kajol's lipstick and coloured her right fingers all orange. Apparently at that moment Rajah remembered a scientist's quote; 'snogging makes life expectancy exceed four minutes.' One could add all the adjectives from the dictionary to describe Kajol. For Rajah only word described her the most. *Beautiful, help me Allah. Be calm, like the wind, go with the flow.* He couldn't remove his eyes from her flawless face. No matter how hard he tried. As if some magnetic force was involved. That's what Rajah was feeling. Hesitating but irresistibly he wanted to take a few snaps of Kajol while she was busy finishing her starter. In seconds he focused the camera on Kajol, positioning himself as a professional photographer. He didn't even wait for the flash and pressed the silver button. Kajol looked up, because the camera flashed. Her eyes widened as the pair locked on Rajah's muted face. She knew in her subconsciousness, she'd seen that face a long time ago. It was a face once seen, never forgotten, despite the adult features, to Kajol. For a second or two Rajah thought, this was a dream. The moment felt precious for both of them. It felt as if they were living together in a parallel world, where they were reincarnated over and over. For minutes, once they realised whatever this was, it was real. Rajah and Kajol stared at each other, without blinking. Like two mannequins facing each other, advertising their clothes in a Chelsea shop window. The guests, bride and groom, waiters and waitresses. No one noticed their naivety and vulnerability, except Hamid.

A waiter served some jalabi (an Indian sweet) to Kajol. That was when she blinked and Rajah went back to where he was sitting. As Hamid approached, Rajah borrowed a pen off him. He was starving, but that could wait. From a passing blonde waitress, Rajah borrowed a piece of paper and wrote;

Dear Kajol,
I apologise for taking a snap of you.
You can blame your own beauty for that.
Now this is very important to me.
If this sound familiar to you,
'tinkle-tinkle little star', then I know
who you are and so should you.
If all this is a nonsense and nuisance,
then please ignore me and I promise
I shall not bother you again.
Rajah Khan.

Rajah was telling the child inside him, to behave. There was no steadiness in his behaviour since he'd seen Kajol. Not to mention he was neglecting his friend's (Hamid) presence. Adamantly Rajah walked straight to Kajol's table and said;

"Excuse me, this is from someone you may or may not know," and left.

The piece of paper was folded into the size of a stamp. What Rajah didn't know was Kajol was thinking of doing

Sons of Jabir

exactly the same. Kajol blushed naturally. She couldn't wait to read the letter, but not there as her parents were around. So she ate half of her dessert and headed for the ladies. When she managed to lock herself inside one of the cubicles only then she read the letter and flushed it down the toilet, after ripping it into bits. She wasn't surprised of its content but had to read the letter twice. Which reminded her of '*marriages are made in heaven.*' She didn't know why she was being over-cautious as the letter didn't have anything that would incriminate her in front of her parents. Since she'd seen Rajah, there was a tingling sensation inside her heart. Despite vaguely remembering nursery. Kajol knew within her deepest feelings, although she couldn't describe it. As her whole body went cold and a candle lit inside her mind telling her that she had fallen in love with Rajah Khan, coincidentally her nursery friend. For Rajah it was love at first sight two hours ago.

Kajol got bollocked off her mother, which was unusual, and;

"Where have you been Kajol?" her father asked, furious.

"Toilet, abba-abbazi" stuttered Kajol.

She was glad Rajah wasn't watching any of this, but Hamid was and she couldn't care less. Manik wasn't pleased to hear;

"I've been looking for you over an hour in that community centre, toilet my foot!" Now something's come up, so pack your clothes, we're going home," said Kajol's father, and coughed, his anger subsiding. He was very possessive of his daughter. The only regret Kajol had, was not having the opportunity of replying to Rajah's note.

Sons of Jabir

Chapter Thirty Nine

Three months passed like thirty years for Rajah. Whilst Hamid now and then talked to Kajol in general over the phone. Rajah decided he would do anything for Hamid, if he could talk to Kajol today.

"You know I don't think, she is my nursery friend after all. Whoever she is, I am very much in love with her" said Rajah, both of them walking to school for their exam results.

"You never told me before you had a nursery friend. It amazes me and I feel a little jealous that you can remember so far back. Especially you must have been what?" Hamid looked at Rajah.

"I was three, I think." Hamid also loves Kajol but as Rajah confided in him first about his feelings towards Kajol, Hamid decided to keep his one-sided love inside him, hoping that Rajah's infatuation turned out to be one-sided as well. Then probably he may have a chance to marry Kajol one day.

Some happy, some sad pupils walked past them, as they approached Greenhill High's large front yard. The sun was full with a slight breeze in the wind. Anxious Hamid and Rajah entered into the school foyer. They re-checked their pockets to check that they had brought some form of identification, in order to collect the results. Hamid brought his British Passport. Rajah brought his Bangladeshi birth certificate and NHS medical card. Rajah didn't know until now, that Hamid was born in Halifax. He always thought Hamid was born in Bangladesh like himself but not probably a premature birth. They walked towards the reception and halted as they faced a queue in front of them, surprisingly quiet.

"Do you think she loves me?" asked Rajah.

"I don't know, why don't you write a letter. I can always get you the address" suggested Hamid. Writing a letter didn't seem appealing to Rajah. He didn't utter for few seconds. A letter may cause trouble for Kajol, and what if she replies saying *'I don't love you Raj.'* That he didn't want to go into now.

"Hammer if you can arrange me to talk with Kajol, then I'm prepared to give you anything you want."

"Anything."

"Yes, anything" nodded Rajah, with a very serious face.

"All right then for starters, I'll have your Spiderman comic books."

"You got it."

Hamid was shocked, Rajah didn't even hesitate.

"So it's true what they say, love is blind" commented Hamid.

"Well are you going to ring Kajol for me tonight then" asked Rajah desperately.

"On one condition."

"What?" Rajah looked at Hamid.

"You can't say I love you over the phone."

"Why not?"

"Because I think it's cheating."

Rajah didn't worry about that, because he intended to state that in his future letter. Besides he wanted to get to know Kajol better and get an answer to his note at Hamid's cousin's wedding.

"Fine." Hamid knew Rajah was smarter than him. At least this time he beat him.

The queue subsided, both of them were letting each other in front, as Hamid gave in.

"Good afternoon lads. Okay name, address and ID please," the temporary receptionist requested. Hamid fumbling got his passport out, and said;

"Hamid Chaudry, ninety three Yorkshire Street and Rajah Khan ninety one Yorkshire Street."

Rajah passed his ID to his friend. Hamid forwarded it to the receptionist with his passport. They were both taken aback by their O-level results. Despite Hamid failing Maths, Rajah got straight A's in all subjects. Hamid realised his friend was gifted.

"Bye auntie, Jabir will be home soon. He's gone to the dentist. If he doesn't get his tea on time, he'll go off his head" Shamina explained and added;

"And thanks for the Nescafe."

She was about to leave Twenty Five Brunswick Street. Monwara walked in with St. Michael carrier bags.

"Affaa kun bala ayso (big sister when did you come)?" Monwara asked in excitement, wearing a satin pink business suit over a navy silk blouse. She recently had layers in her shoulder length dark brown hair. The black leather high heels made her look taller. Shamina couldn't figure out the perfume she was wearing.

"It's been a while," Monwara's mother answered. Somrun Bibi only had one dream and that was to get her daughter married to an educated Bangladeshi citizen.

"So where are you coming from Jazmine?" asked Shamina.

"Work affaa."

"Oh, of course I forgot. Where do you work again?"

"Thomas Cook Travel Agency."

"That's it, of course. Right I'd better be off. Assalamu-alaykum."

"Alikum-salam" Monwara replied as she closed their front door on Shamina.

Shamina wondered why does Monwara (Jazzy-B) have to wear western clothes all the time. I mean she would look much nicer in sarees and salwar kameezes. *It's none of your business, she's not really your sister, whatever?* Shamina hurried home.

For the last twelve weeks Kajol at every opportunity tried her best to answer all the phone calls received in their flat. In the anticipation it just could be Rajah Khan. Her parents weren't curious at all. She was still regretting and partly frustrated at not having had the chance of replying to Rajah's note at the time. Now it was dangerous, but he had to know that she was in love with him, but how, how, how?

"Look I have to warn you, far as I know in Kajol's family, love is forbidden" Hamid said. He made that up.

"I jus' wanna talk to her, that's all Hammer." What Hamid just said made Rajah more anxious. Both of them walked into the South Street BT phone box from their house, quarter of a mile. Hamid having memorised Kajol's number dialled.

"Hey-low" Hamid was greeted by a hollow but sweet voice. And he recognised it.

"Assalamu-alaykum Kajol" replied Hamid.

It sounded sarcastic and he meant it.

"Don't hang up, remember my friend Rajah, he wants to say something." (Kajol's heart skipped a beat.)

Hamid handed the receiver to Rajah. Rajah was glad Kajol wasn't standing in front of him. He was finding it difficult to control his nervousness. *She needs to know, I love her, but how, how, how?*

"Hi, yeh, em-ah, jus talk to me as if I'm Hamid," Rajah suggested. The last thing he wanted was to get Kajol in trouble with her parents.

"Tinkle-tinkle star, isn't that weird I still remember that." Kajol wanted to make sure Rajah knew who she was. Rajah had to laugh at that, Hamid was already regretting arranging this conversation.

"Me too, hey how come you left straight away after the reception?" Rajah for second closed his eyes, and recalled that cattish smile Kajol gave him before she left the Kirkholt Community Centre with her mother.

"Something came up and we had to come home, I really wanted to talk to you then, after reading your note in the toilet" explained Kajol. She could feel a fluttering butterfly inside her heart. Her mind was telling her to scream, *Rajah Khan I have fallen in love with you*. It is not a pity her mother is around.

"Look, I was hoping if I can write to you, that, that is if you don't mind," said Rajah.

Sons of Jabir

"If you want, but type the address on the envelope and use English. Also name it not Kajol but Gulshana Begum Kamali... (Rajah heard a door closing from the other end.) Listen I have to go now, dad's here."

Chapter Forty

"Look" shouted Jabir. He hadn't lost his temper in spite he'd been waiting for both of them for the last three hours, worried. It was two o'clock in the morning. Shamina and Rajah had gone to bed ten minutes ago. As the shout was unexpected, when they came in after opening the door with one of their duplicate keys, Bassha and Suna were startled.

It was the first time their father was not only waiting for them, surprisingly he had something to say. Looking at their father, they remained silent. Bassha and Suna wished Shamina was around.

"I suffer from schizophrenia but I'm not stupid. I'm warning both of you, to get your act together or else, there will be punishments. I mean it. Why don't both of you understand that you are making me look bad. Having studs in your tongues, dyeing your hair blonde. My sons are becoming westernised and I don't want that."

Jabir having lectured and in the fear of there may be a protest, turned round quickly and walked upstairs to bed. At times Jabir felt like kicking them both out. A couple of years ago with Manik's help he remortgaged the house and built a dormer, consisting of two equal sized bedrooms, for each of them, as Rajah had taken over the single bedroom on the first floor. Jabir wanted all his sons to live under one roof with him and Shamina.

Bassha and Suna were shocked. They knew Rajah was their father's favourite son and Uncle Rokiv's favourite nephew. They didn't give a damn because they loved clubbing and partying. They didn't even regret failing their O-Levels second time round. They were sure they would become the next Tyson, Bruno, Mohammed Ali, professional boxers. *Dreams should be big enough, that your friends laugh at them, or else it's not a dream is it?*

"Amma what does Kajol see in Rajah" Hamid asked his mother.

Sons of Jabir

"What do you mean?"

"Well whenever I talk to her, she's always asking about Rajah."

Hamid didn't mention that he had sent a valentine card to Kajol. It was returned unopened.

"Don't worry son, we'll get you a nice wife from Bangladesh. Better than Kajol. Now go to sleep, it's past midnight."

Hamid's mother having said that, left his bedroom.

Rajah understood from his friend that Kajol's father was a strict bastard. So he had left his one-sided love at a side, up until now. He couldn't bear it anymore, the unknown. *Does she love me or not? Does she love me or not?*

"It is time to test my fate," murmured Rajah. He was ready to write the long awaited letter to Kajol. This letter would either bring him happiness or sadness, but he had to find out. To hell with Hamid.

Dear Kajol,

I don't think it is possible to define, what is love. Many people in life experience it. Love is such a precious commodity. Undeniable when you know you have fallen in love with someone. Love its consequences can be painful.

The truth is a decent person. Which I hope I am. I believe in Allah and have faith in religion. I have searched, struggled and endured and have stopped that I have found you.

I shall not waste your time neither do I want to hurt your feelings. In plain simple English. With a lot of feelings and emotions. I say to you, "I have fallen in love with you." I am sorry what I have just said if it has shocked you. But it is the truth. I wish you well even if I die.

R KHAN

Looking at the letter, Rajah couldn't believe it took him almost three years to write. Does he really love Kajol? *No doubt about it. She may hate me, no she won't.* He read the letter a few times to make sure it had no errors. Looking at his watch, one in the morning. He didn't feel too bad about not taking Hasina to Hollingworth Lake. He'd been there so many times in the past years on Eid. It was unfair of Hasina as she was visiting Suna, and Rochdale over the weekend. But Hasina was compatible, whatever Rajah suggested or said, was not a problem for her. Hasina respected Rajah as a big brother. She kind of fancied Suna, but wanted to go out with Bassha.

Rajah was lucky to get a placement in UMIST, coming September, as he only managed six points with his A Levels, Psychology, Sociology and History. It wasn't anything to do with his lack of intelligence. Mostly Kajol's hallucination affected him or else he would have guaranteed himself thirty points and a scholarship to Oxford.

Currently Rajah was doing BSC Psychology. The thing that cheered him last summer was when he passed his driving test, unbelievably, first time round. He was a proud contributor to Psychomania Journal (which published articles relating to mental illnesses.) Eventually fatigue got the better of him. He crawled into bed, leaving the written love letter on his desk.

Complimenting Shamina by saying she was a down to earth person was an under statement. Shamina frequently seemed anxiously frustrated. Not only today but on weekends for some reason Jabir slept less. And she and Rajah had to bear his compulsive rituals, like shaving three times a day, watching television till five o'clock in the morning with loud volume. Shamina never in her nightmarish dreams, dreamt that the future would be like this. Not to mention Rajah her only son was in love with someone, that she hadn't even seen. It couldn't get any worse.

Hasina the teenager was confused, because she couldn't figure out which was the better looking one out of Bassha and Suna. Suna had a good sense of humour. Bassha didn't waste time on gossip. Suna liked Indian food. Bassha loved the Big Mac.

Bassha and Suna had decided to leave home, because they felt unwanted. They felt like Rajah disrespected them. Shamina loves them but it wasn't enough. Their argument was, it's not their fault that they have become westernised. It's Jabir's fault for bringing them to this country. They overlooked the fact that if Jabir hadn't, they would have died of starvation.

Chapter Forty One

Shamina was devastated. Jabir was either hiding his emotions behind the mask of being a strict Muslim or he had come to hate Ayrina's twins. In a way he was glad that Bassha and Suna had left, believing himself that they would come back soon. A couple of days ago, a Bengali girl supposedly Jazmine's friend, ran out on her parents and walked away with an African man escorted by the police as she was under eighteen. So Jabir has hope, but was afraid of his sons ending up with English girls for wives.

The high mileage Nissan Sunny, a King's taxi, parked up in front of Pendennis, a part of the freehold flats council estate. Rajah leapt out after he had paid the driver.

"Abba-amma, I think it would be best if I go on my own and persuade them to come back."

On Rajah's suggestion Jabir and Shamina stayed behind. Rajah blew his nose with a three ply catering napkin that he pocketed from Omar Khayam past Saturday. He also made fifteen pounds in tips as it was really busy. Suddenly he triple sneezed, must be hayfever.

Having reached their mahogany front door, Rajah knocked on 298, a ground floor maisonette. These were new council properties. Rajah remembered his mother saying (it was more of a lecture) "In this country most of the things are free, especially education. But why young people don't take advantage of it. I'll never understand" on one occasion. She was actually referring to Bassha and Suna. *'We are leaving because abba wants us to be like you. We are leaving because amma gets bollocked off abba because of our extra curricular activities.'* Those were some of the words Bassha and Suna barked to Rajah before they moved out suddenly. Rajah wasn't bothered then and now, because he was too drunk in Kajol's love. Kajol that may never become his.

Rajah got tired of knocking and began to bang with his fists.

"Bash, shugi open the door. You guys in there or what? Dammit" shouted Rajah. He triple sneezed again and hated it, the hayfever, or whatever it was. Bassha opened the door within seconds of Rajah's sneezing. Rajah wished he had some more napkins in his pockets.

"Raj common in, what's up?" *What's with the American accent? Tupac's influence.*

Rajah walked past Bassha and sat on their tatty couch in the rectangle lounge with no carpets. A TV, a tea table, and the couch including whatever else furniture in the flat. Everything was bought from a secondhand furniture shop on Oldham Road. Basically the things that people threw away. Rajah promised himself, he would never live like this with Kajol. He will have laminated flooring, vinyl wallpaper, a brand new kitchen, the works. He would probably have to work full time. For Kajol he would do anything.

"Where's Shugi?" Rajah asked.

"Oh he's still sleeping, hangover" answered Bassha. He himself has just snorted some heroin. *What is it? Jack Daniels I suppose*, Rajah wondered disgustedly. Rajah knew well one of his brothers had become an alcoholic and the other had made heroin his best friend. He wanted to tell them, they were throwing their lives away but now all he can think of is Kajol. Love had made him partially blind. It was holding him back, it had made him selfish in a way of not trying to help his brothers, give them advice.

"Right so what's-up?" Bassha added as he walked to the kitchen to put the kettle on.

"Well really amma abba sent me to talk you guys into coming home" Rajah explained.

He just couldn't stop thinking about Kajol. Bassha returning to the lounge (changing the subject) asked;

"Hey Hamid tells me you're in love with this Cockney, is that right?"

Rajah wasn't expecting this, but was ready to tell Bassha about Kajol.

Sons of Jabir

"Well if you must know, it's true. She's a Bengali and beautiful. Her name is Kajol."

"Kajol, I see, is she typical. Narrow minded, westernised, housewife material…"

Rajah had to interrupt and change the subject.

"By the way what happened to the boxing career. Are you and Suna training regularly? I really hoped you guys becoming first division football players."

That from Rajah was a counter attack of slight sarcasm, for Bassha to drop the Kajol investigation. Love for Kajol had made Rajah protective of her.

"Just a minute" said Bassha. He walked back to the kitchen and after minute and a half came back with two mugs of steaming coffee.

Rajah took a mug from Bassha and sniffed the Nescafe aroma.

"Smells nice."

"Would you like some Jaffa Cakes" Bassha offered as he sat on a wooden chair opposite Rajah.

"No it's fine. So what are you guys up to nowadays."

"Well Suna and I are working at the Star of Bengal."

Rajah sipped his coffee. Bassha had drunk half of it already. Rajah found the coffee a bit too sweet and lacking milk.

"That place, how could you work for that scrooge?" exclaimed Rajah.

"You mean Mussabbir."

"Yeh, and you don't get to keep the tips."

"It's a temporary arrangement until we can get a better job."

"Well at least you guys aren't unemployed. Obviously you aren't coming home, but I'll tell amma and abba you're all right, workin an all, taking care of yourselves. Yeh and tell Suna I'll see him another time. I have to be off now, I have things to do."

"Sure na-warries," Bassha replied.

Rajah didn't finish his coffee before leaving.

Sons of Jabir

Chapter Forty Two

"Can't you go to sleep honey. What's the matter?" asked Sandra snuggled behind Rokiv's bare back in her nakedness, on their double bed in their bedroom.

"I have something to, I mean…"

"What is it?" Sandra encouraged. Rokiv turned over facing his wife in the dark. Her breath smelt of bacon.

"Sandra you know I really love Halina. I love both of my daughters. I know you've forgiven me, but I feel so guilty of wanting a son instead of Halina. When she grows up she'll hate m-me…"

"No she won't" interrupted Sandra. "I'll make sure of that" she added.

"But" protested Rokiv.

"Honey don't worry about it, now you go to sleep. You have work in the morning."

The reassurance made Rokiv feel better. Sandra was really worried about her husband. *He'll probably has to see a psychiatrist soon,* she thought. She will suggest that to Rokiv in the morning, for the sake of the family.

Apparently Hasina was happy to have a sister than a brother. They went swimming every weekend with their father. They went dancing every Monday evening with their mother. Halina loved to eat sour than sweet. She liked bumble bees, hated frogs and she couldn't stand the smell of bacon.

Chapter Forty Three

Apparently it was a sunny day for mid-October. The Jumma prayer was over. The Pakistanis and the Bengalis began to come out of the main entrance of Jalalia Mosque at the bottom of Trafalgar Street. The massive crowd subsided.

As soon as Jabir stepped out, he was anxious to go home. He knew a lot of people but none of them he regarded as friends. He'd almost forgotten his friend Chander Ali.

"Jabir" shouted someone above the commotion (most of the Jumma prayer leavers are just having a chit-chat) *noh,* Jabir cursed the person who called his name under his breath. He turned around and was face to face with Karamat Ali, a local resident of Wardle.

"What?" said Jabir. He wasn't very pleased for the interruption.

"Bala asso-ni? (how are you?) huncho-ni (have you heard)…"

"Heard what?" Jabir interrupted.

"Kamal Miar boro furi nu baghiaya gesegi (Kamal's eldest daughter had done a runner.) *Another one*. Jabir didn't like this at all.

"Er-re hunno amora idesho furunthain anaytham na aslam (We shouldn't have brought our children to this country.) It's not their fault, it's our fault" Jabir lectured.

"What do you mean?" asked Ali a bit confused.

"What I mean is, we tell our children to read namaaz, we tell them to recite the Koran when they can. Tell them not to drink alcohol, tell them not to have pre-marital relationships and…"

"Jabir I understand, I'm sorry we shouldn't talk about other people's misery" Ali interrupted.

"That's what I'm trying to tell you. Because we have our own children to worry about. I mean my sons, never mind, I have to go now Ali, I'm starving. Bye."

Sons of Jabir

Jabir left abruptly. He almost made his family problems general gossip for the Wardleworth Bangladeshi community.

"Hammer, I don't want any excuses. You are coming with me definitely tomorrow to Hounslough" barked Rajah to his best friend. For the last few years, and now and may be forever Rajah could only think about Kajol.

"I don't think I can Raj" Hamid replied. Rajah changed the subject;

"You know Hammer you've done so much for me and Kajol. I really never can thank you."

"Du, stop it. It was nothing. Anyway what are friends for." Hamid really didn't mean that. Back to the subject;

"So you are coming tomorrow with me, okay?" reminded Rajah.

"I really really can't," replied Hamid.

What Rajah didn't realise was that Hamid just couldn't confront seeing Kajol and Rajah together. Though Hamid wouldn't have minded driving Rajah's new navy BMW 318 he had to sacrifice his love. Pity it's one sided and still was. That love letter from Rajah to Kajol, Hamid wished he could have sent something like that, instead of a foolish valentine card. He wondered why Kajol hadn't mentioned it to her lover Rajah yet.

"Hamid you gotto come, please I'll let you drive." Rajah was on the verge of pleading.

"Look Raj it's not that, I've got me O-level re-sits. And if I dont pass them this time round my dad is going to kill me for sure" explained Hamid. *(I don't blame him, Rajah thought.)* Now Rajah understood, he'd seen Uncle Manik in a rage. The man's knuckles go white, when and only when, Manik Chaudry loses his temper. But it is about a four hour drive and Rajah wanted company for the journey. So he pleaded;

"Acha-reba (please-please-please)-acha-reba. I beg you we'll be back be..." Rajah got interrupted. Hamid couldn't care less, wasn't even looking at Rajah, pretending to be busy doing trigonometry.

"Look I haven't revised at all, the bluey took most of my time. Now if you'll excuse me I am trying to do some revision here" said Hamid glibly.

Rajah left without a word but he felt the happiest man in the world. Kajol loved him and he loved Kajol. A million pounds cannot replace the experience they are going through, love. *And that is not just a figure of speech.*

"Three hours and twenty nine minutes, ye-es" sighed Rajah looking in his rear-view mirror as he parked his not so hot engine motor vehicle inside the half empty car park of Hounslough Thorpe Theme Park. He would have made it in less time, if he hadn't ended up in North Circular twice, by taking the wrong exit. Thanks to German engineering, at times he drove hundred and ten miles per hour, without feeling his adrenaline. Rajah leapt out, simultaneously stretched and yawned. And went in search for the love of his life. *Alton Towers is better than this.*

"Beg your pardon."

"That'll be naine-nainty-faive sir" said the uniform admission lady, repeating the last four words again, an East End cockney. *Ten fuckin' pounds.* Having purchased an adult ticket Rajah feeling a bit drowsy, headed straight for the theme parks café, without looking up or down.

Suddenly he went flying as if someone pushed him from behind. On reflex he landed on his palms at the entrance glass door. It opened and he fumbled inside gasping for breath he looked back and noticed a banana skin. Wondering could that have been a trick, *don't be silly*, dismissed it instantly. *No harm done.*

Rajah sat down at the nearest table as his panting subsided. Nobody noticed his little accidental incident.

A shabbily dressed dry cleaned uniform waiter, smelling of sweat, appeared.

"Can ay getta ane-theng."

"Jus coffee will do, thank you," ordered Rajah. He wondered is Kajol, does she really have the courage, coming here without her parents' knowledge. It had been a while since he'd seen her in the flesh. Would he recognise her? Of course he would from the photograph she sent him only last month. Not to mention the love letters and telephone conversations between them. Rajah toured his eyes around the café. He gazed at a few paintings of Claude Monet. His eyes rested on the white water lilies, in particular interest. Suddenly the scent around him smelled of Estee Lauder. His face lit up brighter than a Christmas tree.

"Thause wa-tar lellies are beautiful aren't they?" opinionated a sweet voice from behind.

"Fascinating," Rajah replied turning around. As he came eye to sky blue eyes. And much more, a far wider smile, that he had not encountered in Kajol's features before. He irresistibly stared at her paisley black and white cotton sweater, emphasising the most perfect breasts.

"Hey guys leave you love birds, see ya later I'm off," said Saline, Kajol's friend.

Rajah didn't even acknowledge her presence as Kajol nodded goodbye Rajah was not to blame. The couple of years had made Kajol more beautiful than ever.

"C'C, care for some coffee?" stuttered Rajah and gestured Kajol to sit down, trying to sound as if he wouldn't mind if she said no. As expected Kajol said;

"I'd like that very much, Raj."

Kajol shuffled until she got comfortable on the wooden, cast iron legged chair. Her loose long hair got tousled. She was wearing a matching skirt, and hardly any make-up. Which already had impressed Rajah, showing off her voluptuousness.

To avoid the sweaty waiter, Rajah went and got the coffee himself. He returned accompanied with a few flapjacks and croissants with a question on his mind.

"Kajol can I ask you something, promise you won't get mad at me?"

After buttering a croissant, Kajol took a bite.

"O-kay, what is it?"

"At what, what age did you experience your first period." Rajah asked drinking his second cup of coffee.

"Age fourteen, why?" Kajol answered and became naturally curious. For a moment Rajah's mind drifted to his cousin Halina. At the same time he was admiring Kajol's firm breasts. Kajol pretended not to notice.

"Oh just hungry for knowledge."

"Raj, how was your journey?" asked Kajol, trying to sound casual. She found the Kenco filtered coffee too strong. So she made do with flapjacks. Haggardness was showing on Rajah.

"Not bad."

"I am really sorry about leaving suddenly on Hamid's cousin's wedding day."

It was as if Kajol couldn't get over that moment of disappointment.

"Kajol, it's been three years since then, almost. How many times do you have to apologise?"

"I was really dying to see you Raj, today was the only opportunity, thanks to the day trip organised by college."

"Same here, you know I can't get enough of looking at you. That reminds me how is your Travel and Tourism goin'?" Rajah wanted to express himself more, instead Kajol did.

"Fine, Raj you do know that I love you very much. (Rajah nodded vigorously.) And I would be the luckiest woman if I can spend the rest of my life only with you. Be your wife, make you happy, have your children." Kajol stopped as her throat went dry.

Rajah wanted to scream and jump up and down. But that would be foolish within the surroundings. Instead;

"How about getting on a mile together?" suggested Rajah. The two hundred and thirteen mile drive was definitely worth it.

"If you wish" said Kajol.

Their date was nothing like a casual one. Rather like mountains in Himalayas inspiring its surroundings. That was exactly what Rajah and Kajol were portraying. Probably Romeo and Juliet didn't admire each other, when they used to meet, like this. Rajah wanted to snog Kajol and caress her breasts, but that wouldn't be appropriate at that moment. *Maybe later.* Both of them were up and out of the café, for some fresh air.

Kajol and Rajah queued for the CANADA CREEK ride, an open top small locomotive. Kajol insisted, because it moved nice and slow, so she could stare at Rajah and not talk, vice versa. One thing bothered Rajah (has for some time) Kajol's other names. *Gulshana Begum Kamali.* Canada Creek returned to its starting point and the current passengers departed. Kajol and Rajah stepped in with others. Seated themselves facing each other.

"Kajol, I understand Gulshana Begum but Kamali?" inevitably asked Rajah. The ten metre locomotive chugged five miles an hour.

"It's my father. His idea, some sort of prestige thing, I think."

"Could be because you come from lower parts of Bangladesh?" Rajah bit his lower lip. He regretted saying that. Before he could apologise. (Kajol wasn't offended.)

"I don't know Raj but Sharfara is a nice place. A lovely village. In the rainy season, travelling by boats an' all. I love that you know." Kajol pretended not to notice what seemed to be arrogance. She was sure he didn't mean anything by it. *Slip of the tongue.*

"I'm sorry."

"It's fine, by the way I hope to join you at UMIST next year. It's my first and second, and third choice, Manchester." Rajah felt overwhelmed. His eyes lit up, like neon in Las Vegas.

"Now that's great news. At last we will be together. What you said in the café luckiest woman, no – I'm lucky, very very lucky to have you as my life partner."

Kajol blushed a little as Rajah got up, crossed over in one stride and sat next to her. As his left thigh and her right collided, they turned their heads, both facing each other. No words uttered their images reflected in each others' eyes. Their breathing increased and hearts began thumping. Kajol could smell Old Spice on Rajah. She took the initiative of what became an irresistibly intimate situation. No holds barred, she wet her lips and kissed Rajah. He hungrily returned the kiss, turning it into a French one. As their salivated tongues entwined and started to explore the internal parts of each other's warm mouths.

A whistle went off.

"Damn it!" Rajah gasped under his breath.

As Kajol struggled free from Rajah's arm reluctantly Canada Creek returned to its starting position. Rajah felt elated. This encounter would do wonders for him tonight.

"Let's get off then shall we?" Kajol gestured. She looked at her watch and added;

"Am-afraid ad-batter be off Raj." Hesitantly. Now Rajah noticed the Cockney in Kajol.

"But, so soon. I was hoping to finish what you started Kajol."

That changed Kajol's mood.

"Raj, don't forget this so called date has to be kept a secret. Last thing I want is to get caught. We have a special heartfelt relationship here. Maybe not an intimate one yet, but next year, who knows Raj."

Rajah only nodded, still elated. For the third time that day, Kajol saw as if candle flames roared in Rajah's eyes. And Kajol went feeling anxiously happy for the inevitable abandonment. The memories of the French kiss, lingering as she got on the college minibus with Salina. Rajah was nowhere to be seen.

Chapter Forty Four

North Wales may seem far from Rochdale, but it's not. You pass Shotton after Chester and you're in North Wales. Llandudno is ninety eight miles from Rochdale. It took Suna an hour and a half to get there with his new motor, Golf GTi. He was happy to pay eighteen hundred pounds, fully comprehensive insurance for a year.

It was a Saturday evening at the popular Bangladeshi restaurant, the Bengal Dynasty. Suna went into the Bengal Dynasty's chock-a-block lounge. It was only seven and the restaurant's house was full. Suna couldn't believe it. It was like that yesterday as well.

The owners, Manikur Ahmed and Monchob Ali, were proud to have this restaurant. As they boast to their inner circles, that they get a wage plus profit package of two thousand pounds every week. But unbelievably they drive Nissan Sunny's and that's what disgusted Suna the most. *I mean no-one is going to take their money to the grave*, Suna thought. Some people are born to be scrooge.

At the Bengal Dynasty, waiters didn't get to keep the tips. It was meant to be company policy, but the owners told their accountants that waiters do get the tips. It was a cut throat business and Suna was determined to earn a second income. Suna's ideology was simple. What his employers don't know won't harm them or him. Only last week Suna asked for a pay rise, after working there for the last three months. A five pound would have made a difference, but no the fat cats didn't give him a pay rise.

No bother.

"Yow Jamshed, Jack Daniels and Coke on the rocks, table five please." Suna having ordered that at the bar adjacent to the restaurant lounge, jogged to the kitchen (he wished the employers would employ more staff.) *Downsizing my foot*. And shouted;

"Yow chef where is table ten's meal. If they don't get it in the next minute, they have threatened to leave."

"Just give me ten seconds" the chef shouted back. Wet all over from his own sweat. The humidity outside wasn't helping.

"Right, soon as it's ready, bell us. One of us will come and serve it."

Suna, having said that, turned around, checked his trouser pockets, assured himself that he had his loot, it varied everyday, but it was always more than fifty pounds. The procedure was (never mind tips, that's for Oldham boys) you put the front and the back copies of the bill, making sure it was paid cash, in one of your pockets. Put the cash, rounding the amount in your other pocket. Repeat the procedure as often as you can without raising any suspicion.

Now Suna was ready to go back to the staff toilet. He ran up the stairs, which were not a part of the restaurant, as the stairs began from the kitchen and finished at the staff quarters. Suna dashed in the larger bathroom. He quickly closed the door behind him, retrieved his loot from his pockets. He wasn't panicking at all, as if he does this kind of mission elsewhere.

Firstly he ripped the paid customer bills (the evidence) in small pieces as possible, then wrapped it around toilet paper bit by bit and flushed it down the toilet. Then he quickly counted his cash, *one hundred and twenty pounds*, and put it in his wallet. He walked over to the mirror above the sink and grinned at himself. He turned around and returned to the restaurant floor. *Back to business*, it was just eight o'clock.

Chapter Forty Five

What could be worse in life than being ordinary, Rajah thought. And yet he didn't have clear ambitions. Does he want to become a scientist, does he want to become an astronaut? His ambitions weren't clear because of Kajol and his mother wasn't helping the situation.

"You can marry her once you've finished your degree." That's what Shamina had reluctantly said last night.

In the past few days he'd been researching on mental illnesses to help him write his assignment on severe psychological disorders. Again he couldn't think of anything but Kajol. Rajah understood, the sooner his mother proposed to Kajol's parents, and they got engaged, then he will be able to think straight. *Damn this love, it invades your routine of everyday life*, but Rajah knew he was very lucky, unlike Hamid.

"Rajah, dinner's ready!" shouted Shamina from the bottom of the stairs.

Rajah got up in front of his bedroom study, opened his door and shouted;

"Amma, I'm not hungry, leave everything on the table. I'll eat later."

Things were not going well between mother and son. Jabir was now irrelevant to discussions such as, 'Rajah wants to marry Kajol', 'why her not someone else from Bangladesh' why can't he marry Kajol if they love each other?'

Rajah wished his father had a say, because he wanted both of his parents' blessing. Does his father want Kajol as a daughter-in-law? Because his mother doesn't. That's what he felt, he may be wrong. Shamina was proving to be difficult to persuade but Rajah knew he would achieve it.

"No, you will eat now whilst the curry and rice are hot, not later. You said that last night and you didn't," Shamina shouted back. She missed Bassha and Suna. Jabir was devastated that they didn't want to come back.

"Damn it." Rajah having no choice walked downstairs in his lungi and a black crew neck T-shirt. Shamina couldn't wait to ask;

"Are you sure that Kajol loves you. She seems very pretty in those pictures you've shown me. It's just that I don't want to get embarrassed, you know when I propose," Shamina in a way envied Kajol's beauty.

"She does amma, she does love, she said so. You've seen the love letters." Rajah never gave the pictures of Kajol to Kajol, that he took at Hamid's cousin's wedding reception a few years ago. For no reason, Shamina had doubts about making Kajol her daughter-in-law.

"You sure you want to marry Kajol. It's your final decision. There're better and more beautiful girls in Bangladesh for you, you know," Shamina suggested probably for the tenth time in the past week. She was finding it hard to believe that her son wanted to get married at an early age, especially when he hadn't finished his degree.

"Amma please, we are not having this conversation again. I love Kajol very much, and I'd like to marry her by all means, Kajol. No one else. I just can't see my life without her."

"Fine-fine," Shamina said and left Rajah alone to eat his dinner of boiled rice and Madras fish curry. It took him twenty minutes to scrape the plate clean. Remembering his assignment he returned to his organised and tidy desk, or else he would have licked the dinner plate till it sparkled. It was very difficult to stay focused when all he could think of was Kajol. *Why does love demand so much? It's definitely worth it, it's magic.*

Shamina was proud in a way, that a girl as beautiful as Kajol was in love with her son, what seems to be her only son. But one thing was really worrying her, 'what if Kajol takes her son away from her after the marriage', The fear of that was driving her insane, as Bassha and Suna were no longer here.

Sons of Jabir

"Rana darlin', let's go home. I'll drop you off" said Bassha.

He had passed his driving test recently, third time around. He had hoped to pass before Rajah and Suna but whatever at least he'd passed now. And he had got himself a nippy three door Toyota Corolla.

Bassha was very attracted to Rana Begum of Manchester, but wished he could experience love like Rajah. Rana was five-seven, with toffee eyes, round face and had mahogany shoulder length hair. She was in love with Bassha, head over heels. Her father wanted her to marry a forty five year old Bangladeshi Colonel, but that's not going to happen. If it became necessary she would run away from home. She does drama at City college. In spite of the colour of her eyes they are slanted, a reflection of her ancestral oriental heritage. Her nose was like a medium sized button.

"Let me finish my drink then" replied Rana. She drained her flat glass of Pepsi, due to the dancing on the Xanadu nightclub's spacious dance floor with Bassha, beneath hundreds of rotating colourful spotlights. It had made both of them tired, and Bassha felt a bit dizzy.

"Hurry up, I've got a headache." snapped Bassha.

"Don't you talk to me like that!" Rana snapped back.

"Sorry, can we go please?" Bassha apologised. Rana was annoyed.

"Yeh." She didn't even let Bassha hold her as they walked out of Rochdale's busiest nightclub.

Since Bassha met Rana he was trying to get off the heroin. Bassha had a thought because of Tupac's influence. Surprisingly Bassha had a contingency plan. He will enrol in college to learn Barbering, despite Jabir's disapproval;

"My son cannot become a nafith (barber.) It is humiliating" Jabir had said that morning, when he visited him.

Apparently Shamina wasn't up to travelling to London. She got car sick on the motorway. But Rokiv and Hasina, pleaded and as it was the Christmas holiday, assured Shamina it would be a change and would help ease the tension between her and Jabir, leaving Rajah impartial. Rajah couldn't help staring at Hasina's breasts. Despite that in a way it made him feel guilty of cheating on his hopeful future wife, Kajol. He was already dreaming about children.

There were two obvious reasons why Rajah had persuaded his father and was determined to go to London at Christmas. One, Shamina accompanied by his Uncle Rokiv would be proposing for Kajol's hand in marriage to her parents for him. And two, he was hoping to take Jabir to a well known hypnotherapist in Covent Garden. In the past weeks he had been busy with Kajol on the phone and later fantasising in bed.

Everything was packed, doors and windows locked and the house checked. The Khan's set off for the capital. Rajah told Hamid to tell Bassha and Suna to call him in London, if they needed him or amma, abba.

Chapter Forty Six

"I am really re…"

"What happened, tell me what happened?" interrupted Rajah.

"Now sit down over here next to me please. I am very sorry but Kajol's parents refused our proposal." No matter how hard it was, Shamina had to look into Rajah's tearful eyes as Rokiv added;

"I can't believe they treated Sandra like she was an alien or something."

The cold outside was nothing compared to what Rajah was feeling now. Shamina never wished this.

"Wha-wha-wha, what do you mean amma. Her father said noh, noh jus like that. If I want, Kajol will run away with…"

"Now you don't go off doing anything foolish like that," Shamina interrupted. She was glad Athiqul Haque turned the proposal down. Now she could get a traditional Bangladeshi wife for Rajah, who will have to cook better than her.

Sandra was concerned but impartial. Jabir was asleep as usual. Shamina was finding it difficult knowing what to say, what to do, to re-compose her son. Rajah was shedding silent tears, slightly slower than a waterfall. (Halina was staying over at a friends house. Pity thought Hasina.)

"Now you and Kajol running away…" Shamina got interrupted.

"Nephew, I hate to tell you this, but we did. Did mention that you and Kajol are in love. And I, your mother would like Kajol as our daughter-in-law." Rokiv paused.

Rajah was hurt for sure.

"Did Sandra auntie ask Kajol to tell her father that she loves me and…" Sandra had to interject. Apparently she was thinking of becoming a Muslim.

"Rajah I asked Kajol, that does she love you, in front of her mother. In their kitchen, Kajol, she didn't say anything."

"Nephew, that's all irrelevant. Because Kajol's father, Athiqul Haque said to us Kajol's marriage had been already arranged to his nephew in Bangladesh. And he is totally against love. Whatever there is between you and Kajol should be stopped. And he believes his daughter Kajol does not love you."

Rajah wanted to scream out that he'd got letters to prove it, but just as if he had Parkinsons, his hand began to shake, no expression on his wet face. He tried to get up from the sofa. He almost did, but his legs gave way and he collapsed face forward, in front of everyone in Rokiv's lounge.

"Ya-Allah." Shamina's scream woke up Jabir. Rokiv dialled 999 and asked for the ambulance emergency service.

"We have a nervous breakdown situation here," Rokiv explained and gave his address as he hung up.

"Oh-no, oh-no," Sandra sighed.

Rokiv picked Rajah up and carefully laid him on the leather sofa. Rajah was unconscious as Jabir demanded;

"What has happened to our son, Shamina?" still drowsy.

Shamina was weeping. She didn't mean for this. *'Ya-Allah' what have I done.*

"I'll explain later" Rokiv replied to Jabir's demand.

"Look the ambulance is coming. Everything will be all right" Sandra assured the now almost hysterical Shamina.

Rokiv for the first time in his life realised there was a negative side of love. And it can be dangerous to health.

Hasina was worried Shamina may go into shock. No one bothered to notify Bassha and Suna of Rajah's nervous breakdown. It was if they were unreachable.

Who needs an enemy, when they have a friend like me, Hamid thought He had rung for Rajah at Rokiv's flat just for a chat, but Sandra told him the unfortunate news. What happened and why. He felt sorry for Rajah, but not for what he had in mind now.

"Baba-zi, I need to talk to you about something. It's urgent" said Hamid to his father, closing the video shop's door

Sons of Jabir

behind. *Why are you back-stabbing your only best friend? For love.*

"Is it to do with Rajah?" asked Manik, as he was told by Shamina a couple of hours ago. He had offered his sympathies for Rajah's well-being.

"In a way yes."

"What is it then?"

"I-I, I want to marry Kajol – since her father rejected Rajah as a son-in-law." *What Rajah doesn't know, can't harm him. I'll deal with him later, if I have to.* Hamid made a mental note. But this seemed a sensitive subject, and what possibly can be dangerous. Friendship built on, not only childhood could end forever, Manik analysed.

"Only last week you said you didn't want to get married for the next six years, son."

"Baba-zi I know I did, but things have dramatically and circumstantially changed now. Please baba-zi, if you propose to Kajol's father… there's no harm in that."

All this was definitely unexpected and surprising. It showed Manik had no idea of his son's one-sided love, as it just erupted upon him. All that is fine, what about Rajah?

"How madly are you in love with Kajol?"

"A lot."

Manik understood he had to handle this very carefully, because he didn't want his son to have a nervous breakdown also.

"I see. If that's the case then I'll ring Kajol's father right now."

Manik temporarily closed his shop by putting a **BACK IN TWENTY MINUTES, sorry Manik,** sign in his shop window and locked the front door.

"Right now."

"Why not?"

"Okay."

There was a slight tension between father and son now. Hamid wasn't inhibited at all. There was a shred of guilt, but it wasn't his fault Rajah was in hospital. Neither was he to blame because Kajol was more beautiful than imaginable.

Manik dialled from memory. He had to hold for a minute before Kajol's mother put her father on.

"Walikum-salam" replied Manik.

"Sorry I wan in the bathroom doing uzoo" (getting ready for a prayer. Washing one's hands, face, feet, ears and forehead), replied Athiqul Haque after he had religiously (assalamalaykum) greeted Manik.

Manik got straight to the point. After all, despite the far distance, they were relatives.

"What I am about to say, is out of the blue. I was wondering, in fact, that your daughter Kajol, would make a very good daughter-in-law. And that would give us the excuse to visit each other more often. Strengthening our relationship between the families." That came out good as it wasn't rehearsed, thought Manik.

"Manik-bai, I am flattered, but I have promised my brother in Bangladesh. I am giving Kajol's hand to my nephew…"

"If that's the case, there is no problem whatsoever, my blessings. You probably getting late for your prayer, keep in touch. Assala-mu-alaykum." Manik hung up. Pity he thought.

Sons of Jabir

Chapter Forty Seven

For a Bengali girl in her maturity of youth, life could be tough, very tough. When her parents treat her like nothing less than property bought from auction.

Kajol's hopes were high. When Shamina and Rokiv came with the proposal to her father, in positive hope for her hand in marriage to Rajah. But it seemed they weren't made for each other after all. Kajol had to stand her ground, at least for a decent husband.

"Abba-zi, if I'm going to marry anyone, then it's definitely not going to be your middle-age black nephew from Bangladesh."

Kajol for the first time (her whole body was trembling) had spoken to her father like that. But she had to, because if she married her cousin in Bangladesh as arranged, then despite her having a career ambition, she would have to work in a factory, become a general labourer. She would need to buy a house, pay stamp duty. Show habitable accommodation, weekly maintenance. All these things and a few minor requirements. She would have to send to the British High Commission in Dhaka, within a given set period of time. Then, only then a visa would be granted. Going through all that was a nightmare, not only for Kajol but many in her position. Not to mention the process of getting one's spouse over after an arranged marriage, was intolerable.

Hazi Athiqul Haque was in control of his fury, or else he would slay his daughter by now, because of the way she talked to him.

"Look, about Rajah, his father Jabir Khan, is mental, crazy. I can't let you marry a faglor foa (mental's son.) I love you too much for that. How about I find you someone else, in-in, this country not Bangladesh. Try to understand me Kajol."

Was father trying to bribe daughter or was there an indication of emotional blackmail. Whatever it was, not marrying her cousin was an irresistible offer that had taken Kajol aback.

It seemed she did not love Rajah as much as she thought she did. All those promises she made in love, seemed like threads now. COME ON KAJOL GET A GRIP. All she had to do was grab her cherished belongings, dash to the bank, withdraw her savings and catch a train to Manchester Piccadilly from London Euston. And she knew how much Rajah loved her. There shouldn't be any problem. By why the hesitation? But now, there's the element of **faglor foa** (mental's son.)

"Listen…" her father said. Kajol snapped from her trance. "If you're thinking of running away…"

"But…"

"Now don't interrupt me. If you are thinking of running away, then you can – but, I will disown you for the rest of your life. And when Rajah turns out like his father, mental, then your life is going to be nothing but full of misery." Athiqul Haque said his rehearsed speech, which Kajol didn't know about. It was his way of manipulation. He left for his evening isha namaaz (last pray of the day), to the mosque.

Full of self pity, Kajol had a dilemma. Does she love Rajah? Had she ever loved him. Is there a slightest spark of want in her for Rajah. The Rajah that only thinks of Kajol and nothing else, every single moment. The more she thought about this whole love fiasco and reasoned in her mind, the opportunity of marrying someone else in this country, *Britain*, seemed appealing and a relief of not marrying her cousin in Bangladesh. It seemed Rajah in a way helped her achieve this goal. And for that she was going to lie to him.

His eyes were tired of sleep and Rajah opened them. He had no idea how long he had been unconscious. At first everything seemed blurry. Blinking, his vision restored, and his eyes searched for no-one in particular. His mind was focused on one thing only, the love of his life, Kajol, Kajol, Kajol.

"Thank God" sighed Hasina. Rokiv told her to stay behind.

"What, where am I?" asked Rajah, panicking.

"You are at the London City Royal Infirmary."

Sons of Jabir

"How long has it been?" Rajah felt more than lost.

"Five days."

Suddenly there were big fireworks as sparkles flew into the crisp night air outside. Rajah shuddered as it was unexpected. *Kajol, Kajol,* Rajah's mind had become like a broken record.

"What was that cousin?"

It made Hasina jump slightly, but she smiled as she replied;

"Happy New Year and welcome back, Raj."

Rajah was still trying to grasp what had happened to him. Despite acknowledging what the fireworks were for. *Kajol, Kajol, Kajol.*

"I can't have been unconscious for five days in a row, was I in a coma?"

"No the nurse fed yeh, at the times when you were awake, not fully. It seems you don't remember."

"Oh, anyway…"

Rajah took hold of Hasina's left wrist and looked at her Swatch digital (12:01.) Rajah remained quiet, as his recent past came flooding to his unoccupied mind. Except Kajol.

"So what's your New Year's resolution Raj?" asked Hasina.

"Never fall in love" Rajah replied and drifted to sleep.

Chapter Forty Eight

"Look guys, I'm sorry amma abba didn't tell yus about my nervous breakdown because they were there for me and didn't want you guys to get worried" Rajah explained.

He had asked a big favour from his brothers. It didn't matter if they turned it down. *If there's a will there's a way.*

"All that's fine Raj. But forget her, forget Kajol. You can do better than her," Bassha said.

Since when has love entered the beauty competition, wondered Rajah.

"Look are you going to help me or not?" said Rajah angrily.

He was really annoyed with Athiqul Haque, Kajol's father. *Who does he think he is? Juliet's father. Well I 'm not Romeo, I'm a son of Jabir. I'll drive to East End and break all his windows for starters. No Raj, you will not do any such thing because you are not a criminal.*

"What do you want doin'?" asked Suna munching on Cheese and Onion Walkers crisps. Rajah noticed the brand new Dolby surround sound 28 inch TV in his brother's lounge and the new carpet, but wasn't curious because it was not important to him at present.

"I want to kidnap Kajol, I-I mean she will…"

"Kidnap?" interrupted Bassha and added; "Look Raj your problem is you are too soft, you are obsessed with love…"

"You are not sure if she is willing to come with you" Suna interrupted. Rajah realised he was wasting his time.

"Tell you what, forget it, forget the whole thing. If only you'd known what love is all about. Just forget it." Rajah was furious having said that. He stormed out of Bassha and Suna's council maisonette. Bassha and Suna weren't shocked or surprised for some reason. As if Rajah was probably joking about kidnapping Kajol. They realised it wasn't impossible. But if Kajol doesn't truly love him, then Rajah was in big trouble.

Sons of Jabir

"You know something, Hammer, if love is one-sided, it punishes you and if it's two-sided then it's an unforgettable experience. Such feelings and emotions for one another" stated Rajah.

"On that, I couldn't agree with you more. Hey Raj, you know I don't know if this is a good time to tell you. I don't think it…"

"What? Just tell me. What else could be more upsetting than not having Kajol."

Rajah had secret plans for the next twenty four hours. Hamid changed whatever he was going to say.

"Bloody hell, we've been chatting for four hours. It's three in the morning."

"Now don't you go not telling me, what is it Hammer?" demanded Rajah, the second time. Hamid stretched himself, ready to go home to bed, yawning.

"If you want to hear it, okay. I think Hasina likes.."

"She doesn't, she fancies Bassha I think" Rajah interrupted.

"Whatever" replied Hamid, suddenly ignorant and left.

Rajah anxiously set his alarm for seven a.m. That only gave him four hours sleep if he went to sleep within two minutes, unlikely. He ran the procedures of his secret plan of Kajol and him, through his mind. Running and getting away together, hopefully starting a family. Rajah knew, in fact he was confident, that when Kajol saw him she would leave with him straight away. As he had not consulted Kajol of his plan or anyone else, there will be a lot of broken hearts and angry minds. But he can't let go of someone so precious as Kajol. Whatever the consequences may or may not be, he would not let go of Kajol, even for a billion pounds.

Mind checklist; packed clothes, toiletries, petrol and enough cash to last them a month in rented accommodation, until he got a job. Rajah drifted to sleep without switching the alarm on.

Rajah I asked Kajol, that does she love you in front of her mother. She didn't say anything… Rajah jerkingly woke up in perspiration, as his mind restored to the present moment. GODDAM IT RAJ, SHE DOES LOVE YOU, YOU, YOU. In a reflex he jumped out of bed as his eyes glanced away from the alarm clock. Not to mention his erection and a full bladder. Time now, nine a.m. He cursed himself. YOU CAN STILL DO IT. KAJOL FINISHES COLLEGE AT FOUR-FOUR THIRTY. He skipped his shower but shaved. He noticed he needed a haircut, but it could wait. He shaved again and was glad Shamina and Jabir were still asleep.

Everything was in his BMW boot, except cash. Rajah grabbed his jacket and car keys. With a stubble and tousled hair he headed downstairs, checking his inside jacket pocket, making sure his wallet was intact. He was about to open the front door, as coincidentally somebody knocked. Hating what had just happened Rajah opened the door. If it wasn't the postman, Rajah would have been gone by now.

"Hi – I have recorded mail sir. Would you sign here please."

Rajah autographed with the pen given by the postman, where designated.

"That's odd, who'd send me a recorded letter?" Rajah murmured.

"Thank-you, see-ya." The postman was gone. Despite Rajah being very late according to his original schedule of a contingency plan to save his love, he opened the envelope by ripping it at the edge with his right forefinger and thumb. Revealing a hand-written letter on lined A4, unfolding it, the disclosure of the contents made his half swollen eyes widen, as he recognised the address on the top right hand corner. He heard the toilet flush from upstairs.

Rajah decided to read the letter in his car. Then last thing he wanted was his mother to get suspicious. The his best laid plans would be ruined, and his life would be miserable for ever.

Gulshana Begum Kamali
(Kajol)
Bethnal Green
London, E2

2nd Feb 1989
Rajah Khan (Raj)
93 Yorkshire Street
Rochdale
Lancashire OL16 3XJ

Dear Raj

I love you more than Juliet ever loved Romeo. I love you more than Laila ever loved Majnu. I have been getting your messages. I miss you very much.

But since your mother and Rokiv uncle visited our house, regarding our marriage. Which seems impossible. Because now, my father is against love marriages. I understand and can feel, you have gone through a lot. Thanks to Hamid and I am no better. Allah only knows how much I miss you, every day.

What I am about to reveal to you. I assume it will be shocking. When your mother and uncle visited my parents with your auntie Sandra. Your auntie was very polite and nice with me. But your mother told me, that she doesn't want me as her daughter-in-law. And that's what she explain to my father, that I am a loose canon. So I have been exploiting you with my cunning charm and beauty, her son. Since then my father has become a beast. He stopped me going college forever. Keeps an eye on me twenty four hours, seven days a week.

Kajol.

If someone had cut off Rajah's testicles right now, he wouldn't have been so hurt as he was that moment. By learning what seemed to be the truth, after six weeks. For Rajah it seemed as time had stopped and everything around with it. Thank Allah, he was still breathing.

Rajah got out of his car, unlocked the house front door and walked upstairs like a zombie, passing Shamina across the lounge. Reaching his bedroom, he put the letter in his pocket and fell on his unmade bed. Uncontrollable tears rolled and Rajah began to weep. Howling, he let his emotions flow. Louder than a wounded wolf in a full moon. That awoke Jabir.

Shamina burst into her son's bedroom and towering over Rajah asked;

"What's the matter son?" very concerned and worried.

Rajah was still weeping. Shamina wondered could it be a poltergeist but she knew better. It had something to do with Kajol. But what was the reason for this sudden domestic mayhem. Rajah's howling subsided as his mother tried to calm him down. It took Shamina and Jabir almost an hour to calm definitely heartbroken and deceived Rajah. Later, human nature took its course. Fatigue got to Rajah and he drifted to sleep.

Shamina undressed her son with the help of her husband. Both of them tucked him in and left together. I'LL GET HIM A BEATIFUL WIFE FROM BANGLADESH, Shamina planned for the future. Jabir was very worried as he had never seen Rajah in this hysterical state before. But Shamina assured him, since Rajah's nervous breakdown he hasn't been the same. And hopefully everything would be all right. ONCE HE FORGETS KAJOL.

"Who said I'm cheating on you? It's not true Kajol!" exclaimed Rajah, lawned summer green grass around and underneath them. Rajah and Kajol were in Hyde Park, London. Both under a blossoming oak tree, in each other's embrace.

"Raj, I was only winding you up. I know you can never cheat on me, not even in your dreams." said Kajol giggling. The last word made Rajah twitch slightly. Rajah already thinking of the future asked;

"So how many kids are we going to have Kajol?"

"That depends on how much you love me?" Kajol was staring into Rajah's eyes.

"*Whatth* does that suppose to mean?" Rajah tried not to blink as he said that.

"Well if you're horny as much as you love me. No doubt about that. Then we probably have a football team. All boys, I love boys."

Rajah got excited.

"Hey wait. I don't know about that Kajol, boys an all. But when it comes to you I'm very horny." Rajah advanced. As he kissed Kajol passionately on her moist lips, they parted and he entered his tongue down her throat. First base accomplished. Approaching second base. Rajah began to caress Kajol's breasts over her silk blouse. And she wasn't wearing a bra.

Suddenly Kajol, with both palms, pushed Rajah away.

"Raj, I'm sorry I didn't mean to push you so hard. But we can't do this until we are married. It's just I-I don't feel comfortable."

"So no pre-marital relationships whatsoever."

"Yes."

That woke Rajah up from his dream. UNTIL WE ARE MARRIED. HOW AM I NOW GOING TO ACHIEVE THAT. OH KAJOL, HOW MUCH I MISS YOU.

Chapter Forty Nine

No matter how difficult it may be, Rajah was really trying to devise a completely new plan since his last, five weeks ago, to get away with Kajol. Odds were against him because Kajol was not going to college. His nerves weren't helping him. After what he learnt that his mother, Shamina, had done. How could his own mother not love him. What he wants can't comprehend. That just how much Kajol means to him.

The only reason Rajah could think of what Shamina did and why, could be once he'd married Kajol, he probably would have left. But what Shamina didn't know was, her breast milk has more power over Kajol's love. Why? Can't one have both. Love and their parents. It was not too much to ask.

Kidnapping had crossed his mind but that would make things worse, consequently. Rajah was trying to be positive. Can feel it, in his heart. Kajol would never betray him by not betraying their love. She will stubbornly wait for him. Rejecting all the arranged marriage proposals. At least he wouldn't live without Kajol for the rest of his life. Keeping these thoughts at bay and his mind sane. The rain suddenly hit hard on his bedroom window as it melted the morning's snow. d knocked on Rajah's bedroom door with his right fist. It had been ten days since Rajah had been over to his house.

"I want to kidnap her, how much would it cost me?" asked Rajah.

"Four thousand pounds," quoted a Birmingham thug going by the name of Badal (cloud.)

"Four thousand!"

"You have to understand if any, I mean if get caught, then there will be a custodial sentence." Badal toying with his pony tail.

"Okay forget kidnapping for now. Let's plan something frustrating. Got it, smash all their windows back and front. How much would that cost?"

"Four hundre…" Hamid knocked again, harder. Rajah must have dozed off in an attempt to complete a psychology assignment. BADAL, and had a delusionary chat with no one in particular.

"Coming, justa-min-it." He realised time flew but not how much. In thought of Kajol and Allah knows what else, his Papermate lay motionless in the grip of his right arm. Its nib resting on a WHS A4 pad, after the word cognitive. Rajah having come to his senses within his bedroom. Despite the crisp packets and empty chocolate wrappers scattered all around the floor. He realised his door was not bolted.

"Come in, Hammer" shouted Rajah, as he raised his arm dropping his pen, and closing the two inch BSc psychology textbook.

"Was the door open?"

"Yes, anyway what's up?" asked Rajah with an expressionless face.

"You haven't been over, how come." Hamid sat on Rajah's single unmade bed, pushing the quilt to one side. Rajah's bedroom had a damp odour. Hamid thought it would be better not to mention it, as that's the least Rajah would be concerned about, from what he had to reveal.

"I am just trying to get back on track with my temporarily abandoned degree," Rajah explained.

"By the way, Kajol's getting married next month," Hamid blurted out.

The last five words froze Rajah. For almost sixty seconds Rajah was too mortified and shocked to utter a word. He was motionless in furious indignation. When his temporary sudden paralysed vocal chords were working again, all he could choke was;

"Hammer you're joking!"

"Look I know it's April Fool today, but it's no joke" Hamid paused, waiting for some sorrowful reaction. Rajah wished thunder and lightning would strike him, right now. His brain was telling him, there still may be a chance.

"Will you be all right?" added Hamid.

Rajah waved Hamid goodbye subconsciously.

For days on end Rajah's mind was racing. Racing against the deadline of Kajol's arranged marriage. OH ALLAH, only twenty days left, for the actual engagement and wedding ceremony. Once the nikah (engagement) was done, it was over for Rajah.

He just couldn't come up with a bona fide plan. They'd changed their phone number. Even Hamid's father didn't have it. Nothing but out of desperation Rajah had written a few times to Kajol with no reply, as expected. KAJOL PROBABLY WAS LIKE A BIRD IN A CAGE. Another night passed as Rajah drifted to sleep with an anxious heart and a tired mind.

YOUR MOTHER SAID TO MY FATHER THAT I AM A LOOSE CANNON.

"Amma why? Why? Why?, whaaaaaaaah…" Rajah woke up screaming "Why?" six in the morning. Shamina and Jabir came running.

"I'm okay, it was just a bad dream," said Rajah and waved his parents out of his bedroom before they could offer sympathy.

Shamina had realised eventually what was eating Rajah up. If he carries on like this he'll surely die of malnutrition. All for what, love for Kajol. But Shamina wouldn't admit that she didn't try her best to get Kajol for Rajah, her only son. What she fears is does Rajah acknowledge that. There could be nothing worse than your own flesh and blood hating you for not just rest of your life but for the rest of his life, too. The thought of all that had made Shamina very hollow as she went back to their bedroom with Jabir.

06:10 Rajah's luminous digital alarm clock read. Rajah gasped as he sighed;

"Oh Kajol."

The thought of not marrying, not having her as his wife, made him not only shiver but it seemed it was the end of the world. As if America had declared war against Russia. He couldn't care if a meteorite hit the earth and everything banished. If Hitler was back and won world war three and everyone was a German slave. He just couldn't contemplate his life without Kajol. He couldn't bear to think of someone else touching her silky body. And yet there seemed no hope.

Only thing he could do, Rajah joined both his arms and faced them, still in bed.

"Ya Allah my brothers have become westernised, I didn't mind. Ya Allah you have turned my father a mental man, I didn't mind. You gave me unusual illnesses in my childhood, I didn't mind. I grew up without a lot of things other children take for granted, I didn't mind. I adore my mother, in fact worship her. Love her more than anything in this world. And she betrayed me (Rajah now, with his right finger, felt his neck prayer beads.) Ya Allah all I ask, Kajol, Kajol and Kajol in my life, nothing more." Silence stunned upon the damp room as Rajah's prayer finished. This time there were no tears.

Chapter Fifty

Shamina had to admit, Jabir had to be a unique schizophrenic because he loved Rajah dearly. At the same time he was lost in his mental incapacity. He was asleep, nothing unusual for him except his gibberish every fifteen minutes. And not to mention, it was only six thirty in the evening, beginning of a new year. No sun to be seen, darkness outside with January's chilly breeze. Jabir's own odour from urinary incontinence occasionally, doesn't affect his sleep. Unfortunately for him, his mind was full of thoughts of his past.

PRESUMABLY DEAD... YOU CRAZY... DON'T COME LOOKING FOR ME... YOU MENTAL... YOU CRAZY...

"I'll slap you again, shut up" Jabir retaliated in his sleep, as he turned from left to right, his face now facing the wall, as his bed was against it.

Shamina was downstairs in the lounge near the half on gas fire, some prayer beads in her right hand. She came across them when she tidied Rajah's bedroom. Whatever has happened so far, it could have been worse. May be it's all for the best and it's nothing to do with fate Shamina thought. Because she believed in Allah one hundred percent.

In the past nine months she had managed to save near enough three thousand pounds from her part time work, keeping a tight domestic budget. All for what. She hadn't manage to persuade, let alone manipulate her son Rajah of going to Bangladesh, so she could get a daughter-in-law of her own choice. Since Kajol had got married to someone in Kent. And that was nothing to do with Shamina. But Rajah seldom speaks to his mother nowadays.

A key turned. The front door screeched. Rajah walked in from UMIST.

"How come you late futh (son.) You all right?"

"There was an accident on the M62 just off exit A627. I had to take a diversion," snapped Rajah truthfully.

"I hope no one dead. Right what shall I heat up. Fish, lamb…"

"Nothing, I'm not hungry" Rajah snapped again, running straight to his bedroom.

Shamina's heart sank but she didn't drop tears. MY SON WILL COME AROUND. Only thing she worried about Rajah not wearing his prayer beads. She didn't have the courage to tell him off. All she could do was pray to Allah. At times like now, Shamina missed her parents.

Rajah followed his routine. Masturbated and drifted to sleep, despite he was six assignments behind. Eating rice and curry was the last thing he does every day since Kajol got married not to him but to some stranger, to him and her. He was giving himself some sort of punishment. Except now and then, a cheeseburger from McDonalds.

An hour passed. Tears from his bloodshot eyes wet his white pillow. Rajah couldn't rationalise no more. How can he go through another fifty, sixty years of life, which has not yet begun, without Kajol. Was the love of his life. His zaath (caste) has been a barrier. It made Shamina arrogant. She disapproved of Kajol and now he was alone in nothing but misery. WHY? WHY? WHY? He managed to masturbate again and drifted to sleep.

Two in the morning. The hunger woke him up. His desk drawers were full of crisps, chocolates and pop, stocked by himself. So he gobbled three packets of Walkers Cheese and Onion crisps and swallowed a can of Lilt.

Half an hour went by, tossing and turning. Rajah couldn't go to sleep. THERE'D BE HARDLY ANYTHING GOOD ON TV THIS TIME Poor sod tried masturbating again but there was no sperm left in his bank. Without ejaculation there's no real pleasure. Inevitably his mind became unoccupied.

He felt despair, abandoned, no shocked as he lay on his bed wrapped around naked in his quilt. KAJOL IS MARRIED NOW, IT'S NOT TRUE, IT IS. HOW DID THAT HAPPEN? IT HAPPENED WHEN YOUR MOTHER AND KAJOL'S

FATHER, BOTH AGAINST LOVE MARRIAGES, DECIDED AGAINST…Rajah just didn't want to go there, again. To ease his mind, he recited a poem.

"There was time I used to smile. There was a time I used to laugh. If only I could forget you, oh Kajol. But I can't. I don't know why?"

The poem put his mind back to square one. Rajah didn't know who was to blame. His mother, Kajol's father or both. DOES LOVE HURT SO MUCH. That reminded him of another poem.

"Night or day, seven days a week. Twenty four hours a day, I used to feel elated. In your thoughts but with negative premonition. May nobody face these situations in love. Why? My heart does not rest in peace. Impatient so it is, unbearable so it is, intolerable so it is…"

Rajah sighed 'oh Kajol.' At least she could have protested. DAMN-IT, it's a free country. SHE WAS OVER EIGHTEEN. Why do parents demand and equally expect so much from their children. It's as though what they couldn't achieve themselves, they force their children to follow, to fulfil their own dreams.

Athiqul Haque, Kajol's father, never did understand just how much Rajah loved Kajol. How would they, either of them. His mother Shamina or Athiqul. Have they ever experienced love or its boundaries of happiness? NO. He didn't think so. Jabir his father, due to fate, and only Allah knows why, was a schizophrenic. If not things could have been different now.

Rajah had a lot of complaining but he couldn't complain to anyone. At the end of the day Shamina, his mother, kept him in her womb and gave birth after seven months. Thank Allah it wasn't nine months. Breast fed him for two years, nurtured him till he was a teenager, gave him motherly love, even now.

No thanks to Kajol's father, Athiqul Haque. Philosophically not to forget the biological element. That it's one of his sperm from many had entered into his wife's ovary, becom-

Sons of Jabir

ing an embryo. Nine months later concluding another sixteen years, comes out and becomes as beautiful as Kajol. As Titanic was a calamity and those who lost a loved one. And endured the emotional trauma as the years gone by. Rajah losing Kajol was the equivalent. And only Allah knows when he will recover.

Shamina wanted to take Rajah to Bangladesh. Get him married to someone he had never seen before. Are they even going to like each other? Will they be sexually compatible? WELL THAT'S NOT GOING TO HAPPEN. Pity Rajah wasn't a girl. A girl, a daughter would probably be more susceptible to emotional blackmail.

Is fulfilment in love unachievable? Rajah only wanted to marry Kajol, nothing more or nothing less. He didn't want a Ferrari nor become the President of the United States. Only Kajol.

Above all his mother has failed him. There's no worse experience of emotions, when his mother failed him to achieve the only thing he wanted in life. In return he adored his mother very much. Rajah had made a decision in order to keep his mind occupied. And that he was never ever going to get married. Love nor marriage, lust is his salvation to overcome a wounded heart. Feeling horny is that natural in his circumstances? Only time will tell. Rajah, as his mind needed rest, drifted to sleep without masturbating.

"Uncle, please hear me out. I haven't come here to upset anyone. I plead to you, I beg to you. She means a lot to me. She means the world to me. She means everything to me. I will keep her happy. I will give her everything I can afford. If only I can marry your daughter Kajol. Then I will be the happiest man in this universe."

Athiqul Haque was observing Rajah, apparently smiling or may be sneering at him. He wasn't sure but remained silent.

"Uncle I understand. There is a right way to do this and a wrong way to do this. I want to do this the right way. I don't want to take your daughter with me and run away. I love her very much, I respect you too much to do that sort of thing and the last thing I want is to humiliate you. Uncle I want to marry her with nothing but only your blessings." Rajah was on his knees, looking up at Athiqul Haque.

Just the two of them in his flat lounge. Rajah was sure his only wish in the world was about to be granted. Suddenly Athiqul Haque's face turned sullen. His eyes widened with rage. His smile became a smirk. Rajah was so frightened, thinking the devil would probably look better than this.

"Stand up Rajah," said Kajol's father.

Rajah stood up trembling as Athiqul Haque slapped him right across the face.

"How dare…" Rajah opened his eyes, gazed around and went back to sleep again. KAJOL IS ALREADY MARRIED.

Chapter Fifty One

"There are no chemicals in your blood to reason.what has happened in the last two hours could have been its effect. Nor there's any indication of alcohol on your breath. Rajah, I am therefore admitting you to John Elliott Psychiatry" explained the police doctor at Rochdale Police Station, Esplanade.

Rajah hazily nodded as his mind raced through the events of that morning.

Nine a.m., the sun shone through his curtain. He felt the heat on his forehead, forcing him to wake up to a promised hot summer day. For no apparent reason he felt fresh and elated. He emptied his bowels and drained his bladder. Brushed, shaved and showered.

He got dressed and grabbed his car keys. He went out of the front door and sat behind his 318 steering wheel. He put the key in and started the ignition, clutch in with his left foot, into first gear and stepped on it.

It took him eighty five seconds, despite red lights to reach The Butt, Rochdale town centre.

"Like a virr-gin, touch-touch, touch for the very first time. Auoh." He was singing to Madonna. All his windows closed he blasted the music and revved into the one-way system leading towards Rochdale Police Station and Magistrates, The Esplanade. Other oncoming drivers swerved, some to the left, some to the right, to avoid crashing into Rajah, with his dangerous driving. As Rajah, elated, passed the Central General Post Office, suddenly he pulled on the handbrake, the BMW spun round stopping at an angle. That's all he could remember.

"I hope I haven't run anybody over this morning sir."

"Though you could have, fortunately you haven't Rajah."

Rajah was too upset to ask about his BMW, hoping Hamid would take care of it as well as Shamina and Jabir. The wall clock in the interrogation room read quarter past eleven.

NEXT DAY

John Elliot Unit, Psychiatry. A new site, section of Birch Hill Hospital specialising in Clinical Psychology.

Head of Department, Doctor Talbot, browsed through Rajah's medical history from his GP. In contrast the police doctor's assessment and report made a diagnosis possible. Taking into account Rajah's father's condition.

Dr. Talbot gazed through Shamina, Jabir, Bassha and Suna, resting his eyes on Rajah.

"As I can understand you are a sufferer of autism and automatism. What happened over twenty four hours ago, in our profession, it's known as a panic attack or an episode. I hate to tell you, that you have been diagnosed as a manic depressive."

"Manic depeh, what?" said Shamina suddenly. Others remained attentive. *Shit, he's gonna end up like dad*, Bassha thought.

"I understand all this is difficult for a mother" Dr Talbot sympathised looking at Shamina, still sullen.

"Manic depression is characterised by extremes of mood. Periods of deep depression and periods of over-active, excited behaviour known as mania. Some people experience visual or auditory hallucinations or delusions. However when Rajah leaves this ward, hopefully he will be stabilised," explained Dr. Talbot.

"Do you mean cured, doctor?" asked Shamina, as her face lit up.

"I'm afraid not. The illness is a chronic one."

"Meaning?"

"It will be a while before Rajah gets completely better."

Sons of Jabir

Chapter Fifty Two

When Dr. Talbot said 'It will be a while before Rajah gets completely better' that was an assumption based on probability. I mean, I may never get cured one hundred percent. Mind is a dangerous thing, if it takes control over your subconscious. If you have been hurt or betrayed by members of your family or by someone you loved dearly, then it is very difficult to stay sane.

Some can't overcome a broken heart. Some promise they will stay a bachelor for the rest of their lives, I may probably be one of them. Amongst various mental illnesses. I have become a manic depressive from a broken heart. Now I may not be a hundred percent correct because my father is a schizophrenic. So it could be hereditary. But I doubt that because Kajol is the reason, I have become a manic depressive.

What right did she have to play with my feelings, my mother is partly to blame. As she could have tried harder. Proposed to Athiqul Haque till he gave in. No matter how hard I try to reason with the past, if only time travel was possible and not science fiction, but it isn't and I can't change the past. So I have decided to let it go. As time heals all wounds. It's not going to be easy but I have to get over her because she's married. And as time passes by, I'm sure I will, I have to. Maybe I'll find someone special.

To most people in the area I'm a freak because of the dangerous driving incident in town. My family is giving me tremendous support. Bassha, Suna and Hasina believe if I can forget Kajol totally, then I will be cured. I said to them, 'I am trying but memories aren't fading.'

No one can tell that I'm a manic depressive by just looking at me, if they don't know me. Dr. Talbot is a nice chap. He first put me on Chlorpromazine. And now Lithium Carbonate. I was thinking I'd be on Prozak soon but I was wrong.

The thing about Lithium, every three months I'd have to give blood samples. Prolonged use of it will have side effects.

Scary, I know. It's been thirteen weeks and I had enough of the tablets. Once I was working in a local restaurant. As it got busy I forgot to take my medication, inevitably ended up having an episode of depression. I sobbed for half an hour. Can't remember what it was for except that it was a Saturday night. So embarrassed and humiliated. I decided to do something about this unique psychological illness of mine.

I reluctantly asked Dr. Talbot;

"Is there an alternative method of medication or treatment for manic depression?"

He happily replied (but remaining sceptical);

"Rajah there is, it's self therapy. You can find more about it, if you go to the Manic Depression Fellowship on Richard Street, off Drake Street, near the Rochdale Train Station."

I too was sceptical to go at first, that I really can get off Lithium. I was not reluctant. It was more of a, will I be wasting my time.

Once Hamid quoted "faglor foa ar kitha oybo (son of a mental person, what would he achieve in life.)" I was hurt, I thought Hamid was my best friend, best buddy, more than a friend. But he wasn't after all. I didn't know why he was angry with me. Until Bassha told me;

"He too used to fancy, in fact was in and probably still is in love with Kajol the siren."

But why is he taking his frustration, anxiety and hollowness out on me? Anyway, I let it go.

Rokiv uncle and Sandra were really sorry for me, when they came to visit my home a week or two later after my discharge from John Elliott Psychiatry. Apparently Halina was very chatty but something about her eyes I was thrilled of. She looked a lot mature for an eleven year old. Her Bengali was fluent unlike Hasina. All that was fun. I assured Rokiv uncle and Sandra auntie, I will be better in no time as amma abba pray for my well being every day.

Sons of Jabir

Suna surprised me. A couple of days ago he visited me with a bottle of Iron Brew and golden apples. When he left he quoted;

"Falling in love, it can make a person extravagant, lavish and at the same time wasteful."

I was impressed, he must be in love. Good for him because everyone isn't weak as Kajol. Kajol that can't speak up to her father. Kajol that didn't claim their love. But Suna was wearing a Rolex and I couldn't help noticing the two inch gold bracelet around his neck. He must be working overtime unlike Bassha. He did mention, his job at the Bengal Dynasty is a good one. And he is the highest paid Bangladeshi waiter in North Wales.

Monday morning arrived and flew. I have plans today unlike other previous Mondays since my discharge. Afternoon passed in boredom and anxiety as I was trying to read a Jeffrey Archer novel. Waiting was over, almost six p.m., to find out what Manic Depression Fellowship can do for me.

When I arrived at Richard Street in a taxi, I was expecting lunatics, zombies and Allah knows what else. I didn't know why I was thinking like that, they were people just like me, diagnosed with a mental illness. Not ghosts or aliens from outer space.

Amongst eighteen attendants to the fellowship, including me, surprisingly there is a Bengali girl.

I was curious to find out how on earth did she become a manic depressive? I didn't ask her because she turned out to be my auntie. Leaving my curiosity thirsting for water and too afraid to kill the cat, we just talked with each other and everyone else. We exchanged names. She told me her friends used to call her Jazzy Bi. Now she doesn't have friends except the people she knows in this fellowship. She mentioned she's been coming here for the past six months. She still goes and sees her psychiatrist once a month but she's not on any tablets now. When she talked about her mother Somrun Bibi, I remembered my mother talking about her mother being my nani's (grandmother) best friend at times. Now I don't even remember my nani, the nani that raised me from birth to three years old. Never mind her friend Somrun Bibi.

Jazmine was fascinating as she talked about a network marketing company called Amway, an American based company. That promised retirement in five years, if you have the potential. Talking about residual income and therefore having a lot of spare time to yourself.

If you see Jazmine in the street, you will not be able to tell she is a diagnosed manic depressive. She too suffered a nervous breakdown. Evidently we have unfortunate commonalities between us. My first appearance I felt at home. Two hours passed quickly. The self therapy session was over. Everyone departed for home. I thanked Janet for the coffee and Julie for the cookie as they brought it from their homes.

"Nice to see you Raj. Hope to see you next week," most of them said and disappeared, as some drove off in their cars and some in taxis except Jazmine.

I walked Jazmine home as she insisted. It took us about eighteen minutes to arrive at Brunswick Street. As we reached her front door, she offered me a cup of tea. I declined saying; "Some other time Jazz."

After as I walked home, I thought about Amway. Retiring at the age of twenty six was very appealing. But more so I was thinking of Jazmine.

I felt I was attracted to her. She has a radiant smile. She talks fluent English and the western clothes she wears makes her look elegantly beautiful. What I'm trying to say is she is no bimbo. I feel there is some chemistry between us. When we were talking at the fellowship. HOW COULD THAT BE POSSIBLE, I HAVEN'T EVEN FORGOTTEN KAJOL YET? YOU ARE ON A REBOUND, BE CAREFUL BUT I'M NOT VULNERABLE, THAT I AM SURE OF. DON'T BE SILLY, SHE'S YOUR AUNTIE.

Sons of Jabir

Chapter Fifty Three

A year later

It was raining outside and it was cold. Everyone was wearing hooded anoraks and woollen gloves. The cappuccino aroma filled the restaurant floor. Customers were busy in gossip. As the door was open.

"Jazmine I want you, I do" said Rajah.

They were a couple amongst others in the San Remo Italian café on Drake Street.

He added spontaneously;

"I want to marry you. This hide and seek, I don't like it anymore. We've almost been going out for a year now."

Rajah really wanted to marry Jazmine because of lust more than love. But Jazmine truly loved him.

"No, Raj I like you and want you too, but we can't get married because I call your mother affaa (big sister.)" Jazmine hadn't overcome her ex-boyfriend yet.

"Exactly you call my mother affaa. But she isn't your real sister. So we aren't inconveniently blood related because your mother was my grandmother's friend. That's why you call my mother affaa as in big sister." Rajah paused (he couldn't be more thorough.)

"Look I am attracted to you, I like you and want to marry you. I don't want to lose you like Kajol of not taking action at the right time."

"I don't know Raj" said Jazmine sipping her hot chocolate. She was a bit confused of what to do. She knew Rajah will keep her happy but what would Shamina say when this comes out. What will the Wardleworth community think of her and Rajah? How would her own mother react?

"Look we are both over eighteen. We don't need anyone's permission. Let's forget about our parents for once and think of what we want."

That speech made Jazmine's mind up. It became crystal clear that she did want to marry Rajah and spend the rest of her life with him.

Though she never really listened to her mother, nor did Rajah for that matter, both of them were willing to leave their parents for each other. Those parents that gave them birth. Those parents that brought them up since birth into adulthood. It seemed lust is greater than love. Taking into fact the love between them was truly two sided and both of them were willing to contribute towards their own happiness. As they both wanted each other and nothing else.

"Yes I will marry you Raj, but you have to promise me that you will never cheat on me." Jazmine wished Rajah was not on the rebound and truly loved her.

"I will kill myself before I even think of being unfaithful to you."

"Let's get married then." Jazmine became elated. She finished drinking her hot chocolate. For the last ten, eleven months Rajah wanted to ask (he couldn't hold it up any longer).

"Jazminc can I ask you something?"

"What Raj?" Jazmine's elation subsided.

"How did you turn, become a manic depressive?"

"I used to go out with a guy called Shezad Iqbal but he turned out to be a married man with children. And that broke my…"

"Jazmine let's get out of here," Rajah interrupted. (He wanted to ask, was there any intimacy between her and Shezad.) OF COURSE NOT.

Chapter Fifty Four

YOU WILL GET UP AND YOU WILL CONFRONT YOUR MOTHER. SHE CAN'T STOP YOU OR JAZMINE AS YOU HAVE BOTH MADE UP YOUR MINDS. Rajah's overnight headache still lingered. Two five hundred milligrams of paracetamol failed to get rid of it.

Rajah got up, got dressed and without shaving brushed his teeth with Sensodyne toothpaste. He then walked down the stairs and barged into their lounge, wasting no time.

"What do you want for breakfast futh (son)?" asked Shamina as she was watching television.

"Amma I'm not hungry. Amma I wanted to marry Kajol but you didn't really propose properly. If you had today Kajol would be mine, not somewhere in Kent" said Rajah. He knew his mother wasn't all to blame. He wasn't aware that the reason he was talking like that to his mother was because he had become blind in love with Jazmine. How was it possible to fall in love with another woman so quickly when you have been dumped by one earlier. Is it because of some sort of insecurity? Whatever it was Rajah would never know. And he didn't want to know because he wanted Jazmine. He felt that having Jazmine somehow he could get even with Kajol. *'Yeh that's right I'm going to marry someone more intelligent than you, someone better looking than you, someone who is not their parents' puppet.'* There were so many reasons Rajah had to compare Kajol. Rajah understood if someone loved you, they would go all the way in spite of the consequences. So did Kajol love him? He'd never know. Was he bothered? No.

Shamina couldn't believe her ears. This sudden outburst from Rajah seemed a recurring nightmare. She had to reason with Rajah because he may suffer an episode. This manic depression is a tricky psychological illness. But Shamina had to defend herself.

"Futh I did propose properly. Her father just told me to forget it because she was to be married to her first cousin in Bangladesh. But what is it in Kajol than no other woman can match. I keep stressing, why don't we go to Bangladesh and I'll get you someone ten times better than Kajol?" Shamina rested her case. She was shocked what Rajah had just blurted out because he meant it. But she was not hurt because if she was hurt then she will automatically curse her own son. And that she was not going to do, never.

Rajah apparently became ignorant.

"Amma well I don't care anymore about Kajol or you." Rajah paused, hesitated slightly and added;

"The thing is I love Jazmine and I'm going to marry her because she's not a coward like Kajol. She wants me and I want her. She is willing to walk out on her mother for…"

Shamina wished she dropped dead as she said;

"Are you out of your mind, she's your auntie. Ya Allah you have gone mad, craz…"

"Look amma I'm no fool, there is no blood relation between your mother and Jazmine's mother. They were best friends, not any more. So that means I can marry her and none of your emotional blackmail will work on me any more."

Rajah having said that, a kind of a rehearsed speech, stormed out.

Jabir was sleeping as usual. He didn't even hear Rajah's loud bygone speeches. How could Rajah have been so heartless Shamina thought. Her own son had said things to her that Bassha and Suna wouldn't even contemplate to say. Rajah had hurt her but she would not admit it.

Shamina wept for hours. She understood she had no power over Rajah any more. But she had faith in her breast milk that she fed Rajah. And believed Rajah would come back but not under any circumstances would she accept Jazmine as her daughter-in-law. Surprising it was, and she would not forgive Jazmine for luring her son Rajah with the artificial beauty and

Sons of Jabir

snobbishness, because Shamina will pray to Allah for her son's return. As she had been praying for Bassha and Suna's return.

She missed her parents very much. She had hoped of going to Bangladesh in December to get herself a traditional Bangladeshi daughter-in-law. Now the dream was on hold and Rajah marrying Jazmine was a hiccup that had left her broken.

Nevertheless, she will pray to Allah for Bassha and Suna and Rajah, because that's what mothers do. No matter how bad, ignorant, heartless and selfish your children become a mother shouldn't stop praying for their wellbeing. Parents shouldn't give up. She didn't blame Jabir as he is a known schizophrenic. People in the Wardleworth community called Jabir fagol (mental.) She still wondered if Jabir wasn't a schizophrenic then Bassha, Suna and Rajah would probably be at home, because the same community people called them things like faglor foa zaar (mentals son going.)

Shamina had accepted this cruelty and unfairness as part of her fate in her life, a life that may have happiness at the end.

NEXT DAY

Rajah and Jazmine slept in Bassha and Suna's flat overnight. They got married in the morning at the Registrar, Rochdale Town Hall. Bassha and Sun witnessed the marriage. Rajah lost his virginity and was confused about Jazmine. Was she a virgin or not?

For the first time since Kajol abandoned Rajah, he and Jazmine were having the time of their life, as husband and wife. Rajah didn't think it would be inevitable, that he left his parents. He moved out to a council flat in Falinge with Jazmine. Rajah was surprised at Jazmine's clothes and cosmetics. They filled an entire bedroom (small.) Rajah's studies were abandoned. He and Jazmine were trying very hard to make Amway work for them, as they became door to door sales people, mostly selling domestic products. To boost their income Rajah worked part time as a gentlemen's hairdresser at Danny's barbers shop on Oldham Road

On one occasion Hasina said to Rajah over the phone;

"You could have done better cousin."

Sandra and Rokiv said;

"What you did was wrong. All three of you have hurt your mother. God will never forgive you for that."

Rajah ignored the comments.

As weeks passed Rajah was missing his mother's cooking. Especially the ayre fish and tomato curry. He missed his mother too and his father. At nights he wondered how they were coping. For irrational reasons regarding he couldn't marry Kajol he had come to hate his mother.

At least Bassha and Suna visited Jabir and Shamina at every opportunity they had. Months passed and Rajah realised Jazmine was only good in bed. She was useless at washing up, cooking and cleaning. That didn't really bother Rajah. What concerned him was her lack of contribution to their Amway network marketing business.

One evening at their flat in Falinge, Rajah snapped discovering some details of Jazmine's past. He couldn't bottle it up any longer.

"You said you only went out with Shezad on a casual date. But, but yeh you were in love with him as well and he broke your heart as Kajol did mine. But there is more than this isn't there Jazmine?"

"Yes he broke my heart and that was it" Jazmine lied. Calm as a snail. She was fidgeting with the TV remote. Rajah became furious.

"You are lying. I've met Shezad in Daniel's barbershop and he told me everything. The intimacy you both shared. He humiliated me in front of Bassha, Suna and many strangers in the shop."

Jazmine became sullen.

"That he was the one who popped your cherry. Jazmine you could have told me."

Sons of Jabir

Rajah broke into a cry. Heartless and silent Jazmine left Rajah and walked upstairs into their bedroom. She shut the bedroom door and put the bolt on. Rajah dozed off on the couch as his tears dried up. As he remembered Auntie Sandra's and Uncle Rokiv's words, ALL THREE OF YOU HAVE HURT YOUR MOTHER. GOD WILL NEVER FORGIVE YOU FOR THAT.

Chapter Fifty Five

You love someone. Then you leave your parents for that someone special. What do they do? They walk out on you, only because they couldn't face the truth.

Did Jazmine love Rajah? Because if she did then why did she lie to him about her virginity? It wouldn't have made any difference to Rajah, if she had told him before they got married. It wasn't a pity Rajah was inexperienced until now. What hurt Rajah was Jazmine's denial and the fact that Shezad humiliated him in Danny's barbershop in front of Bassha and Suna. Not that it mattered to them but it mattered to him. He felt betrayed and cheated. Whatever dignity he had it was gone.

It had been two days and two sleepless nights and Rajah hadn't left his flat. Despite Bassha, Suna and his mother's phone calls to go over. He didn't even open the door for them. But he did assure them, he needed some time on his own. He may have been on a rebound, he may have been naïve but he never was or is suicidal. Rajah was miserable and alone. Tears flowed down his face as he wept in agony. Why do his genitals desire lust? Was he alone? Is it natural to think about sex twenty four seven? Whatever, Rajah couldn't control his desires but he'd been kidding himself. He wasn't over Jazmine. He was still crazily and madly in love with her. He longed for her smooth silky body and the French perfume she wears. Suddenly the nights had become horrifyingly lonely.

It was a loss, to think she was gone from his life. If only she hadn't lied to him. And yet she will be part of his life as Kajol was in the past. His eyes gazed around the flat, there was only silence. No Whitney Houston playing in the kitchen. No aroma of pot pourri in the lounge. Now he'd never hold her again. He'd never speak to her again.

Why did he have to be so ruthless and demanding with her? Why couldn't he have approached the dilemma with less temper? What did it matter if she was a virgin or not, if he really loved her and wanted her. But it did. The temper at the time, she didn't even let him explain himself. As manic depression was partly to blame.

It felt as if she was dead to him. And yet he desperately missed her. Imagine a life where Jazmine existed but he couldn't see her or talk to her ever again. She said she will be moving to inner London as soon as possible. She said, if he wanted they could be friends. Waves of misery swept over him as he cried helplessly in silence. He cried for what felt like hours. He was trying to unleash emotions in the hope it would wipe out Jazmine from his mind. A mind that has not forgotten Kajol yet. His past was his foundation and he needed to get a grip on it. And try to control his near future. But the tears simply wouldn't stop. At least it was proving to be therapeutic. Gradually Rajah forced himself to stop weeping, as he had no room for liars inside his heart.

Chapter Fifty Six

December 1993, Sylhet

When you break your heart and don't listen to your mother, a second time around, inspite that youth is to blame, you have been foolish, stupid and an idiot. Rajah couldn't imagine just eighteen months ago, he was all three. And not to forget spontaneous.

Recently Rajah had found salvation in reading popular fiction. His favourite authors were Jack Higgins, Sydney Sheldon, John Grisham and Jeffrey Archer. Believe it or not Rajah had decided that he would write a novel. He was trying to sort his synopsis out. Already he had decided on a title, THE PRODIGAL ILLNESS. It would be entirely fiction and about manic depressive patients, as he was one. Now stabilised with the help of anti-depressants and self therapy. Reading more than a hundred thousand words every week was proving to be therapeutic for Rajah.

Shamina's prayers had been repaid. It's been said happy days will return. And Rajah had given himself up to his mother. Reluctantly he had agreed to an arranged marriage. And who knows, he may fall in love with his wife. Whoever it's going to be. As Bassha and Suna would never agree to an arranged marriage, Rajah had made the sacrifice for Jabir and Shamina.

Thunder struck and it struck again suddenly but there was no rain yet. Rajah was anxiously reading Jack Higgins *'The Eagle Has Landed'*, waiting for Bassha and Suna and his parents. They should be home now from Sunamganj. *Speak of the devils.*

"You would not believe this son. Your bride to be is the daughter of my long lost friend Chander Ali. The richest man in Sunamganj. And has become Chander Chaudhury" exclaimed Jabir. Rajah hadn't seen his father so happy since childhood.

Rajah has seen the bride and thinks she will be suitable for him. In spite that he wanted to get married a few years later, so he could complete his abandoned degree. But since his parents had become so happy, he would not let them down. Apparently Bassha and Suna had helped to make his mind up. Shamina was already dreaming of grandchildren. So Rajah said 'Yes' the first time he saw Rowsonara a week ago.

Bassha and Suna utterly hated Bangladesh. The reasons being inadequate sanitation, no footpaths to walk on (in most parts of Sylhet), horrible black mosquitoes and the damn weather was too hot. One thing they did was visit their mother's grave in Srimangal, accompanied by Jabir, Shamina, Rajah, Anwar and Asia. Shamina's parents were over the moon with happiness. To see the family after such a long time was more than great. They hadn't expected to live that long, to witness Rajah's wedding with Rowsonara. Fortunately they still had good health.

Jabir, his sons, in-laws and Shamina were living in the heart of Sylhet in a rented spacious ground floor bungalow. The rent was three thousand taka per month which included the furniture and water. Shamina wished one day she would own her own house or bungalow in Uposhor, the poshest place in Sylhet. Bassha and Suna argued why bother, who's going to come and settle in Sylhet for the rest of their lives. Now Shamina wasn't sure about her future plans. To own or not own anything in Sylhet. Rajah wasn't looking forward to his wedding night, as he was thinking of Kajol and Jazmine. But Asia, his grandmother, encouraged him and pushed him inside into his bedroom where Rowsonara awaited her husband in a pink silk nightdress. She had wiped all her make-up off hours ago, tied her long black hair in a bun. Rajah remained quiet for the moment as he sat beside Rowsonara. Thinking of that morning.

Thanks to Bassha and Suna, Rajah's wedding went as smoothly as it could do. From Sylhet to Sunamganj and back the bride and groom's car was not a Rolls Royce but a 1980, 190E white Mercedes. It cost six thousand taka to hire for the day. And two Honda Accords for the rest of the family. There weren't any guests but no expenses were spared.

Rajah hoped Rowsonara would say something, but she remained silent. They say the mind is a memory bottle and Rajah was trying to forget Kajol and Jazmine. Yet he questioned Allah. Why couldn't he marry the girl he loved? *Kajol.*

Remembering Jazmine, his divorce, the decree absolute only came through last month. At least Jazmine signed on the dotted line without a fight.

Rajah turned his head towards Rowsonara and stared at his new bride, thinking about what to say to break the ice. *Gosh marrying a stranger, this is hard.* It had been thirteen hours since Rajah last slept. The day had taken its toll. Rajah felt exhausted. He desperately wanted to go to sleep but that would be rude.

"So tell me about Sylhet" Rajah said taking his half sleeved cotton shirt off. Wondering should he have asked about something else.

Rowsonara cleared her throat and replied;

"The name Sylhet originates from the word sri-hat…"

"Sorry sri-what?" Rajah got up and switched the ceiling fan on.

"Sri-hat, meaning central bazaar."

Rajah was impressed.

"I didn't know that. (*You learn something everyday.*) What else do you know about Sylhet?"

Rowsonara rubbed her temples, feeling a low-grade migraine percolating, because of lack of sleep. Last night she cried till she fell asleep. Knowing that she would be leaving her parents.

"Sylhet is a tea growing region with more than a hundred and forty tea gardens on over fifty thousand hectares, producing twenty five million kilograms of tea annually." Rowsonara paused, took a deep breath and added;

"Can I request something?"

"What?" said Rajah wondering if it could be about his past. He was ready to tell her everything about Kajol and Jazmine.

"Can we go to sleep and you can have sex tomorrow?" said Rowsonara.

Rajah was gutted. He couldn't believe his ears. Is that what she thought of him, someone desperate for sex. No wonder he hated the idea of an arranged marriage. But he will give it a try for his parents' sake.

"I'm tired too. Let's go to sleep," replied Rajah in a flat voice.

Suna got Rajah a waiting-on job at the Bengal Dynasty in Llandudno. It had been two weeks since Rajah came from Bangladesh, after he had stayed only three weeks. He would have stayed longer if Rowsonara was more affectionate, loving and caring. Rowsonara was still partly a stranger to him. She had phoned a few days ago and notified him she had made her Bangladeshi passport. She couldn't wait to come to Britain. When is he going to apply for her visa. 'I've already done it' Rajah replied and said 'I love you' but she had hung up on him.

Rajah was only working at the Bengal Dynasty because the owners had promised him genuine payslips, which he will post to the British High Commission in Dhaka with other necessary documentation, within four weeks. Hopefully once he gets his wife's visa, he will be leaving the Bengal Dynasty. Rajah wanted to go back to education and complete his abandoned degree. Now that he was married, part time study was possible.

Apparent and unethical it was, when Suna showed him how to do bills. At first Rajah was furious. 'That's stealing' he had exclaimed. But Suna's philosophy 'hundred and sixty pounds per week for seventy hours work is injustice. So what you are worth, you take, because if you ask for a pay rise, they won't give it yah, they probably sack yah' got to him. And they became partners.

Twelve Months Later

It had been eight months since Rowsonara came over. Since she had come, Rajah had been encouraging her to go to college, to improve her English, as she couldn't speak fluently. Rajah was reading a popular fiction novel. He had managed to sort out the synopsis for the novel he wanted to write. THE PRODIGAL ILLNESS. It would consists of fifty five chapters, with a prologue and an epilogue.

Apparently Rowsonara burst out;

"Look I've had, I've had enough of your brothers, your mother and your father."

"Why? What happened?" Rajah replied, still reading *As The Crow Flies* by Jeffrey Archer, partially ignorant. He was glad that they were in their bedroom.

"Your brothers treat me like a servant. Get me this, get me that, all the time."

Rajah knew Rowsonara was exaggerating.

"Sorry" replied Rajah. He sighed and added;

"You were saying?"

"Manche bhandi beti ow ila bangladesho katai-na. (People back home don't even treat servants like this, the way your brothers treat me.) Especially Bassha."

"What's he done now?" Rajah questioned, and marked the paperback novel with a local restaurant business card, as he placed it on top of the bedside cabinet. He turned and faced his frustrating half tempered wife. Rajah felt horny as both of them were naked. But he was hesitating to approach his wife in this mood. Rowsonara's body had become cold and stiff.

Since she'd come over, all she had been doing was cooking, cleaning and cooking, nothing else. Her life had become a dog's life compared to what it used to be in Sunamganj.

"Few days ago there was some guest in the house. A lady, your mother's friend or something. Bassha was watching TV. As I came in the lounge with tea and biscuits for the guest, I didn't have a head scarf on and Bassha told me off. It was humiliating in front of the guest."

Sons of Jabir

"Right, I'll tell amma. She'll have a word with him in the morning. Now let's see if we can make a baby and go to sleep."

Rajah tried to cup his wife's breasts but Rowsonara shrugged him off and said;

"Sorry I'm too tired. I'm going to sleep."

If Rajah had any ego left of his manhood, it was all gone. He was sure there was nothing wrong with his lovemaking ability. But he feared he wasn't attractive to Rowsonara. In spite of his inner feelings of his wife's attitude towards him, he was trying his best to keep Rowsonara happy. Just a few weeks ago he took her to York and they had a fantastic time.

But she seemed as if she has got manic depression. Ironic because Rajah was a diagnosed manic depressive. Just a couple of days ago they made wild love. In spite of her complaints, Rajah admitted Bassha wasn't helping his marriage. But he felt he was unwanted. Whenever he said to Rowsonara 'I love you' she didn't say the same thing in return. Most of the time she changed the subject or had a complaint.

Rajah felt awful, his wife not wanting sex. He felt like castrating himself. Then he wouldn't have any sexual urges left. It was agonising, when you are married and your wife refuses sex, unless she was on her period. Then Rajah surely would understand. But rejecting him by lying to him. He knew very well Rowsonara wasn't tired, because she had slept thirteen hours last night.

Rajah felt like weeping. It wasn't the first time she has rejected him. Rajah wondered hypothetically, could there have been a boyfriend in Rowsonara's life? If there was, she probably wasn't over him yet. Or was she a type of woman that didn't like sex very much? Whatever the reasons, he needed to do something about it, if Rowsonara carried on like this. May be he could tell his mother. He wished he had a sister-in-law to confide in. He probably could confide in Rana, Bassha's wife to be.

Trying to think of something else, he asked himself if love marriages don't work out then his arranged marriage, does it have what it takes? His wife seems to stay away from him. He longed for affection and she was always glib with him. He had to admit there was no chemistry between them. Yet he would not give up.

Rajah was trying to think of nothing and go to sleep.

Rowsonara was snoring next to him. Why couldn't he just doze off like his wife. If he didn't fall to sleep soon, then his past would torment him, in the form of auditory hallucinations. That happened when he worried about his future taking into account the present. Which travels back to his past and questions with no answers haunt him. *What if this? What if that? Why? Why? Why didn't Kajol claim their love? Why? Why? Why did Jazmine lie to him? Are women like that? Most women are bitches.*

Why won't women be frank with him? Kajol, Jazmine and now Rowsonara. Rajah contemplated how would life be if he were single again? His mother sprang to his mind and he dismissed the thought. But why did he agree to this arranged marriage? He could have said no to his mother and left her weeping till she fainted. If he wasn't ready to get remarried then why did he agree? Because of emotional blackmail. Partly this arranged marriage was a sacrifice to make his mother happy.

Is it true when people say, history repeats itself? For Rajah probably it was. Rowsonara was a hundred percent sure she was pregnant but hadn't told Rajah yet. Why not? Except;

"I may be expecting."

"You said that last month and the month before." Rajah had been unnecessarily sarcastic that morning. But he acknowledged she may be right. For some reason he wasn't thrilled of having a child, becoming a father. He was excited of having a child three months ago. As Rowsonara neglected him pretty badly in the past twelve weeks, things had changed.

He asked himself, no matter how hard he tried, could he ever fall in love with his wife? He realised never and that was scary, as he didn't want to be miserable for the rest of his life.

It was another sleepless night for Rajah.

Chapter Fifty Seven

Twenty Four Months Later
Guess what, Rajah had dumped Rowsonara and divorced her later. Not to forget the fact Rowsonara being the daughter of Chander Chaudhury, once upon a time Jabir's best friend. Rajah didn't even hesitate because he felt Rowsonara was unfaithful to him via her heart. She really didn't love him. There was some guilt Rajah would probably carry forever but it was better than being miserable for the rest of his life.

Jabir, a known schizophrenic. The fact his son Rajah had divorced Rowsonara, his friend's daughter, and that his friend didn't even complain nor writes to him anymore, one can argue the friendship was probably over. And so Jabir's condition had become worse. But Rajah wasn't bothered as he had become a selfish individual.

Shamina was already planning to get Rajah remarried again. This time to someone in Britain. Rokiv's eldest daughter crossed her mind. But Jabir would never approve of Hasina because she was a half-caste. Not that it mattered. But Rajah had promised himself, nobody and he means no one, would manipulate or interfere with his personal life from now on. Things like, who should he re-marry? When should he re-marry? After another year, three, five, seven. Shamina didn't know any of this.

Danny's Barbershop on Oldham Road
There was a red and white head sign with capital letters in 3D format, followed by yellow and orange lower case lettering on the rectangle shop window, with details of opening hours and a price list. Wet look gels, Brylcreams and various brands of hairsprays were displayed on the window sill.

Inside there was vinyl flooring from Carpet Right with vinyl wallpaper from B&Q. There were Italian black leather barber chairs with head-rest and foot-rest from Salon Direct in Merseyside. Hairdressing units, scissors, combs and clippers from Alan Howard of Rochdale. The walls lacked models' pictures.

"If anybody loved me then that was Jazmine and I let her go. Rowsonara it was different and letting her go was necessary and yet I feel I betrayed her in a different way. But both of them lied to me, Jazmine about a guy called Shezad and Rowsonara about a guy called Salik. And I don't know who the guys are, I don't want to know and I don't care," Rajah expressed. It wasn't for the first time.

The first six months of the past twenty four, after he had dumped Rowsonara, he was trying to come to terms with the emotional trauma of loneliness at nights. It can be awful when you are used to having a partner besides you. But now looking back it had been worth it. Except Rajah had a daughter ten/eleven months old. And was it selfishness or arrogance he hadn't seen his daughter yet? Neither. Rowsonara hadn't sent him any pictures of his daughter.

"Yeh but you really didn't need to marry Jazmine, she was your, I mean our bloody auntie, Raj" replied Bassha, cleaning his nostrils as Suna broke out laughing and Bassha joined in. Suna sat in the barber chair staring at himself in the mirror.

"Listen she wasn't our auntie. I call her auntie because her mother was a friend of our grandmother, I repeat a friend not a cousin!" said Rajah furiously.

"Hey calm down, he was only joking. It's history anyway" Suna assured. As Suna was having a number one all over (David Beckham hair cut.) Danny was almost finished.

"I was only trying to clarify that Jazmine wasn't our auntie biologically, that's all" Rajah's temper subsided.

"Next" shouted Danny as he took the black polyester cutting square off Suna.

"You not having a trim are you Raj?" asked Bassha grinning at Rajah. He occasionally liked to take the mickey out of Rajah.

"No" Rajah said flatly.

Sons of Jabir

"Will yeh give us a lift to the train station?" Bassha requested. He stopped grinning and added;

"Please."

"Yeh-sure, whatever."

Times like this, Rajah felt like smacking Bassha. No matter how much he wanted to, he couldn't because they were brothers. And it was all right for Bassha to be nosy at times.

Only hours ago Bassha confessed that he was a hypocrite. And realised that his body after all was not invincible. That he too had become a heroin addict. But with Rana's help he would go into rehabilitation.

Suna was in the back listening to Whitney via his personal Sony CD player. Bassha sat in front. Rajah turned left after the Half Penny Bridge as they left Oldham Road behind.

"I have to get a job far away," Bassha said. His whole body was aching as the self induced Class A drug was wearing off from last night.

"What's wrong with Manchester?" Rajah questioned, curious. A lot of things were going through his unoccupied mind. In spite he thinks he probably knew the answer.

"I'm going to end up like Danny. This is like what they call, a ghetto, Longsight and Rochdale."

"What do you mean?"

"It's just that I have to take drugs everyday. I am no exception, I have become an addict," Bassha concluded.

"Hey cheer up, you let Rana help you. You need to face the problem. Getting a job far away won't rid you of your addiction, if you have become one" advised Rajah. This wasn't surprising for Rajah but certainly unexpected. At least he had suggested to listen to Rana. He wished he was there for Bassha. Instead of being obsessed with Kajol and later infatuated by Jazmine. But there's no point regretting over anyone's past. As it can't be changed but one can try to improve his present and look forward to whatever the future may hold.

Sons of Jabir

Chapter Fifty Eight

Falling in love has to be inevitable but there is no guarantee the other person will give love in return. The other person may not be attracted to you. The other person may not have any such feelings for you. Or maybe Rajah was confusing love with attraction, lust and desire. He probably didn't love his cousin Halina. If he did was it anything to do with her being thirteen years younger than him? He hoped not. He hoped if he did love her, then it was genuine in spite that it was one sided at the moment.

At times I wish I had a sister to confide in. To confide about what my brothers are putting me through. I have learnt the hard way (being slightly hypocritical.) And I have told them don't fall in love but if you do don't forget to take advice from me.

I have tried drinking but I never tried hard drugs. (It's not a lie) because, amphetamines (speed) heavy use of that can produce feelings of persecution. Cocaine (coke) more likely to lead to dependence. Heroin (skag/smack) overdose can cause unconsciousness. Regular use can lead to dependence. I tell my brothers all the time. 'You have to stop doing drugs, especially Bassha.' So they stop for a while and start again. I have promised my mother and father I will get them off booze and drugs. Make them clean as a whistle.

Sometimes after midnight, Bassha will blast the ghettoblaster with Tupac Shakur. Ignorant, so he is. I mean people are sleeping for Allah's sake. Other times, when I'm writing relentlessly, he'll ring me on the mobile and ask; "Hey Raj can I have a hair cut tonight?" I feel pissed off and say to myself why did I ever learn to cut hair? Why can't Bassha go to a barbershop like everyone else, because he wants to save money.

I don't mind cutting his hair, despite the fact it's every week. It's when I'm writing I don't like being interrupted.

Sons of Jabir

I tell my brothers forget working in restaurants, as if they would listen. I tell them forget going into partnership with the Abdul's. (It's not a bad idea if it works out) but I want them to go back to college. Get some qualifications, in which case they can get a job with less hours. I tell them to get married and stop sleeping around, not because of the fear of catching Aids. So they can settle down and have kids. Proof of life. Which I intend to do with Halina in a few years' time.

My brothers at present, they are just throwing their lives away. It's nothing to do with religion, it's nothing to do with being westernised, it's nothing to do with own traditions and cultures, it's nothing to do with being rebels, who like upsetting their parents. My brothers do all the silly things for fun. They never take anything seriously.

Our father doesn't blame the influence of the western cultures, clubbing and drinking every weekend. Having one night stands, leave your parents once you are sixteen. Have many girlfriends (boyfriends) as you possibly can. My father doesn't blame Tupac Shakur, or any other American rappers. He blames his own sons. That they are good for nothing, because other people's sons and daughters, have degrees. Have good manners. Respect their religion. And above all have ambition for academic achievement. But what Jabir and Shamina don't acknowledge is, their sons are free spirits. They are living their life, the way they want, individually. Without any manipulation.

I tried becoming a millionaire before twenty five. There were others with me. Jazmine was for one. You know what I did? No I didn't play the National Lottery. I tried robbing the Bank of England. "Sorry that was a joke."

I joined Amway, a network marketing company based in America. Some said it's a pyramid. I wasn't sure of that because their headquarters didn't look nothing like the pyramids in Egypt. Then I realised how stupid I was, as they were talking about some kind of scam that is referred to as 'Illegal Pyramids.' But Amway's regional UK representatives clarified that it was not an illegal pyramid. In fact it was a multilevel international marketing company.

Anyway I abandoned Amway after six months, when I was with Jazmine because I wasn't getting anywhere. I did see Jeffrey Archer live in one of their seminars though. After I tried smaller network marketing companies. Cabouchon, Jewelway UK, Telecom Plus (selling smartboxes but it wasn't easy competing with BT.) Every single one of them was a waste of my time. But my dream of becoming a millionaire wasn't absolutely shattered.

It's possibly in many ways, if I become a Hollywood actor, a best-selling novelist, or I can go to Bangladesh. Take a geologist with me. After some soil and ground testing, I buy acres of land. (It's cheap in Bangladesh, the outback.) It strikes oil, "Hooray." I know it's all hypothetical nonsense but it's possible.

Our mother always prays for Bassha and Suna. You never know they just may drop everything and walk in a straight path. At times I feel like strangling them. At times a couple of days go past without a word between us. Then we miss each other. At times I even miss Bassha's frustration "will you hurry up." "Have you seen my driving licence?" "Allah-kasam, look what you've done to my hair." Once I wanted to shout back; "Bloody hell I'm not your wife," but didn't, as usual.

At times I feel like abandoning my brothers completely. Don't talk to them ever. Ignore them on the streets, don't answer their phone calls. Stop cutting Bassha's hair. Feel as though they don't exist for me anymore. But dad goes; "If you do that you will regret it." Mother goes; "Why are they so irresponsible?"

I replied: "They aren't irresponsible, they are just westernised. That's all."

Rajah loves Halina and wants to marry her. But that doesn't mean he should neglect and ignore Bassha, Suna, Shamina and Jabir at times. He may be glib sometimes. Rajah loves Halina so much he is willing to abandon everyone in his

Sons of Jabir

family, if she did become his wife. But he may not have to because the possibility of marrying his cousin was zero. Halina may already have a boyfriend. But overall Rajah and Halina don't have common ground.

Chapter Fifty Nine

"Listen I have found this place in Carlisle" said Suna, as he took a gulp of his McDonald's hot chocolate. The sons of Jabir were in Sandbrook Park, inside McDonald's restaurant. Rajah was not interested in working in an Indian restaurant again, unless it was absolutely necessary. Bassha and Suna believed the only way to make money was to own your own restaurant.

"Where's that?" Bassha asked, munching on his Big Mac. It was ten to eleven at night and the restaurant was deserted.

"It's in Cumbria. Scotland is only hundred or so miles from Carlisle and Carlisle is about hundred and twenty miles from Rochdale" Rajah explained interrupting. He was sipping his McDonald's coffee, the usual. He believed he had become addicted to it. It was pouring outside. At least English weather was predictable.

"You have found a place for what?" questioned Bassha. The McDonald's restaurant chair was a bit small for his buttocks, yet he wouldn't quit junk food.

"It would make a nice average sized first floor restaurant. By the way I have a partner. His name is Abdul Hakim. He's from Tyne and Wear. But I need both of you to help me financially and become working…"

"I can't," interrupted Rajah, a bit abrupt. He added:

"I mean I can help you financially. Help get a loan, whatever. But I can't work because I have a novel to write and I really wanna become a professional actor, if not I can always end up a teacher. I've got nothing against restaurant employees, it's just that I've made my choices and I'm trying to live my life now. I mean I love writing, who knows?"

Bassha and Suna couldn't argue about that. At the end of the day they were proud of Rajah, as he was trying to make a difference in their family.

"Well that's okay. Bassha and I can work full time. Providing you help us get a business loan for thirty grand. And

Abdul Hakim's brothers, one is an experienced Indian chef and the other is an experienced tandoori chef. We'll be able to manage it." Suna drained his hot chocolate. Bassha finished his Big Mac and his second one.

"That can be arranged by remortgaging Dad's house and personal loans" Rajah concluded. He finished his coffee and wanted another one. He would have, if he wasn't feeling sleepy.

If you believe in the Almighty, ALLAH and help yourself, then Allah will surely help you. Things were looking up for the sons of Jabir. Bassha was trying to get off heroin with the help of Methadone and Rana. Suna had promised Rajah, that he will go to Alcoholics Anonymous. Rajah was dedicated to his writing and determined to finish his novel within twelve months, as he had already written thirty three chapters of it, some forty seven thousand words. And he's probably read more than a couple of million words. Mostly Jeffrey Archer, Sydney Sheldon and John Grisham.

You could say Rajah had had a change of interest, as he had completed a Btec first diploma in performing arts, in which he participated in a Christmas pantomime and in Willy Russell's *Blood Brothers,* the college version. Now he had a sound knowledge of Greek and Elizabethan theatre.

The new Indian restaurant in Carlisle was coming along fine. Jabir was getting stable again with group therapy in Richard Street accompanied by Rajah.

"Bafor ufredi kotha mathiona, bafor ussilay ayso" (don't talk back to your father, your father is the reason you are here in this world.) Jabir's unexpected speech was surprising and partially offensive to Rajah that morning. Rajah just ignored Jabir's male chauvinism and arrogance, because Rajah knew Jabir loved his sons. More than Shamina, more than Chander Chaudhury and more than his religion.

Rajah had come to an understanding that his father Jabir wasn't crazy (fagol) as people referred because those people were ignorant of the fact that in spite that schizophrenia is a scientific delusion, and schizophrenics have problems controlling their thoughts, that is why they say silly things. But with the right anti-depressants and therapy, a schizophrenic can lead a normal life. For example Jabir. But Rajah hoped one day he would like to see his father, Jabir, completely cured from schizophrenia as he no longer had manic depression.

Unfortunately Shamina had a minor heart attack, due to too much cholesterol deposits. Now she has stopped giving too much spices in the curries. Soon Bassha and Suna would be working for themselves. Rajah had spoken to Abdul Hakim a few times over the phone. Sounds a nice fella. It happened Hakim's father, Mr Abdul Baki, was a popular experienced and quality Indian/Bangladeshi cuisine chef. Probably the best in Newcastle-upon-Tyne.

Everything was going smoothly for once in Rajah's life. In spite of his unforgotten past. Till he fell in love again, yes again. *It had to do with his fate.* For Rajah for a while days were practically the same. Tonight was different. Rajah had this urge to write something in his personal diary. (The personal diary was inspired from the college diary, that Rajah wrote being a first year performing arts student.)

Ironically he couldn't find a pen that will write. After throwing three blue biros in his half full waste paper basket. He began to write with a pencil.

Why have I fallen in love with my cousin, for if she finds out, she will be disgusted. Ya Allah I need help. What will Mother think of me now? What will father think of me now? Bassha and Suna they'll understand.

Ya Allah why did you have to give us hearts that will not bleed but only suffer in silence.

Rajah couldn't write any more, he hated this writer's block. I CAN'T MARRY A BIMBO LIKE ROWSANA AGAIN. I CAN'T MARRY A SLAG LIKE JAZMINE AGAIN. I HAVE TO MARRY SOMEONE INTELLIGENT WHATEVER, YOU ARE NOT GETTING MARRIED UNTIL YOU HAVE ESTABLISHED A CAREER. YA ALLAH I KNOW I AM NOT A RELIGIOUSLY CONVICTED PERSON BUT

IMPORTANTLY I ACKNOWLEDGE WITHOUT YOU (ALLAH) I AM NOBODY, NO GOOD, I AM USELESS, I AM NOTHIN', ABSOLUTELY NOTHIN'.

Epilogue

RICHARD STREET CENTRE
(Rochdale Counselling Service)

"What is it that you want to discuss Mister Rajah Khan?" asked Frank Denning, Senior Practitioner, member of the Greater Manchester counselling service. Rajah has been referred by Dr Rimmer from John Elliot, on his own request.

Rajah had a lot of things to talk about. For starters his heart in particular. Why does his heart always fancy the wrong person? But it could be like they say in films, 'she's the one.' So Halina Khan could be the one, his soul mate. And yet he has doubts because he doesn't believe his heart anymore. He doesn't trust his heart anymore. *But, if this, that…*

"Firstly whenever I see my cousin Halina, my heart bounces and for days on end I can't stop thinking about her. I, I, I think I have fallen in love with her. And I feel I can spend the rest of my life with her, only her."

"So I assume this is one sided?"

"Yes."

"So what is stopping you from telling her about your feelings?"

"Because there is a thirteen year gap between us."

"I see and the second thing you wanted to discuss?" Dr Denning paused. Rajah was thinking something. Dr Denning added;

"Mister Khan."

For the past two years a day hadn't past Rajah did not think about his daughter. He had named his daughter Samina after his mother's name. He feels he has committed sins. That Allah may forgive but Rowsonara won't because when he abandoned Rowsonara, he knew she was pregnant with his child.

"I have a secret. I dumped my wife knowing that she was pregnant with my daughter. And I haven't seen my daughter yet. I must be, I am the worst, horrible, terrible father in this world." Rajah burst into tears. He sobbed uninhibited for a few minutes. Dr Denning didn't interrupt. Another minute Rajah regained his posture.

"Have you thought or have considered visiting your former wife and your daughter?"

"I very much want to, especially my daughter but I just can't face Rowsonara after what I've done to her."

"Yes, but what I was suggesting if you go to Bangladesh and ask for forgiveness. I'm sure you will feel much better." Dr Denning is hoping Rajah will take his advice because that's the only way forward. Asking for forgiveness. Rajah thought something and after a moment replied;

"I can start by writing a letter to Rowsonara but…"

"A letter requesting for forgiveness," Dr Denning interrupted assuring. Rajah got up from the old leather couch and left. His mind already thinking of what to say in the letter.

Dear Rowsonara the reason I divorced you because I never loved you. You don't have to forgive me for I shouldn't have married you in the first place…